DAUGHTER OF MINE

Anne Bennett was born in a back-to-back house in the Horsefair district of Birmingham. The daughter of Roman Catholic, Irish immigrants, she grew up in a tight-knit community where she was taught to be proud of her heritage. She considers herself to be an Irish Brummie and feels therefore that she has a foot in both cultures. She has four children and four grandchildren. For many years she taught in schools to the north of Birmingham. An accident put paid to her teaching career and, after moving to North Wales, Anne turned to the other great love of her life and began to write seriously. In 2006, after sixteen years in a wheelchair, she miraculously regained her ability to walk.

For more information, visit Anne's website, www.annebennett.co.uk.

ANNE BENNETT

Daughter of Mine

HARPER

This novel is a work of fiction. The names, characters and incidents described in it are the work of the author's imagination. Any resemblance to actual persons, living or dead, events or localities, is entirely coincidental.

HarperCollins*Publishers*
77–85 Fulham Palace Road,
Hammersmith, London W6 8JB

www.harpercollins.co.uk

A Paperback Original 2005
9

A catalogue record for this book
is available from the British Library

ISBN 978 0 00 717724 0

Typeset in Sabon by Palimpsest Book Production Limited,
Grangemouth, Stirlingshire
Printed and bound in Great Britain by
Clays Ltd, St Ives Plc

I would like to dedicate this book to my second
daughter, Bethany Bennett, with all
my love

ACKNOWLEDGEMENTS

As *Daughter of Mine* is set in a period I have covered before and that is anyway well documented, I didn't need so much help from individuals this time. However, I am grateful to the books Carl Chinn writes, which I find invaluable, and to Amy (UK Villages.co.uk) for help in finding more out about Ballintra and Rossnowlagh, both of which we visited last year, and Paul Lewis, who found out about family allowances for me. I cannot leave out either my special friends Judith Kendall and Ruth Adshead, who helped me in so many ways.

However, without the fabulous team at Harper Collins, I'm sure I would be lost, so I am giving a heartfelt thanks to my editorial director, Susan Opie, my editor, Maxine Hitchcock, my line editor, Sara Walsh, Ingrid Gegner, my exceptional publicist, Peter Hawtin, in charge of Midlands sales, and last but by no means least my agent, Judith Murdoch, who works so hard for me. I appreciate your help, advice and constructive criticism and I take this opportunity to thank all of you immensely.

My family help too through their unfailing support and the fact that they also keep my feet firmly on the ground, if ever I have a temptation to go into orbit, so thanks to my daughters, Nikki, Bethany and Tamsin, and my son, Simon. Thanks must also go to my son-in-law, Steve, my daughter-in-law, Carol, my mother-in-law, Nancy, and my own mother, Eileen Flanagan, who in many ways was an inspiration for this book.

Denis is a very special husband and my partner in crime, and without him my life would be severely curtailed and much poorer, and so I'd like to say thanks to him a million times.

Love, Anne.

CHAPTER ONE

Lizzie Clooney and her cousin, Tressa, almost danced along Colmore Row to the Grand Hotel where both girls worked. 'Imagine, a Christmas social,' Lizzie said, her eyes shining at the thought.

'Aye,' Tressa replied, almost hugging herself with delight. 'And to be held on the nineteenth of December before the hotel gets really busy. I mean, we have to grab this opportunity while we can. It isn't as if we are meeting Catholic men on every street corner.'

Lizzie knew her cousin had a valid point, for although they enjoyed all the delights of Birmingham, the city they'd now lived in for nearly two years, they'd never encouraged any of the boys who'd pressed them for dates, certain they'd be Protestants. Never could Lizzie or Tressa contemplate marrying someone of another faith, for they both knew such a person would never be accepted into their families, who lived in Donegal in the north of Ireland.

Small wonder really, when you looked at the history of the place. Hadn't there been enough trouble between the Orangemen and Catholics there to last anyone a lifetime, without them adding to it? 'Everyone had better watch out,' Tressa said warningly, but with a bright smile plastered to her face, 'for I'm after catching a rich and handsome man at this social.'

'Tressa!'

'Well, I am. Are you not?'

'No,' Lizzie said, and then added more honestly, 'well, not really.'

'Are you mad?' Tressa demanded. 'This is our chance. D'you want to be an old maid all your life?'

'No, of course not,' Lizzie said with a laugh, 'but I don't want to get married yet a while.'

'Well I do,' Tressa declared. 'If one takes my fancy, that is.'

'You be careful,' Lizzie cautioned. 'You'll get talked about.'

'Och, will you listen to yourself?' Tressa said contemptuously. 'We're not in a little village in Donegal now, Lizzie, where everyone knows everyone else's business and would condemn you without judge and jury if the notion took them. I think if you ran naked down the city streets here, there would only be the mildest curiosity.'

'Tressa!'

'Oh don't worry,' Tressa said. 'I'm not intending doing that.' There was a slight pause and then with a twinkle in her eye, Tressa added, 'Not straight away at least,' and the two girls laughed together.

'Think of it,' Tressa said later. 'Our futures might be decided by that night.'

'Heaven forbid!'

'What's up with you?'

2

'What d'you mean?' Lizzie said. 'Why do you want to tie yourself down so soon? For the first time in my life, I have freedom to do as I please, and money in my pocket to spend as I choose. I have bought new clothes, been to theatres and cinemas and dance halls. I don't want to be tied to a house, doing the washing and cooking and cleaning without a halfpenny to bless myself with, for a long time yet.'

'Don't you think about it sometimes?' Tressa asked.

'Think about what?'

'Being head over heels, besotted by someone?' Tressa said. 'And sex and things.'

'Sometimes,' Lizzie admitted. 'I wouldn't be human if I didn't. But I don't dwell on it. Sex an' all verges on impure thoughts, anyway.'

'You don't confess it?' Tressa said incredulously.

'Aye, sometimes.'

'You're mad. No one can help their thoughts and I'm telling no priest what I've been thinking about. It might turn his hair white, or else give him a heart attack.'

'And then he'd fall out of the confessional and roll down the aisle,' Lizzie said, and the two girls collapsed helpless with laughter at the thought, and then, when the laughter had abated somewhat, Lizzie continued, 'I wonder what penance he'd give you when he recovered himself?' and that started them off again.

Through all the hilarity, though, Lizzie realised Tressa's religion sat very easily on her, while she worried about every mortal thing. Maybe she'd fare better if she could view life in the same way as her cousin. But then she'd always thought Tressa had her life well sorted, and that had been the way of it throughout all of their growing up.

They'd been born within two days of each other: Lizzie on the 5th July 1912 on her father Seamus' farm in Rossnowlagh, Donegal, and Tressa two days later above the grocery store in the nearby village of Ballintra, that had become Eamon's when he married the grocer's daughter Margaret. She was an only child and so had inherited the whole business on her father's death.

Lizzie and Tressa had always been the best of friends, but even before they'd begun the national school together in Ballintra, Tressa had been the boss. The point was, Tressa was the youngest in her home. She had two brothers, Will and Jim, followed by two sisters, Peggy and Moira, but then her mother had suffered two miscarriages before Tressa's birth and so much was made of Tressa when she was born hale and hearty. But, as there were no other children after her, she'd been petted and spoilt in a way Lizzie's mother Catherine never approved of. Catherine believed that to spare the rod was to spoil the child and her children were taught to do as they were told and promptly, or they'd know the consequences.

That was the problem. Lizzie had learnt quickly to do as she was told and Tressa had learnt, just as quickly, how to get her own way. Her parents, and certainly her older sisters, had always given in to her and she expected everyone else, and certainly her cousin Lizzie, to do the same. She'd lay plans before her in such a way and coax and even bully until Lizzie would find herself wavering and finally giving in to whatever Tressa wanted.

By the time they'd left school, this was firmly ingrained. But although Lizzie had plenty to do at home, for her mother believed Satan made work for idle hands, Tressa had a different life altogether, for there was no opening in the shop for her. Since she'd left school at fourteen she'd hung about the house, only helping the odd times when they had a rush on.

Her father wasn't keen on her taking on any other sort of job either. 'You'd shame me,' he'd said. 'People will say I can't afford to keep my own daughter at home.'

'Quite right,' Margaret nodded in agreement. She didn't really want this child, this true gift from God, to leave her side. She wanted her near all the days of her life, and when she eventually married Margaret wanted her to marry in the village, where Margaret could take pleasure in helping rear any grandchildren, like she had with the others.

But Tressa had been bored and wanted to go to England. She didn't really care where, she just wanted to sample city life, the sort of life Clara Dunne described that sounded so much more exciting than Tressa's own. Clara was from the village and had got a job in one of the hotels in Birmingham, and Tressa had soon decided that that would suit her just fine and dandy.

'Oh, Lizzie, you should hear her,' Tressa had enthused to her cousin. 'She said you wouldn't believe the shops, and there's a big market called the Bull Ring where you can pick things up for next to nothing. And that's not all,' she went on, seeing that Lizzie was unimpressed so far. 'There's picture houses, with proper moving pictures, and dances, and something called a Variety Hall where there are all manner of acts on. Oh, Lizzie, wouldn't it be wonderful to be part of it?'

'It would, right enough,' Lizzie had said and then had promptly forgotten about it, for she was wise enough not to yearn for things she couldn't have.

However, Tressa wasn't used to having her wishes thwarted, but for once Margaret stood firm and said that she wouldn't countenance the idea of her leaving, and certainly not by herself.

Tressa had no intention of going by herself. She'd automatically assumed that Lizzie would go with her and had said, 'I wouldn't be alone, Mammy. Lizzie would be coming with me.'

'Does she want to go too?'

'Of course she does,' Tressa had said airily. 'She just doesn't know it yet.' But she added this last comment under her breath. All she had to do was convince Lizzie it was a great idea. She'd done it many times before.

But Lizzie had proved to be unusually difficult. 'Don't give in to her this time,' her elder sister Eileen had warned her. 'You're making yourself a rubbing rag.'

Lizzie thought Eileen had a cheek. How many times had she come begging, 'Could you do that pile of ironing for me, Lizzie,' or 'churn the butter,' or 'wash the pots,' or whatever it was. Eileen would always have a good reason for not being able to do it right then. 'I'll pay you back,' she'd promise, but she never did. Even though Lizzie might resent it, she always did it and usually without a word of complaint.

But it was one thing scouring pots, ironing the family wash and making butter. It was quite another to go to a strange country she'd never had a yen to go to, because of a whim her cousin had to see the place. 'I don't know, Tressa,' she'd said.

Tressa hadn't been too worried. Lizzie often had to be persuaded to do things and eventually Lizzie had said, 'If I was to come, and I'm not saying I will, mind, how d'you know there would be jobs for us both?'

Tressa allowed herself a little smile of triumph. 'Clara said that in the New Year two of the waitresses are leaving, one to get married and one to look after her ailing mother, and of course she is getting married herself later. She says the boss likes Irish girls and so do the Americans, and the tips they give are legion. She said she'll miss that when she is married herself,' for Clara was sporting an engagement ring with a huge diamond in the centre of it. 'She's getting married in the spring and moving down south somewhere,' Tressa said. 'We really need to go while she's there to speak for us.'

'I'll think about it,' Lizzie had promised.

A couple of days later, Tressa watched Lizzie working in the dairy, pummelling the poss stick up and down in the churn. Lizzie's arms throbbed with pain and her back ached, and despite the raw, black day she was sweating so much she felt it dampening under her arms and running down her back. It wasn't even her turn to do the churning, she thought resentfully. It was Eileen's, but she had had to mend the tear in the hem of her skirt for the dance she was going to that night.

Lizzie was also going to the dance and she had yet

to have a wash and then iron her own clothes, but it was no good asking Eileen. She'd say she'd do them and then forget.

Tressa, knowing her cousin well, guessed what she was thinking about and so she said, 'They'd manage without you here, you know. Your problem is you allow yourself to be put upon.'

And by you too, Lizzie might have said, but she knew Tressa had a point for there was Peter and Owen to help her father and even Johnnie, at eleven years old, was making a fine turn-out too. Her eldest sister Susan lived not far away and Eileen was on hand to help her mother. And she knew Eileen would have to help if Lizzie wasn't there to cajole and coax and boss about. 'You're right,' she'd said to Tressa. 'I'll go to this place Birmingham with you, directly Clara can get us jobs, and give the place a try-out at least.'

Of course it hadn't been that easy. Lizzie's own parents had to be convinced and give their permission for their daughter to go. 'It's all Tressa's doing,' Catherine remarked to Eileen. 'If that Tressa went to the North Pole and gave our Lizzie the nod, she'd go along with her.'

'Aye, Mammy, I know,' Eileen said with a sigh, annoyed that her compliant sister was even contemplating leaving. 'Still, maybe when all's said and done, she'll not stay long.'

'That's true right enough,' Seamus had put in. 'God knows she hasn't a clue what city life is like and might not take to it at all. Let her get it out of her system anyhow and then she can never claim we were holding her back.'

Lizzie also thought she might not like the life, and that is what she said to console Johnnie, who was so dreadfully upset that she was moving out of his life. Looking at him, Lizzie had thought, was like looking at herself as a small child, for both of them had the dark brown wavy hair and the same deep brown eyes, snub nose and wide mouth. Only that day Johnnie's eyes had swum with the tears that had also trickled down his cheeks. 'Sure, I'll be back before you know it,' Lizzie had said, holding her young brother tight.

Of all his sisters and brothers, Johnnie loved Lizzie most. As she was seven years older than him, when he was younger he had looked upon her as another mother, and, in truth, Lizzie had done a lot of the rearing of him. With her temperament she seldom became angry and had far more patience than Eileen. In the long winter evenings it would be Lizzie who'd play cards or dominoes, or read to him to while away the time, and she was always ready to help him with his homework. And in the finer weather they'd walk together over the rolling countryside, or down to the sea to watch the huge rollers crash onto the sand leaving a fringe of foam behind them. Johnnie knew his life would be poorer without his sister, so he clung to the idea that she'd be soon back. 'D'you promise?' he'd said.

'I can't promise that, Johnnie,' Lizzie had replied. 'I don't know myself how I'll fare. We'll just have to wait and see.' She knew that Tressa had no intention of returning home, but for herself, she wasn't sure how she would cope with any of it.

That morning, in late January 1930, as they'd stood

9

at the rail of the mail boat, watching the shores of Ireland being swallowed up by the mist, Tressa had given a sigh of satisfaction and said to Lizzie, 'I'd say we'll be sure to catch ourselves rich and handsome men in England?'

Lizzie wrinkled her nose. 'Let's have a bit of fun and live a bit first.'

'And Birmingham's the place to do that all right,' Tressa said. 'So, are you glad you came at least?'

Before answering, Lizzie looked down at the churning sea the boat was ploughing its way through, which was as grey as the leaden sky, and she felt excitement beginning to stir in her. She smiled at her cousin and said, 'If I'm honest I'm often glad when you bully me into doing something I'd not given a mind to before. I'm no good at adventures and maybe I never will be. Perhaps I'll always be the kind of person that will have to have my arm twisted to do anything at all. So in all honesty I can say aye, Tressa, I'm glad I agreed to come and I'm so excited I can hardly wait.'

Birmingham lived up to the girls' expectations, although Lizzie had been initially alarmed by the traffic, cars, buses, lorries and trams cramming the roads, and the throngs of chatting and often raucous people filling the pavements. She'd thought she'd never sleep for the noise and bustle around her. She shared an attic room with Tressa and two other girls called Pat Matthews and Betty Green, and on the first night sleep eluded her, despite her tiredness, and she kept jerking awake when she did doze off.

It was a full week before Lizzie slept all night, so

wearied by the twelve-hour shift she'd just finished, nothing could disturb her. From that night it became easier and she began to enjoy city life, and there was great entertainment for two girls with money in their pockets, especially living where they did. They were almost in the centre of the city, where the cinemas, theatres, music halls and dance halls abounded, and at first Clara had taken them in hand to show them around.

She suggested both girls took dancing lessons soon after they arrived, for she said Irish dancing was nothing like the dancing done here. However, Lizzie and Tressa caught on quickly, for they found the years of dancing jigs and reels had given them agility and the ability to listen to and move with the music and to follow instructions.

Lizzie loved to dance and she was so looking forward to the social. Whatever Tressa said, you weren't promising a man your hand in marriage for doing the rounds in a quick step or a waltz and she was determined to enjoy herself. The first thing to do was to find something suitable to wear.

The Bull Ring was the place where bargains were to be had, but in a way Lizzie hated going there. She knew of the slump and the men without work and she'd even seen some of the hunger marches go down Colmore Row. But there was no evidence of deprivation in the hotel, in the food served and facilities offered, for the people who came were, in the main, well-to-do and successful, so Lizzie and Tressa were inured from the poverty.

They weren't aware of the teeming back-to-back houses not far from the city centre where families lived in a constant state of hunger, cold and deprivation, pawning all belonging to them to prevent them all starving to death. It was only in the Bull Ring that these things were brought home to them. Lizzie was sorry for the shambling women she saw there, who were sometimes barefoot, which had shocked both girls at first. They often had a squalling baby tied to them with a shawl and a clutch of filthy, ragged, bare-foot children with pinched-in faces, and arms and legs like sticks. They would dart like monkeys to snatch at anything falling off the barrows before the coster could pick it up. The barrow boys would shout at them and often raise a fist, but they were too hungry to take any notice and it tore at Lizzie's heart to see them.

Tressa laughed at her softness when one day she gave a group of children her saved pennies to buy a pie each so that they could have a full belly for once. 'They needed it more than me,' she said in defence when Tressa chided her. 'That eldest boy was about the same age as Johnnie. Think of the difference.'

'And what of the razor blades, shoelaces and hair-grips you buy nearly every time you're let out alone? We have enough in now to stock a shop.'

'Ah, Tressa, doesn't it break your heart to see those poor men with trays about their necks, and many of them blinded or with missing limbs?' Lizzie said. 'They fought in the war-to-end-all-wars and now have no job. They're like debris, thrown out on the scrap heap. I have to buy from them.'

There were always more of the poor about on a

Saturday, hoping to snatch a bargain, but that afternoon, two weeks before the dance, the girls were on a mission. Tressa wouldn't let Lizzie look to left or right and led her straight down the cobbled streets from High Street into the melee and clamour of people and the costers shouting their wares above the noise.

The place had a buzz all of its own and there was always something to see, but that day there was no time to stand and stare. They skirted the flower sellers, around the statue of Nelson, shaking their heads at the proffered bunches and the market hall where the old lags were with their trays. The old lady stood outside Woolworths as she did every day, shouting her wares: 'Carriers, handy carriers,' and they passed Mountford's, where the smell of the meat turning on a spit in the window would make your mouth water.

The rag market was where they were making for, and when they entered it, it still had the familiar whiff of fish lingering, for it sold fish in the week. But now, goods of every description were laid out on carpets or rugs on the floor. Lizzie got a bronze satin dress with lace underskirts: the bodice was decorated with beads and fancy buttons and cut to show the merest hint of cleavage. She even picked up a pair of bronze shoes and a brown fur jacket at the second-hand stall and was well-pleased.

Tressa was equally as happy with her dress of dark red velvet bound in black, for with her blonde hair she suited red. The smart black jacket fitted like a glove and the two-tone shoes were a find. If they pinched a bit, so what. She just had to have them. They made the outfit. The girls were well satisfied and as Tressa said when they dressed up in their room later and spun around before the mirror, 'Don't the pair of us look just terrific?'

The days seemed to drag, but eventually it was time to lift the dresses down from the picture rail where they'd been covered by a sheet, and the two dressed in their finery. Even Lizzie, never one to give herself airs and unaware of her beauty, was stunned. The skirt, which reached the floor, rustled delicately when she walked; and the beads on the bodice, shimmering in the light, brought out the beauty of her creamy skin and made her eyes dance and sparkle. Tressa's gown was pretty enough and she did look beautiful in it, but it was Lizzie's that drew the exclamation from Pat and Betty, who'd demanded to see them both before they set off.

CHAPTER TWO

Lizzie and Tressa stood in the doorway and peeped in. Streamers interspersed with balloons were draped around the walls and hung from the ceiling, while around the edge of the room were small tables. Each one had a lighted candle in a gold-coloured candlestick and it gave a magical feel to the night. At one end of the hall was a band setting up with their instruments, and, to the side, a more than adequate bar.

'Isn't it wonderful?' Lizzie said, as the band struck up the first tune of the night, which was a slow foxtrot to the tune of 'My Foolish Heart'.

'Aye,' Tressa agreed, taking a seat at one of the tables. 'But I hope we are asked up by someone and before too long. Wouldn't it be a desperate situation altogether if we were left sitting at the table by ourselves all night? I'd die of shame.'

There was little danger of it for the girls' entrance had caused quite a stir, and both were asked up almost immediately. As Lizzie spun around the room with one partner after another she began to thoroughly enjoy herself.

They discovered punch early on in the evening and, thinking it to be non-alcoholic, drank plenty of it. Unbeknownst to them, they had been watched for about an hour by two men at the bar, who smiled to themselves and then to each other as they saw the girls fill up their glasses once more and go back to the table for a well-earned rest.

As soon as the men detached themselves from the bar and began to move towards them, the movement drew Tressa's eyes. 'There's two gorgeous fellows heading our way,' she whispered to Lizzie. 'Absolutely terrific, so they are.' And then, as Lizzie was to turn her head for a swift peep, Tressa hissed, 'Don't look around. They'll know we're talking about them.'

Have we to be totally unaware of the two men walking towards us so deliberately, Lizzie thought. It seemed that way, and they'd reached the table before Tressa appeared to see them and Lizzie had her first good look. Both were tall, she noticed, and one had sandy-coloured hair and grey eyes and his mouth was wide and full, his whole attitude one of laughter and fun. His friend, though, was a different kettle of fish altogether, his countenance graver and his attitude altogether more serious. His hair was nearly black, his nose long and mouth thin, but his eyebrows seemed so prominent they almost hid his deep brown eyes.

Lizzie didn't take to him at all, but the other man seemed to have eyes only for Tressa. They asked if they might sit for a while and talk to the ladies, and as Tressa was more than willing there was little Lizzie could say. They introduced themselves: the one enamoured with Tressa was Mike Malone, and the other one, Steve Gillespie. Lizzie sat and sipped her punch and listened to them talking. Both came from a place called Edgbaston, they said, only a short distance away, where they lived just a street apart. They'd been friends since their first day at St Catherine's School and both were in full-time work, in the brass industry. 'We're lucky,' Mike said. 'And we know it, with so many unemployed now.'

They heard of Mike's two elder sisters, now married and away from home. 'I'm the youngest too,' Tressa said. 'Lizzie says I'm spoilt.'

Lizzie opened her mouth to say something, but Mike forestalled her. 'Never,' he said. 'Such a beautiful girl cannot be spoilt. And I love your accents.'

'Your names sound Irish too,' Tressa said. 'But your accents don't.'

'Our dads were both from Ireland,' Steve answered. 'But we've been brought up here. My father has no love of Ireland, for he had a hard time there after he was orphaned at the age of seven.'

Lizzie would have asked more questions, but Mike would not allow it. He forbade all talk of sadness and fetched more punch for the girls and a Guinness each for themselves, before leading Tressa onto the dance floor.

Steve watched Lizzie's eyes as they followed Tressa and he said, 'You don't want to dance, do you?'

It was said ungraciously and Lizzie didn't want to dance, at least not with Steve. She didn't even want to sit with him. He unnerved her. She wanted to say she needed the Ladies, but she could hardly skulk there all night, and anyway, Tressa would root her out and be furious with her. So she said, 'No, no, it's all right.'

'Your glass is empty, I'll get us a refill,' Steve said, and Lizzie was surprised. She couldn't remember drinking the punch at all, but she took a big drink of the glass that Steve brought her as he talked of his father, who'd fought in the Great War as a volunteer. 'He was injured, my father,' Steve went on. 'Had his leg shot to pieces and it probably saved his life.'

'Have you any brothers or sisters?' Lizzie asked. Her voice, she realised, was nothing like her own. It was thicker and the words were harder to form.

'Yeah, one brother, Neil. He's five years younger than me. I'm the golden boy, though, even above my father in my mother's eyes.'

'Oh.'

'Oh yes. If I told my mother to jump, she'd just say, "How high"?'

'I pity the girl you marry then.'

'Oh, I don't know,' Steve said, and his hand caressing Lizzie's made her insides jump about uncomfortably. 'I have good points too, Lizzie Clooney,' he said in a husky whisper. 'And many ways of making a woman very happy.'

Lizzie withdrew her hand and Steve laughed, and Lizzie drained her glass of punch, for she didn't know how to react. But when he took her by the hand and led her onto the dance floor, she went willingly. Even when she felt his hands slide across her bottom as they waltzed to 'The Blue Danube', and his lips nuzzle her neck in the darker corners of the room, she found she didn't mind at all. In fact, she liked it.

Tressa was happy to dance with Mike for the rest of the night, and Lizzie thought dancing with Steve wasn't so bad and better than sitting on her own at the table. At some stage, as the night wore on, Lizzie was brought more punch, and after she'd drunk it she found it hard to stand up, let alone dance, and Steve took her outside. 'You'll feel better with some air,' he said.

Lizzie hoped she would. She felt distinctly odd. Her legs refused to obey her and so did her mouth. She wondered what was the matter with her and she was glad of Steve's arm around her.

Steve Gillespie had been attracted by the young girl since he'd first spotted her, and though he'd seen that Mike had been smitten with her cousin, she was nothing besides Lizzie. Lizzie was a real beauty.

Steve also knew the girl was virtually untouched, probably never even been kissed properly. She was now very drunk and he could guess that it was probably the first time she'd been in this state too, and she would be putty in his hands, if he so desired it. However, he didn't want to scare her off altogether and so he decided he would proceed very slowly. So, when they reached the darkened entry, he kissed her, but gently on the lips and held her close.

Lizzie responded to Steve's kisses. It was her first sexual experience and she felt faint urges tugging at her. Steve wasn't used to such innocence and usually he was out for all he could get with a woman, but he felt an attraction for Lizzie that he had never experienced before. He felt a thrill of excitement when Lizzie groaned as he kissed her neck and throat. He kissed

19

her more passionately, though he didn't prise her lips open with his tongue, feeling that would frighten her. He felt the kirby grips she'd fashioned her hair up with fall to the floor as he held her head, and then he ran his fingers through the freed locks and buried his face in Lizzie's neck. 'Oh, Lizzie.'

The name, whispered so huskily, awakened her a little more and, greatly daring, she put her hands either side of Steve's face and kissed him hungrily. She'd never had a real kiss, but for all that she was excited by feelings she didn't understand, and when Steve ran his hands over her she didn't object.

Steve was surprised, and supposed it was the alcohol she'd consumed that was making her so compliant. When she continued to kiss him and pressed her body close against his, he could not resist trying to go further. With his arm around her, he cupped one of her breasts, and when Lizzie didn't push him away he felt the heat of desire flow through his body and his fumbling fingers began unbuttoning the bodice of her gown.

Lizzie, even in her hazy state, reacted strongly. 'Stop it, Steve! What are you doing?'

'Showing you how much I care for you,' Steve said huskily, tightening his arms around her. 'Ah, come on, Lizzie? Don't stop now.'

'No,' Lizzie said, pulling away from him. 'I'm not that sort of girl.' She began to do up the buttons, unaware in her tipsy state that she'd clumsily buttoned herself up wrongly and left two buttons undone entirely. 'I want to go back in now,' she said, and Steve didn't protest. He knew he had gone too far and too fast, and he also knew if he wanted to have a chance to see this beautiful girl again he would have to proceed slowly.

Tressa, coming into the hall, intending to look for Lizzie, saw them come in. When she saw the state of Lizzie, her flushed cheeks, messed-up hair falling about her face and unbuttoned bodice, she thought Lizzie and Steve had been up to far more than they had. She was mightily glad Mike hadn't come with her and there were no other witness either, and also glad the Ladies led off the hall. With a glare at Steve that should have rendered him senseless on the floor, she shoved Lizzie into the Ladies to try and repair the damage.

'You bloody little fool,' she admonished as she wiped Lizzie's face with her handkerchief, which she had dampened under the tap. 'You haven't the sense you were born with. Why did you agree to go outside with him in the first place?'

Lizzie looked at Tressa with an inane grin on her face. For the life of her she couldn't understand why Tressa was cross. 'For air,' she said. 'I was hot.'

'Hot, my foot,' Tressa cried. 'The state you're in, Steve Gillespie could have taken advantage of you.' Might have taken advantage of you, she thought, but didn't put in to words.

But what she said got through to Lizzie's befuddled brain. 'No,' she replied. 'I'm a good girl, Tressa.'

'Aye, course you are,' Tressa said sarcastically, buttoning Lizzie's bodice up correctly. 'Turn round and I'll see if I can do something with this hair, and then I'm getting you a big glass of water and you are going to drink it. That punch is alcoholic, you know; Mike

21

told me. I took to orange afterwards.' Lizzie heard the words but they didn't seem to matter. Nothing did, and she just grinned again. Tressa sighed and said wearily, 'What's the use of talking to you? Turn around and let me see if I can work some sort of miracle.'

There were not enough grips to put Lizzie's hair up the way it had been and Tressa was forced to leave some of it loose, but it looked good even so. When Lizzie had obediently drunk the water, Tressa, surveying her, thought she'd done the best she could in the circumstances and led her back onto the dance floor.

Steve was sitting with Mike, and when he saw Lizzie framed for a moment in the doorway he thought he'd never seen anyone lovelier. Her face was no longer flushed and she had regained her creamy complexion, and her hair, though tidy, was now allowing waves to fall down her back and tendrils of it framed her face. He stepped forward quickly to claim Lizzie before someone else did, a large glass of punch in his hand. She lifted it to her lips, her eyes met Tressa's, who raised hers to the ceiling as Lizzie took a large gulp.

The next morning, when Lizzie opened her eyes because Tressa was shaking her, she felt as if she'd fallen into the pit of Hell. A thousand hammers were beating in her head, her eyes throbbed and she felt sick. 'Leave me alone.'

'No way will I,' Tressa said. She was glad the other two girls that shared the room were not there, for they were on breakfasts this morning while she and Lizzie weren't on duty until six, and looking at her cousin's comatose frame she was glad of it.

Tressa expected Lizzie to feel bad. Mike had said she'd have a bad head when she woke in the morning. They'd had to nearly carry her home and she'd almost tumbled down the stairs as Tressa forced her up them, her arm around Lizzie's waist; and now she lay like one dead, while Tressa's insides were filled with delicious excitement at seeing Mike again, and she was letting no drunken cousin spoil it. 'Get up!' she commanded, giving Lizzie a shove.

'I can't.'

'You can and you bloody will. We've got Mass at eleven o'clock and the fellows are going to meet us outside.'

'The fellows! What fellows?'

'God, Lizzie! What fellows do you think? Mike and Steve, of course. We arranged it yesterday. Don't you remember?'

Lizzie shook her head, but gently. She remembered very little, but she recalled her earlier feelings about Steve. 'I don't think I like Steve much,' she said.

Tressa looked at her scornfully. 'Oh aye,' she retorted sarcastically. 'Is that why you danced with him all night and went out with him into the night, arm in arm, and came back with your hair looking like you'd been pulled through a hedge backwards and your bodice nearly unbuttoned?'

Lizzie sat bolt upright in the bed, putting her hands to her aching head as she did so and fighting nausea. 'I didn't,' she breathed, horrified. 'Say I didn't?'

'You did. You were all over him and his hands were everywhere when you danced and you never said a word. You couldn't get close enough. Even when we

23

sat down, you sat on Steve's knee and nuzzled into his neck. It was embarrassing. Do you remember none of it?'

'No. Oh God!' Lizzie said. 'I can't even remember how I got home.'

'They walked back with us,' Tressa said. 'I could never have managed you on my own. I told you that punch was alcoholic, for all the good it did. You just kept knocking it back.'

Lizzie couldn't remember Tressa telling her that, couldn't remember anything much. But, whether she could remember it or not hardly mattered. According to Tressa, those glasses of punch had caused her to do God knows what with a person she had just met and in her sober moments hadn't cared for. The evils of drink – Jesus Christ! Her mother had been right all along.

And she felt so ill. 'Tressa, I feel like death. I don't think I'll make Mass this morning,' she said.

Tressa laughed. 'You're hammered, and for the first time in your life, I bet,' she said. 'Your mother would be scandalised.'

'It's not funny.'

'No, it isn't,' Tressa said. 'And you're not spoiling my Sunday off because you got drunk last night. We wouldn't have got home at all if Steve hadn't nearly carried you to the door, and I nearly broke my neck getting you in the room. When we got here, you lay on the bed and began to laugh. The other girls were none too pleased being woken up, I can tell you.'

'I woke them up!'

'Not just them I shouldn't think,' Tressa said with gusto, laying it on. 'God, you were in a state. I undressed

24

you because you were incapable of doing it yourself. I put on your nightdress and tucked you up, and you owe me. So get on your feet.'

'I can't, Tressa, I'll throw up.'

'Well then, throw up,' Tressa said unsympathetically. 'Didn't your mother ever tell you it was better out than in? And when you've been sick, take a couple of aspirin, clean your teeth, wash your face and put on your clothes for Mass.'

'Did anyone ever tell you how aggravating you are, and a bloody prig into the bargain?' Lizzie said, getting to her feet with difficulty and a degree of caution. She was unable to wait for Tressa's response to this, though, for she had to run to the bathroom, her hand to her mouth, while Tressa's tinkling laugh followed her down the corridor.

Steve noticed Lizzie's pallor as soon as she emerged from the church and guessed the reason for it. He felt sorry for her, certain that the previous night had been her first brush with alcohol.

She was so embarrassed in front of him. She could scarcely meet his eyes, and though he thought she'd remember little of the previous night, he knew her cousin would have filled in any gaps and probably with embellishment.

'Where shall we go?' Mike asked. 'The day is too raw for walking much. I fancy a pub somewhere.'

'Somewhere where we can get food would be nice,' Tressa said. 'My stomach thinks my throat is cut.'

'Of course, Communion,' Mike said. 'What about the Old Joint Stock?'

Tressa made a face. 'No, they don't do food. Anyway, it's too close.' It was just down the road from the hotel, near to Snow Hill Station. 'Half the hotel go in there from time to time.'

'What about The Old Royal in Edmund Street?'

'I don't know if they do food either. I've never been in.'

'What about you, Lizzie? Have you a preference?'

Oh God yes, she had a preference. It was to go back to the hotel, crawl into bed and let the world go on without her, that's what her preference was. Catching sight of Tressa's face, she knew that if she voiced those thoughts her life wouldn't be worth living. 'No, not really.'

'Tell you what,' Steve said suddenly, 'let's go down Digbeth Way. We can cut down by the Bull Ring and there's hundreds of pubs there and we're bound to find one doing lunches.'

'Aye, and the walk will give us an appetite.'

'God, I don't need to walk to give me an appetite,' Tressa said. 'If I don't eat soon I might go mad altogether.'

'What d'you mean, *go* mad?' Mike said with a laugh, and when Tressa went to hit him with her handbag he caught her around the waist instead and kissed her on the lips.

Lizzie was shocked at Tressa behaving that way in daylight and in front of a church too. She saw Mike now had his arm around Tressa and both were laughing and looking at each other in such a way that Lizzie felt suddenly shut out.

Steve saw it too. When he draped an arm over her

26

she wanted to protest at the familiarity, but then she remembered Tressa's account of how she'd behaved with the selfsame man just the previous evening and felt she could say nothing.

'How about you, Lizzie?' Mike asked. 'Are you hungry too?'

Lizzie gave a brief shake of her head, but regretted it immediately for it started the thumping pain again. 'No,' she said with a sigh. 'I'm not hungry at all, and even the thought of food makes me feel sick.'

'You need some of Uncle Steve's medicine,' Steve told her.

'Uncle Steve's medicine? What's that?'

'You'll soon find out,' he said with a smile.

'Brandy,' Lizzie said. 'I've never had brandy in my life.'

She felt the nausea rise in her throat as Mike said, 'You've not lived. Drink it down, it'll settle your stomach.'

She looked around at them all watching her in this little old pub called The Woodman, chosen because it had a restaurant on the side, and she wondered if Steve was right, for the different smells of alcohol, cigarette smoke and food cooking were making her feel incredibly sick. She'd die of embarrassment if she was sick in front of everyone, and Tressa would kill her altogether.

Lizzie picked up her balloon glass and looked at the amber liquid. 'There's an awful lot of it.'

'I asked for a double,' Steve said. 'I thought it an extreme case. Get it down you.'

'It smells awful,' Lizzie moaned, putting the glass down. 'I couldn't.'

'Course you could,' Tressa snapped. 'For God's sake, Lizzie, you're not putting it up your nose. Don't be such a wet blanket.'

Steve put his arm around Lizzie and said gently, 'Trust your Uncle Steve, he's had more hangovers than you've had hot dinners, and I know this will make you feel better. Hair of the dog, d'you see.'

Lizzie didn't see at all, but suddenly she put the glass to her lips and took a gulp. It was like the very worst medicine she'd ever tasted and it burned her throat and made her eyes water, but even as she coughed and spluttered she felt the warmth of it trickling down her throat.

'Treat it with care,' Steve said, touched by Lizzie's naivety, his arm still around her. 'Sip it.'

Lizzie warmed to Steve for his patience and understanding, and when she had emptied the brandy glass she had to admit it did settle her stomach, but it went straight to her head and made it swim. However, that felt quite pleasant and was better by far than the pounding ache.

When Mike came back with the news that he had a table booked for one o'clock, even Lizzie didn't dread it so much; and when Steve bought her and Tressa a port, the drink Tressa had had previously, Lizzie took it without a murmur, and liked the dark, slightly sweet drink much better than the brandy.

Lizzie and Tressa had been introduced to wine with the meal and neither were keen. Lizzie drank sparingly anyway, for the port and brandy had made her feel strange enough and she hoped they weren't to stop in

there all afternoon, though it was no day to be outside either. Mike and Steve must have felt the same,
for as they finished their apple pie and custard, Mike
said, 'How d'you two feel about the pictures?'

Lizzie was delighted. Since arriving in Birmingham
she'd been many times to the pictures with Tressa and
liked nothing better. 'What's on?' she asked. '*The Blue
Angel* is on at the Odeon on New Street,' Steve said.
'I noticed on the way here. It stars Marlene Dietrich.
Fancy that?'

'Oh yes,' Tressa said. 'Neither of us have seen that.'

Steve was very attentive to Lizzie as they prepared
to leave, fetching her coat and helping her into it, and
taking her arm once outside. The wind had come up
and icy spears of rain were attacking them, and Lizzie
was glad of Steve's arms encircling her, holding her so
close she was able to semi-bury her head into his coat.

Steve felt ten-foot tall holding this slight-framed girl
in his arms. He'd had many sexual experiences and
with a variety of women, for he was a highly sexed
man, but never had his heart been stirred before. But
it was stirred now all right, in fact it had been churned
up right and proper, and the prospect of her beside
him in the dark of the cinema filled him with excitement.

Lizzie was delighted by the chocolates Steve presented her with in the cinema, but puzzled when he
led her into the back row. Nevertheless, she presumed
he had just followed Mike and Tressa, who were in
front of them, and she sank into the seat in contentment.

No one had ever bought her a box of chocolates

before and she took off the wrapper and looked in amazement at the selection. 'All right?' Steve asked.

'More than all right, much more,' Lizzie said, and, leaning over, she kissed Steve on the cheek. 'Thank you.'

Steve felt expectation fill his body and Lizzie gave a sigh of contentment as the lights dimmed and she sat back to enjoy the film.

Evidently, Steve was uninterested in the film, for it had barely started when she felt his arm trail around her neck. She made no protest, though, until his hand cupped her breast, and then she gasped in shock. She shrugged her shoulder, hoping to dislodge his hand without disturbing the people in front of them. Steve, thinking Lizzie's gasp was one of pleasure, began kissing and then gently biting her neck.

Lizzie threw Steve's arm off roughly and moved away, sitting up straight in her seat. 'Stop it.'

'What? Stop what?'

'All that sort of carry on.'

'Oh for God's sake, Lizzie.'

'Look, whatever impression you had of me at the dance, I'm not that sort of girl.'

'You could have fooled me.'

'Yes, well, now you know.'

'You agreed quick enough to come into the back row.'

'Ssh,' said someone in front of them. 'Go and have your row someplace else. We've bought tickets for this film and want to see and hear it.'

'Sorry,' Lizzie responded, flaming with embarrassment.

Steve was smiling, but in the darkness she couldn't see that. 'Look around you,' he whispered in her ear.

She did, and though she could see little she knew some of the people were in very odd positions altogether and her eyes widened in shock when she thought she saw Mike's hand inside Tressa's clothes. Maybe, she thought, you said you were up for things like that when you agreed to go into the back row. She didn't know the rules for this place. They'd never had any type of cinema in Ballintra, but she had no intention of forgetting herself.

'We'll hold hands,' she said.

'Hold hands!' Steve cried in dismay. He'd forgotten to lower his voice and the people in front glared around at them. 'I'll have a word with the usherette if you don't pack it in.'

Mortified, Lizzie grasped Steve's hand firmly. After all, she told herself, she hardly knew the man and he wasn't her type at all. Holding hands was really all he could expect.

Steve held hands, knowing he'd get no further and would only worsen things if he was to insist or try and force Lizzie; but never had he sat and just held hands before, especially if he'd bought drinks and chocolates. This time he'd even splashed out on a meal as well. Most girls would be more than grateful and not averse to a bit of slap and tickle themselves. Look at Tressa with Mike. Christ, he envied him, but his Lizzie sat rigid and he knew if he wanted to win her he'd have to play by her rules, for now at least.

CHAPTER THREE

Because of the girls' shifts, it was the 23rd of December before Tressa and Lizzie saw Mike and Steve again, when they were taken to a theatre called The Alex to see *Snow White and the Seven Dwarves.*

'A fairy story!' Lizzie cried in disbelief.

'It's a pantomime,' Steve said.

'What's a pantomime?'

'You'll see.'

And Lizzie saw. She saw a sort of play with music, where the principal boy was a girl dressed up and the crowd were encouraged to boo and hiss and cheer and clap and some of the jokes were so suggestive they made her face flame. She wasn't at all sure if she enjoyed it or not, but the others seemed to and so she said nothing. Then, they were taken to the Old Joint Stock for a few drinks before being delivered back to the hotel.

Tressa was happily tipsy and confided to Lizzie when they reached their room that she was in love with Mike.

'How can you be?' Lizzie demanded, shocked. 'You've only just met.'

'Sometimes a person just knows these things.'

Lizzie was still doubtful, but whether Tressa was in love with Mike or not, Lizzie knew that with their shift rota there would be little chance of her seeing Mike before the New Year. Christmas was almost upon them, one of the busiest periods of all at the hotel, where time off was minimal or altogether non-existent, and any free time they did have was usually spent sleeping the deep sleep of the totally exhausted.

All Tressa could talk about, though, was Mike. 'I love him,' she declared. 'Wait till you love someone, you'll sing a different tune then. It'll hit you like a ton of bricks, I bet.'

'Maybe,' Lizzie said. 'We'll have to wait and see. It hasn't yet anyway, and remember, when you marry it's for life, Tressa.'

'I know that,' Tressa replied, 'but if I wait a lifetime I'll want no one else. How d'you feel about Steve?'

'He's all right.'

'Come on, why don't you give the man a chance?'

'I have. I am. I just don't feel that way about him.'

'He's smitten with you.'

'How d'you know?'

'You just do, the way he looks at you. His eyes never leave you. You must have noticed.'

Had she, and refused to acknowledge it? She didn't know, but it was obvious Tressa was right because when they next went out with Mike and Steve in January, Steve asked her to tea the following Sunday to meet his parents, as she was free until seven o'clock that evening.

'Why don't you want to go?' Tressa asked later. 'I'm going to see Mike's.'

'I know, but you and Mike . . . well, it's different.'

'Lizzie, all you have to do is smile and be polite. What's so hard?'

'It's not that. It's the complexion Steve will put on it. It means something, surely, when you meet the parents?' Lizzie bit on her thumbnail in consternation. 'I mean, maybe it would be better to end it now, stop him getting ideas.'

No way did Tressa want Lizzie doing that, but she didn't say this. Instead, she said, 'How will you tell him? Do you know where he lives?'

'No, well, only vaguely.'

'So, you're going to wait until he comes, when everyone's gone to the trouble, made tea and all sorts, and you'll let him go back alone to face their ridicule and scorn?'

Lizzie hadn't thought of that. 'You think it's better to go through with it then?'

'I think it's the only thing to do now. You should have told him straight at the time.'

'I meant to. He sort of took me aback a bit.'

'Well, I think you've got to see it through now,' Tressa told her, and Lizzie knew in her heart of hearts that Tressa was right.

Edgbaston was Lizzie's first experience of back-to-back housing. Steve and Mike had come to meet the girls and as they alighted from the tram on Bristol Street, which was another first for them both, they all went up Bristol Passage, and at the top both girls stood and stared. Lizzie was in shock, and so, she saw, was Tressa. Nothing in their lives so far had prepared them for anything like these cramped and crowded houses, squashed together in front of grey pavements and grey cobbled roads. And so many of them: they went on and on, street after street of them. Even when Lizzie had seen the beggars and poor in the market, she'd not thought of them living in places like this. She'd not think of anyone living in places like this. Her father's calves were better housed.

The two men didn't seem to notice the girls' disquiet. 'We've come to the parting of the ways now,' Mike said. 'You go straight up Grant Street, so we'll see you later.'

When they moved off, Steve put his arm around Lizzie. 'All right?'

Whatever she felt privately, Lizzie told herself this place was Steve's home, and she hadn't any right to criticise it. How would she feel if she took him to Ireland and he tore her family's farm apart? And so she said, 'Aye, I'm grand.'

'It's bound to be a bit strange at first.'

'Aye.'

'And it's natural to be nervous.'

'Aye.'

'Can you say anything other than "Aye"?' Steve said with a grin, and Lizzie smiled back and answered in the same vein: 'Aye.'

Steve's parents' house was number thirty-five, halfway up the hill, and it opened onto the street. 'We'll go in the entry door,' Steve said, and led the way down a long, dark tunnel between two houses, where there was a door on either side. He turned the handle and went in, but not before Lizzie had had a glimpse of the cobbled yard the entry led to with washing lines criss-crossing the place and three toddlers playing in the dirt and grime.

Steve, following her gaze, said, 'Normally this place is teeming with children. The bad weather today is keeping most of them inside.'

'Aye,' Lizzie said again, and ignored Steve's sardonic grin as she wondered where in God's name the teeming children played. But she had no time to frame this question, for Steve had gone inside and Lizzie had no option but to follow.

To the left of the entry door was a scullery of sorts, with a sink with lidded buckets beneath it and shelves to one side. There was no tap, and Lizzie wondered at that. Yawning cellar steps were directly in front of her and there was a door to the side which was ajar, and which was where the family were assembled to meet Lizzie.

Lizzie saw there was just one small-paned window letting light in, and that was covered with curtains of lace and heavier curtains of blue brocade hanging on either side. 'So you're here then,' said a thin, sour woman Lizzie assumed to be Steve's mother.

'As you see, Ma, as you see.'

Now she had time to study the woman, Lizzie saw she had many of the same features as Steve and thought it odd that though they turned Steve into a handsome and presentable man, they turned his mother grim-faced and surly looking, unless it was life itself that had given her that discontented air.

Steve's father was introduced as Rodney and was just a little taller than his wife, and Steve's brother Neil was the same. Both had sandy hair and pale brown eyes, their noses had little shape and they had slack lips and an indeterminate chin, while Steve's was chiselled and firm. Lizzie wondered if Neil resented his brother at all, for he was obviously at the back of the queue when good looks were given out. Beside his tall, brawny brother, he looked like a wee boy, and when he shook her hand his was clammy and limp and his father's little better. It was like shaking hands with a warm, wet fish.

But she was to soon learn much of Neil's rancour was caused by his mother, and it had nothing to do with looks or size, for, as Steve had boasted the first time Lizzie had met him, Flo only had eyes for her eldest son. He was the light of her life, and in case there should be any doubts, Flo went into a litany of how good, honest, upright, decent, respectable, etc. Steve was. What a marvellous son, a tremendous man altogether, and, she inferred, Lizzie was lucky to have him.

The point was, Lizzie didn't want him. Flo could keep him by her side a wee while longer, but now wasn't the time to say so.

It was a comfortable and well-furnished room, Lizzie had to admit. A brass clock was set on the mantelshelf below the picture of the Sacred Heart of Jesus, that familiar picture in all Catholic homes. A selection of brass ornaments were either side of the clock, and a shop-bought, fluffy blue rug was before the gleaming brass fender. Dark blue armchairs and a matching settee, each scattered with cushions of pale blue and cream, were pulled in front of the fire, which was roaring up the chimney. The linen, lace-edged arm covers on the chairs matched the antimacassars draped across the backs of the chairs and settee. Against the wall was a sideboard with a runner across the length of it and a large oval mirror above. Brass candlesticks stood each end of the runner with a potted aspidistra in the middle.

Lizzie guessed the table against the other wall matched the sideboard, for the ladder-backed chairs around it certainly did, but it had a tablecloth of lace covering it.

In one of the chimney recesses were shelves holding some books and a few toby jugs, but the wall the other side was covered in photographs of Steve. The brothers were so unlike each other, both in looks and stature, there was no mistaking them. There was just the one picture Lizzie could see that had been taken when Steve looked to be about ten and Neil about five. The rest were all of Steve: one of him as a baby on a lambskin rug, then as a toddler and a schoolboy. Steve's First Communion was also documented, as was his Confirmation, and him in his new suit for the occasion, and another where he wore new overalls, checked shirt and shiny new boots, probably for his first day at work. There were none of anyone else.

The visit could not be considered a success. She knew afterwards that, whatever she'd done or said wouldn't have been right, for the talk was stilted and false, and though the tea was adequate and well-prepared it felt like sawdust in Lizzie's mouth. I pity the girl who eventually takes Steve on, she thought, for Flo will make her life a misery. Thank the Lord it's not going to be me!

Eventually, Lizzie ran out of things to say and there was an uncomfortable silence for a minute or two before Rodney Gillespie began on his favourite topic: hatred of the Irish generally and Ireland in particular. 'I was found by the parish priest when I was but seven years old,' he said, 'and all about me were dead or dying of TB. He took me in and tended me and apprenticed me to a brass worker in Birmingham the week after my eighth birthday.'

Lizzie did feel for the old man for Steve had explained some of the work they did the night they'd gone to the Old Joint Stock after the pantomime. He'd told Lizzie how the copper and zinc were turned into molten brass in furnaces that burned white-hot, and how they had to carry heavy ladles of it to pour into crucibles. He spoke of the heat and the danger and the way hands grew cracked and calloused and how bare backs ran with sweat all the day long, and of how his father had been at the work since he'd been a young boy.

'Ah, God, for a wee child to be in such a place,' she'd said.

'Yeah, it was a hard life for him I think,' Steve told her. 'The apprentice was always the whipping boy, the one who got the toe of someone's boot in his behind if he slackened at all, or spilt precious metal. Yet he has a love of England and brass, for he says it's given him a home. There was always enough food for us, bags of coal and warm clothes and boots for the winter and blankets for the bed. My mother has never had to pawn.'

Lizzie had never heard the word pawn, so Steve had explained it to her, but she'd understood the rest: how a young boy was given the gift of life, and a good life, though a hard one. But now she saw he was revelling in this story that he must have told often, almost enjoying it, when life for many was hard then. So when he said, 'Ireland took everything from me: parents, brothers and sisters,' Lizzie said,

'I thought it was tuberculosis did that?'

And then she nearly jumped out of her skin as Rodney's hand slammed the table with such ferocity the crockery rattled. 'Tuberculosis wouldn't have taken hold if they'd all had the right food, and a decent cottage rather than the stinking hovel we had, and money for medicines,' he thundered. 'Ireland is no friend of mine.'

No one said a word after that, and the silence was strained. Lizzie left as soon as she decently could.

'Don't start my father on about Ireland if you don't want a tirade,' Steve warned later as they made their way to the tram stop. 'He's a mild-mannered man in most things but that, and he can't bear being contradicted.'

'Well, we might not meet again, so it will hardly matter.'

'Of course you will, you silly girl.'

Lizzie decided she couldn't let Steve go on in blissful ignorance of how she felt, and so she said gently, 'Don't read too much in to this, Steve.'

'In to what?'

'This visit to meet your parents.'

'What're you on about?'

'I'm not ready for anything serious, not with you or anyone yet.'

'Don't be stupid,' Steve said. 'When you agreed to come it meant . . . well, it means something. Why did you come if you feel like that?'

The tram pulled up then and Steve waited until they were seated before he said, 'It was him, wasn't it, that put you off: the old man, and our poker-faced Neil.'

'No, it wasn't them.' Lizzie tried to explain without hurting Steve's feelings too much. 'I admit I was alarmed by the way your father reacted, but that isn't the reason I've said I don't want anything serious. I . . . I just don't want to be tied down.'

'I ain't in no hurry for marriage,' Steve said. 'But you can still be my girl, can't you?'

'No, Steve.'

'Look, it's how it is: Tressa and Mike, and me and you.'

'Tressa and Mike have got nothing to do with us. We're separate people.'

'Mike won't see it that way. We're marras, mates, like, and if I tell him this he'll chuck your cousin without a thought.'

'He wouldn't.'

'Yeah, he would.'

Lizzie wondered if Steve was right. She remembered Tressa's face earlier that day, the adoring looks she kept giving Mike. She had it bad, Lizzie knew that, and she also knew she couldn't live with herself if she was to be the cause of the break-up.

'Look,' Steve said. 'Do you dislike me; find me physically repulsive?'

Lizzie shook her head, for her initial dislike of Steve had frittered away, and he was a very good-looking man.

'Do you like me, even a little?'

'Of course I like you, but as a friend.'

'That will do, Lizzie. I have enough love for both of us.'

'No, Steve. It isn't like that.'

'I know, but sometimes feelings take time to grow,' Steve urged her. 'Give it a few more weeks, eh? Give me a chance. For God's sake don't pull the bleedin' rug from under me already. We've only known each other a short time.'

'And then what, after a few weeks?'

'You'll be madly in love with me.'

'And if I'm not?'

'I don't accept failure,' Steve said.

Nor does he accept 'No', Lizzie thought. He's like Tressa. He wants his own way all the time, for he's used to it.

But she said none of this, for the tram had pulled into the terminus in the city centre and Steve put his arm around Lizzie as they walked along. She didn't object, because she was thinking over Steve's words. Would it be any better if she told him in a few weeks' time? She didn't know, but at least then he couldn't say she hadn't given it a fair crack of the whip.

'I'll give them all what for when I go home,' Steve told Lizzie, convinced, whatever Lizzie had said, that it was his family's behaviour that had made her say what she had.

'Steve, there's no need.'

'There's every need,' Steve snapped. 'They'll behave better next time, I promise you. I'll even have a go at the old woman. She could have been more welcoming.'

'She loves you, Steve,' Lizzie said. 'She doesn't want anyone, especially any woman, to be more important in your life than she is.'

'She'll have to learn then,' Steve said. 'Silly cow. She'll do as she's bloody well told.'

'Hush, Steve. Try and understand her point of view,' Lizzie said, though she had no love for the woman herself.

'She should bloody well understand mine,' Steve growled. 'And she will. I'll see to it.'

Lizzie had had quite enough of Steve's family. 'I'll have to go in, Steve,' she said. 'I'll be late and then I'll catch it.'

She was glad to go, for this bad-tempered Steve unnerved her more than a little. She almost felt the anger coursing through him as he drew her into his arms. The kiss was like a stamp of ownership. It was a hard, unyielding kiss, which bruised Lizzie's lips and pushed them against her teeth, but Lizzie bore it without complaint, for she was too nervous of Steve to protest much.

She was changed and ready to go on duty when Tressa dashed in, red-faced both from the cold and the warmth of Mike's embrace, and the kisses which had left her breathless. She was prepared to make light of any trepidations Lizzie might have had about Steve and his family problems, though she was pleased that Lizzie had agreed to go out with Steve a little longer. Lizzie felt she was being inexorably drawn into a future she didn't want and felt filled with apprehension as she and Tressa went down to the kitchen.

The following Saturday morning, the head waiter, who had a soft spot for Lizzie, approached her as she was finishing her breakfast stint. 'You and your cousin were down to work tonight, but you can have the night off if you like.'

'I thought we had a big party in?'

'We did have, but so many have come down with flu they've cancelled, and the hotel isn't exactly bursting at the seams at this time of year. So, do you and Tressa want this or shall I offer it to one of the others, because the manager won't pay for half of you to be doing nothing?'

Lizzie didn't need asking twice and neither did Tressa, who insisted on letting the boys know. Lizzie would have preferred for the two of them to do something together, as they used to, but she told herself she had to get used to the fact that Mike was now the most important person in Tressa's life. She also knew that Tressa was quite capable of throwing a mammoth sulk if Lizzie refused to do what she wanted, and then the value of the Saturday night would be lost to the both of them. And so they travelled up to Edgbaston to tell Steve and Mike.

They met that evening in the Old Joint Stock again, because it was easiest, and when Tressa and Mike sloped off after the one drink, Lizzie and Steve weren't surprised.

'So, what do you want to do?' Steve asked.

There was no hesitation. 'I'd like to go down to the Bull Ring,' Lizzie said. 'I've never been at night, but all the other girls have told me how good it is and the entertainment to be had there on a Saturday.'

Steve had no problem with that and Lizzie was filled with excitement as she stood at the top of High Street and saw it all arrayed below them. She was glad too that she had Steve's arm around her, for the night was a chilly one.

It was all so different from the daytime, though just as full of people. Now it was lit up by spluttering gas flares and looked almost magical. There were still the poor, hoping to get meat or vegetables cheap, but they were hidden by the darkness. The flower sellers had gone from their usual space around Nelson's statue, along with most of the old lags selling their wares from trays around their necks, and there was no little old lady outside Woolworths urging people to buy a carrier bag. However, others had taken their places, and one was a stall selling cockles and mussels and jellied eels. 'Are you hungry? D'you want some?' Steve asked.

'Ooh no, thank you,' Lizzie said. She had no liking for cockles or mussels, and as for jellied eels . . . 'I've tried them just the once,' she said. 'They're slimy.'

Steve laughed. 'That's the idea,' he said, and he smacked his lips as if he was going to enjoy a great feast, as he soaked his dish liberally with vinegar. He lifted one to his mouth and sucked it in with a slurp, laughing again at Lizzie's look of distaste. 'Lovely,' he said. 'Slips down the throat a treat.'

'You're welcome to them,' Lizzie told him, wrinkling

45

her nose. 'Give me a hot potato any day.'

'I'll buy you one if that's what you want,' Steve said. 'Might even get one myself to fill a corner.'

'Fill a corner!' Lizzie said scornfully. 'You're always filling corners, you.' She was right, for Steve had a voracious appetite. 'I think you have worms.'

Steve roared with laughter. 'Worms! Don't be so daft, woman. There's a lot of me to fill. I'm a big strapping chap.'

He was right there, Lizzie thought, as with the eels finished he draped a heavy arm around Lizzie once more. His fingers resting on her shoulder smelt of vinegar and fish and she turned her face away, but she said nothing and they went on through the crowd.

There was a man tied up in chains demanding more money in the hat before he tried to get free. Lizzie thought he looked decidedly uncomfortable. 'Have you ever seen him get out?' she whispered to Steve.

'Never,' he said, tossing a florin into the hat, 'though I've paid enough to, over the years. Mike says he's seen it, but I doubt it.'

They got fed up waiting in the end and walked on. 'I think it's all a con, anyroad,' Steve said.

'How?'

'Them chains can't be real, can they? I mean, how could anyone get out of real chains when they are trussed up like he was?' And then, seeing Lizzie's crestfallen face, he gave a gentle laugh and tightened his arm around her. 'Spoilt your illusions, have I?'

Lizzie didn't answer, for her attention was taken by two stilt-walkers moving effortlessly amongst the crowds and between the stalls and barrows, and standing so immensely high that her mouth dropped open in amazement.

But Steve pushed her on to where the boxing ring was set up. 'Me and Mike had a go here when we was lads,' he said. 'Knocked on our backs, the pair of us,' he added, laughing at the memory. 'Wouldn't be so easy for him to do that to me today.'

'Like to try your luck, sir?' the man in the black top hat and red jacket encouraged, seeing Steve's interest. The assembled crowd turned to see who he was addressing and shuffled their feet in anticipation of a fight. 'Five pounds if you beat the champ,' the man said.

Steve looked at the glowering champ sat in the corner of the ring. He was broad and hefty, terrifying to him as a boy, and he remembered the way the big man with fists like hams had felled him with one blow, and how he lay on the ring floor with the breath knocked out of his body and thought every bone and joint had been loosened. But the champ was running to fat now, and Steve, full-grown, well-muscled and strong, reckoned he could give the bruiser a run for his money.

'Don't, Steve.'

'Five pounds is five pounds, pet,' Steve said. But it wasn't the money. It was the thought of the fight wiping the supercilious smile off the champ's face, maybe making Lizzie proud of him. He didn't know that such an action would not make Lizzie proud; that she hated violence.

'I could beat that bastard with one hand tied behind my back,' Steve sneered, and Lizzie pressed against him and felt the excitement pounding through his body.

The champ snarled at him. 'Words is cheap, mate. Come up here and prove it. I'll pound you into the ground, you cheeky young pup.'

'Right,' Steve cried, and tried to disentangle himself from Lizzie, but she held on to his coat. 'No, Steve. Please don't.'

'Come on, darling, it's only a bit of fun.'

'Please, I can't bear it. For my sake, don't do this.'

Steve was pleased that Lizzie was showing such obvious concern for him. He hadn't been aware she felt so strongly about him getting hurt and it gave him a glimmer of hope. No way was he going to risk upsetting her, so he smiled ruefully and said, 'We'll have to settle the score some other time, mate. I've got my orders for the moment.'

There was understanding laughter amongst the crowd and Lizzie was embarrassed by everyone looking at them. 'Come on.'

'I would have been all right, you know,' Steve said when they were out of earshot.

'I don't care.'

'You didn't want me face messed up, is that it?'

'I didn't want you hurt at all,' Lizzie said.

'I didn't think you cared.'

'Of course I care.'

Steve pressed her close. 'You don't know how good it makes me feel when you say things like that.'

Lizzie's heart gave a lurch. She didn't mean it that way at all, but before she was able to explain this Steve had grabbed her arm. 'Look, there's the man who lies on the bed of nails,' he said, and taking her hand he pulled her into the ring of onlookers watching the man, lying seemingly unconcerned.

'Who'd like to stand on my stomach?' the man said as they approached, scanning the women in the crowd. 'You, darling, or you? Come on. Don't be shy. Promise I won't look up your skirt.'

Eventually, a girl stepped forward. She would have been about Lizzie's age, and she was out with a crowd of similar-aged girls who were egging her on. In horrified fascination, Lizzie watched the girl remove her shoes and step gingerly onto the man's stomach. Lizzie was glad of Steve's arm around her, glad that she could bury her face in his coat and not see the nails sinking into the man's flesh to the sympathetic 'ooh's and 'ah's of the crowd.

Coins splattered into the bucket, but Steve led Lizzie away. The accordions and fiddles had begun their tunes, and as they passed the hot potato man, Steve bought them one each, served in a poke of paper folded into a triangle to protect hands.

The tunes being played at first reminded Lizzie of Ireland and they lifted her spirits. She had the urge to lift up her skirts and dance the jigs and reels of her youth, but she didn't, for she guessed Steve wouldn't like her to make such an exhibition of herself. She contented herself by leaning against Steve and tapping her foot to the music as she ate her potato. Then they changed to the popular songs of the music hall that Lizzie had learnt during her time in Birmingham. They began with, 'By the Light of the Silvery Moon' and went on to 'Just a Song at Twilight', before changing tempo to, 'I'm Getting Married in the Morning'. By the time they'd got to 'Daisy, Daisy' the crowd had begun to sway and they really belted out 'Roll Out the Barrel', 'It's a Long Way to Tipperary' and 'Knees up, Mother Brown' before the musicians ended the impromptu concert with 'The Old Bull and Bush'.

Lizzie had had a wonderful time, finishing off her visit to the Bull Ring singing the hymns with the Salvation Army band until they marched back to the Citadel with the tramps and the destitute trailing behind them, confident of a good feed. She acknowledged that Steve had been kind, generous and good fun to be with. He'd also been the perfect gentleman and had not done or said anything even mildly suggestive, and so she relaxed against him as they sauntered back to the pub for a drink before Steve would leave Lizzie at the back door of the hotel.

Steve had also felt the difference in Lizzie, but he put a totally different interpretation on her behaviour, especially when he remembered how she'd reacted at the boxing ring when there was the possibility he could have been hurt.

In the pub, they talked easily of that night and the things they'd seen, and they discussed the budding romance between Mike and Tressa. As they made their way back to the hotel, Lizzie realised she might have had a totally miserable time without Steve, for she'd not have wanted to tag along after Mike and Tressa, even if they had allowed her to, so at the doorway she said, 'Thanks for tonight, Steve.'

'S'all right. My pleasure.'

'Well, I truly appreciated it,' Lizzie continued. 'I've had a wonderful time.'

It was on the tip of Steve's tongue to say he could think of a more satisfactory way of finishing the evening, where she could show him just how appreciative she was. But he bit the words back. Nor did he force her lips open when she kissed him goodnight, though he was so filled with desire that he shook slightly, and his groin ached so much he knew he'd have to seek relief before he made for home that night. And yet, despite his frustration, he went home whistling because he really thought Lizzie was warming to him, as he'd prophesised she would in time.

CHAPTER FOUR

The days slid one into another and the girls went out to the pub, theatre, music hall, cinema or dancing, and when Lizzie could stop feeling guilty about leading Steve a dance she enjoyed herself immensely.

When the two girls had first come to England and explained they were cousins, the office staff had tried to work it so their free time co-ordinated. As they had each other, they didn't need to make deep friendships with the others, though they liked them well enough, and Lizzie knew that if she hadn't had Steve she'd have been a lot lonelier.

However, she didn't think that was a good enough reason to go out with someone, but Steve seemed happy with it. What he wasn't happy with was the way he'd got no further than a kiss on the lips, linking arms as they walked along the street and holding hands in the cinema.

He knew Mike was getting much further with Tressa, because Mike had told him, boasted of it even. Lizzie knew it too, but she wasn't going down that road with a man she was dating almost as a convenience. So, when Steve asked her to go again to tea, she hesitated. She had no desire to go near the place, but she pleased Steve in so very little and he was incredibly generous buying drinks, dinners and tickets for the threatre or cinema with money he near sweated blood for. 'Won't they think . . . I mean we're not a committed couple, are we?'

'Who gives a sod what they think?'

'Well you must. They are your family and they don't seem to have taken to me at all. Not that that matters, except that I don't know why you want me there.'

'I just do,' Steve said obstinately. 'And it would please me if you came. They will behave better this time, I guarantee it. I've warned them all.'

Against her better judgement Lizzie went, and she found the atmosphere much as before. This time, in an attempt to stop Flo extolling the virtues of Steve, she tried to get to know his brother Neil. She didn't like him much, for he'd been surly and barely polite at their first meeting and he hadn't improved. But, she excused him. Surely such blatant favouritism of the first-born, who already had everything going for him, would affect anyone?

She knew Neil hadn't gone into the brass industry like his father and brother, but had been taken on as an apprentice in a bespoke tailors' in the Bull Ring. Steve had told her that and said it was a bone of contention in the family, but after the tea, which had been eaten in almost total silence, Lizzie asked Neil about his job. 'We can make up a suit, with a waistcoat thrown in, for thirty bob,' Neil said with a hint of pride. 'You wouldn't get me near brass. Makes old

53

men out of young ones. You should see the state of this pair when they gets in of a night.'

'It's a living, ain't it?' Rodney growled.

'Some living.'

'You ungrateful sod!' Rodney exploded. 'Many of the barefoot, bare-arsed and starving kids around these doors would have been glad of their fathers working any damned place, and most of the poor buggers out of work that cluster on the street corners would give their right arms to earn half as much as me. You don't get that kind of money sitting on your arse stitching clothes for toffs.'

'Yeah,' Steve put in. 'Just how much do you put into the house, our kid?'

'I know I don't earn much yet,' Neil said, 'but when I finish my apprenticeship in two years I'll be on a good enough wack.'

'You mind they don't finish you then,' Rodney warned. 'Happens in the factories all the time, and the bloody shipyards.'

'They won't.'

'You're sure of yourself,' Steve said. 'I hope you're right. Sometimes you haven't money to bless yourself with, never mind give a woman a good time.' He put his arm around Lizzie, who was by his side. She didn't shake him off, she wouldn't shame him that way before his family, but she did wish she'd never started the conversation that had developed into these heated words. In fact, if she was totally honest, she wished she'd never set eyes on Steve Gillespie and his dysfunctional family at all.

'Give a woman a good time,' Neil said sarcastically.

'I know what manner of good time you like to give a woman. Maybe some of us are more choosy and like to keep it in their trousers more.'

Flo clouted Neil on the side of the head. 'Less of that dirty talk.'

Neil looked across the room where Lizzie stood, her face crimson. 'Dirty talk, Mom, dirty talk!' he cried scornfully. 'Why don't you complain about the dirty deeds your sainted son gets up to.'

'Shut your mouth!' Lizzie felt the anger flooding through Steve, so even the arm he had around her shoulders trembled slightly and she saw the whitening of his fisted knuckles.

Neil ignored his brother and, addressing himself to Lizzie, said, 'See, our Steve here likes variety, goes down the streets like a dose of salts, sampling them all.'

'I said, shut your gob, or by Christ I'll shut it for you.'

Lizzie put a hand on Steve's arm and said gently, 'It doesn't matter.' But Steve could tell by Neil's sly eyes what he was going to say next unless he put a stop to it. He and Mike both had very high sex drives and when between girlfriends, or going out with girls that gave them little sexual satisfaction, or perhaps just for a change, they often frequented places where they could pick up a woman of the night. They never considered it a problem and it meant they didn't have to force the girls they were dating to go further than they wanted to.

Often, after Steve left Lizzie he'd be so worked up that he'd be forced to seek solace elsewhere. How had

Neil found that out? Steve did not know, but he saw Neil knew all right: he could see it in the little shit's eyes. He also knew that if Lizzie was made aware of it, he'd never get near her again.

Neil smiled at his brother. It was good seeing him squirm for a change. 'Lizzie has a right to know what she's taking on,' he said. 'Does she know, for example, that some of the women . . .'

Steve had dropped his arm from Lizzie's shoulder and was across the room in an instant. He almost lifted Neil from the floor with his left arm, while his right fist powered into Neil's face.

Lizzie watched, horrified. No one seemed surprised or went to the aid of the boy, who slid down the wall as Steve released him. Neil's mouth and nose spurted blood and Lizzie noticed that one of his teeth had been knocked clean out.

Flo, with a sigh, crossed to the fire and filled a bowl from the kettle to the side of it, got a clean rag from the line above the hearth and carried it over to Neil. 'You asked for that,' she said as she handed it to him. 'Why couldn't you stay quiet when you had the chance?'

'Why should I?' Neil's words were slurred because of his thick lips but his eyes still held contempt. 'Just because big brother says so?'

'If you want more of the same, I'm willing to oblige,' Steve growled out. 'Only this time I'll not stop at one punch, you little shit. I'll beat you to pulp.'

Lizzie crossed to Steve. 'Please, don't fight any more.'

She was totally shocked. The angry, hate-filled words had been bad enough, but fighting! And yet the family took it almost as a matter of course, so much so that

Rodney hadn't even raised his head from where he sat, staring into the fire.

Steve looked at Lizzie and regretted she'd seen any of this. 'Get your coat,' he snapped.

'What?'

'Are you deaf? Get your coat!'

Lizzie hurried to obey him. She knew it wasn't her that Steve was so cross with, but she was still unnerved by the angry, curt way he had spoken.

They walked side by side in silence, Lizzie knowing anything she said would be wrong. She didn't care about Steve's past, she didn't really care about his future either, because she wasn't going to figure in it. This had decided her. She'd dallied long enough and really had made a monkey of the man, and the sooner she came clean the better. Neil's phrase – 'what she's taking on,' – had filled her with dread. Someone else would have to fill that role; it would certainly not be her.

She kissed Steve when he left her at the hotel, but on the cheek only, and turned without even a hug and opened the door to the stairs.

Christ Almighty! Steve thought. He knew the rage, still burning within him, needed some outlet. Sex would fit the bill nicely and he turned to make for one of his familiar haunts, where he knew one or two of the women liked him to be a bit rough.

Lizzie waited for Tressa to come in that night, not a thing she did now as a rule, but she needed to talk to her about Steve. They both had the whole evening off and so, after tea with the family, Mike had probably taken Tressa out somewhere. Steve might have done the same if that distressing scene at the house hadn't happened. It seemed to have upset Steve totally, and whether he'd forgotten Lizzie had the evening off or whether he'd wanted to be by himself, she didn't know nor care. In the few hours she'd been with the family, she had had enough of them all; enough to last a lifetime. How could one simple question start such a barrage? She was glad to reach the peace and quiet of her room, for her nerves were still jangling, and she lay down on her bed fully clothed and thought about it.

She was woken by Betty and Pat, who'd been on duty, coming in and complaining about their feet. They'd turned the light on before they noticed Lizzie.

'Sorry!'

'That's all right,' Lizzie said. 'I must have dropped off.'

'You're back early.'

'Aye, let's say it wasn't a total success.'

'Oh!'

'Aye, Steve had a row with his brother, which turned into a fight.'

'That's men all over,' Betty said. 'Solve everything with their bloody fists.'

'Well, I was glad to leave anyway,' Lizzie said. 'It's not my idea of a pleasant Sunday afternoon. I'll wait for Tressa and see what she makes of it.'

'You won't see your cousin for some time yet,' Pat said.

'How late is it usually then?' Lizzie said. 'I never hear her come in.'

'I know you don't hear her,' Betty told her. 'You must be a deep sleeper. It's always the early hours when she arrives home. She's woken me a few times. She has an arrangement with the night porter to let her in when she knocks in a certain way.'

'The early hours!' Lizzie repeated. 'What does she do till the early hours?'

The two girls giggled. 'Don't you know about the birds and the bees?' Pat said with a smirk. 'I'd have a good guess at what she's up to, her and that feller she has. Lead you on, blokes do. You've got to keep your wits about you. I tell you, Lizzie, it would be good to warn her, like. A girl needs to watch herself.'

'Yeah, and she's in a state sometimes,' Betty put in.

'A state?'

'Yeah, drunk, like, or very near it, anyroad.'

'I had no idea, though I know she's hard to rouse sometimes, but then she has never been easy to get up.'

'Thought you hadn't guessed,' Betty said. 'Glad to have told you. You're the only one to have a word. She'd not listen to us.'

'She'll probably not listen to me where Mike's concerned.'

'Well, at least you'll have tried,' Betty said. 'Sorry, I won't be able to keep you company if you're set on sitting up for her, I'm jiggered.'

'Me too,' Pat agreed. 'And me feet are burning.'

'I don't need company,' Lizzie said. 'You get to bed, you've been at it all day.'

She lay quiet until the girls' even breathing told her they were asleep and then she got softly out of bed. The clock at St Phillip's Cathedral tower, opposite the hotel, said nearly eleven o'clock, and she decided to get herself ready for bed and then if she did drop off in the wait it didn't matter.

Before half-eleven she'd finished her ablutions and was undressed, her Sunday clothes put back in the wardrobe and her uniform for work in the morning hanging on the picture rail. She was in her nightdress and tucked up in bed, with just the lights on her side of the room lit, and was reading a book she'd bought from a stall in the market.

Twice she got up to go to the toilet and looked at the clock, and twice she dropped to sleep, the book still in her hands, and was jerked awake. By half past one she decided Tressa could go hang herself for all she cared, she was too tired to wait any more and both of them were on earlies the following day. She put the book down, padded across the floor to put out the light, and climbed into bed, pulling the covers over her.

The light flooding the room pulled her back from the edge of a wonderful dream and she opened her eyes wearily, blinking in the sudden brightness to see her cousin standing there. Her face was aglow, as if a light had been lit behind it, and there was an inane grin on her face. Betty's words came back to her.

'You're drunk,' she said.

Tressa giggled. 'Maybe,' she replied. 'We were celebrating.'

The blood in Lizzie's veins suddenly felt like ice. 'Celebrating what?'

'Getting engaged!'

'Getting engaged!' Lizzie repeated, relieved it wasn't something worse.

'No ring yet,' Tressa said. 'I mean, Mike asked me

to marry him tonight, and I said "yes" of course, and then he said he must ask Mammy and Daddy and do the thing properly, but that won't be a problem. I've told them about Mike every week and how wonderful he is.'

'You're so young to be engaged.'

'No I'm not,' Tressa protested. 'I'll be twenty in July. We're not getting married yet awhile. We have to save quite a bit first, Mike said. But an engagement is a commitment.'

'I'll say,' Lizzie agreed. She got out of bed and crossed to the window. 'It's turned two o'clock.'

'Who cares,' Tressa laughed, turning a pirouette in the room. 'Mike bought a bottle of champagne.'

'Put a sock in it, why don't you,' Pat's weary voice said from the other side of the room, and Tressa, her face still wreathed in smiles, put her finger to her lips in the exaggerated manner of a drunk. 'Ssh.'

'Tressa, get to bed, we've work in the morning,' Lizzie advised.

Tressa tossed her head and went on, but in a whisper, 'I care nothing about tomorrow. It's another day. What I care about is Mike, I love him so much I ache. I want to be near him all day and lie curled around him every night.'

'Tressa!' Lizzie said in dread. 'Tressa, you haven't . . . ?'

'No, I haven't,' hissed Tressa. 'But it's hard, bloody hard. I won't feel as scared when I have the ring on my finger.'

'It's not a wedding ring, Tressa,' Lizzie reminded her.

'I know that. The wedding ring will follow.'

'Please, Tressa, be careful.'

'Careful!' Tressa said scornfully. 'That's for old bones, careful. I'm so happy I could die, and you tell me to be careful.'

There was no use talking to her. She was drunk on love and champagne and that wasn't a combination that would produce any sort of sense. 'Well, stay happy, Tressa,' Lizzie said, 'and if it's what you want I'll be happy for you, but for now I'm too tired to feel anything much. You stay awake all night if you like, but I must sleep.'

'I'm too buoyed-up to even close my eyes.'

'Then don't,' Lizzie said softly. 'But stay awake quietly, will you?'

Tressa didn't answer. She was too busy pirouetting at the end of her bed, her arms outstretched, and Lizzie gave a groan and hid her head under the covers.

Later, she heard Tressa bumbling away, bumping into the bed, and once after she'd put the light out she thought she heard her fall onto the floor. She didn't look and Tressa giggled again so Lizzie knew she wasn't hurt. God, I wouldn't have her head in the morning for all the tea in China, she thought, and remembered how she'd felt the day after that fated Christmas dance. For all the urging of Mike and Steve and even Tressa, she'd never got in that state again, nor anywhere near it. She had the feeling she had to keep a grip on herself and stay level-headed with Steve, but Tressa obviously didn't feel the same. However, that wasn't her concern. She wasn't her cousin's keeper, and that was Lizzie's last thought before sleep overtook her.

'Tressa, wake up!' Lizzie hissed urgently.

'Leave me alone.'

'I can't. Come on, you'll be late and you won't half catch it.'

'I'm ill. Tell them I'm ill.'

'I'll do no such thing. Anyway, they'd not believe it, and if the night porter tells them the time you came in and the state of you, you might get your marching orders. Come on, you're hung over and I bet it's not the first time either.'

'Shut up!' Tressa said, pulling the cover tighter around her. Lizzie had a measure of sympathy for her, for she knew how Tressa would be feeling. But Tressa had shown little feeling for her, Lizzie remembered, and she'd got that way by accident whereas Tressa had known what she was doing. But Lizzie also knew the state Birmingham was in with regard to jobs, and if Tressa lost this job she'd have a long wait for another, especially if the manager refused to give her a reference.

Lizzie couldn't allow that to happen and so, grasping the covers with both hands, she yanked them clean off the bed. Tressa gave a shriek and the other two girls, who'd been fast asleep, jerked awake. 'If you don't belt up, Tressa,' Betty said fiercely as she sat up in the bed, 'I'll come over there and knock your bleeding block off. It's not on, this. You come home in the early hours as drunk as a Lord and wake us up, and then again in the morning. What's your problem, anyroad?'

'I'm ill.'

'Ill my Aunt Fanny! Get up and go to work and give us all a bit of peace, or I'll throw a basin of water over you.'

63

Lizzie could see Betty meant what she said and she honestly couldn't blame her. Tressa knew it too and, whimpering, she got to her knees and gingerly put her feet to the floor, pulling herself up by the bedpost. 'God, I feel awful! I won't be able to stand the sight of all those greasy breakfasts, I feel sick already.'

Lizzie had had enough. 'Get yourself to the bathroom,' she commanded. 'Clean your teeth, wash your face and get your uniform on. We're running late already.'

'You don't understand. My head's pounding.'

'Then take an aspirin,' Lizzie said unfeelingly. 'I'm away. I'm not putting my job on the line for you.'

'Lizzie!'

'No, Tressa. Sort yourself out. You didn't give a monkey's yesterday and I don't today, so I'll see you later.'

Tressa couldn't believe Lizzie had gone. She'd never done that before. When she'd been a bit groggy and hung over in the past, though she'd never felt this bad, Lizzie had done the lion's share of the work and always covered for her. 'Thank God. The worm's turned at last,' came Betty's voice from the bed.

It angered Tressa. Who the hell did Betty think she was? She didn't know how it was between her and Lizzie. Tressa was unable to say this, however, for when she opened her mouth she was assailed by nausea and had to hurry, as much as she was able, to the bathroom.

She was late reporting in the kitchen and got told off for that and for the state of her hair, which she'd been too clumsy to manage. Her face was pasty white and there were blue smudges under her eyes. The head waiter knew what was up with Tressa and he had little patience with her. 'You can't go into the dining room with hair like that,' he snapped. 'And kindly remember lateness and this slapdash manner won't be tolerated here. Lizzie, can you help your cousin, for her hair looks as if it has been pulled through a hedge backwards.'

'Don't say I told you so,' Tressa pleaded when the two girls were in the staff cloakroom.

'I had no intention of it,' Lizzie said, pulling off Tressa's cap and attacking the tousled locks with the brush that she kept in her handbag in her locker. 'I could say you're a bloody fool, but you probably know that and it would serve no purpose. Just keep your head down and do nothing else to annoy the waiter, because he'll be watching you like a hawk and he's the power here. If he complains to the manager, you'll be out.'

Tressa knew it, and despite feeling like death she tried, but for all that the head waiter shouted at her and berated her for every little thing and she was glad when her shift was over and she could reach the relative safety of her room. Betty and Pat were out and Tressa was glad of it as she sat on the bed and dissolved into tears. 'I hate him.'

'Come on, Tressa, he's not the worst,' Lizzie said. 'You annoyed him and he made you pay, that's all.'

'That's all! You weren't on the receiving end of it.'

'Well it's over now,' Lizzie said soothingly. 'He'll have forgotten by this evening, and if I were you I would get some sleep, you'll feel heaps better if you do.'

'I don't know that I could,' Tressa said. 'My stomach's churning like one of those washing machines in the laundry.'

'How much did you drink, for God's sake?'

'Lots,' Tressa admitted. 'We went to a party after we'd been to Mike's house, some friend of Mike who has rooms off the Belgrave Road. Steve knows him too. We expected the two of you to turn up.'

Lizzie made a face. 'Something else turned up for us.'

'Oh, what?'

'Tell you later. Go on.'

'Well, unbeknownst to me, Mike slipped out before closing time and bought this big bottle of champagne and then, as the party was beginning to fold up, Mike took me into the hall of this place and asked me to marry him.

'I was ecstatic and already tipsily drunk, but after I said yes and we kissed and all, he produced the champagne and we drank it between us.'

'Oh Tressa.'

'I know,' Tressa said. 'It was bloody stupid, but it seemed like a good idea last night.'

'I bet,' Lizzie said with a grin. 'Never mind, you've survived the morning – just. Nothing will be as bad as that.'

'No,' Tressa said with feeling. 'Now you. What went wrong with you and Steve?'

And Lizzie told her. 'I can't go on with this charade, Tressa, really I can't. It isn't fair. It's nothing to do with Steve's family, but God knows they're bad enough; it's Steve himself, and before you say it there's nothing wrong with him either. He's a fine man, handsome, generous, good company and he has a good, steady job. He could make some girl a first-rate husband, but that girl is not going to be me. I'm wrong to keep him hanging on, hoping.'

Tressa knew that this time Lizzie was serious. She'd hoped Lizzie would fall for Steve and she knew Mike did too, but she saw now that what they hoped for wasn't going to happen. 'Could you wait until we're properly engaged?'

'Oh I don't know, Tressa.'

'Please.'

'It could be ages.'

'No, it won't,' Tressa said, and added, 'Look, Lizzie, Mike has planned a big night for our next Saturday off, because it's the day before Valentine's Day. We're meeting you two for a few drinks early and then Mike's taking me to the theatre to see Gracie Fields and afterwards we're going to dinner. Once the ring is on my finger you can say what you like to Steve.'

'I don't see what difference having the ring will make. You're committed anyway.'

'Just do this one thing for me,' Tressa said. 'Steve is going to be upset when you tell him – and I know that's not your fault, I'm not blaming you. But, what if Mike decides to postpone the engagement to comfort his mate and try and get him to forget and all that, and you know he could do just that.'

Lizzie knew he could. 'Somehow, I don't think he'll feel the same if his ring is on my finger,' Tressa went on. 'He's made his choice publicly then and that choice is me. Please, Lizzie, don't mess it up for me. If I don't have Mike, I will die. I might as well, for never as long as I live will I love someone as I do him. It's less than a fortnight I'm asking for.'

Lizzie looked at her cousin and knew if she was to do anything to jeopardise this romance Tressa would never forgive her, and she'd not forgive herself for Tressa's heart would be broken. 'What if you don't hear from Ireland before then?'

'We're going ahead anyway. With or without their permission or blessing, we are getting engaged on the thirteenth of February, come hell or high water.'

Steve knew all about the engagement plans and he was filled with envy.

'Amazing, the powers of a ring,' Mike said to Steve one night as they returned from a date with the girls.

'Have you gone all the way yet?' Steve asked.

'Nearly, but not quite,' Mike said. 'The ring will clinch it. I'll give Tressa a good time, and bingo! Christ, I can hardly wait.'

Steve was silent, trying to cope with the frustration eating at him, and Mike said, 'Aren't you thinking that way yourself – engagement, I mean?'

'Lizzie's not ready yet,' Steve answered shortly. Mike had no idea how little he and Lizzie did together and Steve had no intention of telling him. Tressa had said nothing either, because until she was securely engaged it was in her interest to pretend things between Steve and Lizzie were hunky-dory.

'Maybe when she sees the ring she'll change her mind,' Mike commented. 'You know how women are about rings.'

God! Steve thought, it would need more than a ring to alter Lizzie, for she was worse if anything. And she was worse, because for all her promise to Tressa to say nothing to Steve until the fateful engagement day, she felt as if she was leading him on by still going out with him. She tried not to let this affect her, but of course it did, and that evening, Steve, remembering how unsatisfactory things had been of late, said to Mike, 'I'm not going home yet, Mike. Be seeing you.'

Mike knew where Steve was heading. In his pre-Tressa days he'd have probably been alongside him, but now he said, 'Why d'you have to go to those places when you have a lovely girl you've just spent the evening with?'

'Mind your own business, Mike,' Steve spat out angrily. 'I don't have to answer to you.'

'I was just saying.'

'Well stop just saying,' Steve said, 'because I've stopped listening.'

Mike shrugged as Steve turned away from the streets and headed back to one of his favoured haunts in Varna Road.

The good news approving the engagement came after a week. Tressa read it out:

> *It is obvious you are smitten with each other and as this Mike Malone gives a good account of himself, you have our blessing so far. However, you are young and there is to be no marriage until we have met your intended. We suggest you come home in the summer and introduce us.*

'Isn't Mammy a pet,' Tressa said, spinning around in delight.

'It seems all fine for you, right enough,' Lizzie said, but she was a little saddened for she knew she would be quite lonely when she told Steve she didn't want to see him any more, but despite this she would wait no longer than the thirteenth. She owed him that much.

That day, the girls were on duty until three o'clock and Tressa got dinner and sweet orders mixed up, laid tables the wrong way round, forgot the cruets and sauces and dropped so many things in the kitchen that the chef yelled at her. She didn't seem to care; excitement had taken hold of her and her nerves were jumping about inside her body as she watched the clock anxiously, willing the time to be gone so she could go out to meet her man.

'We just have three hours,' she told Lizzie in their room. 'Do you want the bath first?'

'Why just three hours. Surely we're not meeting them at six?'

'Aye. The theatre performance is at seven thirty.'

'Even so.'

'They're going to be in town anyway,' Tressa explained. 'They're buying the ring today.'

'Didn't you want to choose it?'

'No,' Tressa said. 'I wouldn't know how much Mike would have to spend. I told him to surprise me.'

It had surprised Steve, for he'd seen Mike part with the best part of three weeks' wages to buy the diamond cluster he'd set his heart on.

'Some price, man,' he said as they left the shop.

'Tressa's worth it,' Mike said. 'Think of it, Steve. This is my passport to freedom.'

'Yeah,' Steve remarked gloomily. 'Let's go and sink a few pints.'

'You're on,' Mike replied.

That evening there was a spring-like feel to the air. There was even a little warmth in the setting sun and across the road, around St Phillip's courtyard, Lizzie glimpsed the heads of snowdrops and crocuses peeping through the soil as the girls scurried along the road, for they were meeting the men at the Old Joint Stock.

Judging by the glasses on the tables, Mike and Steve were finishing their third pints when the two girls went into the pub. Lizzie's heart sank, for when Steve was drunk he was unpredictable and could sometimes be difficult to handle. But she could hardly tell Steve what to do, and more drinks were ordered as soon as they spotted the two girls and no one listened at all when Lizzie said she'd have an orange. This was Tressa and Mike's moment and she decided she'd not spoil it by making a fuss.

Tressa was rendered speechless by the ring and Lizzie let her breath out in a sigh. 'Oh, Tressa, it's gorgeous,' and it was gorgeous, for the large diamond in the centre was surrounded by smaller diamonds that shone and sparkled in the lights of the pub.

'Do you like it?' Mike asked, made self-conscious by Tressa's silence.

'Like it? Oh, Mike, I haven't words . . . Oh, thank you. I never dreamed you'd buy me something so exquisite.'

'Nothing in the world is too good for you,' Mike said, and he leant across the table and the two kissed.

'Ain't love grand,' Steve said sarcastically and then added quietly, 'You only have to say the word, Lizzie, and I'll buy you a diamond twice the size of that.'

Lizzie's heart skipped a beat at the hopeful look in Steve's eyes, and so though she shook her head she smiled as she did, and leant across and squeezed his hand as he turned to Mike and said, 'I'll not congratulate, but commiserate. Another good man down. There's few of us bachelors left, you know.'

He was putting on a good act for his friend, Lizzie thought. Making the best of it. *I wish I could make his day now, by agreeing to be his girl, but I'd be fooling myself and not being fair to him.*

Some of the hotel staff used the pub and insisted on buying rounds of drinks when they heard the news of Tressa's engagement, but Lizzie insisted on drinking only orange. She felt she needed her wits about her for what she must say to Steve, and neither her nor Tressa had eaten since about eleven o'clock. They'd hoped to grab a bite after the lunchtime rush, but hadn't had time, and she was feeling decidedly peckish.

Eventually, Mike and Tressa got up to go and Lizzie noticed Tressa was none too steady. Not to worry, she thought, we're not on duty till three tomorrow.

'What d'you want to do?' Steve asked, for he knew Lizzie didn't like staying in the pub all evening.

Lizzie ran her tongue over her lips, which had become unaccountably dry, and said, 'I need to talk to you, Steve.'

He was unaware of the undercurrent, totally

unprepared. 'Talk away, then. Shall I get us another drink in?'

'No,' Lizzie said, grasping his arm. She looked around the noisy pub, with a good number of the hotel staff already there, and knew it wasn't the place to tell anyone anything important. 'Not here. Can we walk? It's a fine evening and quite warm.'

'It that's what you want.'

Once in the street, Steve pulled Lizzie close, and as she didn't protest his heart beat faster. Women were a funny breed. Maybe Mike was right. Maybe an engagement ring on the finger of one woman was a powerful inducement for another. Was that what Lizzie was going to tell him tonight?

He had always had remarkable success with women. In that, Neil had spoken the truth, and Steve had often had trouble shaking them off in the past, though until he'd met Lizzie he'd never been properly in love. However, he was assured of his attractiveness to the opposite sex, and when he'd claimed Lizzie would love him too after a few weeks he'd truly believed she'd be unable to hold out against his charms indefinitely.

'Come on, darling girl,' he said. 'The night is young and you can talk till your heart is content.'

CHAPTER FIVE

Lizzie knew the centre of the town would probably still have people on the streets, couples like themselves, many of them entwined together, planning their night out or making their way to one of the many entertainment venues, and the Bull Ring would be full of people for a few hours yet. What she had to say needed as much privacy as she could get and so she led the way across St Phillip's churchyard to Temple Row, and from there into a deserted and semi-dark Needless Alley.

There she stopped and faced Steve, and he smiled to himself. In his book there was only one reason a girl stopped in a dark and quiet place. He was right, Lizzie had fallen for him good and proper, and he decided he'd not go home tonight too frustrated to sleep. Desire, fuelled by the beer he'd consumed, rose in him. A man could only stand so much, he told himself, and by God Lizzie had had things her own way for long enough. He reached for her, pulling her into an entry, and was quite surprised when she twisted out of his grasp.

'Steve, please. I need you to listen.'

'Listen be damned,' Steve cried. 'The time for talking is past,' and he grabbed her again roughly, holding her so tight she was unable to move, her chest so crushed she had trouble drawing breath, let alone crying out. Steve was kissing Lizzie madly, forcing her lips apart, his tongue darting in and out, and she wriggled and fought, tossing her head from side to side.

Eventually, she freed one of her hands and was able to push Steve away from her. She realised he'd misconstrued her actions in bringing him here, and so she forgave him his frantic lunge and said gently, 'Steve, I came here tonight to tell you it's over between us. I did what you asked and gave the relationship more time, but my feelings haven't changed. I can't go out with you any more. It wouldn't be fair.'

Steve was knocked for six. It was the very last thing he'd expected Lizzie to say and he felt the hurt of it flow through his body. 'What have I done?' he asked in an effort to understand. 'What's the matter? I love you with all my heart, you know that. Christ, Lizzie, you only have to say what you want, anything, and I'll get it for you. I love you; I adore you.'

Tears squeezed out of Lizzie's eyes, for she knew her words had affected Steve deeply. Although it was too dark to see his face, the pain was apparent in his voice. She was angry for allowing herself to be coaxed into continuing to see this man when she knew she felt nothing for him but friendship, and she shook her head sadly. 'It isn't you, Steve, it's me. I'm sorry.'

Steve had never begged, he'd never had need to, but he begged now. 'Please, Lizzie. You don't know what you are doing to me. I don't think I can bear not to ever see you again.'

Lizzie shut her eyes and let the tears trickle down her cheeks.

'Anyway,' Steve went on stubbornly, 'I don't know why you're saying these things cos you don't want to. I can hear it in your voice.'

Lizzie felt for Steve's fingers and held his hands. 'You do hear sadness,' she admitted, 'because I am sad that I don't feel the same for you as you feel for me. I care for you, Steve, I do truly, and I wish I could feel more, but I can't.'

'I don't believe you,' Steve said again. 'How can I? Look how you behaved the first night I met you.'

Lizzie was dreadfully ashamed of that night. 'I was drunk and I can remember little about it. I am really sorry if I gave you the wrong impression of me.'

Steve's eyes narrowed. He knew nothing had happened that night, but Lizzie had admitted she didn't remember it. He was hurting to his very soul and he hit back. 'Well you did give me the wrong impression, and not just me, I might add. People were scandalised by your shameless behaviour. And when you suggested going outside there was no holding you. I was good enough for you then all right. There isn't much of your body I haven't explored already, so what you're being so prissy about now beats me. As for being drunk, my old woman always says that what's in a man sober comes out when he's drunk, and I reckon it's the same for a woman, so don't play the bloody innocent with me.'

Lizzie listened, appalled. She didn't doubt the truth

of what Steve said. Hadn't Tressa hinted at something similar? But to hear the words dripping from Steve's tongue. God, it didn't bear thinking about.

But Steve hadn't finished. 'It was you begging me to go on then,' he said.

'My God!' Lizzie thought. The disgrace of such behaviour engulfed her and she held her head in her hands.

Steve was enjoying her obvious discomfort and went on: 'Ripe for it, you was. It took all my willpower, I'll tell you, not to take you that night, for you wanted me to. Bloody fool that I am, I didn't want to take advantage, like. I did think, though, after that performance, you'd be little goer like your cousin, but you turned into an ice maiden. By Christ, you're a prick-teaser all right.'

Lizzie was mortified. Never in her wildest dreams and however much she had drunk would she have believed she could have conducted herself in such a way. If her parents knew any of this they would disown her. She was so burdened down with the things Steve had told her, the total embarrassment of it all seeping out of the very pores of her skin, that she was unprepared for Steve, who chose that moment to make a grab at her.

She tried to wrench herself from his arm, and though she managed to push him away, one of Steve's hands held on to the neck of her coat and the blouse beneath. She was suddenly scared of Steve for the first time. 'Let me go, Steve, for pity's sake?'

Steve didn't answer, but Lizzie heard his breath coming in short pants. She knew she had to get away and quickly. The sudden lunge she gave took him by surprise and she heard some of the buttons from her coat fall to the ground and felt the blouse tear and Steve's fingernails rake the back of her neck.

But it mattered little for she was free, and she began to run as she'd never run before, up Temple Row and across the churchyard to the hotel, expecting any minute to hear footsteps pounding behind her or clawing hands reaching for her.

She almost sobbed with relief as she reached the door of the hotel, and as most of the buttons had been ripped from her coat she wrapped it tightly round her before opening the door. Even so, Ron, the night porter, looked at her strangely as she made for the stairs. 'You all right?'

'Aye, I'm fine,' Lizzie said. But she was far from fine. She was trembling all over and she wanted to be by herself in her bedroom and safe.

She was quiet, for both Pat and Betty were fast asleep, and she didn't even put the light on. She was glad no one was up to see her take off the torn blouse, which she threw to the back of the wardrobe. She was in no mood for Tressa coming in enthusing about the night; she knew she'd see her in the morning, and so she turned over and tried to sleep.

Tressa was disappointed to find her cousin in the land of nod. She'd wanted to relive the night again, confide in Lizzie that her virginity was gone and forever and how wonderful the experience was. She was tempted to wake her up, but Lizzie slept deeply when she did go off – and what if, in trying to waken her cousin, she also roused Pat and Betty. She reckoned they'd string her up if she did that again. They'd been very stiff with her after last time.

So she lay on the bed and went through it in her mind and fell asleep with a smile on her face and dreamed of making love to Mike over and over again.

Tressa felt very delicate when she woke somewhere around mid-morning, but Lizzie didn't look too hot either, she noticed. In fact, she looked dreadful. Tressa gasped when she saw the score marks on the back of Lizzie's neck as she pulled her nightdress over her head.

'Who did that to your neck?'

'Who do you think?'

'It was never Steve?'

'Oh yes it was,' Lizzie said grimly, 'after I told him it was over,' and she went on to describe exactly what had happened. 'He frightened the living daylights out of me,' she said. 'And yet nothing really happened and I didn't wait around to see if it would. But now . . . oh, I don't know, I think it was partly my fault.'

'How in God's name did you work that out?'

'Maybe I told him clumsily,' Lizzie said. 'You know, maybe I should have led up to it more, not just told him like that, straight out.'

'He still shouldn't have done that to your neck.'

'He didn't do it on purpose,' Lizzie said. 'He was holding on to me, holding my coat at the neck, and when I pulled away quickly his nails sort of caught me.'

'Even so . . .'

'Tressa, he wasn't himself and he was so dreadfully hurt. I felt a heel. I should never have let it go on so long.'

Tressa could see the guilt settling around her cousin. She knew her well and was aware how that guilt would eat away at her. 'Come on, Lizzie,' she said. 'Put this behind you now.'

'I'm sorry, Tressa,' Lizzie replied. 'How did it go with you and Mike?'

'Do you want to know, after your night ended so badly?'

'Course I do,' Lizzie said. 'I'm not that small-minded.'

'Well I'll tell you in the bathroom.'

'Bathroom?'

'Aye,' Tressa said. 'I'm going to run you a hot bath. It will do you the world of good.'

'Tressa, I'm feeling a bit groggy.'

'Then a hot foamy bath is just the thing,' Tressa declared, and went on with a smile, 'come on, and while you are soaping yourself, I'll tell you about my night of passion.'

Lizzie forced a smile from her reluctant lips and began collecting her toiletries together.

The girls were tired when they returned to their room that night. It was Valentine's Day and there had been a special menu, so the place had been bursting at the seams and they'd been run off their feet, for they'd been on the go since three o'clock. Lizzie sat thankfully down on the bed with a sigh when they'd got back to their room. 'What time is it?'

Tressa consulted her watch. 'Just turned eleven.'

'Oh, Hell, and we're on earlies tomorrow.'

'You don't have to tell me.'

There was a lot of noise outside for a Sunday night and someone was yelling something out in the street. 'Sounds as if someone's celebrated a bit too well,' Pat said from the other side of the room.

'Aye,' Tressa said, crossing to the window, and then she exclaimed, 'God Almighty! Lizzie, it's Steve.'

'No!' Lizzie crossed to the window and saw Steve, off his head with drink and leaning against Mike, who seemed to be trying to remonstrate with him.

The other two girls crowded behind them to see. 'Ain't that your feller?' Betty said to Lizzie.

'He was,' Lizzie said. 'I finished with him yesterday.'

'Doesn't seem to have taken it too well then,' Pat remarked.

Lizzie watched him shake Mike's hand away, totter a couple of steps and, looking straight at her framed in the window, he screamed, 'Lizzie! Come out, you bitch. You hear me, Lizzie?'

'Tressa,' Lizzie said, 'I must go down.'

'There is no way you are going near that mad man in the state he's in,' Tressa said firmly.

'Tressa, I'll lose my job if the manager finds out.'

'He won't know it's you,' Tressa said. 'How many staff do you think the boss can name?'

'He'll tumble to it eventually. He's not stupid.'

However, the manager was tired and longing for his bed and had no patience with any drunk that the waiter said was screaming abuse in St Phillip's churchyard. The whole incident would probably disturb his guests, who'd come to him in the morning with a list of complaints. It was not to be borne. 'Phone the police,'

81

he told the head waiter. 'It's their business, so let them deal with it.'

Within minutes, the watching girls saw two policemen approach Mike and Steve. 'Now, now,' said the younger one. 'What's all this about?'

Steve, staggering on his feet, said, 'She's a bitch, a bloody bitch.'

'I'm sure she is, sir,' said the older man, 'but I think it would be best to discuss it in the morning.'

'It's all right,' Mike said, stepping forward. 'I'll see to him.' He'd seldom seen Steve as drunk as this. He could handle his drink, could Steve, but then he'd been drinking nearly all day.

Mike had had no idea Lizzie was to finish with Steve the previous evening, and when Steve told him at The Bell that lunchtime he was shocked and felt sorry for him. Getting drunk had seemed a damned good idea. It was only when Steve started muttering about going into the town and what he'd do, both to Lizzie and the bloody hotel she worked in, that Mike had decided he'd better go with him.

'Come on, mate,' he said now, his arms around Steve.

'Get off me.'

Steve's hefty swing nearly had Mike on his back and the young policeman said, 'Steady, sir.'

'Steady, sir. Steady, sir,' Steve mocked. 'Why don't the pair of you fuck off.'

'We can't do that, sir,' the older policeman said firmly. 'You either go home now, or you cool your heels in a cell.'

'Look, there's no need for this,' Mike remonstrated. 'I've told you I'll see to him,' and he tried again to put his arm about his friend. 'Come on, mate, let's go home, eh?'

Home. The word registered in Steve's befuddled brain. He wasn't going home. He wanted to speak with Lizzie; make her see she couldn't just finish with him like that.

Again, Mike was sent reeling. 'I'll go home when I'm bloody well ready to go. After I've talked to Lizzie. I've got to see her.'

The policemen had decided enough was enough. 'Come along, sir,' the older one said. 'You can't see people at this time of night. Leave it to the morning, eh?'

'Get your hands off me.' Steve's flailing fist caught the younger policeman's helmet and it rolled into the road.

'That's it,' the older man said. 'You're coming with us.'

'There's no need for this,' Mike protested again.

The younger man retrieved his helmet and said warningly, 'If you don't want to accompany him, I'd get yourself home and tell those he lives with he'll likely be out in the morning.'

And that's all it would have been, if Steve hadn't reacted so badly to the older policeman's efforts trying to put his hands behind his back to put cuffs on. In the fist that slammed into the policeman's face was the pent-up rage that had been building all day, fuelled by alcohol, and the policeman was knocked clean out.

'Oh dear God,' Lizzie breathed, watching the scene with tears streaming down her face. The younger policeman had handcuffed Steve and, holding him firmly, blew the whistle in his mouth.

Suddenly, a paddy wagon screamed to a halt and a policeman, with coshes raised, manhandled Steve into it with little ceremony. 'And him?' he then asked, indicating Mike.

'No,' the younger copper said, helping his stunned mate to his feet. 'He was trying to calm the mad bugger down. Go home,' he advised Mike again. 'And tell his people, because he'll be on a charge in the morning for this.' He indicated his mate, who would have fallen without his support and stood swaying and shaking his head from side to side.

Mike knew he had no option but to do as the policeman suggested and he looked up at the window to see the faces framed there and gave one wave before making for home.

The Gillespie house was in darkness, and Mike hesitated. But they had to know. No tabs were kept on Steve, but they'd be worried if he wasn't in his bed in the morning; and then there was work. He had no choice but to lift the knocker.

It was Rodney who came, his trousers obviously pulled hurriedly on, for the braces hung either side. His top and feet were bare, and behind him on the stairs Mike could see Flo in a dressing gown with her curlered hair tied up in a turban.

'What is it, man?' Rodney barked.

Mike glanced up and down the street. He could see no one but he knew many would have been disturbed by the sudden knock in the quiet street and might even now be peering out at the commotion on the Gillespie doorstep, and so he said, 'Can I come in?'

'Yeah, of course,' Rodney said.

Flo, seeing who it was, followed them into the living room and demanded, 'Where's our Steve?'

And Mike told them both as succinctly as possible what Steve had done and what the consequences were.

Flo knew Steve would have been drunk, for he'd had a skinful at lunchtime, but she had no idea what had brought it on. And now, prison. God, such a thing had never befallen any one of them before. 'He'll be out in the morning, though, won't he?' she said.

Mike shrugged. 'He would have been, I think, till he hit the copper.'

'But what was it over?'

It was no good Mike not telling. It would come out anyway. 'Lizzie finished with him yesterday,' he said.

Neil, who'd come down to see who the nocturnal visitor was, gave a hoot of laughter at that. 'Oh, I bet that dented the big bugger's ego,' he said in delight. 'The boot's always been on the other foot. Love 'em and leave 'em has been that sod's rule.'

'Will you shut up!' Flo cried. 'Your brother's in jail and might be up on a charge. Have you no sympathy?'

'Not a jot,' Neil said. 'I hope they throw the book at him, and now I know I'm off back to bed. Night, all.'

Mike, watching Neil go, knew the boy had a point, for Steve had scattered broken hearts willy-nilly over the neighbourhood and never lost any sleep over it. 'I'll be off then,' he said. 'I just called in to tell you, like.'

'Will you not stay for a cup of tea?' Flo asked, as she moved to put the kettle on above the fire, which she poked into life.

'No, thanks all the same,' Mike said. 'I need my bed.'

'What about work in the morning?' Rodney asked. 'What shall we say, for we can't tell the truth – the lad will be out on his ear and jobs are like gold dust?'

Mike knew that. The unemployment rate was now touching two million and Steve couldn't afford to lose his job. 'What d'you want to say?'

'We'll say his stomach is upset.'

'They'll think he's had a skinful.'

'Then they'll be right, but they won't know it all and maybe they'll not need to.' Rodney glanced across at Flo and said, 'You go along to the police station tomorrow and see what's what. Just so we know where we stand an' all.'

Flo nodded. She knew she'd have to. There was no one else and she knew she could expect little help from Neil.

But Flo didn't follow her husband to bed after Mike had left. Thoughts of her boy in a prison cell would keep sleep at bay and she knew who was to blame. The same girl that had caused a row each time she was here. And now for that piece to throw her son over! She had no desire to lose Steve to any woman, but for one to indicate he wasn't good enough! That wasn't to be borne at all.

What else did Lizzie want in a man? Flo thought. True, he had a temper at times and a liking for the beer, but in that he was like a great many other men;

and as for the women . . . Well, he was a normal man, after all, and the women usually chased him. You couldn't blame a man for taking what was on offer.

Everything that had happened to her son that night was down to Lizzie Clooney, and Flo knew she'd never forgive her for as long as she lived.

Steve felt panicky when he came to the next morning and realised where he was. He couldn't bear being cooped up and he had the desire to hammer on the door, but when he tried to stand, nausea caused him to vomit into the bucket by his bed.

The breakfast they brought him he couldn't face, but he was grateful for the cup of tea. By lunchtime he'd not been sick for some time, but the headache continued to bother him and he was in no mood for the grinning face that appeared at the hatch.

'Ready?' the policeman asked, unlocking the door.

'Ready? For what?' So far no one had told him anything.

'You're before the magistrate, mate, so on your feet.'

Steve got to his feet gingerly. His head felt as if it were on fire and his red-rimmed eyes burned. The young policeman laughed. 'You look a pretty sight, I don't think.'

Steve shut his eyes for a moment against the pain. God, how he wanted to send the young copper's teeth down his throat, but now he was sober he knew better and he was in no fit state anyway. But what was he talking about, before the magistrate? Just for getting drunk? He thought they'd tell him off and let him go.

'What have I got to go before the magistrate for?'

'Ooh, now let's see. Little string of offences we have. Drunk and disorderly, causing an affray, assaulting a police officer.'

'Assaulting a police officer?' Steve said incredulously.

'No recollection of it, mate?' the policeman said with a grin. 'Well, that won't save you. Come on, let's get going.'

Flo could have wept when she saw her son. His face was grey and his eyes were bloodshot and had black pouches beneath them. His hair stood on end and his Sunday suit was crumpled and stained.

Steve was fastidious about his appearance. His suits were regularly cleaned and returned to the wardrobe under a plastic cover and he was fussy about his shirts, which had to be pristine white and ironed just so, and on Sundays his tie always matched the handkerchief poking from his pocket.

But in the dock, Steve had no tie and no sign of the handkerchief either. He looked a beaten, crestfallen man and it tore at Flo's heart.

When the police officer read out the charges against him, Flo saw him shake his head from side to side, as if he couldn't quite believe it, and she knew he could remember little or nothing of what had happened. That didn't seem to matter and the magistrate tore into him. 'Assaulting a police officer is a serious offence and one that can carry a custodial sentence,' he told Steve. 'But as you've told the court you're in steady employment we don't think it would be in the country's best interests to lock you up.'

Steve let his breath out in a sigh of relief. He'd never even thought of a jail sentence.

'But, we don't want to be considered as treating this as a trivial matter,' the man went on. 'No indeed, and if you come before me again there will be no doubt about the custodial sentence. This time, however, you are fined seventy-five pounds.'

Seventy-five pounds! The sum reverberated in Steve's head. How in God's name was he going to find that sort of money? Christ! The image of Lizzie staring out at him from the window of the hotel suddenly floated before him, and he knew just who was to blame for the state he was in. He'd never forget it for as long as he lived.

Steve and Flo weren't the only ones blaming Lizzie, for she already did an adequate job of this herself. She thought she'd never get over the sight of Steve hauled into the van, handcuffs holding his hands behind his back, especially as she still thought it was her fault, at least in part. She certainly didn't want to come across him, not for a while anyway, so when Tressa met Mike in her free periods, Lizzie would sit in her room and hem the sheets and blankets she had picked up cheap in the Bull Ring.

'Come out with us,' Pat urged. 'We go to the flicks, or dancing at Tony's Ballroom up the West End.'

But Lizzie would shake her head, thinking that at the moment it was best to lie low. Tressa worried about her, and in the end Mike reluctantly agreed she could come out with them a time or two, but she wouldn't do that either. 'She's frightened of bumping into Steve,'

Tressa said, 'and making things worse for him.'

Nothing could make things worse, Mike thought, for Lizzie's decision had upset the man totally. He was paralytic each night, not tipsy or merry but falling-down drunk, and before he got to that state he'd tell any who would listen about Lizzie and how much he had loved her and how he wished he could make her see that. He was hurting, and Mike was well aware of that, but he told Steve he had to keep well away from Lizzie. Steve knew that already and he drank himself into oblivion because that was the only way he could cope with it.

Then, he'd started becoming friendly with a man called Stuart Fellows, who lived at the bottom end of Bell Barn Road. They'd all been to St Catherine's together, but as Stuart was considered a troublemaker, Mike and Steve had kept well away from him. But now, with Mike meeting Tressa as many nights as he could, they'd sort of been thrown together, and Mike could hardly blame Steve for that.

Stuart was only too willing to go after the women with Steve, despite having a steady girlfriend of his own. 'Don't it bother you?' Mike asked him when the three of them were together one day. 'What if your girlfriend finds out?'

'She won't,' Stuart said confidently. 'Anyroad, if she does, so what? It ain't hurting her, it's helping.'

'How d'you work that out?'

'Look, she don't want to go all the way, frightened of finding herself pregnant; and she's right to worry because I think her old man would kill the pair of us. This way I don't have to push her.'

'Tressa wouldn't see it that way,' Mike said, shaking his head.

'You sleep with Tressa,' Steve pointed out.

'Well, we're engaged.'

'I ain't going down that route, mate,' Stuart replied quickly. 'Have fun while you're young, that's me. But I don't think it would stop me if I was engaged, or even married.'

'Talk sense, man.'

'Look,' Stuart explained, 'you can't do nothing to stop having kids, can you, cos the Pope says so. Well, I wouldn't want a houseful of kids and a wife like an old hag. Some of these women having a baby every year and living hand to mouth would take it as a bonus to have their old man dip his wick elsewhere once in a while, I'll tell you.'

Steve thought about that. Next door to them lived Bob and Chrissie Roberts. They'd been married thirteen years and Chrissie was pregnant with her tenth child. All the children were pitifully thin, dressed in rags and usually barefoot, and Steve had heard them crying with hunger and cold.

And countless times he'd heard Chrissie pleading with Bob to leave her alone and the resultant slaps and thumps and punches, followed by her muffled moans and the rhythmic thump, thump, thump of their bed-head against the wall, and later in the quiet of the night he'd often hear Chrissie sobbing.

The young, once beautiful girl was gone for good. Her golden locks were dark, lank and greasy and her skin had lost its earlier bloom and was heavily lined and sallow and thin. Added to that, her body was shapeless and she'd lost a lot of teeth. And the woman was too poor and wretched to take joy in anything. Would you want that for any woman you married? No, by God you wouldn't.

So, when Stuart said, 'Seems to me the church has you by the balls every which way, and I'll go on the way I've always done, wife or no wife, and no bloody church will tell me different,' Steve could see the reasoning behind it.

'Well, I have no wife, no girlfriend, no nothing,' Steve said. 'And I'm not doing without female company a minute longer. Are you coming along with us, Mike, or are you not?'

Mike shook his head, and the other men laughed. 'Suit yourself,' Steve said, and with a wave they were gone.

CHAPTER SIX

'You said it would be all right,' Tressa said accusingly to Mike as they wandered arm in arm down Colmore Row.

Mike was still getting to grips with the news that his lovely, beautiful Tressa was carrying his child, and yet he knew she had a right to be angry with him. He had promised she'd be all right and that he would see to it. He knew he couldn't wear anything to prevent pregnancy, the Church's teaching was clear, but he'd intended to pull out before any damage was done. He hadn't realised how difficult that would be, how carried away he'd become, so that he'd be virtually unable to do that. So the condition Tressa was in was entirely his fault.

He wasn't aware she was crying until he felt her shoulders shaking. 'Don't cry, pet,' he said, 'please don't.' He turned her away from the city centre into one of the deserted side roads and kissed her gently. 'Now,' he said, facing her. 'You are sure about this?'

Tressa nodded her head. 'My monthlies were due a week after we became engaged, but nothing happened and it's been the same this month, and it's nearly the end of March now.' She looked at Mike and added, 'It must have happened that first time.'

Bugger! thought Mike, and he knew it must have. That time he was so buoyed up with the culmination of his dreams, and drunk with lust as much as the drinks he'd consumed, he could no more have stopped than he could have turned back the tide, and this was the result. 'We'll get married sooner rather than later, that's all,' he said reassuringly.

'We haven't money enough,' Tressa cried. 'Where will we live and everything?'

'Look, Tressa, many start with less and manage,' Mike told her. 'We have a bit saved between us and I know you've been picking up bits and pieces in the market. I'll put in for any overtime going and as long as you are feeling all right you can work a wee while yet, till the wedding at least.'

'Where will we live?'

'We might have to stay with my mom and dad for now,' Mike said.

Tressa gave a shiver of distaste. Mike's parents were almost as bad as Steve's and Mike's two sisters also adored their baby brother. They'd resented Tressa from the beginning, sensing how Mike felt about her. They were too clever to do this in front of Mike, when they were icily polite, but they had plenty of opportunity to give digs and make comments to show Tressa she wasn't welcome in their family. Tressa never complained about this to Mike, for she knew the high regard he held his family in and she told herself it was Mike she loved and was marrying, not his family. But then she'd never envisaged living with them.

Mike, catching sight of her face by the light from the lamppost, said quite sharply, 'It's no good looking like that, Tressa. It's my parents or the streets as far as I can see just now.'

'I know, I'm sorry. It's just not what I imagined.'

'D'you think I did?' Mike snapped, and then he put his arms around Tressa. 'God, I'm sorry,' he said, kissing her gently. 'I'm a brute yelling at you. It's all my fault, because I know you would have waited.'

Tressa knew Mike spoke the truth. However hard it was, she would have held out to keep her virginity till the wedding night if Mike hadn't wanted it so much. That first night, the night of the engagement, she'd done it fearfully to please him, because she knew he expected it, and she'd been totally bowled over by the experience. Few of the women she had spoken to had mentioned any enjoyment they got from sex, never mind the exhilarating, mind-blowing rapture Tressa had felt. After that first time she'd been as anxious to repeat the experience as Mike was, and so she said, 'No, I loved you too much to want to wait.'

'Well,' Mike said with a rueful grin. 'See where our loving has got us both?'

'Aye.'

'You've had time to think and worry about this,' Mike said. 'To me it's like a bolt from the blue. Who else have you told?'

'No one,' Tressa said. 'But I think Lizzie suspects. I've been sick a few times in the morning, you see. I've even seen Pat and Betty looking at me oddly a time or two. But they've said nothing and neither have I.'

'We need to get things organised,' Mike decided. 'I

think we should tell Mom and Dad straight away.'

Tressa quailed inside at the thought of that and yet she knew they'd have to know, and fast, for a wedding had to be arranged speedily. 'What about my mammy and daddy?' she asked suddenly. 'They'll have to give permission; I'm not twenty till July. I'll have to tell them face to face. We'll have to go over on a flying visit.'

'First things first,' Mike said. 'Let's tell my parents tonight and at least get that over and done with.'

'She looked at me like I was some sort of slag,' Tressa cried later to the three girls grouped about the bed. 'She said . . . she said it . . . it was all my fault; that . . . that I'd trapped her son, snared him in some way.' She looked at them all, her face red and awash with tears, twisting a sodden handkerchief in her agitated hands. 'It wasn't like that. Mike and I love each other.'

None of the girls were surprised. Mothers seemed to care more for sons than daughters and they all knew how Mike's family behaved towards Tressa for she'd told them bits before, but now wasn't the time to remind her of that.

'Come on, bab. Don't take on,' Betty said. 'These things happen. She's likely in shock.'

'At least your man's standing by you,' Pat added. 'That's summat today.'

'That's not all,' Tressa said. 'She says we can't stay with them. That she'd never live with the shame and that she's writing to her brother Arthur and his wife Doreen, to see if we can live there after the wedding. I don't even know the man and he lives in Longbridge.'

'Where's that?' Lizzie asked.

'Bloody miles away,' Pat said. 'You don't even know these people?'

'No, but apparently they've always had a soft spot for Mike,' Tressa said. 'They had four daughters all growing up when Mike was a boy and he used to go and stay with them both. Mike told me this Arthur always wanted him to go into the car industry with him, but Mike said he'd have to live with them and he knew his parents would have been hurt. And,' she added bitterly, 'then they might have been. Now, they can't get rid of him quick enough, and God alone knows what my parents will say when we go over and tell them.'

'So, if they agree, you'll go to live in Longbridge?' Lizzie asked, and suddenly realised how she would miss her cousin. They'd lived only a few miles apart since they'd been born and had lived in the hotel together for two years. They almost knew the secrets of each other's soul.

But, she told herself, this was no time to think of herself. There was a wedding to arrange, and hurried forward or not, Lizzie was determined to do all she could to make the day a wonderful one for Tressa and one she could think back on with pride.

Saturday, 14th June 1932, and the wedding reception, held in the back room of The Bell, was in full swing. Lizzie had worked hard to keep her promise to make this a day to remember, but she doubted Tressa would look back on it with any sort of pride, though she'd probably remember the glowering looks Mike's sisters and parents cast in her direction.

But then Tressa's parents, though they had been bitterly disappointed with Tressa when she and Mike had gone over to tell them they had to get married and speedily, were inclined to blame Mike. Before Tressa had gone to England she'd never even dated a boy, never mind kissed one. And now!

'The man must have taken advantage of her,' Eamon said. 'She was young and innocent and had her heart turned.'

'Well at least he'll marry her,' Margaret had said with a sigh of relief.

When they came over and saw the fawning way Mike's parents and sisters behaved towards him, they'd been even more incensed, and when the two families had to speak to each other you could almost feel the disdainful animosity between them.

Lizzie wished she could tell them both to behave, for Tressa and Mike's sakes, if for no one else's. Neither of the two young people had meant to hurt and disappoint anyone, they had just let their feelings overwhelm them. It wasn't as if they'd never intended to get married, for goodness' sake.

Tressa, far from enjoying her day, seemed to be constantly agitated, buffeted as she was between her parents and her new in-laws. Lizzie came upon her in tears in the hall a few minutes after she'd seen Mike's mother speak sharply to her about something. 'For God's sake, Tressa, stop crying,' she said impatiently. 'Don't you see it's what the old cow wants?'

'I never knew you were so unfeeling.'

'I never knew you were so feeble,' Lizzie retorted. 'For God's sake. You wanted Mike and you've got him.

You know, whenever it was done, Mike's mother would never have fallen on your neck in gratitude. Here,' she said, pulling a compact from her bag, 'wash your face and put this under your eyes to hide the puffiness, pinch your cheeks to give them colour, paint a smile right across your face and go and talk to Mike's Uncle Arthur.'

Lizzie liked Arthur and Doreen. She saw they thought a lot of Mike, but in an understanding type of way, not as if he was a creature from another, and much superior, planet. They didn't even seem that shocked about the pregnancy. 'In my day, young girls were chaperoned a bit more,' Doreen said. 'And even then ... takes you by surprise, those feelings, and when young people are alone so much, well, it's human nature really, isn't it? They were engaged, after all, and you just have to look at them to see they are made for each other.'

And they were. Despite the atmosphere of the place and the families grouped on opposite sides of the hall, their love for each other shone and sparkled between them.

All in all, Lizzie thought, Tressa had fallen on her feet. Mike's uncle had told her he was a sort of boss in the car factory at Longbridge and had already secured Mike a job on the assembly line. He also had a large terraced house, where there were two rooms downstairs and a breakfast room/kitchen and they said Tressa and Mike were to be given one of the rooms downstairs for themselves, and were to have one of the four bedrooms on the first floor.

'When the nipper's old enough, there's two attic

rooms above,' Arthur told Tressa. 'Plenty of room for all of us. Tell you the truth, me and Doreen have rattled about in the old house since the girls grew up and moved on, and Doreen at least will be glad of the company. She's that excited about a baby in the house, and I'll be glad to get Mike out the brass industry, I'll tell you.'

'But it's so far away,' Tressa complained to Lizzie.

'You'll soon settle down,' Lizzie said. 'How far was this place from Ballintra and we settled here fine.'

'Aye, but we had each other.'

'And now you have Mike and an uncle and aunt who'll welcome you, and soon a wee baby too, all of your very own. You won't be lonely then, and you'll be too busy to blow your nose, never mind miss anyone.'

And so she could reassure her cousin, but she knew that when Tressa left there would be a gaping hole in her own life. When, later that evening, Arthur said to her, 'You'll miss Tressa,' she could do nothing but nod her head, because she couldn't trust herself to speak.

She was glad Pat and Betty had been invited, but not that keen to see Steve, who'd been Mike's best man. It was the first time she had seen him since that awful business in February, when he'd taken a swing at the policeman, and she knew by the glares he was casting her that he hadn't forgotten either.

Tressa had said that, according to Mike, Steve had taken up with someone called Stuart Fellows, and Lizzie supposed he was the man keeping Steve company at the bar. She wasn't terribly impressed with him, but she told herself it was none of her business if Steve Gillespie went about with a man from Mars. Anyway, she'd probably not see Steve again when this day was over, and that would suit her just fine.

'You should have dropped dead with the look that old woman's giving you,' Betty said suddenly, and Lizzie glanced up. 'Oh, that's Steve's mother,' she said. 'Flo was never keen on me, and Mike told Tressa she blames me for Steve getting locked up that night in February.'

Betty remembered the night well, and Lizzie went on, 'Tressa said some of the neighbours gave her a hard time about it, but most of that was her own fault. I mean, she's been blowing Steve's trumpet for years. You name it, he had it and in dollops, far more than any other boy born this side of paradise, and that understandably put a lot of women's backs up. They must have thought when they read in the papers that he'd been charged, for assaulting a policeman no less, and for being drunk and disorderly and causing an affray, they had something to make Flo squirm with for a change, pay her back for her bragging. I can't say I blame them.'

'How does Steve feel?'

'I don't know and don't really care.' Lizzie said emphatically.

'He seems near welded to the bar with that other fellow.'

'Aye,' Lizzie said.

As the girls were discussing Steve, so he was saying to Stuart, 'I was crazy about her, you know.'

'I can understand it. She's a looker,' Stuart said.

Steve shook his head. 'I don't know. I mean, when

I remember the prison cell and all. God, she did nothing, she just stood at the attic window of that hotel and watched them dragging me away. She didn't come down and say it was partly her damned fault. Part of me can't ever forget that.'

'Put her out of your head, mate,' Stuart advised. 'She's bad news.'

'That's it. I can't,' Steve said. 'Despite it all, I still love her like mad. I don't know why either.' He didn't go on to say that when Lizzie had told him it was over he'd wanted to die. You didn't share that, even with a mate. He'd think you'd gone soft in the head.

Steve looked across the room. Lizzie was still wearing her bridesmaid's dress of peach-coloured satin with the long lacy sleeves, and she looked breathtaking. The headdress was gone and her hair was drawn up into an elegant chignon, showing her slender neck, and he felt the blood pound in his brain.

He knew he had to at least talk to her. If he lost this opportunity he'd probably never get another and he'd always regret it.

'Oh God, Steve's coming over,' Lizzie said to Betty.

'So what? You'll have to meet him sometime.'

'Why? Anyway, he's been drinking.'

'Course he bloody has. It's a wedding, ain't it?'

'Yes, but . . .' There was no time to say more for Steve was suddenly beside her.

'Hallo, Lizzie.'

'Hallo, Steve.'

Across the room, Flo dug Rodney in the ribs. 'Go across and tell our Steve to get away from that Lizzie!' she demanded.

Rodney was too drunk to care who Steve was talking to. 'For God's sake, woman, he's a grown man.'

'Are you going or not?'

'Not. Go yourself if you're so concerned. Rescue your wee, innocent son why don't you?'

'Useless, you are! Bloody useless!' Flo cried, and she marched across the room.

Lizzie saw her coming. 'Your mother's on her way,' she just had time to say to Steve before Flo was in front of her demanding,

'What d'you want of my son now, you brazen hussy?'

That was rich, Lizzie thought, seeing that it had been Steve who'd come over to her, but she didn't bother saying this. This was Mike and Tressa's day and she wanted no scene, so she smiled at Flo. 'Just exchanging pleasantries,' she said and Steve urged, 'Go on back to Dad, Mom. This doesn't concern you.'

'Oh, so it doesn't concern me that this dirty little trollop caused you to be taken in by the coppers?'

Scene or no scene, Lizzie wasn't standing for that. 'I did no such thing, and I won't be called names I don't deserve.'

'You do deserve them and more, you brazen, trouble-making bitch.'

'Mom, that will do.'

'I'll decide what will do,' Flo snapped. 'That one will have you for a fool and throw you to one side when she's done with you.'

'Mom, shut up!' Steve said, his voice rising in agitation.

'That's a fine way to speak to me.'

'Oh for Christ's sake,' Steve said, exasperated, and he took his mother by the elbow and steered her across the floor to where his father was. Lizzie took the opportunity to slip outside and hoped the night air would cool her cheeks, which were flaming with embarrassment and anger. She leant against the wall. It was still as light as day outside, but some of the heat had gone and she was glad of the little breeze.

'Thought I'd find you here.'

'Steve!'

'Lizzie, are you scared of me?' Steve asked, worried about the wary look that had come over Lizzie's face and her widened eyes.

Lizzie looked him full in the face. 'What do you think?' she asked. 'If the boot was on the other foot, wouldn't you be scared? Look at the size of me to the size of you, and that night . . . well, I'm not sure what you would have done if I hadn't got away. And quite apart from that, you could have lost me my job.'

'I know, and I understand how you feel,' Steve said sincerely. 'I've regretted that night often and wish I could turn the clock back, for it was never my intention to hurt you. All I can say in my defence, and it is no excuse, is that I was angry and drunk, for I'd seldom drunk as much in such a short space of time. My head was reeling, and then, when you told me it was over . . . Christ, I think I really went clean mad for a bit. I'm real sorry about it, Lizzie.'

Lizzie saw the true regret and more than a hint of shame in Steve's eyes and so she said, 'I do understand that I hurt you a great deal that night, Steve.'

'Until that moment I'd never pleaded with a woman,

you know,' Steve said. 'I suppose I was angry that you'd made me look like a bloody fool. Then the next night I saw you all laughing at me as they led me away.'

'No one was laughing, Steve, believe me,' Lizzie said. 'I wanted to come down, but Tressa wouldn't let me. I watched only because I was concerned. It gave me no satisfaction to see you taken away in handcuffs.'

'I'm glad of that at least.'

'Let's put it behind us now, shall we?' Lizzie said. She put a hand on Steve's arm and went on, 'You are a lovely man and you could find a girl much more worthy than me, one who'd love you back.'

Steve could have told Lizzie there and then he'd tried a variety of girls, all willing, and he'd near drunk the pubs dry, but it had only blurred the image of her from his mind. In his sober moments each day she was there at the forefront of it, tantalising him.

But he didn't say this, and Lizzie went on, 'Steve, we knew each other for some weeks, and apart from those two awful nights – the one where I told you it was over, and your reaction and the incident the following night, which was linked to it – we had good times. Let's at least part as friends?'

That wasn't what Steve wanted, but it was a step in the right direction. 'If that's how you want it,' he said, and he took Lizzie in his arms as one might a friend and kissed her lightly on the cheek.

Lizzie gave an inward sigh of relief and the guilt she'd felt towards Steve shifted slightly. 'I must go in,' she told him. 'Tressa will be leaving soon, according to her uncle. Will your mother attack me if I go back?'

'She'd better not. I've told my father to keep her at the table and to sit on her if he has to.'

'I'd like to see that,' Lizzie said with a grin, and she went back inside and Steve followed.

Three weeks after Tressa's wedding, a bouquet of twelve red roses was delivered to the hotel. Lizzie had been serving breakfasts when the receptionist sent for her. 'Someone has an admirer,' she said, handing Lizzie the bouquet.

Lizzie had never received flowers before. '*To Lizzie, from your very good friend. Happy Birthday. Love Steve,*' the card read.

'Friend, my Aunt Fanny!' the receptionist spluttered. 'If any fellow sent me flowers, I'd know he'd want to be more than a friend.'

Betty and Pat were agog when she came into the room carrying them, and the flowers did give Lizzie a welcome boost, for she'd begun to feel very low. Before Tressa's wedding it had been rush and bustle, arranging everything, and then there'd been the wedding itself, and though she'd accepted the fact she would miss Tressa, she hadn't realised how much until everything was over.

'Is that the same Steve who was at the wedding?' Betty said, scrutinising the card.

'Aye.'

'Is he aiming to get back with you or what? You said you was just friends.'

'We are,' Lizzie declared, and hoped Steve still saw it that way and he wasn't harbouring false romantic hopes. But surely, she told herself, I am overreacting.

106

He had sent flowers for her birthday. It was the sort of thing friends did. 'No,' she said. 'Steve knows it's over. I think it's his way of saying he is sorry that it ended the way it did.'

'Oh. Right,' Betty said, and her eyes met those of Pat's. Both thought the same thing: if Lizzie really thought that, then she definitely was as green as she was cabbage-looking.

Lizzie sighed as she went down for the loan of a vase for the flowers. Although she had no desire to begin any sort of relationship with Steve, she knew the days ahead would be lonely ones for her.

What made things worse was the fact that Betty and Pat had got themselves steady boyfriends and seldom went out with each other, never mind having Lizzie tag along. She didn't know the others in the hotel well enough to ask if she could be part of their group, and anyway, most of the girls of her age were like Betty and Pat and courting strong.

She tried to rouse herself, but even going to the pictures on your own was no fun, though better than the music hall and you couldn't turn up at a dance alone and unescorted. As for pubs, well she knew what sort of women hung around in those places. So she ended up going on long, solitary walks.

Every week she went to see Tressa. Tressa, now a married woman and getting heavier by the week, was steeped in domesticity. She didn't seem like the sort of girl that had gone tripping over the cobblestones of the Bull Ring arm in arm with Lizzie, picking over the bargains and cheeking the costermongers. Nor did she seem the same sort of girl who'd once spent two weeks' wages on a pair of shoes from Marshall and Snelgrove's – that she really 'had to have'. Lizzie remembered how they used to giggle as they tried on the fancy hats in C&A Modes and acted all lah-di-dah and how they searched the racks of clothes to find something new to wear to go out in that night.

For Tressa, those days seemed so far away they might never have been, and she had no interest in hearing what Lizzie had done or seen. Most of her sentences now began, 'After the baby is born . . .' and Lizzie realised that Doreen, who awaited the baby's birth with the same excitement, was now more important to Tressa than she was, and it was a blow to take.

Lizzie began to feel increasingly lonely, but she tried to keep any self-pity out of her voice in the letters she wrote home every week. That October she went alone, Tressa being too near her time, to the marriage of her sister Eileen to Murray O'Shea, the man she'd been after for years. Lizzie didn't know why she wanted him, for, as her father said, the man would neither work nor want. But there was no accounting for taste, and Eileen was blissfully happy. Lizzie, not wishing to spoil the day for her, wore the bridesmaid's dress she thought she looked hideous in without a word of complaint. Back home in Birmingham she felt more alone than ever, and she viewed the coming winter with depression, knowing soon even her walks would be curtailed.

One evening in early November, Lizzie was queuing alone at the Odeon cinema to see *Cavalcade*, which many of the girls at the hotel had enthused about, when she spotted Steve in the crowd in front of her.

She was pleased to see someone she knew and she called to him. He was with Stuart and two chattering, giggling girls, but she saw that too late and he was already pushing his way through the people towards her. 'Lizzie,' he breathed. 'How have you been?'

'Oh, grand, you know,' Lizzie said. 'I didn't realise you were with friends.'

'That's all right.'

There was an uneasy silence and then she said, 'Thanks for the roses in July. I meant to send a note.' She had agonised over what to say and in the end decided to say nothing, and she wasn't to know how longingly Steve had waited for some acknowledgement.

'Were they all right?'

'They were beautiful. Every girl in the hotel was envious,' Lizzie said, and then, seeing Stuart's neck craning over the queuing people, she said, 'Shouldn't you go back to your friends?'

'They're not,' Steve said. 'I mean, they are just two girls we picked up in the pub. I'll just put Stuart . . .'

'No, wait. Steve . . .' But he'd gone and the crowd closed about him. In minutes he was back.

'Right, sorted that. Now where shall we go?'

He didn't say that Stuart had called him the stupidest bugger he'd ever seen. 'We were in for a good night here, mate, with these little goers.'

'Come on, man, I'd do the same for you.'

'Oh go boil your head, Steve. You need it looking at.'

'I'll keep it in mind.'

Steve betrayed not a word of this altercation on his

face as he stood before Lizzie and said, 'Just say the word, Lizzie. We'll do whatever you want.'

'What d'you mean?'

'D'you fancy going dancing up West End?'

'With you?'

Steve looked around him with exaggerated care. 'Well,' he said at last with a grin, 'I can't see any other bugger offering.'

It was on the tip of Lizzie's tongue just to say no and thank him. And then what? She could hardly go into the cinema with Steve now, after he'd apparently dumped one of the girls he was in the queue with to be with her. And yet . . .

'Come on, Lizzie,' Steve pleaded. 'It will be as a friend. Straight up.'

If she didn't go, ahead of her was a lonely night spent in the bedroom of the hotel, and she loved dancing. But it was going out with Steve again. 'As a friend only, nothing more,' she said at last. 'Promise me?'

'As a friend only,' Steve said, drawing her away from the crowds surging into the cinema. Then he lifted his finger and gave it a lick. 'See this wet, see this dry,' he said with a smile, 'cut my throat if I tell a lie.'

Lizzie gave him a push. 'Fool!'

Steve laughed and grasped Lizzie around the waist and felt his heart thudding against his chest.

Steve behaved like a perfect gentleman that night, and the night he took her to the pictures and she saw *Cavalcade* in the end, and the time he took her to see the hilarious but saucy Max Wall at the Hippodrome. One night they spent a quiet evening at the pub, and though Lizzie allowed herself two port and lemons before switching to orange juice, Steve didn't complain or urge her to drink something more exciting.

Gradually, she began to relax in his company and remember the good times of their earlier courtship. It was a novel experience for Steve to try and please a lady knowing there would be nothing in it for him, and Lizzie didn't know what it cost him to keep his hands by his sides when he longed to encircle her and to kiss those lovely lips he watched yearningly.

Without his street women, he couldn't have managed, though now he'd begun to feel guilty about going from Lizzie straight to the bed of another. He didn't tell Stuart this, though, for he was aware that Stuart already thought him clean barmy. 'Variety, man,' he said, when they were both making their way home after such a night. 'Spice of life. Nothing quite like it.'

Tressa's son was born on Wednesday, 7th December, and Steve came that evening to tell Lizzie the news after it had been phoned through to The Bell public house and the landlady had come up with the message. 'We could go up of the weekend,' he said.

Lizzie hesitated. She wouldn't like Tressa and Mike to get any ideas about her and Steve, and yet she was off-duty all day Saturday until seven o'clock, and she had to go and see Tressa sometime and ooh and ah over the child. It would be silly for her to go on her own, and so she nodded. 'All right.'

In the end, she was more affected by the child, Phillip,

than she ever thought she would be, and she didn't have to pretend to be awed by the diminutive but perfect little person Tressa gave her to hold, with his tiny fingers and even smaller toes. His skin was flawless, his lashes making perfect crescents on the top of his cheeks as he slept, and Lizzie smelt that very special baby smell. Suddenly she was filled with a deep longing for a child of her own, a feeling that took her totally by surprise.

'Are you and Steve . . . you know?' Tressa asked when the men had gone off to wet the baby's head.

'No, but we are friends,' Lizzie said. 'Mind how I told you we had a talk about everything at your wedding?'

'Aye, I remember all right,' Tressa said. 'And I hope you know what you're doing. Steve doesn't seem to be looking at you with the eyes of a friend, if you know what I mean?'

Lizzie told herself Tressa must be mistaken. Steve never touched her besides holding her shoulders gently and giving her a kiss on the cheek. Surely if he thought of her any other way he'd have tried something else. She hoped he never went down that road, for then she'd have to put a stop to it straight away, and she had to admit that going out with him was far better than sitting alone in the bedroom of the hotel.

Lizzie barely saw Steve once the Christmas festivities got underway, and she was surprised to receive a package on Christmas Eve. She took it to her room and opened it out. There was a velvet box inside, and in it, resting on a nest of navy silk, was a beautifully fine gold bracelet. When she lifted it out there were gasps from Betty and Pat and Marjorie, who now occupied Tressa's bed.

'Will you look at that?' Pat breathed.

'Who's it from?' Marjorie asked.

Pat and Betty exchanged knowing glances. Lizzie had explained away the birthday roses, and apparently to her satisfaction, but this was something else entirely. Lizzie was naturally reticent and too worried about being teased to tell Pat or Betty about her meeting with Steve in November, and the fact she had been seeing him since. It wasn't hard, for their times off rarely coincided and they were too preoccupied with their own love lives to worry overmuch about Lizzie's, and Marjorie had no idea of any of it. So, as far as Pat and Betty were aware, this bracelet had arrived out of the blue.

It was like a statement, Betty thought; like saying, *To hell with being friends. I want something more.* And so she said to Marjorie, 'It's from Lizzie's feller.'

'Steve's not my feller,' Lizzie protested.

'Oh no,' Pat said, with a hint of derision. 'Let's say I wish some non-feller of mine would send me something half so nice.' And she pulled the card from the box '"*All my love always, Steve*",' she read out. 'Like I said, some friend that Steve.'

The card unnerved Lizzie and she knew she should have a talk with Steve as soon as possible. She withdrew the bracelet and played it though her fingers. It was gorgeous and she knew it would have been expensive. 'Maybe I shouldn't accept it.'

'Don't be such a bloody fool,' Pat admonished.

'I need to talk to him about this,' Lizzie said. 'Set the record straight.' But she knew that was a vain wish. The guests were arriving any time after four o'clock that afternoon, and from when they stepped into the hotel until they checked out on 1st January she knew she'd hardly stop running. The hours would be long, sleep a luxury she could only dream of, and time off virtually non-existent.

In a way she was glad of it. She was able to push the problem of what to do about the bracelet to the back of her mind.

On 3rd January Steve took her dancing at the Locarno. She spent some of the tips she'd earned over the festive season to buy a dress from C&A Modes. It was of rose velvet with a scooped neckline and fell to the floor, the bottom section gathered in little pleats. She had her hair piled on her head with combs the same colour as the dress, and peeping from beneath it were dainty high-heeled shoes. On one of her slender wrists was Steve's bracelet. He was so pleased. He hadn't been sure she would accept it, especially after what he'd written on the card.

Everything pleased him that night. Lizzie thanked him warmly for the bracelet and said truthfully it was the prettiest thing she'd ever owned, but she chided him for spending so much on it. 'And who else would I spend it on?' he asked. 'Now, Lizzie, my money is my own and I must choose how to spend it.'

Lizzie kissed him gently on the lips in gratitude and friendship and he felt his body grow hot with desire, but he told himself to go easy. Lizzie had noticed

114

nothing untoward and she removed her jacket and said, 'Do you like the dress? I treated myself.'

'It's beautiful,' he said, surveying it. He was bowled over by the strength of his feelings coursing through him and excited by the prospect of being able to legitimately hold Lizzie in his arms as they danced. He put his arms gently around her and said, 'And you're beautiful, Lizzie.'

Lizzie, though embarrassed, was warmed by his genuine praise and realised she'd missed not seeing him over Christmas. Don't depend on him, she'd warned herself, but the alternative if she didn't go out with Steve was a dismal one.

She had a wonderful time, so wonderful that when Steve left her back at the hotel she kissed him again on the lips. 'Thank you, Steve.'

'You deserved a treat tonight,' he told her. 'You've been working like a Trojan at this place. You're thinner than ever.'

'Och, Steve, don't worry, I'm as strong as an ox.'

'Oxen don't come in such pretty packages,' Steve said. 'Look after yourself.'

'I will, don't worry.'

CHAPTER SEVEN

The following morning Lizzie didn't feel a bit like an ox. In fact, she woke feeling very strange indeed. She was dripping wet with sweat, her head was thumping and she felt as if she had a tight band around her chest. She was due to serve breakfasts with Marjorie and she struggled to get out of bed, though the room tilted in a most alarming way.

She slumped back on the bed again, and Marjorie, coming back from the bathroom and beginning to dress, said, 'God, are you all right? Your face is as red as a beetroot.'

Lizzie wasn't surprised. She could feel the sweat standing out on her forehead, trickling down her back, and seeping between her breasts. She opened her mouth to say she felt a little strange, but she was taken unawares by a fit of coughing.

'God, Lizzie, I don't think you'd better go downstairs like that.'

'No, I'm all right, I'm fine,' Lizzie said in a husky voice.

'Don't be bloody stupid,' Marjorie said, putting her

feet into her shoes. 'Stay here, I'll have a word with someone.'

Lizzie tried to tell the doctor that the manager had summoned that she was all right too, between bouts of coughing and gasping for breath. The doctor was Scottish and one to stand no nonsense and he said, 'Please let me be the judge of that, young lady. I wouldna dream of telling you how to serve breakfast now, would I? Open up the front of your nightie and let's have a wee listen to that chest of yours.'

Acutely embarrassed, Lizzie undid the buttons at her neck and the doctor sounded her chest with the stethoscope. 'Hm, hm,' was all the comment he made, and then he straightened up and said, 'Pull it right off.'

'What?'

'I need to listen to your back.'

'I can't.'

'I'm a doctor, lassie,' the man barked. 'Here to see how ill you are, not to look at your body. Now pull off your nightie.'

Lizzie did as the doctor bid, glad they were alone, and the doctor listened and he also gave her back little taps. Eventually he said, 'All right, put your nightie back on.'

'What is it, Doctor?'

'Bronchitis,' the doctor replied, 'and a bad dose I might add. Need to take care of it.'

To the manager he said more. 'Have to see it doesn't turn to pneumonia. Needs careful nursing, for that girl might have little resistance and she's as thin as a rake.'

'She's never had a day off sick before.'

'Well, she'll have more than a day now.'

'I have a hotel to run.'

'I am aware of that.'

'What I mean is, I can't have her here,' the manager said. 'With one down anyway, I won't have the staff to nurse her and I presume she won't be able to stay in a dormitory with the others?'

'It's not something I would recommend.'

'Well then . . .'

'The only place for her, if you're adamant, is the hospital.'

'See to it, can you?'

The doctor, grim-faced, saw to it, and when he told Lizzie that she was to go to the General Hospital, she shed bitter tears. She'd never been in hospital in her life and didn't want to go now. Surely to God she wasn't that sick. People died in hospital.

Lizzie sent a note to Steve to tell him what had happened and he turned up at the hospital a couple of days later. Lizzie had deteriorated during that time and it tore at his heart to see her fighting for breath, the beads of glistening sweat on her forehead lending a sheen to her face, despite the ministrations of the nurses.

Knowing she had little breath to talk, he did the talking, and for hours. Much of what he said went over her head, but she liked the sound of his voice and it was nice to have someone near, holding her hand.

Betty and Pat came, and even Marjorie popped in one day. Tressa came too, but obviously without Phillip, so she couldn't stay long, but Lizzie was pleased she had made the effort, for it was quite a trek.

Two days after Tressa's visit, Lizzie was in the throes

of delirium when Steve called at the hospital. 'What is it?' he cried, seeing the hospital staff scurrying about and Lizzie hardly aware of anything as she was being transferred to a separate single room.

'Are you a relative?' the doctor asked.

'Sort of,' Steve said. 'All her people are in Ireland. I'm her boyfriend,' and then, thinking it might have more clout, he added, 'her fiancé really. I just haven't got around to buying the ring yet.'

'Well,' the doctor said, 'in view of that, and her family not being here, I'm sorry to have to tell you that Miss Clooney has developed pneumonia.'

Ah Jesus Christ, Steve's mind screamed, thinking of that killer disease of his youth, and his mouth dropped open with shock. 'Will she . . . Will she . . . ?'

The doctor shrugged. 'We'll do what we can and it will depend on her resistance to fight. I'm sorry I can offer you no further hope.'

'Shall I inform her people?'

'It can do no harm,' the doctor said, and those words more than any other conveyed to Steve the seriousness of Lizzie's condition.

Lizzie felt as if she were surrounded by sticky treacle and across her chest was a hot, tight band, so that she found it hard to breathe. She was semi-aware sometimes of someone sitting by her side, holding her hand, talking to her, but it was as if she were outside of it. Strange images disturbed her dreams, mixed up with her home back in Ireland, the hotel, and, most of all, Steve.

He'd arrived every evening since he'd been told Lizzie had pneumonia. 'We have got a visiting policy,' the matron had said to the nurses, 'but I haven't the heart to turn him away. And after all, it's a private room she has, so he's disturbing no one else.'

'He wouldn't disturb anyone else anyroad,' one of the nurses replied. 'He just sits there. God, to have someone love you like that.'

Lizzie's mother, who'd come over to see her daughter, while desperately worried about her was also impressed by Steve's diligence. When she was informed he was Lizzie's fiancé, she believed it, though thought it odd. Lizzie had not asked their permission and she said as much to Steve.

Steve had no wish to alienate Catherine and yet was unable to tell her the truth in case he might not be allowed to see Lizzie any more, but he was anxious to assure her their relationship was above board. 'Neither of us had the time to ask your approval,' he told Catherine. 'We were just toying with the idea of becoming engaged, with your blessing of course, when Lizzie became ill.'

Catherine accepted Steve's version of events and the hospital gave a very good account of Steve Gillespie; and while his cronies at The Bell and the women of the street could have painted a different picture, even they would have had to admit that since this business had started he'd been a changed man.

Catherine was staying at Longbridge with Arthur and Doreen, whom she'd met and got on well with at Tressa's wedding. It was a long haul every day into the city centre, and while she stayed with Lizzie most of the day she tended to leave the evenings free for Steve, which suited him fine.

He hadn't told Flo where he went every evening after a swift wash and a bite to eat, but the news filtered through to her at last. Flo wanted to tell her son to waste no time on the girl, that it would be better if she died altogether, but the sorrow on his face checked her and, uncharacteristically, she made no comment.

'The crisis will be reached in the early hours,' the doctor told him when Lizzie had been in hospital a fortnight. 'Sometime between two and four.'

Catherine had been informed too, and that night they sat either side of the bed, holding Lizzie's hands, watching her struggling to breathe, the sweat pouring from her. Steve was bone-weary for he'd sat there many days now, but he felt that if he took his eyes off Lizzie for one moment she would die.

It was the early hours when Catherine got to her feet. 'God, I'm stiff,' she said, 'and I need some air. I feel as if I'm suffocating in here.'

Steve had barely noticed, but when she said, 'Would you mind if I pop out for a few minutes?' he nodded. He'd be glad for a few minutes alone with Lizzie to speak of what was in his heart.

He began as soon as the door had closed behind Catherine. 'Come on, Lizzie. You must fight this, for God knows I can't live without you. You know that. I love you. Jesus, I've always loved you. I'd lay down my life for you, Lizzie, please . . .' On and on he went, in the same vein.

Lizzie felt as if a furnace blazed within her and her eyes burned too, and she was so tired she had the feeling she could just float away, but always that voice

121

would drag her back. She liked the sound of it. It soothed her, though the words were indistinguishable, and she liked the feel of a large hand encircling her own. Maybe, if she could raise her other arm from the bed, she could tell whoever it was she could hear them and that she liked what they were doing.

But her arm felt like lead. She couldn't lift it. She tried again and again and eventually, slowly, her fingers moved. Steve wasn't aware of the slight movement straight away, but when her arm lifted oh so slightly, he jumped from the bed as if he'd been shot and was out of the room in seconds, yelling for a nurse.

He stood at the threshold of the room, unable to see her for the doctor and two nurses grouped about the bed as Catherine returned to the ward. She hurried when she saw Steve standing outside the room, but before she was able to frame a question the young doctor came out of the room towards them, and he was smiling. 'The fever has passed,' he said. 'The crisis is over and she is sleeping normally. I won't tell you how worried I was. She will be weak for some time, but she will live.'

'Oh thank God! Thank God!' Catherine said fervently.

Steve thanked the Almighty too, but in his head. He couldn't speak for the torrent of tears pouring from him. Catherine put her arms around him and they cried together and took comfort from one another.

It seemed to Lizzie that nearly every time she opened her eyes, Steve was by her side, his large muscular hands holding hers, especially after her mother had returned home. Her mother and the nursing staff had often referred to Steve as her fiancé and she'd not corrected them and wasn't sure why she hadn't. Maybe, like Steve, she'd thought he wouldn't be able to visit so often, and she'd not have liked that. In fact, he had become very important to her and she longed to see his large frame almost filling the doorway each evening and his heavy strides across the floor to sit by Lizzie's bed, when he would take her small hand in his and talk to her.

She'd been in hospital a month when the manager of the Grand Hotel came in one afternoon with a hamper of fruit, and when he told Lizzie he was very sorry but he couldn't keep her job open any longer, she wasn't really surprised.

'I'm sorry you've been ill and everything, and I am delighted you'll make a full recovery in time,' he went on to say. 'But, you see, it's Easter in a few weeks. We're coming up to our busiest time and with you off I'm one member of staff down already.'

It was only what Lizzie expected and she could see the man's dilemma, but she knew when she left hospital she would have to work at something and jobs were desperately hard to find. Finding somewhere to live that she could afford would be just as bad and she was nervous and scared of the future.

She told Steve her concerns that same evening, but he told her not to worry, something would turn up. He had plans of his own for Lizzie and they involved her marrying him so he could look after her for good. But first he had to find a place to live, for he couldn't really expect Lizzie to move in with his parents and Neil. Time enough then to ask her to marry him.

In early March, Steve heard of a house in a courtyard off Bell Barn Road that would be coming vacant in a month or two, when the old man living there alone would be moving to stay with his daughter. It wasn't much more than a few hundred yards from his parents' house in Grant Street, but that couldn't be helped, for many would give their eye teeth for any sort of house at all.

That night at the hospital, he took Lizzie's hand in his. 'Lizzie, you once told me you didn't love me. Is that still true?'

'Ah, Steve. Don't do this. Why torture yourself?'

'Please, I need to know. There is a reason.'

Tears sprang to Lizzie's eyes and she opened her mouth to say she didn't love Steve and she still felt the same, but then she stopped. Once she definitely hadn't, it was true, but people change and circumstances can alter the way a person views things. There was no doubt that she liked his company, had depended on it while in the hospital and longed for him to come in each evening. Wasn't that a kind of love? True, it wasn't the aching, bittersweet passion enjoyed by Tressa and Mike, but she and Steve were different people, so the way they loved would be different too, surely. 'I don't know how I feel about you now, Steve,' she answered honestly.

'Do you like me?'

'Of course I like you.'

'A lot, or just a bit.'

'A lot, bighead.'

Steve gave a sigh of relief and knelt beside the hospital bed, but still kept hold of Lizzie's hand. 'Marry me, Lizzie?' he pleaded. 'I love you more than life itself.'

'Oh, Steve . . .'

'Please think about it!' Steve begged. 'I know this isn't ideal and you didn't want to get married so young, but your illness changed a lot of things and I will have a house for us to move in to.' And then, as Lizzie's eyes still looked troubled, he said gently, 'If you refuse me, what is the alternative?'

And Lizzie couldn't answer that. She had no job and no place to live, and even if she had both, Birmingham was a lonely place where she knew no one. Tressa, as a friend to go out with, or even as a confidante, was almost lost to her. Betty was getting married, Pat would soon follow, and Marjorie had never been a true friend.

'Can I think about it, Steve?'

'Oh yeah, bonny girl,' Steve said, delighted that Lizzie hadn't said no outright. 'You can think about it. But don't keep me waiting for weeks.'

'I'll not do that to you, I'll give you the answer within the next few days,' Lizzie promised.

The following day, she was leaving the hospital and had been offered a temporary home with Mike's aunt and uncle at Longbridge, till she was on her feet and could decide what to do. Arthur and Doreen had taken to Lizzie at the wedding and Doreen had gone to see her a few times in the hospital after Catherine had left. Catherine had told them Lizzie wasn't keen on going back to Ireland at all and yet there was little else for her to do as far as she could see. That had decided Doreen. 'The girl can bide here a wee while until she is fully recovered and then she can decide what is to be done,' she declared one evening.

Arthur nodded his head sagely, knowing agreement was the only and safest course to take with his wife over certain issues. He collected Lizzie the following evening after work, and Doreen saw how white-faced the girl was with tiredness.

After the evening meal, with the men away to the pub, Lizzie said, 'I can't thank you enough for asking me to come here for a while. Mammy wanted me to go home, but I had the feeling if I left these shores I'd never come back.'

'Think nothing of it,' Doreen said. 'You can stay as long as you like.'

'Aye,' said Tressa. 'It will be like old times.'

'Not quite,' Lizzie said with a smile. 'Those days will not come back, I'm afraid. Maybe my carefree days are over too.' And then, in a quieter voice, she said, 'Steve asked me to marry him yesterday.'

Tressa's mouth dropped open in surprise. Because she hadn't been able to visit the hospital much she didn't know the role Steve had played. The last she'd heard, Lizzie had told her firmly that they were just friends. 'What did you say?' she asked.

'I said I'd think about it.'

Doreen, who'd had many a chat with Catherine about Steve, gave a sniff and said, 'What's there to think about?'

'I'm not sure I love him,' Lizzie said simply.

'Love! Bumpkin!' Doreen said disparagingly. 'Love, let me tell you, flies out of the windows when the bills come in at the door. And it's a good thing that man didn't waste time to think about it when you were lying half-dead in a hospital bed.'

'I know that.'

'He has a good job, he'll be a good provider,' Doreen said. 'Is he generous?'

'Aye, very generous and considerate. He has a temper though.'

'Not with you, surely?'

For a second, the scene when she told Steve it was over flashed through Lizzie's mind, but she decided to say nothing, for Steve had apologised profusely and since then he had been kindness itself. 'No,' she said, and added, 'He fights mainly with his brother.'

Doreen gave a snort. 'What brothers do not?' she asked. 'But they'll probably get on better when they have wives and children of their own. It's a very gentling experience becoming a father. I've seen it many a time. Tell me, Lizzie, do you like Steve?'

'Oh aye.'

'Well, let me tell you that liking is often more sustaining and fulfilling than love. When love dims, liking will survive.'

'So you think I should say yes, Doreen?'

'I do, my dear.'

'What about you, Tressa?'

'It's entirely up to you, Lizzie,' Tressa said, 'but do you not want a home and family of your own?'

Unbidden, Lizzie remembered little Phillip, the

perfectness of him, and she knew she yearned for a baby and the decision was made.

The wedding was in Ballintra on 18th June 1933, just three weeks short of Lizzie's twenty-first birthday, and her family pulled out all the stops to accommodate Steve's family, who came over for it.

Lizzie herself was consumed by excitement as the wedding drew near. She'd bought the dress in Birmingham, though her parents had paid for it, and it was the talk of the place for days. It was pure white, the shimmering satin of the skirt held out with six lace petticoats, caught up at intervals with white rosebuds. The bodice fitted her slender figure to perfection and the entire dress was covered with beads that caught the light in the room as Lizzie spun round to admire herself in the mirror.

It brought a lump to Catherine's throat to see this, her youngest daughter, and one who had been dangerously ill not so long ago, looking so radiant, so happy. She was thrilled that the man she had chosen was honest and respectable and that he had shown Catherine that he loved Lizzie to distraction. She was also glad that Lizzie had respected herself, that she had earned the right to wear the white dress.

However, it wasn't in Catherine's nature to praise her children, and so now she said chidingly, 'How can I get this headdress on with you spinning around like a dervish? Be still now.'

Lizzie obediently stayed still, though her insides continued to perform somersaults as her mother fastened the veil in place, pinning it securely to the plait she had in a coronet around her head. The effect of it all caused Eileen, coming into the room at that moment, to catch her breath. 'God, Lizzie,' she said. 'You look just fantastic. Doesn't she, Mammy?'

Catherine blinked away the tears from her own eyes and said almost brusquely, 'Aye. You chose well, Lizzie. The dress an' all suits you fine.'

Neither Lizzie nor Eileen were put off by Catherine's manner. It was her way, and both had spotted her glittering eyes and they smiled at one another across the room.

'Thank you, Mammy,' Lizzie said, suddenly overcome with it all. 'Thank you for making it so special for me, the dress, the flowers, the cake, and for arranging it all. No one could ask for more, or better parents.'

And then, mindful not to crush the dress, Catherine took Lizzie in her arms and kissed her lightly. 'And why would we not want it special for you?' she said. 'Aren't you the last daughter to see to, and one I love dearly.'

Seldom had Catherine used such gentle tones and never could Lizzie ever remember her mother saying she loved her and it brought a lump to her throat.

'Don't be blubbing now,' Catherine warned, seeing her daughter's eyes brimming, 'or your face will puff up and your man will go for me for upsetting you. Go on now with Eileen. Your daddy will be waiting on you.'

Later, when Lizzie stood at the church door, one arm through her father's and the other holding the beautiful array of flowers, her three little nieces who her sister Susan had got ready in place behind her, the strains of the wedding march filling that familiar church, she felt she could burst with happiness.

She kept her eyes averted from the malicious glare of Flo as they began the slow walk down the aisle and instead fixed them on her man waiting for her before the altar, with Mike his best man beside him. As she drew closer, Steve risked a peep at her and he felt for a moment as if his heart had stopped beating. At the look on his face, Lizzie's own heart turned over and she stepped forward to be joined to Steve until death would part them.

Margaret confided to Catherine that she wished Tressa's wedding could have been in the village too, but in the circumstances it was better done in Birmingham where none knew them. Even now, she'd had a few with knowing glances and nudges saying that the baby had made a great turn-out, seeing as he was so premature.

Lizzie knew this, for the same had been said to her, and she knew her mother was puffed up with pride that she hadn't been in the same condition as Tressa when she married. In Catherine's opinion, Lizzie had done well for herself. She was marrying a fine strapping man in a well-paid job and the only haste to the wedding at all was because they had a house waiting for them.

Margaret would know the manner of house it would be. She'd seen the streets of them when she had gone over for her daughter's wedding. The pub where the reception had been held was actually in Bell Barn Road, but when Catherine had been over when Lizzie had been so ill, she went only from the hospital and out to Longbridge each day and had no idea. Margaret was glad, at any rate, that her own daughter was out of those crowded, disease-ridden streets. She couldn't really describe it: you had to see the place, smell the stink in the air and hear the noise to understand it at all. But she didn't say any of this and Catherine was only worried about one thing, as far as her daughter was concerned, and that was Flo.

'You may have trouble there, Lizzie, for she thinks Steve can do no wrong.'

'Oh, you've noticed then?' Lizzie commented dryly, for Flo's obsession with her son was obvious even to the most casual observer.

'Does she live far from you?'

Lizzie wrinkled her nose. 'Not far enough!' Then she added, 'In fairness, Steve did his best. Housing is at a premium and some have to make a start in a couple of rooms.'

'Aye, you have a good man there,' Catherine said. 'And God knows, he can't help his mother. Eileen's chap, young Murray O'Shea, doesn't treat her half so well as Steve does you, but nothing would do her than marry the man.'

And Lizzie knew Steve was good. Even after she'd agreed to marry him, he'd not urged her to go further in their lovemaking than fondling and kissing her. She didn't know what it cost Steve, and Lizzie hadn't admitted to him that she often wanted things to go further, nor told him how she longed for fulfilment on their wedding night.

And when it came, it was wondrous, rapturous, a

131

feeling that superseded the sudden sharp pain, and afterwards she cried with joy, glad she'd waited and that her wedding night was all she'd wanted. Steve lay curled beside her, delighted he'd pleased her. He'd taken his time because he'd wanted her to enjoy it. It was a long time since he'd slept with a young, tight virgin and he'd also wanted to savour the moment.

There were many things about Steve that Lizzie hadn't been aware of, and many a woman could have warned her that you never know a man fully until you marry him.

She didn't know he drank so much, for instance, nor that he wanted to drink almost every night. He could carry his beer well most nights at least, and though he was not sober when he came home and sometimes a little unsteady on his feet, their lovemaking, which Steve wanted often, was almost as good as it had been on their wedding night. However, on the fairly rare occasions that Steve was really drunk it was a different story. He'd be so unpredictable; Lizzie would be afraid to say anything much in case he took it the wrong way, for he could be aggressive and belligerent and he'd be rough and unfeeling later in bed and often hurt her.

She didn't bother complaining for she knew this was the lot of many women. She met her neighbours: Violet, who lived beside her with her husband Barry and their two teenagers, Colin and Carol, and the others down the yard: Ada Smith, Gloria Havering, Minnie Monahan and Sadie Miller, who she met at the tap and in the brew house, where they helped her with the weekly wash in the early days of her marriage.

Between herself and Violet there was a special bond. Violet felt sorry for the girl with none of her own beside her and became quite motherly towards her, and Lizzie was glad of it, of all the women's company. All the women complained about their husbands and only Violet's and Gloria's besides Lizzie's were in work. Quite a few also complained about the amount the men drank. 'He's always down the boozer and I'm always down the pawnshop,' Ada would say.

'Yeah, and when they comes home bottled, they can't think of owt but getting their leg over,' Minnie put in.

'Mine don't get owt if he comes home bottled,' Gloria said with a sniff. 'Told him I'd brain him with the frying pan if he comes home again in that state. I'm having no drunken pig in my bed.'

'Mine wouldn't stand for that,' Sadie said, and there was a murmur of agreement.

'He had to stand it,' Gloria retorted. 'He has to tie a knot in it some nights when I'm not in the mood, anyroad. I've told him, I'm not a brood mare.'

'Jesus,' Minnie cried. 'My Charlie would have the priest up to me so quick his feet wouldn't touch the floor.'

'That's the trouble with you papists, hidebound by the priests,' Gloria said witheringly.

Lizzie knew that for most of them sex was a duty and done for their husbands' sake. They never spoke of enjoying it themselves and when Lizzie mentioned it to Violet, she'd said, 'It's not done to say you enjoy it, Lizzie. Most women don't, or else say they don't. If you enjoy it, you're lucky, but keep it to yourself.'

133

So Lizzie kept to herself the times she enjoyed sex, and put up with the bad times. Sometimes she was able to encourage Steve to do something other than drink himself stupid every night and entice him for a walk, or even to go to the nearby Broadway Cinema on Bristol Street.

Flo had been scathing of that when she got to hear. 'You're a married woman now,' she'd screamed, 'not a kid playing at it. Your gallivanting days is over and your place is in the home looking after it and seeing to your man.'

Lizzie honestly couldn't understand Flo's anger. 'We only went to the pictures.'

'"Only went to the pictures",' Flo mimicked. 'And his father waiting on him at The Bell.'

'He works with his father every day,' Lizzie answered, and added a little bitterly, 'Anyway, he's at The Bell every other night.'

'Oh so that's your tack, is it,' Flo said. 'Stopping a man having a drink after he's been at work all day.'

'No, but . . .'

'He's always enjoyed a drink, like his father before him. Brass workers need to drink. They're all the same.'

Flo was right there and not just about brass workers either. The Bell would be full of men most nights, and while the women might moan and nag their men a little, in the main they put up with it.

Flo was the thorn in Lizzie's life that her mother had prophesised, coming around and always complaining. She was jealous of the friendship developing between Violet and Lizzie, which meant Lizzie wasn't depending on her as she'd thought she would be. Lizzie could have told her she'd never have leant on her anyway. She'd rather rely on a viper than her mother-in-law, or muddle through on her own before she'd ask her to do a hand's turn.

Flo also constantly complained of Lizzie's house-keeping skills. Steve's shirt collars weren't clean enough, nor stiff enough in her opinion, and her ironing left a lot to be desired. She ran her finger over the mantel-piece and clicked her tongue at the state of the grate, and made disparaging remarks about Lizzie's cooking. If there was washing on the line she'd sniff her disapproval and say she wasn't maiding the things well enough and had she boiled up those sheets?

'How do you keep your patience?' Violet asked her one day.

'Oh she's just a bag of old wind,' Lizzie said. 'And Steve hates me to argue with his mother.'

That was an understatement. One day, when she'd had an up and downer with Flo, his father was quick to make Steve well aware of it that night at the pub. 'Your mother was proper put out,' he said. 'Your Lizzie really flew at her, she said, and all she did was make a comment, like.'

Later, a drunken Steve went for Lizzie. He said the last thing he wanted to cope with was arguments between her and his mother. Lizzie had to understand Flo's position. 'Can't you show some consideration? You knew she would be jealous.'

Lizzie knew she should let Steve rave on, knowing he hated to be criticised, argued with, and especially when he had a load on, but the unfairness of his accusations got to her. 'Why doesn't she show me any understanding? She's always moaning, complaining and finding fault, and I'm sick of it.'

Steve grasped Lizzie by the arms and shook her as if she was a rag doll, shook her till she felt as if every bone in her body had loosened. 'She needs to show no consideration for you, you stupid bitch. You respect her because she's my mother, or I'll want to know the reason why.'

Lizzie, shocked to the core and frightened, said not another word but got into bed, and later, while Steve slept, cried herself to sleep.

The next morning he was contrite when he saw the dark blue and black bruises ringing both arms. 'Sorry about that,' he apologised. 'I know I was a bit too rough, like, but dad went on and on, and God, she is my mother. I can't have my wife treating her badly.'

Lizzie didn't bother with a reply and kept her arms hidden from Violet and the others. They'd have sympathised, but would be unable to lift a finger to help her. Lizzie had heard of women near killed by violent husbands, and within the bosom of the community, where everyone had been aware of it and those in the house adjoining must have heard every blow, every shuddering scream through those paper-thin walls, and yet none had gone to their aid. So, what price sympathy?

When Lizzie told Steve she was expecting, she could have done anything to Flo he was that delighted with her. Later, at Phillip's first birthday party, Lizzie found out Tressa was pregnant again too, both babies due towards the end of May, but Steve seemed to think no one had ever been pregnant before.

Lizzie was a little annoyed with Mike turning the conversation around to less joyful things, like the Jews who'd marched through London to draw attention to the persecution of their race, which they claimed was happening in Germany.

'What the hell are we supposed to do about it?' Steve said. 'Declare war for a handful of Jews, when we've not recovered from the last one?'

'I don't know,' Mike answered. 'But I don't like this Hitler. Anyway, I'm getting a wireless, see what is going on in the world.'

'You can, man, you have the electric in.'

'You can get one too,' Arthur said. 'Even without electric. You get one with a battery and get an accumulator with it for power, like, and get it charged up every so often. They do it at any garage.'

'I'll certainly look into it,' Steve promised. 'I suppose it's probably as well to know.'

Lizzie began having pains just a few days before Christmas and her knickers were stained with blood when she went to the lavatory, so she went for Violet.

She was in the bed, warmed by the hot-water bottle, when Doctor Taylor arrived, closely followed by a frantic Steve.

'She might be miscarrying,' Doctor Taylor said, 'and then again it might be a warning that she's doing too much. Only time will tell. Call me if you're worried.'

Worried! Steve was beside himself. But he needn't have fretted quite so much for the neighbours were all willing to give Lizzie a hand with things till she was on her feet again, and the doctor was pleased when he called again. 'It might be better,' he told Steve, 'if sexual activity were to cease for a little while. Best to be on the safe side.'

Steve wanted this child as much as Lizzie, and wanted it, son or daughter, to be born hale and hearty; and yet, 'God,' he confided to Stuart, 'it could be months. I'll be a raving loony by then.'

'There's an alternative,' Stuart told him. 'Like I've said before. You're often doing the woman a favour.'

'Oh I don't know, I've not been with another woman since . . . well, for months.'

A month later, Steve was burning up with frustration. 'She won't know owt about it,' Stuart encouraged. 'How could she, and how would it hurt her anyroad?'

'You're right,' Steve decided. 'She needn't know a thing about it.'

But Lizzie did know, or at least had reasonable doubt, for the odour of cheap perfume lingering around Steve and the smell of cosmetics on the shirt he'd worn were apparent enough. Later, she had further evidence, for she knew the marks on his neck that she saw when he stripped for his wash had nothing to do with her. However, Lizzie was too ashamed to voice her suspicions and far too nervous of Steve to challenge him about it, and so she drew a veil of secrecy over it all.

CHAPTER EIGHT

Niamh Mary Gillespie was born on 30th May 1934, a day before her cousin Deidre was born to Tressa, and Steve's delight was sincere and enthusiastic.

He was a wonderful father, who never objected to minding Niamh if Lizzie was busy, even if he'd just come in from work. Flo was shocked one day, seeing him do this while Lizzie was sorting the hot water for his wash, but Steve paid her no heed. 'I see little enough of her, Ma,' he said, cradling her in his arms. 'This is no hardship to me.'

Nothing he did for his daughter seemed a hardship to him, and every fine Sunday afternoon Steve would forego the lunchtime binge with his mates and walk out with his wife and baby, pushing Niamh proudly in the pram he'd bought from Lewis's when she was just a few days old.

'When she's older, we'll take her to the Lickey Hills,' Steve would promise as they wheeled the child through Calthorpe or Cannon Hill Park.' My old man never did much with me or our Neil, and I intend to be a better dad than that to mine.'

How could Lizzie resent the few occasions when she'd known he'd sought satisfaction elsewhere, when under doctor's orders she'd been unable to have sex before she'd had the child? There had been times she had burned with frustration herself and she'd missed the cuddles they used to have in bed, but Steve said you never knew where that might lead. He was right, but it had been hard, and if she'd found it difficult how much worse must it have been for him? Men couldn't really do without sex like women could, it was a well-known fact, except for priests of course. She resolved to put those past incidents out of her head and let them both take joy in their child.

Niamh was over three months by mid-September, old enough to make the trip to Ireland, and so, desperate to show her daughter off, Lizzie went to see her mother. Steve didn't go with them, so he was able to indulge himself with all the street women he wanted as soon as Lizzie's back was turned.

She was none the wiser for Flo had looked after Steve in her fortnight's absence, loving the opportunity to once more cook for her son and wash for him. If there'd been telltale smells or marks of make-up on his shirts they were effectively obliterated and nothing was said.

But, on the whole, Lizzie was a contented wife and considered she had a happy marriage. She never argued with Steve, but then he wasn't an unreasonable man about most things. He loved Lizzie in the only way he was able to love anyone, and he would give her anything she wanted if he could. He was proud of her and liked her to wear nice clothes on their jaunts to the park.

When she smiled, it was for him alone, for Lizzie was his, she belonged to him. Often, when he made love to her she'd cry out with joy, and he lived for those moments. The street girls he dallied with was just sex, as Stuart said, and even if Lizzie was aware of them she needn't concern herself, for they meant nothing to him and had nothing at all to do with his marriage and the vows he'd made.

When Tressa gave birth to Sally in August 1935, when Deidre was only fifteen months and Phillip was four months before his third birthday, Steve said, 'The Malones must be trying to populate the earth by themselves. I don't want the body pulled out of you like that,' he added. 'I'd not like Niamh to be brought up by herself, but time enough yet.'

Lizzie agreed, but wondered why, with Steve's voracious sexual appetite, she hadn't become pregnant immediately Niamh was born. But Steve had told her he would deal with that part of things and not to concern herself.

Lizzie didn't, and when she had suspicions that Steve was seeking pleasure elsewhere, she told herself that she was imagining things. Was she going to think Steve was straying every time he stepped down the road for a pint? she asked herself. If she was not careful, she'd turn into a nagging, jealous wife and maybe cause arguments between them when there was no need. It was better by far to say nothing at all.

When Niamh's brother, Thomas Patrick Gillespie, was born on 5th October 1936, Lizzie did wonder what sort

141

of world he'd been born into. She was finding the wireless that Steve had bought not long after Phillip's first birthday party brought world events right into the living room and so she heard of the Civil War, which had begun in Spain in the summer of that year, when the government was fighting against some group called Fascists that Steve said were no better than the German Nazis.

At home, things were no better. King George V had died in January and his son Edward seemed to take his kingly duties flippantly. Tales about his lavish and extravagant lifestyle abounded, as did his association with an American divorcee, Wallis Simpson.

Then, on the very day of Tom's birth, two hundred unemployed men set off from Jarrow, to present a petition to the Prime Minister. 'Too frightened to see them,' Steve said a couple of days later, when the Prime Minister refused to even speak with the men and they had massed in Hyde Park in disarray. 'Frightened of anarchy, see. They don't give a monkey's for the likes of us. They need overthrowing, the whole damned lot of them.'

There was talk about arrests being made if the men from Jarrow didn't disperse and go on their way, and that incensed Steve. 'Arrest innocent men on a peaceful rally,' he exploded. 'If they are that keen to arrest someone, it should be that bloke Moseley and his British Fascists' Party, leading an anti-Jewish march down the Mile End Road in London, inciting trouble.'

Britain everywhere appeared to be in a terrible state, and it seemed the last straw when Edward, asked to choose between Wallis Simpson and the Crown, made a speech from Windsor Castle on the eleventh of

December:

'... I have found it impossible ... to discharge my duties as King as I would wish to do, without the help and support of the woman I love.'

'Rat's deserting the sinking ship,' Violet remarked to Lizzie when she popped in later and commented on it.

'Don't you believe it,' Violet's husband Barry said. 'Oh, he was dashing and handsome and said to be popular, but too friendly with the Krauts for my liking. His brother George will do nicely for me, especially if he can conquer his bloody stammer.'

'He can't help his stammer, Barry.'

'Well, he'll have to try. God, he can't lead this country to bloody war and stumble over his words.'

'You think it will come to that?'

'Course it'll come, now that madman Hitler is in total charge of Germany.'

Lizzie shivered, but she knew it would be worse for Violet and Barry, for their son Colin, having left school, had kicked his feet in idleness for eighteen months or so before declaring he didn't intend to spend his life on the dole and gone off to join the Royal Navy. Violet had tried to dissuade him. 'But what could I tell him?' she'd asked plaintively. 'It wasn't as if he had some golden future lined up as any sort of alternative. I mean, Barry has tried at his place, but they're not setting on, not even at the foundry.'

Colin had been in the Navy six months and Violet worried about him and would be frantic if there was a war.

'Our Carol's leaving school in the summer,' Violet went on. 'God knows what she'll do, though sometimes it's easier for girls and women and she has a mate left school last year that has a job at Cadbury's and she says she'll have a word. What good it'll do I don't know, but then worrying never did much good either.'

But you can't help worrying with children, Lizzie thought, and keeping them well-clad and well-nourished enough to fight any disease was of paramount importance to both her and Steve. Steve gave her plenty of money for groceries and there was always money for footwear for herself and the children and they all had good warm coats. She hadn't ever had to visit the pawnshop, like many of her neighbours, and when she lay in bed and waited for Steve, wondering what state he would be in, or picked up the shirts reeking of cheap perfume or stale make-up, she still told herself she had much to be thankful for.

In February 1937, Tressa gave birth to her second son, Sam, and just two months later, the Germans, who sided with the Fascists in Spain under Franco, bombed the Basque town of Guernica. It was Market Day and half past four in the afternoon when the church bells began to peal. The town was filled with its own people, those drawn in by the market and refugees fleeing from other towns, and Guernica was nearly destroyed and many ordinary people killed or injured.

'Why?' That was the question asked. They were civilians and Steve knew that under Hitler's domination no one would be safe. 'If war comes,' he said to Lizzie, 'will you go home to your mom's?'

'What? I don't know. I'd not thought of it.'

'It's just with raids like that . . .'

'Surely to God we'll have shelters of some kind?' Lizzie said. 'The Spanish people weren't prepared, there was no provision.'

'Mike is determined to take Tressa home,' Steve said. 'He said as much when we went up a couple of months ago to see the new baby.'

'I don't know,' Lizzie mused. 'It's a bit like running away, but then there's the weans and I couldn't send a couple of babies away on their own. Oh, don't let's talk about it any more. It frightens me.'

In March of the following year, German troops marched into Austria and were welcomed by the government and the two nations were united in the Anschluss. Hitler then turned his attention to Sudetenland, a part of Czechoslovakia where many German people lived. The whole world seemed poised on a knife's edge.

Lizzie was glad to go to Ireland that year, away from the doom and gloom. She went every year, only missing 1936 because Steve had said she was too near her time to risk it. Catherine, who'd often been quite sharp with her own children, doted on Niamh and little Tom, and they were great favourites too with their aunts and uncles and cousins.

In the main, most of their cousins were older than they were, but put up with their little Brummie relations with tolerant good humour. But their favourite was Johnnie, who loved them like they were his own, he supposed because they were Lizzie's. The bond between him and Lizzie had never been broken, despite Lizzie being so far away, and every year he longed to see her.

'No girl on the horizon yet, Johnnie?' she'd asked him that year.

'No, the girl I wanted is already married to another.'

'Oh, I'm sorry,' Lizzie said. 'Who is it? Do I know her?'

'Aye, very well, I would say,' Johnnie said. 'For it's you.'

'Johnnie!' Lizzie said with a laugh, giving him a push.

'It's right,' Johnnie protested. 'When I was wee, I always told myself I'd marry you. It was a while before I realised I couldn't and you up and went to England. God, if Steve hadn't been such a fine fellow, I'd have hated him with a passion.'

'You are a fool.'

'I know it,' Johnnie said with a grin. 'It's not so bad if you're aware of it.' But Johnnie was only half-joking, for every girl he was interested in he compared to his sister.

He was glad Steve was good to her, and he obviously was, for she looked well and so did the children, and dressed more than just respectably. Added to that, the children plainly adored their father. Niamh talked of him often and in glowing terms and he'd take a bet that Tom would be the same when he was a wee bit older.

Aunt Margaret was envious of Catherine seeing her daughter every year, for since Lizzie's marriage Tressa had either been too pregnant to travel or had a baby too small, or else was unable to come so far with little ones. Margaret always came to see Lizzie soon after her arrival to get news of her daughter, things that maybe she wouldn't tell her in a letter. She was worried by the number of children Tressa had and the small gap between them all. 'I know it's wrong to plan your family,' she said one day. 'But, God, she must have the life pulled out of her the way she is.'

She did often look drawn, Lizzie thought, but it wouldn't help to say so. She'd also gone extremely plump and seemed to get bigger with every child. Mike didn't seem to mind. He said jokingly there was more of her to get hold of and they still did seem to adore each other. But Lizzie wondered if Tressa ever thought back to the figure she once had just a few short years ago and hankered for the young woman who'd turned matronly and looked older than her years.

'She's coming over if there's a war, you know,' Margaret went on. 'And you will, I suppose?'

'Um, I don't know yet.'

Lizzie didn't really want to go home, not to live there for months, maybe years. She was a wife and mother now and had ways of doing things and ways of rearing the children that her mother did differently. For two or three weeks a year she could take her children being spoilt and herself treated as a wean with half a brain, but for longer . . . no thanks.

Tressa, on the other hand, would slip easily back into the mould of spoilt baby of the family and be happy for her mother to rear the children any way she saw fit. But Lizzie wasn't sure the children would take to it so well. At Longbridge they had two attic rooms to sleep in and a large garden. However, the Clooneys' shop opened directly onto the main street of Ballintra and there was but a yard out the back that was usually full of boxes. Added to that, the living accommodation was cramped for a woman with four children who was expecting another in September.

She didn't share these thoughts with her aunt. Anyway, it might come to nothing in the end. The papers were full of the news of Chamberlain going to Munich to see Herr Hitler.

And then it was over, all that worry and speculation, Chamberlain was back. He'd given Hitler that place Sudetenland that he was so keen on, so now there would be 'peace in our time', as the headlines said. There was a picture of Chamberlain waving the document ensuring this in nearly every newspaper in the land.

Tressa had a third little boy they called Bernard just days after Chamberlain's announcement. She now had five children and the eldest was only six. It was a good job, Lizzie thought, that Doreen was such a help.

'You trying for a football team, mate?' Steve said to Mike when they called that weekend to see the new addition.

'Might be,' Mike replied, a smile of pride playing around his mouth. 'Long way to go yet, eh, Tressa?'

'Aye,' Tressa said, but Lizzie noticed that her eyes were nearly glazed over with tiredness and she knew Tressa would get no rest with the children cavorting about the room.

'Come on,' Lizzie said. 'Let's go out into the garden

and let your mammy sleep now the wee one's settled.'

Tressa looked at her gratefully. 'Will you be all right?'

'I'm certain sure I will be,' Lizzie reassured her. 'Doreen will give me a hand. You rest yourself. And I suppose,' she added to Steve, 'you'll be away for a pint or two.'

'Well, if you insist,' Steve answered with a grin. 'Come on, Mike. Ask Arthur if he wants to come.'

Much later, going home in the bus, Steve said, 'Glad you haven't gone to seed like your cousin. You're still shapely and I still fancy you.'

Then why do you need others? The retort was on the tip of Lizzie's tongue, but she bit it back. Mike might be faithful, Lizzie thought, but she wouldn't change places with Tressa for all the tea in China. 'I'm fair jiggered,' she said. 'And Tressa has that day in, day out. And Mike's little use.'

She had noticed that Mike seemed to think his job as father was done on implantation of the seed and the rearing of the children was totally up to Tressa.

'Ah,' Steve said with a smile, as he jiggled Niamh on his knee. 'Not all women are as fortunate as you.'

'No,' Lizzie agreed ruefully and in spite of all Steve's faults, she truly meant it.

In November, Lizzie was listening to some music on the wireless one evening when it was interrupted by a news broadcast.

'Reports are coming in of great disturbance in Berlin. Shops and houses of the Jewish people are being looted and burned and the people thrown onto the streets.'

The details came later. It was known as the Kristallnacht, or Night of the Broken Glass, and it went on for three days, when it was said that Berlin's skies were blood red with the number of synagogues set alight. It also caused a domino effect throughout Germany and many people in other towns and cities copied the activities of those in Berlin.

Lizzie crossed to the window one late and dusky afternoon and saw the icy spears of rain hitting the cobblestones, and she shivered for the Jewish families cowering in the cold streets while their homes were being destroyed.

'And do we just watch?' Lizzie asked of Steve later.

'That's about the strength of it,' Steve said. 'Do you want war?'

'No, of course not.'

No one did, so Lizzie tried to put it out of her mind.

In March 1939, the Czech government, intimidated by the Germans' aggression on their borders, demoralised by the lack of support from the United Kingdom and frightened by the threat of the blitz they'd seen in Guernica, handed over the independence of their country to Hitler. The Spanish War finished just days later, with Franco, another dictator, the victor.

'I think,' said Steve, folding up the paper one day, 'it's only a matter of time now.'

Lizzie, helping Tom spoon up the last of his dinner, looked up. 'War? Surely not? What about "Peace in our time"?'

'What about it?'

It seemed Steve was right. Everywhere people seemed

to be getting prepared. Even in her mother's last letter, Catherine had told her that Aunt Margaret was clearing out the two back bedrooms in readiness for Tressa coming home. Was Lizzie making similar arrangements? Catherine asked, especially if Steve joined up as Mike intended to do.

Lizzie was undecided. Around her, people seemed to accept that war was inevitable. Violet's Colin would be in the front line as it were, and now Carol, though she had a job at Cadbury's, was hankering to join the Women's Air Corps, wanting to do her bit. 'I don't know,' Violet said, wiping her seeping eyes with the hem of her apron, 'You struggle to give birth to them, rear them up to be fine and healthy, and then send them off to war to be shot to pieces or blown apart.'

'Ah come on, Violet, nothing's decided yet.'

'Even you can't think there's an alternative now?' Violet said. 'All Hitler has got to do now is invade Poland and we're in.'

And of course he would. Everyone knew he would.

Brick-built shelters, reinforced with sandbags, sprang up everywhere, and deep trenches were dug in parks. People were advised to criss-cross their windows with strong sticky tape to try and reduce injuries by flying glass in the event of a bombing raid, and to register for a gas mask. It was terrifying and yet people's lives had to go on.

Niamh, who celebrated her fifth birthday in May, was due to start at St Catherine's after the holidays, and yet before the schools officially opened there was talk of evacuating children from the area.

Violet and Lizzie went to the Bull Ring for blackout material, for the blackout was to come into force from 1st September. Lizzie had bounced the big pram down from the attic, for she didn't use it much now, and they came back with bales of material and other produce packed around the chuckling Tom, to see the headmaster of St Catherine's at the door.

'No, Mr Steele,' Lizzie said once he'd spoken to her. 'I couldn't bear the thought of Niamh going to strangers. If I send them anywhere at all it will be to my mother's in Ireland and I feel they are a little young for that yet – after all, Tom isn't three for over a month.'

'You wouldn't consider going with them?'

Lizzie had considered and rejected it. She thought about the men rushing to join the Territorial Army and registering for the Home Guard, Violet's two youngsters anxious to play their part and Steve and Mike expressing their determination to enlist in the event of war. She knew if the men were up to fighting to try and stop Hitler, it was up to the women to roll up their sleeves and get on with keeping the country going. They couldn't all scuttle away like frightened rabbits.

Carol Barlow wasn't scuttling anywhere either. She'd now firmly set her heart on joining the WAACs. Lizzie knew all about it, for Carol had confided in her, but both knew Violet wouldn't see it the way Carol did. However, as Lizzie said, there was nothing to be gained by delay and it was always best to take the bull by the horns. Carol agreed: there was no way she was going to back down and the sooner her mom realised that the better.

'This ain't just a war for the men,' she told her weeping mother after their evening meal that night. 'Not if we're going to win it, anyroad.'

'It ain't for kids neither, our Carol.'

'I ain't a kid,' Carol protested. 'Not any more. I feel as strongly about this as our Colin does and you never even tried to stop him.'

'I did try,' Violet protested. 'You might not remember, but I tried. I begged and pleaded. But there weren't no other option open to him. He didn't have a good job like you have.'

'Well, he'd be in it now, anyroad,' Carol said.

Violet knew Carol was right. The boys of twenty years old had been called up from April and Colin was just two months off his twenty-first birthday.

'People are saying there should be conscription for women too,' Carol told her mother.

'Heaven forbid!' Violet cried. 'For pity's sake, girl.'

'There won't be time for any pity in this war,' Carol said grimly. 'Look at Guernica. Who pitied them?'

'I know that,' Violet said, 'and I know that might come here too, but I just don't see how you running off to join the services is going to help.'

'Neither do I till I get there,' Carol said. 'But what if girls like me were given jobs, usually done by men, thereby releasing them men to fly or summat?'

'Barry!' Violet cried, exasperated. 'Haven't you got anything to say about all this?'

Barry had been calmly reading his paper before the fire, taking no part in the heated discussion around him, and he folded it and laid it on the chair beside him before addressing his wife. 'I got summat to say all right, but you won't like hearing it.'

'What then?'

'Just this,' Barry said. 'Every one of us in this world has got to do as they see fit, and as kids grow up the decisions they make has to be their own.'

'So, you think we should just let her go?'

Barry winked across the room at his daughter. 'Daresay we couldn't really stop her, old girl' he said, and crossed the room and put his arm around his distressed wife. 'What I say is, let her go with our blessing.'

Carol let out the breath she'd been holding, for she knew she'd won. Her father was a quiet man and seldom made a stand, and so when he did it was even more powerful and Violet always listened and rarely went against him. Her mother looked suddenly defeated and Carol felt a stab of sympathy for her as she sort of sagged against Barry and he held her tighter. 'Do it then,' she said. 'You've made your mind up already, anyroad.'

Carol resisted the temptation to give a whoop of joy.

Later Carol relayed the conversation to Lizzie, although there was no need because she'd heard the entire altercation through the walls. Nevertheless, she congratulated Carol warmly and her determination to do her bit strengthened Lizzie's own resolve to stay put, at least for the time being.

That night, the *Evening Mail* carried the story and pictures of seventy Jewish children arriving from Poland, who would stay with foster parents until they were eighteen. What a desperate thing, Lizzie thought, to send your children to live with strangers in a country where the whole language and culture would be totally alien to them. A parent had to be panic-stricken to agree to such a course of action.

Two days later, on Friday, 1st September, Poland was invaded and a sad little group of children left St Catherine's School with a case, haversack or carrier bag with their clothes in and a gas mask slung around their necks as they boarded the buses to Moor Street Station. Many adults dabbed at their eyes at the sad sight and some mothers cried openly. 'Poor little devils,' Violet said. 'No one has a clue where they are going.'

But Tressa's children knew where they were going, and later that same day Mike helped her transport the entire family to Donegal, where they would be safe. Lizzie couldn't blame Tressa, for she had a lot of children to see to if there was bombing of any magnitude, but, despite Steve's urging, she decided to wait and see for herself and her own.

By the following day, German tanks had flattened the Polish towns of Krakow, Teschen and Katowice, and Warsaw too was suffering heavy bombardment. Chamberlain issued an ultimatum to withdraw immediately from Poland but there was no response from Germany.

'This is really it, ain't it?' Minnie said, meeting Lizzie on her way to put rubbish in the bin.

'Looks like it,' Lizzie replied. 'Steve says he'll join up.'

'Aye, mine too,' Minnie said. 'I told him he's likely

be the first casualty. Bloody daft bugger. He wheezes like an old steam train when he walks to the boozer at the end of the street to see how many pints he can down before he falls over.'

'There won't be the money for much of that,' Gloria added, coming out to join them. 'I don't think army pay is that good and they have to send most of that to the women, especially if there's kids, like.'

'And no chance of nicking it out your purse when your back's turned either,' Minnie said.

Lizzie was shocked. Steve would never have taken a penny piece from her. He got good money, though he worked for it and she realised he wouldn't get anything like the same money in the army. They'd all have to pull their belts in a bit and she wouldn't be the only one.

'Blokes is all the same,' Sadie put in from her doorway. 'Puffing and blowing and threatening to join up, like they was off to some boy scouts' jamboree.'

'Oh, I think they give it a bit more thought than that, Sadie,' Lizzie said with a wry laugh. 'They know war isn't any sort of picnic.'

'I think half of them won't do it in the end.'

'Well, we'll soon see,' Lizzie said. 'The Prime Minister is going to be on the wireless just after eleven o'clock tomorrow. Steve's coming to the children's Mass with me at nine so we'll be back in plenty of time. Anyone coming in to listen?'

'You bet,' said Minnie and Ada together.

'Violet's coming in too, for all she's got her own set,' Lizzie said.

'Bit daft that, ain't it?'

'I don't know. It's sort of nice all being together to hear news like that,' Lizzie mused.

'I'll come up after,' Gloria said. 'When I get the roast in the oven. What about you, Sadie?'

'No,' Sadie answered. 'I'm going to our mom's up Latimer Street. She's dead upset at this talk of another war. She can remember the last one that took my dad. He was killed at a place called Wipers in 1915. I was only a nipper, can't remember him, and I know my mom had it tough bringing up three kids. Jesus, we sometimes had to live on fresh air, and there ain't much of that round here.'

'It was hard after the last war,' Ada added. 'There was no work, and all those men thinking they was coming back to a land fit for heroes. Well, they came to the dole queue and the means-test people assessing every bloody thing in your house and telling you to sell everything before they'd give you a penny piece.'

'And the bums tipping you out on the street if you fell behind in the rent,' Minnie put in.

'They must really feel as if they was cheated,' Gloria said, 'cos wasn't it supposed to be "The War to End All Wars", and here we are again.'

'Mind you, at least we get full employment now,' Ada said. 'Even my bloke's found work. He used to say the dole was like a living death.'

'Well, there is going to be a lot more deaths before we're done, I'd say,' Lizzie said. 'As you said, Ada, there is full employment now, but most of the jobs are war related. Making things to help kill and maim people.'

It was a sobering thought, and, as the women went

about their business, in the forefront of all their minds was the Prime Minister's broadcast in the morning, though most knew that now war was inevitable.

It seemed as if everyone was holding their breath. In the Birmingham streets where Lizzie lived, the crush of humanity meant they were seldom free of noise. Now, though, not a person spoke, no children cried, no dog barked, and there wasn't even a yowl from a stray cat.

The rumble of traffic and clop of horses' hooves you could often hear from Bristol Street had ceased, as if everyone was listening, waiting, although they knew what was to be said.

'I am speaking to you today from the cabinet room of ten Downing Street . . .

. . . Consequently, this country is at war with Germany.'

There was a collective sigh and then people began speaking again. Lizzie's door had been left open to the yard, for not everyone could crowd into the living room, and now those in the yard pointed out the menacing-looking barrage balloon that had appeared, floating in the air above their heads as the air-raid siren blared out.

It proved to be a false alarm, but it unnerved Lizzie and many more, because she hadn't been ready, not sure what to do, with no plan of action. God knows what might have happened if it had been real. That day, she put together a shelter bag, and into it she put identity cards, Post Office books and treasured photographs. Later she would add ration books, and she was to find that nearly every woman had a shelter bag which went with them wherever they chose to hide away from the raids.

'Are you ready then?' Violet asked.

'Are you ever ready for war?' Lizzie replied. 'But I'm as ready as the next, I suppose. Now we'll just have to wait and see what the Germans intend to do.'

CHAPTER NINE

Just five days after war had been declared, Steve, Stuart and Mike went off to Thorpe Street barracks and enlisted in the Royal Warwickshires, as they'd declared they would. Many men and boys followed the same course and others were called up, and so, within a month or so, the streets were very different, stripped of many of the young, fit males.

The women drew even closer together, and never was Lizzie more grateful for Violet's support and that of the others down the yard. They looked out for one another and drew strength from being in this together.

Everyone had someone to worry over. Violet's Barry was too old to be called up, but Carol, having finished her basic training, was now based at Castle Bromwich aerodrome, learning to maintain and repair the Spitfires and Wellingtons, which were made at the Vickers factory across the road. 'Each night the road is closed off by the military,' she told Violet and Lizzie one day, while briefly at home on leave, 'and the planes are pushed across the road. It's a sight, not that you can see much, like, with the blackout as well.'

'Blackout, huh . . .' Violet began, but Carol hadn't finished and she went on, with a glance at her mother, 'Some of the girls are training as pilots,' and her eyes were dreamy.

Violet's own opened wider in shock and horror. 'Pilots!' she shrieked. 'I'll not have you . . .'

'Not for fighting, Mom,' Carol said with a giggle. 'They fly the planes down to the airfields in the south and that, and then take the train back. There's not so many at the moment, but one of the officers told me he can see a time when they'll need more planes and I'll get my chance then if I'm really keen.'

'You get on well with them all then?'

'Oh yeah. 'Specially the Americans.'

'Americans?'

'Volunteer Air Force. There's a small company of them based there. Full of charm they are. Think they're God's gift, some of them.' She thought for a minute and went on, 'in the main, the black ones are nicer.'

'Black ones!'

'Yeah, like the ace of spades they are, and when they open their mouths their teeth look real white. Not that they ever say much to us, like.'

'Are there many?'

Carol shook her head. 'Just a handful, and the white Americans are not always nice to them.'

'Why not?'

Carol shrugged. 'Search me. Cos they're black, I suppose. Mad, ain't it? I mean, ain't we got enough to do fighting the flipping Germans without scrapping amongst ourselves.'

Lizzie couldn't agree more. She was horrified when

Steve came back after just seven weeks away at a training camp and whispered he thought it was embarkation leave. He looked very smart in his uniform and the children were impressed, but Lizzie knew an army at war isn't made up of military parades and polished boots and the ability to make up a bed with proper hospital corners. 'It's so soon,' she said.

Steve laughed. 'Hitler has rode roughshod over Europe and is still coming,' he said, and added, 'Maybe Churchill should have a word. Hold your hand there awhile, man, and play the game. Give our chaps a chance to have six months' training before we engage in hostilities.'

'No, but . . .'

Steve kissed her on the nose. 'I'm as well-prepared as the next man.'

'Are Stuart and Mike home too?'

'Yeah, Mike went straight over to Ireland,' Steve said. 'She's up the pole again, your cousin.'

'No,' Lizzie cried in disbelief.

'Yeah, due in February, Mike said.'

'She must be mad, and so must he. That will be six.'

'Yeah, well maybe she'll have a wee bit of a break now, if he's away for a bit,' Steve said. 'It's up to them, anyroad, but I want better for you.'

Lizzie sighed and leant her body against Steve and he bent and kissed her. Desire rose in her at the sweetness of that kiss, and if it hadn't been for Tom, who'd turned three the previous week and was playing on the floor with the toy cars his mother had managed to find and buy him, Lizzie would have turned the key in the door and led her husband upstairs, though it was the middle of the afternoon.

She wished she could do this, for soon Steve would be gone and in danger, and suddenly she knew that, despite his faults, she cared for Steve greatly and wanted no harm to come to him. He took her in his arms and kissed her again. 'I love you, Mrs Gillespie.'

'Ah, Steve.'

'You know why I'm doing this, don't you? It's for you and the kids, you do know that?'

'I know that.'

'Sometimes I've thought that I was daft joining up straight away,' Steve admitted. 'You know, with me a family man and all; and then I think, if this madman is to be stopped, everyone has to do their bit. We can't run and hide and let others fight our battles for us and keep us all safe.'

'I know, Steve,' Lizzie said. 'Don't worry. I know where you are coming from – and knowing you as I do, it's what I expected of you. I don't ever imagine there was a time in your life when you let others fight your battles.'

'No,' Steve said. 'But if I'm honest I did enlist in a fit of patriotic zeal, with me mates Mike and Stuart, like we was off on some great adventure. I know really that war ain't like that. Sometimes you sort of wake me up when you get up in the morning to see to the children and I listen to you all and know I might lose all that I hold most dear.'

Lizzie knew he was right and he wouldn't be the only one, but the die was cast now. There could be no turning back. All they could do was savour every moment of that precious leave together.

One dark, dismal, rain-sodden night in late October, the Royal Warwickshires were part of the British Expeditionary Force that sailed across the Channel, and Lizzie settled to life without her husband, with the additional anxiety that he was now in the firing line.

She was finding, like many people, that the blackout was the worst thing of all to contend with. Often any stars in the heavens would be hidden by the smoky Birmingham air, and if there was a moon at all it was usually obscured by cloud. She'd helped paint the white line down the side of the road as the Government had advised. 'As if a bloody white line helps, when the night's as black as pitch,' Violet said contemptuously, but continuing to wield her brush.

Lizzie knew Violet had a point, for there were more people killed and injured in those first dark days, weeks and months of the war than from any type of military action. She didn't see how white lines painted on the edges of pavements were going to help in stopping people falling off them, just as she couldn't see how a white line around lamp and pillar boxes were going to prevent people walking in to them.

'I keep out of it as much as I can,' Ada said. 'Make sure I'm back in the house well before dark.'

'We all do if we can,' Gloria said. 'But what about the poor souls out at work all day.'

'Yeah, must be dead depressing, that.'

'What depresses me is those bloody awful black curtains at the windows,' Minnie said. 'The warden, the

164

son of her up the entry, told me the fine's two hundred pounds. Claimed he could see a chink of light from my window. There was nowt when we were both in the yard, though. Told him he must have imagined it.'

'Anyroad,' Sadie put in, 'How can one chink through the smoky Brummie air light the way for enemy bombers?'

'What bombers?' Lizzie said. 'There's been nothing yet.'

That's what made the whole thing seem so pointless. 'It's Hitler's secret weapon,' Barry said one day. 'He ain't bothering going to war at all, he just said he was, and now he'll wait while we all kill ourselves on the bleeding roads.'

Eventually, the government announced vehicles could use shaded headlights. Shielded torches could be used too, though batteries for them were soon like gold dust. It was an improvement, but not much of one, and it was hard to find anything to be optimistic about as Christmas approached. There was little food in the shops and talk of rationing in the New Year. 'Rationing what?' Lizzie said, looking at the sparse array of food on the table. 'Half of what I want now is unobtainable.'

'Yeah, and if you say owt they remind you there's a war on,' Violet said. 'As if we don't know. Like you was dropped in from another planet or summat.'

There was very little festive stuff to buy at all, and virtually no toys. Lizzie scoured the Bull Ring and the little shops in side streets to find a yo-yo and skipping rope and a couple of colouring books and crayons for the children. And so, Christmas for them was the usual magical time, and they had no idea of the headache Lizzie had to produce the dinner they tucked in to with gusto.

Rationing came into effect in January and ration books became a way of life, although, as Lizzie prophesised, even your allotment was sometimes unavailable and she had to be more inventive to provide nourishing family meals. Every women's magazine ran articles and recipes and there were even snippets in the paper and in the cinema, people told her, slotted in between the first mediocre film and the main one, and just after Pathé News.

'It's riveting stuff, all right,' Violet remarked. 'Fifty million ways to cook swede, turnips or carrots.'

Lizzie laughed, for it was a bit like that. The public were bombarded with advice and encouragement to eat home-grown produce. 'The Kitchen Front' gave out recipes each morning after the eight o'clock news and millions tuned in to Radio Doctor, who told people what foods were good for them and how to cook them. Potato Pete was only rivalled by Doctor Carrot, and one or both of these vegetables turned up in nearly every recipe in one form or another.

People were being urged to 'Save Our Ships', meaning the merchant ships bringing British imports from other countries, which with enemy action was always a hazardous procedure.

To cut down on imported goods, more food had to be grown. The phrase 'Dig for Victory' became popular, and to this end, next to the trenches, many parks now had furrowed rows growing all manner of things. Many of those lucky enough to have gardens had used some of their lush lawns, and flowerbeds too had been given over to growing cabbages, potatoes and the like.

'So we won't starve to death, like,' Violet said. 'But if I eat much more of them root vegetables, I just might be bored to death.'

'Aye,' Lizzie said with a smile. 'Or be blown up by the gases inside you.'

Tressa had a baby girl on 26th February that she was calling Nuala. Lizzie wrote a long letter to her and said she'd be over maybe in the summer.

But then news came in of the German invasion of Norway and Sweden on 9th April, and the countries' subsequent collapse was worrying. But there was soon a greater worry when Lizzie heard on the nine o'clock news that Hitler had invaded Belgium and Holland and inflicted great hardship on the people.

'What does it mean?' she asked Violet, but Barry answered.

'It means the Maginot Line is bloody useless,' he said. 'Like I said it was from the beginning.'

'What is the Maginot Line anyway?' Lizzie said. 'All I've heard since the beginning of the war is that this line, whatever it is, can't be breached.'

'It can't,' Barry said. 'Well, not at least without great loss of life. The Maginot Line is a long line of deeply buried fortifications that were erected along the border that France shares with Germany after the last war,' he explained. 'But it stops at France's border with

Luxembourg and Belgium. If you were a German, what would you do?'

He'd bought the *Evening Mail* on his way home from work and he spread it out on the table. 'There's a map in its centre,' he said. 'And the line is marked clearly.'

Lizzie studied it and then said slowly, 'if I was a German, I'd go through Holland into Belgium and across the border to France.'

'And me,' Barry said grimly. 'And that's what the German Army has done.'

'Can't they fight them off?'

Barry shrugged. 'Only time will tell.'

No letters came from Steve, the papers made grim reading and Lizzie could scarcely bear to listen to the news reports. Flo was at her door every day, asking if she'd heard anything – as if Lizzie would keep such a thing to herself – and she was wailing and bemoaning all the time. Lizzie was desperately worried and trying to keep a lid on it for the children's sakes. She wished Flo wouldn't show such open emotion in front of them. They knew nothing definite yet.

'Why is Granny always crying?' Niamh asked at last. She'd come home from school to see her grandmother in floods of tears again.

'She's upset. It's nothing.'

'It's about Daddy. She said so.'

'She's just concerned.'

'She was crying her eyes out,' Niamh said flatly. 'Where is daddy? Why is she so worried?'

'No one knows where he is, that's why your granny

is upset,' Lizzie admitted, because she couldn't think of a plausible lie.

'We all know where daddy is,' Tom declared.

'Do we?'

'Yeah, killing Germans, bang, bang, bang.'

Lizzie gave a sigh and picked her son up and held him close to hide her glistening eyes from the inquisitive Niamh. 'Of course he is, Tom,' she said. 'Now why didn't I think of that?'

She saw Niamh wasn't satisfied and in a minute would start a barrage of questions, and so to forestall her she said, 'How would you both like dripping toast?'

Niamh was starving, she always was when she came home from school, and dripping toast sounded just the thing. 'Oh yeah,' she said with glee. 'And bagsy I have the toasting fork first. Tom's no good anyway; he always drops the toast in the fire.'

'I don't!'

'Yeah you do.'

'Don't.'

'Do.'

'Stop it,' Lizzie said sharply. 'Or neither of you will do it.' But in reality she was pleased Niamh's attention was diverted.

If only hers could be diverted so easily, Lizzie thought during the next few days, for neither papers nor wireless had anything remotely cheering to say. She roused herself to make an effort for Niamh's sixth birthday, although any festive food was hard to find. The cake had to be baked without eggs and with extra sugar and margarine ration donated by Violet, and the only present she had was a doll which had once been Carol's, though Niamh didn't know that the doll was second-hand and she was delighted with the knitted outfits Lizzie and Violet had made for the doll she called Maisie.

The day after Niamh's birthday, the veil of secrecy lifted at last. Allied soldiers were trapped on the beaches at a place called Dunkirk and the navy were having trouble rescuing so many, for the waters were too shallow for the big ships. They'd already comman-deered some boats capable of crossing the channel to take the men from the beaches to the naval ships lying at anchor in deeper waters, but more were needed.

Once the dilemma was known of, more boat owners set off on their own, risking life and limb to bring home as many of the soldiers as possible. Soon the papers were full of pictures of men alighting from landing craft of all shapes and sizes, or disembarking from the bigger naval ships. There were pictures of them smiling for the camera as they accepted tea, sand-wiches and cigarettes from the women of the WVS, or cheering from the railway carriages taking them home.

It was all over by the 4th June, and on the 5th Lizzie received the buff telegram. She opened it full of trepi-dation, steeling herself, and then went into Violet's, needing to tell someone. 'He's alive,' she cried. 'Steve's alive! Injured, but alive, and at a military hospital in Ramsgate.'

It was then she noticed the tears pouring unchecked down Violet's face and the telegram crushed in her friend's gnarled hand. 'Colin isn't,' she said. 'He was stationed on a gun boat, *HMS Mosquito*, and now he's missing, presumed dead, and I bet them German bastards blew the thing clean out the water.'

'Oh God, Oh Christ, Violet, I'm sorry,' Lizzie cried, holding Violet's shuddering body tight. She'd liked Colin, with his cheeky grin and infectious laugh. He'd worn his uniform with pride and was more prepared for war than many, but in the end did that count for anything?

Steve had had one of his legs and one of his arms badly crushed and was riddled with shrapnel, and Lizzie had gone down to see him in Ramsgate before he was transferred to Dudley Road Hospital. Stuart was also injured, but Mike had escaped virtually unscathed.

While Steve was in hospital, the Battle of Britain raged in the skies. Britain teetered on the edge of defeat. Invasion seemed imminent. The Home Guard no longer seemed ludicrous, though few people had any faith that the motley crew of old, young and disabled could take on the might of the highly disciplined German army, who'd trampled their way unchecked across Europe.

Signs were removed from roads and railway stations and posters told you that, 'Careless Talk Costs Lives', and advised, 'Keep Mum'. At railway and bus depots, others asked, 'Is Your Journey Really Necessary?'

People were told to disable cars and bicycles not in use, to hide maps and to 'Be Vigilant'. Across the water there were reports of Hitler massing boats and landing craft ready for invasion. 'We've only got the RAF now,' Carol told her parents, still devastated by Colin's death.

But Carol couldn't help being excited. Factories like Vickers were working around the clock to produce the planes as speedily as possible. Fighter pilots couldn't be spared and so Carol got her wish. Many of the girls like herself had a crash course in learning to pilot a plane and then climbed into the cockpit and took it to Biggin Hill or wherever they were needed.

She never told her mother much about this work, but she often popped in for a word with Lizzie when she had a spot of leave.

'So you're enjoying yourself then?' Lizzie asked, seeing Carol's shining eyes.

'Yeah,' Carol said. 'You don't think me awful, then?'

'Why ever would I?'

'Well, you know, with our Colin dying and that,' Carol said. 'I did miss him. Still do. I keep expecting him to come in the door and start taking the mickey and that or ruffle me hair, cos he knew that used to get me real riled up.'

'The way I see it,' Lizzie said, 'is that you are doing a valuable job. I didn't know Colin like I've come to know you, but even I can guess he would be very proud of you and tell you to go for it if he was here today. Wouldn't he?'

'That's exactly what he would say,' Carol said. 'I can almost hear him say it.'

'So, that's what you must do, and don't worry either about enjoying yourself, like many do when a loved one dies' Lizzie told her. 'Grab life with both hands, Carol. We only get the one go at it.'

'I always feel better when I talk to you,' Carol said. 'You're so sure of yourself.'

'Sure of myself?' Lizzie repeated, surprised. 'I was never sure of myself when I was younger. I was always being pushed about by other people: my cousin, my family, particularly my elder sister.'

'I bet you wouldn't let that happen now, though.'

'Probably not,' Lizzie agreed. 'But you are much braver than me, Carol. I could never go up in one of those planes. Aren't you ever scared?'

'Ah, no, never,' Carol said. 'It's wonderful, exhilarating, and the view is tremendous. What isn't so nice is seeing the destruction at the airfields as we fly over them; dirty great craters in the runways and sometimes the planes still smouldering or reduced to mangled heaps of metal. It's heartbreaking, for every plane is needed so badly, but some of the airfields are under almost constant bombardment. But don't tell mom that, will you.'

'Don't worry,' Lizzie said. 'She has enough to worry about without me adding to it.'

They all had. The coastal towns – Portsmouth, Southampton, Ramsgate, Dover and Plymouth – were being bombed indiscriminately, and so were the ships bringing valuable supplies into Britain.

The day that the Luftwaffe sank seven ships on their way to Weymouth was the day before the first bomb fell in Birmingham on 9th August. It took everyone unawares and no sirens sounded. Many thought the lone bomber was looking for Fort Dunlop or Castle Bromwich aerodrome, but instead he dropped three bombs on houses in Lydford Grove, Montague Road and Erdington Hall Road, killing one boy on leave from the army and injuring countless others.

On 13th August, Castle Bromwich and the aero-drome were heavily bombed, as well as areas near the centre of the city. It happened again the next night, and the next. Many of these were too far away for Lizzie to take shelter, although she did go to the shelter in Bristol Street on the 23rd August and stayed there till the 'All Clear' sounded some seven and a half hours later, when she struggled home with two overtired, hungry and fractious children to snatch a few hours' sleep.

Two days later, Violet and Lizzie were back in the shelter while the city centre was pounded. Barry wasn't with them as he was fire-watching and people around were grumbling about the sirens not sounding soon enough. They had a point, Lizzie thought. You often heard the crump and crash of explosions before the sirens warned you, and a policeman on a bicycle, blowing a whistle and shouting for people to 'Take Cover', didn't have the same sense of urgency.

But, just then, Violet said to Lizzie, 'I'm taking a job, starting Monday.'

'A job?' Lizzie repeated, aware suddenly that she would miss popping in for a cup of tea and a chat whenever the notion took her, and how good Violet was at minding the children a time or two.

However, the light of determination was in Violet's eyes. 'I'm making shell cases,' she said. 'It's at Arkwright's up Deritend way. Her on the corner gave me the wink there was some jobs going, like. I mean, I've been thinking everyone must do what they can to win this damned war, or my Colin and thousands like him have died in vain. I mean, yeah, it was great so many men were rescued from Dunkirk, and yeah, it were a miracle, like, but what about the equipment left? They can't fight the whole of the German army with pop guns, and if there ain't the men to make them then the women must.'

Violet was right of course, and though women had worked in war-related fields since the start, now there was a drive to get more of them involved. Lizzie knew she'd consider it herself if she hadn't the children to see to – and Steve, of course, for he was coming home for a period of convalescence and some physiotherapy on his arm and leg, and she looked no further forward than that at the moment.

The last raid had torn through the city centre and ripped the roof from the Market Hall in the Bull Ring and done extensive damage elsewhere. The following night set the Snow Hill area alight as far as the Jewellery Quarter, liquid fire running along the streets, licking at the warehouses that were mainly made of wood and destroying factories. Lizzie wondered if the Grand Hotel still stood.

Steve returned home the next day to a world of blackouts and shortages, and a wife wearied by lack of sleep and hardly able to cope with a traumatised man who was often in pain and snappy because of it.

He seemed totally different to the man who'd walked away that day in October. He had a shorter fuse and often shouted at her, and his violent outbursts would cause Niamh to put her hands over her eyes and Tom's bottom lip to tremble.

But Lizzie forgave him, for as well as the pain he was

175

so obviously in, she'd seen his haunted eyes and heard the screams he gave sometimes in the night. But she did miss having Violet next door, whom she could have a good old moan to and know it would go no further. She lived in hope that when Steve had had some rest away from it all, he would improve. It was hard, though, to get away from it, for the raids were almost a nightly occurrence. At these times Steve would seldom seek shelter and would instead go to The Bell. Stuart Fellows's family had moved while he was in France, for when their house, much further down Bell Barn Road, was caught in a blast and declared unsafe, they were offered a home with an elderly uncle who lived near the back of the airfield at Castle Bromwich. If Steve took himself off to see Stuart he'd often not come home all night, and he was so wearing and unpredictable when he was there that Lizzie was often glad of it when he stayed away.

Steve knew he was being unfair yelling at Lizzie. He was really yelling at the unfairness of life and the things he'd been subjected to and the suffering witnessed at Dunkirk, which was so brutal and terrible he couldn't talk about it, but which he knew would stay with him as long as he lived.

Those last few days in action never left Steve. While retreating, most of The Royal Warwickshires were set to guard the right flank just outside a small town called Wormhout. They'd gone on hour after hour. They hadn't hoped to win this battle, outnumbered as they were, but every minute, every hour, meant more of their comrades might make it to relative safety back home in England.

Steve had felt as if he was in the pit of Hell, with whistling shells erupting around him and whining machine-gun bullets getting their target more than enough times. Before he went to war, he'd have said he was afraid of nothing. He was six foot in his stocking feet, broad-shouldered, well-muscled and as strong as an ox, a man to be reckoned with. But in the fields of France and Belgium he'd tasted fear. It was in his mouth, his nostrils, flowing through every fibre of his being.

Suddenly, a shell, closer than any other, had burst amongst them, taking out both the machine gun and those that manned it. There was another shell and another, and Mike and Stuart and Steve were thrown to the ground with the force of the blast.

When the smoke cleared and they were able to see, they realised they were alive and uninjured. Without a word they began slithering away from their dead and dying companions, wriggling on their bellies through the long grass till they reached the shelter of trees at the edge of a little copse.

It was suddenly remarkably still.

'What's happening?' Mike asked.

Steve, spread out on the ground, risked a peep. 'They've surrendered,' he said. 'There's Officer Crabtree, look, with his hanky on a bit of a stick, and the rest behind him with their hands up.'

'Be a prisoner-of-war camp for them then,' Stuart said, but the words hadn't left his lips when the German machine gun spat out once more and first the officer, and then the men behind him sank to the ground in rows. 'Dear God,' Steve said in an awed whisper. 'They've shot them.'

'And we'll be next if we bloody hang about,' Mike hissed. 'Come on.'

And, tired though they were, they began to run though the trees to the road. Dunkirk was miles away, but better to take a chance on making it than wait to be shot to pieces or impaled on a German bayonet.

They walked all night, and it was about mid-morning of the next day when they came upon a party of refugees on the road in front of them, the flotsam of bombed villages. These were the old and infirm, and mothers with babies and children. Some carried the contents of their homes on their backs, others had a pram piled high or a cart pushed by them or pulled by a donkey or small pony. Steve saw one child cradling a kitten and noted the pet dogs running alongside.

They turned at the soldiers' approach, their eyes full of despair and fear but with a little glimmer of hope when they saw the men were British. However, when Steve, Mike and Stuart opened their hands helplessly, the refugees gave a shrug and parted to let them pass. The little caravan of people turned into a field, obviously to rest. It was ringed with trees and had trenches dug all around it. Mothers settled thankfully against the trunks of the trees and some put their hungry babies to the breast, while the other children cavorted and played together, the dogs running between them, and the ponies and donkeys were released from the shafts to graze on the grass.

Minutes later, the planes were overhead. Steve scanned the road. There was no cover anyway. They moved to the side where the ditch was and knew the Germans would pick them off one by one.

But the planes didn't go as far as the men, though they couldn't really miss them. Instead, they circled the field where the frightened people were. Steve raised his head from the ditch and saw the bombs hurtling downwards and the blast on impact. He saw pet dogs, ponies and donkeys mangled to a million pieces, babies torn from their mothers' arms and blown into bits that littered the lush grass, the bodies of the children and the elderly blasted into the air. And following after the Heinkels came the Stukas, flying in low, machine-gunning any the bombs had missed, until nothing even twitched in the field of death, whether human or animal.

'Christ Almighty,' breathed Steve, as Mike vomited beside him into the grass. Steve and Stuart knew just how he felt.

Mike wiped his mouth and said, 'Shall we go back?'

'What the hell for?' Stuart demanded. 'Even if we found one person alive on that bloody field, what could we do, eh? Best thing is to get the bleeding hell out of here, and quick before Jerry comes back to finish us off an' all.'

It was the only thing to do and they started out again, fear lending speed to their pace. But Steve knew he'd never blot those images out of his mind. It was so senseless, so barbaric. Those people had been defenceless and vulnerable and he knew with absolute clarity that if the Germans were to win this bloody war, a similar fate might await his family, and he was determined to make it at least to the beach, and from there home, if at all possible.

*   *   *

They heard the non-stop clamour from the beaches long before they reached them, and smelt the smoke. the acrid tang of it mixed with the stink of cordite, and over it all the salty sea breeze.

And then it was before them, and Steve saw the pier that looked as if it were comprised of army trucks. There was a little regatta of boats queuing up there and, despite the constant bombardment, the boats' crews continued to lift soldiers over the sides and take them out to the Royal Navy Destroyer *HMS Havant*, which was waiting at anchor in the deeper water.

The sands were already littered with bodies and parts of bodies and discarded equipment. The noise all around them was ear-splitting and relentless, the crashes and boom of the bombs, the shrieking Stukas diving, low guns blazing, the ack-ack guns hastily set up on the beach blasting into the air. All mixed with the shouts, cries and screams of the men.

Nothing in Steve's training or experience so far had prepared him for this, and he stood and watched in horror. 'What d'you think of our chances, mate?' asked a voice behind him.

The soldier was just past boyhood – eighteen or nineteen, no more. 'Bugger all,' was on Steve's lips, but he didn't say it. Instead, he said encouragingly, 'You'll get through, lad. You're young and fit and England will need you again before long.'

'Ain't got much choice, anyroad, have we?' the boy said. 'Germans up our arses and the sea before us. Mind you, rather than fall into German hands I'd take the sea and swim to old Blighty.'

'That's the spirit, lad.'

Steve saw the boy once more after that. It was impossible to hurry in the soft sand clawing at your boots, but he tried, and he and Stuart and Mike were together. They passed the dead and dying, some dismembered, some in bits, some still twitching, others screaming or crying in agony, and on they went. The boy that had claimed he'd rather swim to England was in a pit, both his legs blasted away and his life blood seeping into the sands, and Steve had to turn away from the look in his eyes.

Time and again they had to fling themselves to the ground and try and bury themselves into the sand to avoid the Stukas, but at last, when dusk descended rapidly, they'd almost reached the pier head when Stuart gave a cry and went down, and Steve saw a Stuka had got him and ripped into his leg.

'Leave me,' Stuart said.

'Bugger that for a lark,' Mike had replied. 'We're nearly there, man.'

An officer was at the pier head, keeping order and directing the men, and Steve and Mike, dragging Stuart between them, took their places in the queue.

Stuart was being lowered gently into a motor launch when someone gave a shout. Five Messerschmitts came from behind the clouds and began releasing their filthy harbingers of death at *HMS Havant*. Despite the ship's spirited response, it was over in minutes and nothing remained but floating cargo and wreckage and many, many dead bodies.

It sobered everyone. All those men rescued, at great human cost, and for what?

And then another destroyer moved into place and

the rescue went on. There was no time to spare, no time to grieve and mourn, to reflect on what was happening. Stukas came at them then, and the suddenness of the attack caused Steve to slip into the water, where he was peppered with shrapnel from a bomb exploding nearby and had his leg crushed by two army trucks. He'd been unconscious when Mike pulled him from the sea and onto the next boat home.

Had he been able to tell Lizzie this, she would have understood his fears and maybe helped him overcome them, but he saw admitting to fear as a sign of weakness. In fact, he wanted to bury those experiences in the darkest recess of his mind, and because of this he was happier in Stuart's company than anyone's.

Stuart left hospital at almost the same time as Steve and was welcomed home as a conquering hero. When he explained what a good mate Steve had been after he'd been injured at Dunkirk, Stuart's family couldn't do enough for him either.

Steve felt the need to prove he was alive, the same strong, virile man he'd once been, able to drink men twice his age under the table and with the ability to pull the women. There were many hanging around the pubs ringing the airfield, and when there were no pilots to give them a good time, a Dunkirk survivor did just as well. Many didn't mind him being a bit rough, which was just as well because all softness and gentleness had been stripped from him, left behind on the journey to Dunkirk.

He was unfeeling with Lizzie too and she was worn out trying to please him. She knew in her heart of hearts it wasn't all his fault. He'd been damaged by what he'd witnessed, but she longed for him to be declared fit and healthy and able to rejoin his unit, although she felt guilty about thinking that way and knew she would worry about him every minute he was gone.

CHAPTER TEN

Steve went back to his unit on the 26th September and Lizzie tried to keep the relief out of her face and voice as she bid him goodbye.

The next day, the Germans launched the first of their daylight raids and Fort Dunlop was hit, but though there was damage there was no one injured. Not content with this, though, the tram stop by Dunlop's was full of people when they were strafed with machine-gun fire.

This was the first of many reports of such indiscriminate shooting. Bus stops and tram stops and vehicles themselves were attacked, as well as people in streets and parks. There was one incident of a lady with a baby in her arms and another older child hanging on to her skirt who ran to the park, the nearest open space, after her house had been bombed, and all three were killed by machine-gun fire.

It could so easily have been Lizzie that she felt shocked to the core and wondered for the first time if she'd been wise to keep her children at home with her. Tom passed his fourth birthday in early October and she talked it over with Violet.

She hadn't come to any decision by the time Clementine Churchill visited Birmingham on 14th October. She visited two factories and one neighbourhood that had been extensively damaged by the bombing. The *Mail* had a picture of one of the people, whose home had gone, who'd defiantly placed a Union Jack on top of the rubble and told the lady, 'Our house is down, but our spirits is still up.'

Clementine Churchill was impressed by this demonstration of unflinching courage in this typical working-class district and said that she found the same everywhere she went.

This Brummic courage was needed in the nightly raids that followed Clementine Churchill's visit. Lizzie got used to getting a meal together quickly and maybe letting the children have a few hours' sleep before needing to rouse them again. She was grateful for the siren suits that she'd bought for each of them, which could go over other clothes to keep them warm as the cold autumn nights began.

On Thursday, 24th October, there was another massive raid, the way lit for bombers by sticks of incendiaries dropped first. A shelter in Cox Street was blitzed and the Carlton Cinema and the Empire Theatre, and Tony's Ballroom next door burned out completely. Lizzie remembered that she and Steve had always intended to visit the Empire Theatre, but they never had made it. She'd been to Tony's Ballroom lots of times with Tressa in the early days and later with Steve, and she was saddened it was there no longer.

New Street had received many attacks, including

one on Marshall and Snelgrove where it was reduced to twisted black girders sticking up through the rubble and assorted debris. Lizzie remembered window-shopping there, which was all she could ever afford to do.

'Does no harm to look,' she remembered Violet saying one day. 'Even that snobby lot can't charge us for just looking.'

Well, they would look no more, and Lizzie felt desolation seep through her. She wondered if at the end of it all there would be any of the city left, for after that one raid the papers reported one hundred and eighty-nine major fires had begun.

The next night was another of Hell. Kent Street's baths were hit and fires burned in Barker Street, Summer Hill, Constitution Hill and Holloway Head. As the 'All Clear' sounded, Lizzie gave a yawn. She shook Niamh awake, for both children had dropped asleep on the bunk. She then took Tom in her arms, though he was a weight, and Niamh scrubbed at her eyes and stumbled sleepily to her feet. Lizzie looked at her face, white with exhaustion, and knew she was doing the children a disservice keeping them with her. Both of them deserved better than this. They stepped into a night that glowed with the flames of many fires and stank with smoke that swirled around them, and Lizzie said to Violet, 'I'm not letting the weans stand any more of this. I'm taking them to Mammy.' But she said it in a whisper, for Niamh had ears on her like a donkey.

'I don't blame you, girl,' Violet said. 'By Christ, it gets to you after a while. Will you stay there yourself?'

'No,' Lizzie said firmly. 'I won't run away. I'll come back and take a job some place. Do my bit, like everyone's saying.'

'Good on you, girl,' Violet said warmly. 'I could get you set-on at my place if you like?'

'Oh that would be good,' Lizzie said as they reached the entry. 'I'll see about the trains and things in the morning and we'll go from there.'

'Will you send a letter?'

Lizzie shook her head. 'I won't take the time, I'll send a telegram. One thing I know, Mammy won't refuse. She's been dying to get her hands on the weans since it began.'

With Violet at work, Ada willingly minded Tom while Lizzie went into the town to book their passage to Ireland. No one blamed Lizzie for her decision; in fact, Gloria said if she had relatives in the country, regardless of where it was, she would have hers away there like a shot, and the others agreed with her.

'It's sending to strangers I couldn't abide,' Minnie said. 'But one of your own, especially your mother, that's different altogether. I know this is no place for kids and babbies, but how would I know they was being looked after proper if I was just to send them away. Now yours . . .'

'Will probably be spoilt rotten, knowing my mother,' said Lizzie with a laugh. 'She's much softer as a grand-mother than she ever was as a mother.'

'That's usually the way of it,' Minnie said. 'Anyway, better that way than the other, and you'll soon knock them back into shape when this little lot is over and they can come home again. And at least this way they will be safe.'

Safe, thought Lizzie, as she scurried through the city centre later, and she decided to go along Colmore Row to see the destruction for herself as she had taken the tram to Steelhouse Lane. She was delighted to see the Gaumont still stood, but behind it the whole area was a sea of blackened, scorched rubble. The front of Snow Hill Station was there, but behind that was a blistered landscape of brick, masonry, glass, and twisted and buckled train lines.

Along the road there were gaping potholes and craters and piles of rubble where there had once been shops and offices, but the sandbagged structure of the Grand Hotel still stood, and St Phillip's on the other side of the road. She went down through Chamberlain Square and Paradise Hill, taking in the top end of New Street where the scale of the destruction was so apparent. Burst and sodden sandbags lay bleeding onto the pavements; here and there, snaking hosepipes still dribbled into gutters, and blackened mounds were everywhere. Here, the smell that she'd noticed as soon as she'd alighted from the tram was stronger, a scorched and acrid smell of burning and smoke, mixed with the stink of cordite and a definite whiff of gas.

Oh yes, Lizzie decided, her children were better out of this for a while, and she hurried on to New Street Station to make the arrangements.

Catherine was delighted to have the children, but couldn't understand why Lizzie couldn't stay there too.

'It's a good enough place to land your children in, but not good enough for you. Is that the way of it?'

'No, Mammy. It's . . .'

'Tressa seems happy enough.'

But Lizzie wasn't Tressa. 'Can you understand why I feel I have to go back, Johnnie?' she asked her brother.

'Aye,' he said, 'though I hate to think of you in danger. But you're right. Everyone can't just run away, and I'd say for now the weans are better here.'

'What will Steve say about you going back to that place?' Catherine asked.

'You forget, Mammy, his own family are in the thick of it too,' Lizzie said. 'He'll be fine about it.'

And Steve was fine about it. He knew as well as any that although three hundred thousand French and British soldiers had been rescued from Dunkirk, masses of equipment had been left to rot on the roads and beaches of France. There was an even greater need for more bullets, tanks, lorries and planes, and he was aware of the recruitment drives to encourage women to join the workforce. Lizzie was only one of many doing her bit. He was proud of her stand and wrote telling her so.

Lizzie hated the job, but was pleased with the little nest egg she was building up for herself in the Post Office. She was often more than tired, exhausted from the raids, which were virtually every night. Sometimes, if she was lucky, she was able to grab a couple of hours' sleep, and sometimes she wasn't. The raids weren't always that close, but she'd lie awake, waiting and tense, knowing they could be overhead in minutes. Other nights they had a respite, but Lizzie, like many others, would still lie awake or doze fitfully, waiting for the sirens' strident wail. Everyone was feeling the strain, but most women turned in at the factory the next day, knowing the work they did was essential for the war effort.

On 15th November there was a memorial service for Neville Chamberlain at St Martin's in the Bull Ring, though his funeral had been held in London. 'I ain't going,' one girl stated. 'Stupid bugger, anyroad, to be led up the garden path by bloody Hitler.'

'Don't be too sure of that,' Violet said. 'My Barry says he knew all the time and it was a ploy cos we wasn't nearly ready, was we?'

'No? And why not?' another put in. 'Cos Hitler made no secret of it, did he? I mean, that Olympic Games in 1936 was nowt but showing off, what he had and that, and his bloody goose-stepping army, and still we did nowt about it.'

'I bet some of them poor buggers in Coventry wish we'd acted sooner,' another girl said.

Everyone knew what she meant. News had been filtering through all day of the terrible raid that had been inflicted on Coventry the night before, where the destruction and loss of life was said to be colossal, and all the women fell quiet thinking about it.

Lizzie and Violet had bought a paper on the way home and later spread it out over Violet's table and looked at it horror-struck. Within a square mile, eighty per cent of buildings were destroyed and five hundred and sixty-eight people killed, with thousands more injured. A new word had been coined in Germany, the paper reported: 'Coventration' which meant razing to the ground.

'Well,' said Violet, looking at the photographs of destruction. 'They've done that all right, ain't they?' She folded up the paper and looked at Lizzie grimly. 'Next it will be our turn.'

'What do you mean, Violet?' Lizzie snapped. 'Our turn. It's been our turn since bloody August. That raid we had last night was scary enough for me.'

'It weren't nothing like Coventry,' Barry put in. 'And Violet's right, Lizzie. Mark my words, we'll suffer summat similar. We make too much for the war for the Luftwaffe to pass us by.'

It began four nights later, on Tuesday, 19th November, and the hooter for the end of the day in the munitions factory hadn't gone. Those who lived near set off for home, but Violet and Lizzie, along with many of the workforce, made their way to the cellars underneath the factory.

'If it goes off, we'll make a dash for it if you like,' Violet said.

Lizzie nodded.

But it didn't go off. Lizzie had experienced many raids, but few as fierce or furious as this. The bombs seemed to hurl themselves from the droning aircraft above, one blast or explosion following another, shaking the cellar walls and the ground she'd sank down on to in utter weariness. The noise, even muffled as it was, seemed incredible and relentless. Together with the boom and burst of the bombs and the crash of disintegrating buildings, they heard the frantic ringing bell of the emergency services tearing through the blitzed city, and the tattoo of anti-aircraft fire, and this was over the chatter and forced laughter and shouts of terror from the sheltering people.

This is what the people of Coventry must have felt like, Lizzie thought, as the blood ran through her like ice. The walls shook so hard with each crash that mortar was dislodged and dribbled down the bricks, and Lizzie tried not to panic, but she did wonder if the cellar she'd fled to shelter in might turn out to be a tomb. She imagined the factory being hit – surely it couldn't escape the mayhem outside, and then it would fall in on them, crushing them, trapping them.

People said if your number was up then that was that. Christ! Fear was etched on everyone's face, and in the stale and fetid air it was almost tangible. Violet's hand, which sought Lizzie's, was shaking.

Then there was a massive explosion. It lifted people off their feet and shook the entire building and plunged it into darkness. Those with torches in their shelter bags used them, and pencils of light pierced the gloom to see people shouting, crying, praying. Lizzie played her torch on the walls, expecting to see plaster seeping from the ceiling prior to it descending on them, and saw it seemed as solid as ever. But that bomb had landed somewhere close.

One of the men, torch in hand, went up the cellar steps to look. 'It wasn't us,' he said minutes later. 'It was The Fountain pub. People are trapped in the cellars, I'm going to give them a hand getting them out.'

Other men detached themselves and followed the

first into the teeth of the raid that went on as fast and furious as before.

The rescuers had not returned by the time the 'All Clear' went, and Lizzie was quite surprised that she had survived the night. Upstairs, the blast had broken all the windows in the factory and covered everything with dust and ash, and the stink in the air made her feel sick. 'Take tomorrow off,' the supervisor told them. 'We'll have to get this lot cleaned up and the machines checked for safety before we can set up again.'

'Thank Christ for that,' Violet said as they set off for home. 'God, I'm so tired I could sleep on a washing line.'

'And me,' Lizzie said with feeling.

They knew they'd have to walk, no buses or trams would run so early in the morning, but they skirted the city centre. Much of it was impassable anyway, for even as they cut up Jamaica Row they could see the tongues of orange and yellow sparks spitting into the night sky. They heard the roar of the flames and smelt the stink from the charred buildings, mixed with dust and smoke, cordite and gas. And neither woman spoke of it. It didn't need words.

They walked along streets annihilated by bombs. There were gigantic mounds of rubble, all that was left of a terrace of houses or shops. Often those mounds still smouldered, grey smoke curling into dull, dusky dawn sky. At others, people clambered over them, painstakingly removing bricks to release those trapped beneath, with the help of the glowing orange sky and shielded flashlights.

Lizzie and Violet stepped over sandbags, often seeping and dripping wet, and dribbling hosepipes that littered the pavements, and which often ran with water. They saw roads with gigantic craters in them, others where the tar had melted and slid into the gutters, leaving the tram lines warped and distorted.

They went up Bristol Passage and stopped dead, for one side of Bell Barn Road and all of Grant Street was one massive sea of rubble. People were moving over it, searching for survivors.

Please God, let Flo be dead! As soon as the sentence popped into Lizzie's head she disregarded it and prayed for forgiveness, but Violet, guessing her thoughts, said to one of the rescue workers, 'Where were the injured taken?'

He shrugged. 'Into town, but the General was hit too. People say Lewis's has opened its basement.'

And there they found Flo and Rodney, though there was no record of Neil. Lizzie and Violet weren't allowed to see them as they were heavily sedated, but the nurse told the women to come back the following day when the doctor had seen the injured and they'd have a better idea of the state of their injuries.

They were nearly home again when they came upon the woman. They knew her: her name was Sandra Hearnshaw and she'd lived above Flo in Grant Street. Her girls Dianne and Dora had often played out in the street with Niamh, being of similar ages, and they had a wee brother, William, just six months old.

Even in that light, Lizzie could see how bedraggled the three were. Sandra's arms were ominously empty and the girls trailed behind her. 'Can I help you?' she said.

Sandra looked at her with vacant eyes. 'Help me?' she said, as if she'd never heard of such a thing. 'No, no one can help me. Blown right out my arms he was. I couldn't do owt.'

Sudden fear clutched Lizzie. Surely to God . . . But this wasn't the time or place to stand firing questions. 'Come on,' she said as she reached her entry. 'Come in and have a drop of tea and something to eat.'

The woman allowed herself to be led down the alleyway and followed Lizzie into the house. Violet lit the gas lamps and Lizzie saw the little family clearly for the first time. Their clothes were in tatters and not really suitable for the elements, and over everything was a film of dust and ash, ingrained into their skin and coating their hair. Down the girls' faces were cleaner tear trails, but it was in their eyes that Lizzie saw the panic and petrified terror.

The story came out slowly as the children drank the cocoa Lizzie made and munched the toast. 'I was sheltering under the stairs,' Sandra said, 'cos Billy, he'd had a touch of bronchitis, like, and I didn't want to risk the shelter. People say under the stairs is the next safest place, don't they?'

Sandra was asking for assurance and Lizzie said gently, 'Aye, they do.'

'Anyroad, there was this bomb, like,' Sandra went on. 'And Billy, he was pulled from my arms, like, and flung across the room, and the house collapsed on him, on us all. I couldn't get to him, me and the girls was trapped. They dug us out like, but the babby . . . he never stood a bleeding chance. Warden wouldn't even let me look. He said . . . he said I wouldn't want to see him like that. I mean, Lizzie, what harm's a baby done, anyroad?'

Lizzie, the tears seeping from her own eyes, shook her head helplessly. She held Sandra's shuddering body against her own for a minute, but practicalities had to be discussed. 'Have you anywhere to go?'

Sandra shook her head. 'There's only me and the kids. I mean, there's Malcolm, like, but he's away in the army.'

'Your parents?'

'Both died of TB,' Sandra said. 'I was brought up by my gran. She died the day war was declared. She remembered the Great War, see. Said it killed my granddad. Now everything's gone. The house I worked for and my little babby. God, I don't feel I want to go on any more.'

'Come on, Sandra,' Lizzie urged. 'You can't give in. Think of the two wee ones you have left.'

'I can't.'

'You must,' Lizzie said firmly. 'Look at them, for Christ's sake. Who have they got now if you give in?'

Sandra looked at the poor, suffering children, as if seeing them for the first time. She was suddenly smote with pity, and got up from the chair and, bending down, put her arms out. The relief on the girls' faces as they rushed into their mother's arms brought tears to Lizzie's eyes again.

'What are you going to do?' Violet asked her quietly.

'Put them to bed. What else?'

'I mean after?'

196

'They can stay here. I've the room an' all.'

'Have you thought about this? Your mother-in-law . . . ?'

'Has somewhere to go,' Lizzie said. 'If she survives, she has a sister Gladys who's as mean-spirited as she is herself. She nagged her husband to death, Steve always said. Anyway, she rattles about by herself in a big house on the Pershore Road. Plenty of room for the in-laws, and Neil if he survived it all. I couldn't have them all here, anyroad.'

'What about Steve?'

'I'll square it with Steve,' she said. 'You know how he loves kids? I'll stress the fact that Sandra hasn't a soul belonging to her and neither have the children.'

Lizzie found out the next day that Flo was in fine fettle and good voice. Firstly, though, she had gone into town and got clothes for Sandra and the children at the Mission Hall, and then the family trailed up to the Town Hall for new identity cards and ration books, for Sandra's shelter bag had been buried in the rubble. They ate from a WVS van and then Lizzie went along to Lewis's to see how her in-laws were, while Sandra went to see about her money in the Post Office and the insurance policies.

Flo looked anything but pleased to see Lizzie, and Lizzie reminded herself that her mother-in-law, who was getting old, had had a terrifying experience and maybe had no news of Neil. But before she could say a word, Flo snapped, 'You took your bloody time.'

'I came as soon as I found out, last night, but I wasn't allowed to see you,' Lizzie said. 'You were sedated, they told me.'

'You'd be sedated an' all, girl, if you'd been through an ordeal like that.'

'I know,' Lizzie said, genuinely sympathetic. 'It must have been terrible. Violet and I hadn't left work, so we took shelter in their cellar.'

'All right for some,' Flo growled out. 'And why ain't you at work today?'

'There was damage,' Lizzie said. 'It wasn't hit, but some of the buildings around were, and the factory was caught in the blast.' She shrugged. 'Might be back tomorrow.'

'Well, I shall be out in a few days,' Flo said. 'So you'd best prepare yourself. Rodney's worse, poor sod. Our Neil's been to see him and told me.'

'Neil?'

'He weren't with us last night,' Flo said. 'He was at the shop and he took shelter at a mate's house, so he d'ain't know about the house till the morning. Said his dad's in a bad way.'

'I'm sorry.'

'No you ain't,' Flo snapped. 'Never give us the time of day, you. Well, things will change when I move in with you, I'll tell you.'

That was Lizzie's worst nightmare, and though she wouldn't have wished a minute's harm on Sandra's family she blessed the fact she had a house full. But Flo wasn't interested in Sandra Hearnshaw, like she wasn't interested in anybody but herself and Steve. She didn't listen to the tragic tale of the dead baby and dispossessed mother and her girls, who hadn't a soul belonging to them.

'I can't believe you have the audacity to stand there and tell me you've given house-room to some strangers over your own flesh and blood,' she shrieked. 'By God, girl, you take some beating.'

Lizzie almost recoiled under the blast, issued with such venom. 'Come on, Flo, be reasonable,' she pleaded, but she knew, even as she spoke, that the woman had never been reasonable in the whole of her life. 'Sandra has no one and she needs support.'

'And I don't?'

'Aye, yes, but you have Gladys.'

'Gladys! You know I never could abide our Gladys,' Flo snapped. 'Anyroad, it's not for you to tell me where to lay my head. I'm family, and you owe me.'

'I haven't room,' Lizzie said firmly. 'I can't turn Sandra and the two little girls out into the street. Gladys will take you in, I'm sure she will, and there'll be room for Neil. He'll hardly want to bide at his mate's forever.'

'You don't want us, that's the truth of it.'

Too right, Lizzie thought, but what she said was, 'It's not a question of wanting or not wanting. Sandra has nowhere to go and you have.'

Flo's eyes narrowed. 'It ain't your decision,' she growled. 'You tell Sandra bloody Hearnshaw not to get her feet too far under your table, for she'll have to take them out quick when I write and tell our Steve about you.'

'Well,' Lizzie said with a sigh. 'We'll have to wait and see.'

'Yeah, we will. We'll see all right,' Flo said

malevolently, and went on, 'I tell you, I rue the day my lad ever saw you, for you've brought him nothing but heartache. He might have forgotten that you once got him locked up in a cell, but I never will. Christ Almighty! But I'll have my day with you yet. You just see if I don't.'

Despite herself, a shiver of fear ran down Lizzie's spine at Flo's words and the vindictive way they were spoken. She looked at the woman in the bed, her face contorted with hate, and knew she was eaten up inside with bitterness and misery. She should be able to feel sorry for her, but she couldn't and she wouldn't stay a moment longer to be abused.

She forced herself to speak calmly. 'I must be going, Flo.'

'Oh that's right, run away. Truth hurts, so they say.'

Lizzie refused to rise to the bait. 'I'm running nowhere,' she said. 'I've a lot to see to and may be back at work tomorrow. And I want to see how Rodney is.'

She thought Flo might call after her, but she didn't, and gradually Lizzie felt her shoulders relax and her pounding heart slow down a little.

Rodney was very ill. As Lizzie was a relative, one of the nurses told her he had little chance of survival, and when she looked at the semi-conscious, delirious man in the bed, she didn't doubt it. 'His internal organs are all damaged,' the nurse told her. 'Crushed, mainly. All we can do is try to keep him pain-free. It won't be for long.' She put a hand on Lizzie's arm. 'I'm sorry.'

'It's all right,' Lizzie said. 'I'm sure you've done your best. I must away now and write to my husband. God knows whether he'll be allowed leave or not.'

She wrote that day, telling him of the raid and the injuries of his parents. She went on to highlight Sandra's plight, playing on the tragic death of the baby and the distressed state of the children, knowing he would be affected by that, and suggested that Flo go to her sister's when she left the hospital, sure that Gladys would welcome her.

Your mother isn't at all keen, but I really think this will be for the best. Sandra hasn't a soul to call her own.

She'd barely finished the letter by the time the sirens blasted out their warning and Sandra's children began to scream in fear.

By the time Steve's reply came, his father Rodney had lost his tenuous hold on life. Flo was almost ready to leave the hospital and Lizzie and Violet and quite a collection of other neighbours had watched a wee coffin with the remains of Billy Hearnshaw being lowered into the black earth in Witton Cemetery.

Lizzie, as a Catholic, was unable to attend the service, but she was glad she was at the graveside to support the weeping and distraught Sandra. She wished Malcolm could have got leave, but it wasn't to be, and she felt so sorry for the woman, no older than herself, so distressed and full of grief.

The next day, Steve's reply came:

I'm sorry about the old fellow, for all we've never been that close, and I know Ma can be dif-

ficult at times. I'm sure you're right about her living at Gladys's, it will be more comfortable for her, anyroad, with her getting on, and she'll see that in time.

You're right to offer Sandra a place. I'm a mate of her husband's, Malcolm, and he's a good sort. I know I'd want someone to do the same for you if the positions had been reversed. Terrible about the babby, though. Christ, Lizzie, you did the right thing sending ours away.

Don't worry, I'll write to Ma, telling her to go to Gladys's. After all, this is war and everyone has to make sacrifices. I doubt I'll get home, even for the old boy's funeral. It's madness here and I think I'm for overseas again, God knows where.

Try to look after yourself.

Love, Steve

Lizzie saw that her mother-in-law had had a similar letter by the set of her grim mouth and the doleful glint in her eyes when she went to the hospital that evening. Gladys and Neil were both there too, and they discussed Rodney's funeral arrangements with the hospital authorities.

By the turn of the year, Flo and Neil were safely ensconced at Gladys's and had no desire to leave, even when Sandra agreed to be evacuated with her girls. Lizzie was glad, for she'd seen the girls' reaction to air raids since they'd been almost entombed on the 19th November. When the city had again been attacked in force on the 22nd November they'd been reduced to blubbering wrecks. God, it had been enough to frighten stronger people than those two wee mites she helped Sandra comfort.

That raid had fractured the water pipes coming into Birmingham. No one was told, but everyone seemed to know. Everyone prayed they didn't have a raid the next night, knowing if it happened that the city would have been burned to the ground. But Hitler's planes had pummelled the south coastal ports instead.

After that there had been a lull until December, and though the raids then weren't too fierce, even with those raids the children had been beside themselves with fear.

The doctor gave them a tonic, 'for they need building up,' he said. 'But, that's only for the short term. In the longer term I would suggest you get them away.'

'You mean evacuation?'

'Yes, I do, Mrs Hearnshaw, for the mental health of your children.'

Sandra could hardly argue with that, but Christmas was around the corner, and when the New Year was heralded in with another big raid on the 1st January, it straightened her resolve and she went to see about it. She left on Saturday, 14th January, and Lizzie and Violet went to New Street Station to see her off to some unknown, but presumably safer, destination.

Lizzie hadn't wanted Violet to go with her, for she had a hacking cough. She'd had it since just after Christmas, and even Carol, home for a few days, had been worried about her, although Violet told everyone not to fuss.

The draughty platform was really not the place for her that raw winter's day, but she was as stubborn as a mule. 'I'm all right, Lizzie,' she said impatiently when Lizzie glanced at her as a spasm of coughing shook her frame and caused her eyes to water. 'Everyone knows a cough lingers after a cold. I'll be as right as rain in a day or two.'

In a day or two, Violet was in bed, and there she was to stay, the doctor said firmly. The 'persistent cough' turned out to be quite a severe case of bronchitis and she would be away from work till he gave her the say-so to go back.

Lizzie laughed as she looked at Violet's mutinous face as the doctor left. 'No good looking like that,' she said as she tucked the covers around her. 'You've met your match and no mistake. Now, lie quiet for once in your life, and I'll make you some beef tea as the doctor ordered.'

'Doctor's orders,' Violet said scornfully. 'Huh. What's he know anyway?'

'More than you in this instance,' Lizzie retorted, but she knew Violet hated being idle and she was smiling as she closed the bedroom door.

CHAPTER ELEVEN

It was a cold day, the sort of cold that caught in the back of a person's throat and made teeth ache, and though Lizzie was glad the hooter had gone she wasn't looking forward to the journey home, especially when one of the girls said, 'I bet the trams won't be running, there's a proper pea-souper out there.'

'As if the bleedin' blackout ain't enough to cope with,' someone else said.

Lizzie couldn't have agreed more, for the day was dark as pitch outside and it would be a miserable and lonely trek home if the trams weren't running.

'Ain't you got a torch?' someone asked as Lizzie set off into the gloom.

'Aye, for all the good it is,' Lizzie answered. 'Gave out on me coming in this morning. I knew the batteries were going, but I couldn't get any more, not for love nor money. I should have knocked at Violet's and taken a loan of hers.'

'Well, she'd hardly have need of it,' the first girl said. 'How is the old codger, anyroad?'

'Ready to slaughter you if she heard you call her

that,' Lizzie replied with a wry smile. 'She's getting better slowly. All set for coming back, but it depends on the doctor.'

'Well, bronchitis can be treacherous. Turns to pneumonia in no time if it ain't caught early and treated proper.'

'I know that,' Lizzie said. 'But it's getting on for four weeks now and she don't honestly know what to do with herself. She's snapping the head off Barry and for little or nothing, and even young Carol got it in the neck for something stupid when she came home on a few days' leave last week. Believe me, everyone will breathe a sigh of relief when she is eventually signed off.'

The women laughed. 'Oh that would be right,' one said. 'Couldn't never bear to be idle, Violet.' And then she added, 'You all right going home with no torch? I could walk with you a bit of the way if you like.'

Lizzie would have valued company, but she knew the woman had worked a full day like herself and was probably just as tired and hungry and longing for her own fireside. She couldn't ask her to walk with her and then come all the way back, so she said, 'No, it's all right. I'll go steady.'

'If you're sure?'

'I am, really.'

The woman called their goodnights to each other as they went their separate ways, and though Lizzie longed to hurry she knew she risked breaking a limb if she did that. The darkness was so intense she felt she could put out a hand and touch it, and though she couldn't see the fog she could feel the cloying dampness of it and smell the smoky stink of it in her nose and seeping into her mouth, despite the scarf wrapped around the lower part of her face.

There were no trams or buses and precious little else on the roads either. It was curiously quiet, the fog successfully muffling sound and the darkness hiding people and obstacles until they were suddenly before her in the gloom. She'd apologised to a tree and a pillar box before she'd gone very far. At least Jerry will give us a break tonight, she thought, and once I get home I'll not have to leave it again till the morning and I'll sleep the night through in my own bed.

That was something, for though the raids had eased a little and were no longer every night, as soon as people began to relax there would be another one, like the one just three nights before. Only on nights like this could a person be sure of a break.

Lizzie breathed a sigh of relief when she turned up Bristol Passage. She was bone-weary and starving hungry, but at least she felt more confident on her own territory. Even so, she nearly passed the entry and had to retrace her steps holding on to the wall.

Almost as soon as she'd stepped into the cobbled yard she cannoned into someone. 'Sorry,' she said, wondering why the person had no torch, but then maybe they had the same problem with buying batteries as she did. They were like gold dust to get hold of. 'Can't see a hand in front of your face, can you?'

There was no reply and she thought that odd. Everyone in the yard knew each other and there was no reason for anyone else to be down there. She opened her mouth to say something else and then was filled with fright as the person clapped a hand across her mouth. It was a big hand, a man's hand, and smelt faintly of oil. As well as being fearful, Lizzie was also surprised and angry. She began to writhe and struggle and stamp on where she imagined the man's feet to be, trying to wrest herself from his iron grip and demand to know what the hell he was playing at.

But then she felt a pain in her side so acute she tried to cry out against it. It was agonising, like a red-hot poker was burning her insides out. She felt her head swim as she sank to her knees with a gasp of agony. The man had released his grip on her mouth, and yet she was incapable of calling for help, or anything else either. Waves of blackness threatened to overwhelm her, and then she felt her head held tight by those big, muscular hands and her forehead was slammed hard onto the cobblestones. She crumpled in an unconscious heap and the man lifted her coat up and lay down on top of her.

An hour or so later, Violet, muffled up, on her way to the lavvy, tripped over the unconscious figure on the ground. She grumbled slightly, thinking one of the children had left something there to trip up decent folk about their business, and she shone her shaded torch over the offending item.

When she saw who the unconscious figure was she felt as if her heart had stopped beating. In a moment she was on her knees beside Lizzie and feeling her neck. Her relief when she found the pulse was immense and she wondered if Lizzie had fallen over something in the yard, or tripped on the uneven cobbles. Christ, that was easy enough to do in the bleedin' blackout.

But she was suddenly aware of something soaking through her lisle stockings, and when she directed the torch there and saw she had knelt in a patch of blood that was still dribbling and seeping from Lizzie's coat, she sat back on her haunches in shock. Dear, sweet Almighty Jesus, what had happened to Lizzie?

And then she was on her feet and crashing through the house, shouting for Barry to, 'Come quick.' Between them, they got Lizzie into the house and laid her on the settee. 'You go for Doctor Taylor,' Violet told the startled Barry, who stood staring at his injured neighbour with concern. 'He should be at his surgery in Bristol Street and tell him to come as quick as he can.'

When Barry left, she looked with concern at the crimson stain spreading across Lizzie's coat. She hesitated to take the coat off in case she would make whatever it was bleed more, but she stemmed the flow with linen pads she had in the sideboard.

She hoped to God that Barry stressed the urgency to the doctor. She looked up at the clock and then put the kettle on, knowing whatever ailed Lizzie, hot water wouldn't come amiss.

It was as she filled the kettle that she remembered Lizzie had had no bag with her. It was likely still in the yard and she went out to look. She saw it almost immediately, but there was something else beside it too, and as she picked it up she saw it was Lizzie's knickers. No need to share that with the entire yard, she thought, and as she'd not taken time to remove her coat she stuffed them in her pocket.

* * *

Doctor Taylor was well-known in the neighbourhood and had been a regular visitor at Violet's house because of her bronchitis. When his receptionist said Barry Barlow was waiting, he thought Violet had taken a turn for the worse, for she wasn't out of the woods yet by any means, whatever she said.

But it wasn't Violet that Barry had come to see him about, but their neighbour. Barry could tell him little. 'The missus found her in the yard, on her way to the lavvy,' he said. 'Nearly went flying over her by all accounts. Anyroad, she's bleeding from somewhere. It's all over her coat and that. We didn't hang about, like. Violet said to fetch the doctor quick, like, so I don't know no more.'

The doctor knew by Barry's agitated manner that the matter was a serious one, so the two were soon hurrying back as fast as the blackout would allow.

Barry was very fond of Lizzie and hoped to God she was going to be all right, but he wasn't to find out straight away, for when the doctor saw the young woman and said he had to remove at least the top half of Lizzie's clothes before he could examine her, Violet despatched Barry to the pub. 'I'll send for you if you're needed,' she said. 'It's not right you should stay when we're stripping Lizzie.'

'Are you sure you're up for it?' Doctor Taylor said, for he'd seen the two spots of colour on Violet's cheeks and heard her laboured breathing.

Violet made an impatient movement with her head. 'I'm grand, Doctor.'

The doctor knew she wasn't grand, but he hadn't time to go into it. The young woman needed attention and fast; the pads were saturated with blood and he had to find out why. He washed his hands quickly, glad that Violet had had the foresight to have water boiling, before extracting a large pair of scissors from his bag. 'I'm going to have to cut some of the clothes from her,' he told Violet. 'I want to disturb her as little as possible, at least until I've located the source of the bleeding.'

Violet nodded and she unbuttoned the coat. When it lay open she heard the doctor give a whistle at the blood pumping from somewhere, soaking the side of Lizzie's jumper. Without further ado, the doctor, anxious now, sliced up the jumper and vest from hem to neck with his scissors, and Violet saw the gaping hole in Lizzie's side. 'God Almighty!' she cried in shock. 'What's happened to her, Doctor?'

'She's been stabbed, Mrs Barlow.'

'Stabbed! Surely not?'

'I've seen enough stab wounds to know,' the doctor said grimly. 'Could I have some of that water in the basin? I need to get this cleaned up before I stitch it.'

'But . . . but . . . Doctor, who would stab Lizzie?' a shocked Violet asked.

'That's a question she might be able to answer,' the doctor said. 'But she can thank God for that thick coat. Whoever did this meant business and that coat probably saved her life, but still, she's lost a fair bit of blood already.'

The doctor cleaned the wound carefully with cotton wool and Violet stood ready with a clean bowl for him to drop the soiled pieces into. She saw plainly, once the wound was washed clear of blood, where the knife had sliced through the skin.

She felt rather sick suddenly, and the doctor, noting the slight movement she made, glanced up. 'All right?'

Violet chided herself. This was no time to think of her own sensibilities. 'I'm fine, Doctor,' she said.

'Good woman,' the doctor replied, admiring Violet's pluck. 'Now, if you get rid of that cotton wool and stand at her shoulders. It is Mrs Gillespie, isn't it?'

'Aye, Doctor, Lizzie Gillespie.'

'Well, stand there and hold on to her shoulders, but gently. I'm going to stitch the wound now and it might rouse her. It's important that she lies still, so if she starts to move you hold her tight. Okay?'

Violet smiled a little, feeling it strange hearing 'okay', that Americanism, from the doctor's lips. But she answered in kind. 'Okay, Doctor.'

There wasn't much to smile at after that, because gentle though the doctor undoubtedly was, Lizzie did come round and began to thrash and try and dislodge Violet's hands holding her down, turning from side to side. At one point her back arched and the doctor swore. And then Lizzie's arms began to flap about madly and Violet pleaded, 'Lie still, Lizzie. Please, lie still. It's me, Violet, and I'd not hurt you for the world, you know that.'

Lizzie became quieter and the doctor nodded approvingly. 'Go on.'

Violet went on. She told Lizzie about finding her in the yard and the shock it had given her and about sending for the doctor, and all the time Violet talked, Lizzie lay still and listened.

Later, she was to tell Violet she lay in a sort of semiconscious state and, with Violet inadvertently helping her, tried to piece together what happened after she left the factory. But from when she'd bumped into the large black shape she could remember nothing.

The doctor finished and snapped off the thread. 'Now,' he cautioned Violet to hold steady. 'I must dab the wound all over with iodine and it will sting. But it will also stop infection.'

However, Lizzie made no movement, though her face grimaced in pain and her eyes flickered open. 'Hallo, Mrs Gillespie,' the doctor said, and because he saw that her glazed eyes looked frightened, he went on, 'You've had a bit of an accident.'

'Accident,' Lizzie repeated.

'That's right,' the doctor said. 'And your good friend Violet sent for me.'

'Violet?'

'Aye, cock, I'm here,' Violet said, and because she was so agitated and worried she went on, 'Some bugger stabbed you. Who was it?'

Lizzie couldn't comprehend it. 'Stabbed?', and she looked at Violet aghast. 'Stabbed!'

'Yeah, stabbed. Done for you an' all, the doctor said, if it hadn't been for your coat.'

The doctor, seeing Lizzie's mind trying to come to terms with all this, motioned to Violet to be quiet and spoke to Lizzie. 'I will put a dressing over the wound for tonight,' he said, 'in case it should weep, and I'll come back tomorrow to attend to it.

'Now,' he went on, 'I noticed the bump and slight graze on the back of your head, but are you injured anywhere else?'

Lizzie hesitated. Since she'd come to, she'd been

aware of stickiness between her legs and the fact she had no knickers on, but she didn't want to mention that yet, and so she said, 'No, Doctor, I don't think so.'

But Doctor Taylor had seen the pause and he said, 'Are you sure, Mrs Gillespie? There's nowhere else you were hurt?'

And Lizzie held his eyes. 'No, Doctor.'

She was extra glad she'd said this when the doctor went on, 'You realise I'll have to inform the police?'

Even Violet jumped at that. She'd never had police at her door and didn't want them now, and nor did Lizzie. 'Is it necessary?'

'I think so,' the doctor said. 'We can't have a madman with a knife taking advantage of the blackout to hurt, maim and kill people.'

'But all I can remember is a huge black shape that I collided with,' Lizzie protested. 'After that it's a blank till I woke up here.'

'Even so,' the doctor said. 'I'm bound to mention it. But not tonight, because I'm going to leave you a draught to help you sleep. Are you going to stay here?'

'Course she is,' Violet put in. 'Where the hell else would she go? She can share the bed with me – that's if you can make the stairs, Lizzie?'

'Yes, but Barry . . .'

'Barry can have the settee,' Violet said decisively, and went on with a grim laugh, 'God knows, it might be all he's capable of when he comes in. Now, it's decided, Lizzie. And you need someone on hand in case you need owt. Don't she, Doctor?'

'It would be advisable.'

'There y'are, settled,' Violet said. 'I'll pop a hot-water bottle in the bed now to warm it up, and I'll go next door for your nightdress and stuff and get you all comfy in the bed. Snug as a bug in a rug, as my old mother used to say, and with what the doctor gives you, you'll sleep like a baby till morning.'

It was as the door closed on the doctor that Lizzie remembered her knickers. God, if they should be lying in the yard somewhere the doctor's flashlight might pick them out and then he'd be back, would insist on examining her and telling the police, and she said to Violet, 'Did you see anything else in the yard?'

Violet knew what she was asking. 'There was your handbag,' she said. 'And your knickers.'

'Oh, thank God.'

'So, he . . .'

Lizzie nodded. 'I have no memory of it, but there is stickiness between my legs.'

'And why else would he take your knickers off anyway. You didn't want to tell the doctor?'

'No,' Lizzie said firmly. 'I want to forget it ever happened. I'm not telling the police and I want no one in the yard to know either. They'll have enough to talk about with me being stabbed without having that to gossip about as well.'

'I agree with you, bab,' Violet said. 'And don't you worry, I'll not say a word.'

The policeman had to interview Lizzie in the bedroom because Violet said she wasn't fit to be up. Lizzie had no desire to get up. She seemed to be affected by a feeling of lethargy, so that opening her eyes and talking

215

to the policeman was almost too much of an effort.

It was an effort to no avail as well, for Lizzie could tell them little.

'You're sure it was a man?'

'I assumed it was a man. From what I remember, my last memory is of a large black mass that I bumped into. The darkness was dense.'

'And this man – person – did not speak?'

'Not a word.'

The policeman leant back and looked straight at Lizzie. 'Mrs Gillespie, have you any enemies that you know of?'

'No, none.'

'Your husband is . . . ?'

'Overseas,' Lizzie said. 'And my children are in Ireland with my mother.' Lizzie gave a sigh. 'Violet and I usually go to work together, but Violet hasn't been in for over three weeks. She's had bronchitis.'

'So, all your workmates knew you'd be alone?'

'Aye, but I get on with all the people I work with.'

'You enjoy the work?'

'No, I hate it, but I like the money. Most of the women are like Violet and myself and we all get on. Most of the men we work with are young lads, or those getting on a bit, or else they're handicapped in some way.'

'Hmph. It might be worth interviewing them infor-mally anyway,' the policeman mused. 'So, you walked home alone in the blackout?'

'Aye. My torch batteries had given out that morning.'

'You haven't had anyone move into the area lately that you've had words with?'

'No.'

'You see, Mrs Gillespie, I don't think this was a spur-of-the-moment crime. Whoever attacked you seems to have been lying in wait for you.'

Lizzie shook her head. 'I can't think of anyone that would do such a thing.'

'If you do think of anything I'd be obliged if you'd contact me. My name is Inspector Lomas,' the policeman said, handing her a card. 'In the meantime, the number of beat officers are being increased and they are being warned to be extra-vigilant. It's all we can do with nothing to go on.'

'I understand, I'm sorry.'

'It's hardly your fault, Mrs Gillespie. But if you think of something . . .'

'I'll contact you, I promise.'

But when the inspector had gone, Lizzie lay and thought about his words. She thought back to every chance remark she'd made, any complaint or rebuke, however mild. Oh, this is ridiculous, she told herself. No one can examine their life like this. Why did the man attack her? She didn't know; the police didn't know. Maybe she'd never find out. But what if he came back to finish the job? The doctor said the coat had saved her; maybe next time she wouldn't be wearing a coat.

When Violet said she was to stay with them until she was better, she was relieved. She had no desire to live by herself, though she insisted on moving into the attic and letting Barry back into his own bed. The doctor said she'd hardly be fit for work for weeks yet, and Lizzie was glad. It crippled her just to stand and she couldn't wear proper clothes because of where the cut was. She knew the factory had been informed of what had happened to her, and this had been verified by the police visit.

'Are you going to write to Steve?' Violet asked her the following afternoon.

'Not about this,' Lizzie answered. 'What good would it do? It would worry him and it's not as if he can do anything about it. I'm not telling Mammy and Daddy either, because they'd only fret.'

'What about Steve's mother?'

Lizzie gave a sigh. 'I'll have to tell her eventually, but I'm not able for Flo yet awhile. She'll be round here fussing and moaning and won't be in the house five minutes before working out that it was somehow my fault.'

Just over a week after Lizzie's attack, on 14th February, Violet got the all-clear to return to work. Lizzie didn't want Violet to go anywhere at all and knew she would be more afraid and feel far more vulnerable without Violet downstairs. Although she knew the women in the yard would be in and out and would do anything for her, it wasn't the same as having someone in the house all the time. She couldn't say any of this, though, it would sound extremely selfish, so when Violet asked her if she felt all right about staying by herself, Lizzie scoffed gently at her concern. 'I'm a big girl now,' she said. 'I'll be grand and the neighbours are golden, you know they are.'

Violet knew they were. When they'd heard about the attack on Lizzie they had been appalled, and they'd all felt very sorry for her. They had each been in to see her and offered their help if she needed anything, so Violet was able to start back at work with an easy mind.

The slightest thing still seemed to tire Lizzie. She started going downstairs through the day when Violet began work, but only to sit in a chair, because it was agony to stand and she couldn't get dressed because even underwear caught. The doctor told her not to even try until her wound had healed over. 'The last thing I want is for you to get an infection in it,' he'd said. So Lizzie stayed in her nightdress and dressing gown and slippers all day.

She knew she really should get a message to Flo, despite her initial reluctance, because two weekends had passed now and she always went over every weekend and would often see Flo and her sister at Mass. Flo would write and complain to Steve, if she hadn't already done so, Lizzie thought, and I can do without a sermon from him on how to treat his mother.

The point was, she didn't know if she was strong enough yet to cope with Flo, and she was sitting there one morning thinking about it when there was a knock on the door.

Immediately, her whole body stiffened. She wouldn't answer. Who would it be? No one knocked in these courts. No one, at least, that Lizzie would want to see.

She heaved herself to her feet painfully, tied the belt around her dressing gown loosely, crossed to the fire and lifted the poker. She'd not be attacked so easily a second time, she decided. She was surrounded by people. If she hollered loud enough someone would come, especially in view of what she'd suffered already. But if she never went near the door it would be safer still.

She carefully pulled the curtain aside and she saw Father Connolly step back from the door into the yard and look up at the windows. She gave a groan. Oh God, anyone but him. Father Peters was a kindly man, but Father Connolly hadn't a kind or considerate bone in the whole of his body.

And yet she couldn't leave him stood in the yard. She walked heavily to the door and drew back the bolts and turned the key in the lock.

Father Connolly looked at how Lizzie was dressed, in her nightwear and at this hour of the morning. 'Are you not well?' he asked, walking past her into the room. 'One of my parishioners spoke of an accident of some sort and said you weren't back at work after it yet, and that you were living with a neighbour, and I find you here in your nightwear.'

Lizzie knew she'd have to tell him and so she said, 'It was no accident. I was attacked, Father, twelve days ago, on my way from work.'

'Flo didn't say anything when I asked her last Sunday.'

'I haven't told her, Father,' Lizzie said. 'I didn't want her fussing around me, I wasn't well enough. At first I slept most of the time.'

'But why were you attacked?' the priest asked. 'Did you know your attacker?'

'I wouldn't know, Father,' Lizzie said. 'With the blackout, together with the thick fog, the night was as black as pitch. I didn't see who it was, but he seemed to be waiting for me in the yard.'

'Why you?'

'I don't know. The police are baffled too.'

'It's not some man you've encouraged?'

'God, you priests are all the bloody same,' Lizzie spat out, too angry to care. 'I was attacked and somehow I must be to blame.'

'I never suggested . . .'

'You may as well have. It was an insinuation,' Lizzie retorted.

'Calm yourself,' the priest said sternly. 'This does no good at all. Maybe a cup of tea?'

The glance Lizzie threw the priest should have rendered him senseless on the floor, but holding her stomach and walking bent over to ease the pain in her side, she did manage to pour more water into the kettle from the bucket and put it back on the gas before turning back. 'He didn't just push me over, this man,' she said. 'Didn't just slap me about a bit. He stabbed me.'

'Stabbed you!' the priest repeated, horrified.

'Aye, stabbed me. He meant business all right. The doctor said I probably wouldn't be here today if I hadn't been wearing a thick winter coat. As it is, I had to have fifteen stitches in my abdomen.'

'Why didn't you send for me?'

'I didn't need you,' Lizzie said bluntly. 'I needed a doctor and they informed the police.'

'Police!'

'Aye,' Lizzie said. 'The way it was explained to me, they can't have a madman with a knife terrorising women in the blackout. They've put more men on the beat now too, so I understand. They think this man, whoever he is, might have another go at me when he knows he's failed.'

'And you have absolutely no idea who he was?'

'I've already told you, no, none at all,' Lizzie said. 'The police have nothing to go on.'

'And how are you feeling now?' Father Connelly asked, accepting the cup of tea Lizzie gave him.

Lizzie wondered if she should admit to terror. An all-consuming, petrifying fear, deeper even than any other fear she'd had in the air raids, for this attack was personal, for her alone and by a person unknown to her. But no, she decided, she'd admit to no such weakness before this man, and so instead she said, 'I'm still a little sore and have been advised by the doctor not to wear proper clothes at the moment. It's uncomfortable anyway because of where the wound is, but more importantly he said it could cause infection.'

'Oh, I see,' said the priest, and Lizzie knew he had been wondering. 'It must have been a terrible ordeal for you, though?'

'I'd rather not discuss it any more, Father,' Lizzie said firmly, and was surprised when the priest just bowed his head.

'As you wish, Lizzie, and it's best if you can try and put this whole distressing business behind you,' he said, draining his cup and getting to his feet.

'I do try,' Lizzie said. 'It's not so easy when I think this unknown assailant might be lying in wait anywhere to have another go at me. But I will get word to Flo now that I am a little stronger. It is right that she should know.'

* * *

Before Lizzie had time to get word to her mother-in-law, Flo came to the house herself two days after the priest. Lizzie was by then back in her own house, because, welcoming as Barry and Violet were, she felt she'd imposed long enough and her side was healing nicely, though she still wasn't dressing through the day.

Flo didn't bother knocking, but burst through the door and faced Lizzie angrily across the room, 'What's this about an attack and why wasn't I bloody-well told?'

Lizzie looked at the woman who'd shown Lizzie she disliked her from the first moment they'd met, and suddenly she was sick of trying, so all she said was, 'Who told you, the priest?'

'No,' Flo snapped. 'It was one of my neighbours who's aunt to a woman at the end of Bell Barn Road. She'd just got to hear of it herself. Made me look a right fool to know not a thing about it.'

'What was the point of worrying you?'

'Never mind all that clap-trap, I had a right to know.'

'Why? What could you have done?'

'That's neither here nor there. I'm your mother-in-law. I would have come down.'

Lizzie tried to hide the involuntary shudder that went through her. 'I bet that old crone next door was right in there with her tea and bloody sympathy while the family was shut out,' Flo went on sneeringly.

Violet was more than Lizzie's friend, she was her mother figure, her confidante and now possibly her life-saver and so she said sharply, 'Aye, Violet knew.

It was her tripped over me, for I was unconscious, laid out in the yard.'

Flo hadn't known it had been that serious. 'Why were you unconscious?'

'It might have had something to do with the fact that I was stabbed,' Lizzie said, and saw by Flo's face she'd known nothing about that either.

'Stabbed!' Flo cried.

'You want to know about it,' Lizzie said almost scornfully. 'Well, I'll tell you. I was attacked by someone in the blackout. The darkness was too intense to see who it was and I was rendered unconscious. The doctor said my thick coat saved my life. That and Violet finding me lying bleeding onto the cobblestones before I froze or bled to death. If you look at the coat carefully, you'll see the mark where it was sewn at the cleaners, where Violet's husband took it because it was saturated with blood; and I don't want you writing all this in gory detail to Steve and worrying him half to death.'

Flo gaped at her. 'He needs to know. He is your husband.'

'I'll tell him, but in my own time and in my own way,' Lizzie cried. 'He doesn't need to know that even now I'm scared stiff of going to the lavvy.'

'Well, then you'd best come and live at my sister's for a bit,' Flo said. 'She won't mind in the circumstances, if I put it to her, like.'

Over my dead body, Lizzie thought, but she said, 'No thanks, Flo. I must master this fear.'

'You need to be with family. It's what Steve would expect of me,' Flo insisted. 'We've got the room. Neil can bugger off to his mates for a bit, like he did afore. He'll be getting his call-up paper anyway any day now I reckon.'

Poor Neil, Lizzie thought. But then maybe the army would be the making of him. At least he'd start on a level playing field with the rest.

She said none of this to Flo. What she did say was, 'No, Flo, really. It's kind of you, but I need to get over this on my own.'

Flo gave a disapproving bob of her head and said, 'Oh, stay here then. It's obvious to me that that woman means more to you than your family.'

And with reason! God, she'd nearly said the words out loud. 'Come on, Flo,' she pleaded. 'Don't be like this.'

She knew if Flo left her in this mood she would write to Steve, a letter full of complaints about Lizzie, and she never knew how Steve would react. He really had enough to worry about without believing that her and Flo were at each other's throats every minute, and Lizzie usually ended up trying to placate her mother-in-law.

But that day it wasn't working. 'Don't be like this,' Flo said scornfully. 'What else way should I be? When for all your fancy words I know you prefer that woman to anyone else in the land and she's not even a Catholic. Steve has never liked her, and when he's home for good he'll see to it you have less to do with her. He told me so in a letter he wrote.' She wagged a warning finger in front of Lizzie's face and said, 'Mark my words, she'll cause trouble between you and my Steve before you're through.'

Lizzie watched Flo stride away and knew the woman would write to Steve and straight away. She suddenly felt helpless and vulnerable and so very, very tired and she put her head in her hands and wept.

CHAPTER TWELVE

Slowly, Lizzie did begin to recover her health and strength and come to terms with the attack made upon her, and she returned to work on 9th March and was even welcomed back by the boss, who said he was glad to see her looking so well.

After the autumn raids, which had virtually crippled Birmingham and killed and maimed countless numbers of people and made others destitute, there had been a little lull from 1st January to 4th February, just three days before the attack on Lizzie. After that there were sporadic raids, often far enough away to be able to stay in bed; which was just as well, for after the assault on Lizzie, fear prevented her leaving the house and touring the streets for shelter in case she risked bumping into the madman, intent on finishing what he had begun.

However, the raid on 11th March saw Lizzie and Violet scurrying through the night together, for Barry was again fire-watching. 'Thought he'd finished with us,' a woman in the doorway said as they picked their way across the sandbags.

'Not likely with London getting it every night,' another put in.

'Ah, and they have less shelters than us according to the paper,' said an old man in the corner. 'They're holding out in underground stations and deserted warehouses and all sorts.'

'It ain't right, is it? I mean, before governments lead a country into war, you'd think they would make sure their people was safe.'

'Not the likes of us, they don't,' another commented. 'Haven't you heard the term "cannon fodder"? That's what we are. And if a few of us get killed, what's the odds?'

'That's an awful outlook to have.'

'True, though.'

And it was true. Lizzie had often thought brick-built shelters were little safer than a house. She envied those with cellars big enough to hide inside. Oh she was glad she'd got the kids away. She'd made the right choice. Christ Almighty, what if they'd still been in Birmingham when that madman went for her. They could have seen it. He could have turned on them too.

She gave a shudder at the thought and Violet was surprised, for the raid wasn't that severe. 'All right?'

'Aye,' Lizzie answered. 'I was thinking of the weans.'

'You surprise me,' Violet said dryly, for she knew Lizzie thought of little else, but she couldn't wonder at it, for they were young to be growing up without their mother, however good her parents were. She sighed and said to Lizzie, 'I know you miss them, bab, but they're best out of all this.'

'I know,' Lizzie said. 'Nights like this I'm doubly

sure. But even when there are no raids, you know, Violet, I look at the rations sometimes and can't seem to summon up the energy to cook something I know will be barely edible when I've made it.'

'I know what you mean,' Violet said with feeling. 'It's the boredom that gets to you after a while.'

'Aye, Woolton pie is almost tasteless.'

Violet gave a wry smile. 'You said it.'

Woolton pie was a meatless pie, pioneered by Lord Woolton. Each time Lizzie heard of a merchant ship sinking, she'd think of the tons of foodstuff lying on the sea bed and feel depressed.

Her children, on the other hand, had as much food as they wanted. She remembered how she'd once taken for granted the rashers of bacon, thick and sizzling in the pan, served with eggs with bright yellow yolks, collected in just that morning, or the succulent chicken, who'd been strutting about the yard just a couple of hours before. Even the soda bread was delicious, spread thickly with creamy yellow butter and perhaps topped with home-made jam. Jam was something Lizzie hadn't tasted for months, and you could only afford a smear of butter or margarine to try and make the grey, stodgy national loaf more edible.

She sighed again and lay back against the bunk she and Violet shared. Violet had her eyes closed, but Lizzie doubted she slept. She couldn't sleep while a raid was going on. It was far enough away that it didn't make you jump every time a bomb landed and think every moment was your last, but too near for her to risk going home yet awhile, though some had. She knew from experience how quickly the raid could turn to be directly above them and so she stayed put.

She closed her eyes too and thought of her home in Ireland, a sort of paradise for her children, with fresh air to breathe and fields to play in and the babbling stream that fed into the rolling sea no distance at all from them. She contrasted that with the life the children had here. The bare streets and dusty courts had once been their only playground, but now there was a sea of bombed rubble, which was like a death trap. More than one child had cut themselves deeply on the glass shards poking up between the beams and masonry debris, or had fallen onto the broken bricks, or gotten small fingers crushed or legs twisted, and yet it drew the children like a magnet and why wouldn't it? It was like an adventure playground on their own doorstep and they swarmed over it like ants.

The next thing she was aware of was Violet shaking her, 'Come on, sleepy head,' and she woke to the reassuring sound of the 'All Clear' blasting over the city. 'Was I asleep?'

'I'll say,' Violet said. 'Snoring like a good'un!'

'I wasn't,' Lizzie said, horrified.

'No,' Violet assured her. 'But you was well-away for all that.'

'God, I'm stiff.'

'You would be, the way you was lying, but I didn't want to disturb you, like. Ready?'

'You bet,' Lizzie said, glancing at her wristwatch. 'I want my bed, even if it is only for an hour or two.'

Lizzie felt herself begin to relax coming home from work. Part of this was due to the fact they now came home in full daylight as the days lengthened, and any air raids were sporadic and too far away to warrant dashing to the shelters.

Then there had been no word of any other women being attacked. The police were as baffled as ever, but they'd told Lizzie when they'd called to see her one evening as she'd just got in, that even if the frenzied assault had been directed at her, it didn't seem as if the man was going to repeat it, or he would have tried by now. 'Maybe he had a fit of conscience, or of course he might have been injured or killed in one of the raids.'

'Well, we wouldn't know, would we?' Lizzie said. 'But God knows, if he was, he's no loss.'

'Indeed,' the policeman said. 'And I don't think you'll be troubled further, but just in case, keep alert, and lock and bolt your door at night.'

'I always do now, since.'

'A wise move. And if you want our help at all, you know where we are.'

About this time, Lizzie noticed a metallic taste in her mouth and she mentioned it to Violet on her way to work. 'It's all them root vegetables we're forced to eat,' Violet said with a smile. 'They've fermented in your stomach and are giving off gases.'

'Aye, and I shouldn't be a bit surprised,' Lizzie said. 'One of these days I know I'll wake up looking like a turnip.'

'Well,' said Violet, pulling away from Lizzie slightly so she could look her full in the face, 'now you come to mention it . . .'

Lizzie gave her a shake. 'Fine friend you are,' she

said with a laugh. 'But, joking apart, this makes everything taste awful, and you know me and how I love a cup of tea? Well, I can't bear the taste of it now.'

'Oh, now why didn't you say so,' Violet said with mock horror. 'God Almighty – not being able to have a cup of tea. Life threatening, that is.'

'Will you be serious for a minute.'

'Well, I ain't a doctor, am I?'

'I can't go to the doctor with a funny taste in my mouth.'

'Maybe you've got a bad tooth.'

'I don't think so. I've had a poke about with my tongue.'

'That won't tell you owt. Why don't you pop down the dental hospital and ask them to take a look?'

Lizzie made a face. 'I hate dentists.'

'I doubt anyone likes them much. But if you've got a bad tooth it's better out than in.'

'I know that.'

'Well then,' Violet said. 'Or you could buy a mouthwash, the chemist would put you right about what to use.'

'Now, that is a good idea,' Lizzie said. 'And I'll have a go at that before I go to any dental hospital.'

It was later in the canteen that one of Lizzie's colleagues, seeing Lizzie accept a glass of water instead of tea at tea break, remarked, 'What's up with you, Lizzie, giving up tea for Lent?'

'It's this funny taste she has in the mouth,' Violet said before Lizzie had a chance to speak.

'Funny taste?'

'Aye, like metallic,' Lizzie said. 'Makes everything

I eat and drink taste funny. Even this water.'

'I had that,' Nancy, one of the women, burst out. 'When I was expecting our Audrey. It went off after a bit, but it was awful while it lasted.'

For a split second everything in the canteen seemed to be at a stand-still. People were laughing and joking and chatting just the same, but it was as if Lizzie wasn't a part of it, removed from it by a terrifying fear, while her mind screamed denial.

Because Lizzie had no recollection of any rape, she'd refused to accept it had happened. She hadn't been totally sure the man had penetrated her and hadn't wanted to think about it; the whole idea made her feel sick, so she'd pushed it to the back of her mind. She certainly hadn't thought there might be any result. Even when her period hadn't come when it was due, a week after the attack, she was still recovering from the trauma of the whole thing. The doctor had told her she was suffering from shock and that, he said, could do dreadful things to a person. She'd had more on her mind to try and cope with to even think about her periods. But now, she suddenly realised her period hadn't come since either.

That day, that minute, she knew with a sickening lurch to her stomach that the sadistic sod who'd stabbed her hadn't just left her with a scar, and the enormity of the consequences of that night seemed almost to paralyse her.

Violet saw the blood drain from Lizzie's face at Nancy's words and suddenly knew what she feared. That good, honest girl stood to have her life ruined because of that one attack by a vicious and heartless thug. 'Come on, God,' she silently admonished the Deity. 'She's one of your own, for Christ's sake. The one true religion, she says. Give the girl a break. If the story of them miracles is true, this should be a piece of cake for you.'

But in case God didn't work instantly, Violet knew she had to shield Lizzie as much as she could, answering questions the others asked her before the silence grew too uncomfortable and someone realised Lizzie Gillespie had barely opened her mouth, maybe then linking her unusual behaviour to the conversation.

There was no opportunity to talk in the factory, and Lizzie longed for the hooter signalling the end of the day. She wanted to talk to no one, not even Violet, but to go into her own house and bolt and bar the door and stay there and pretend this God-awful thing wasn't happening to her.

She knew it wasn't to be of course. Barely were the two women through the works gates when Violet said, 'Well?'

Even then she parried. 'Well what?'

'You know what, you ain't stupid. You heard what Nancy said about when she was having Audrey. She had that taste in her gob as well. Have you had your monthlies or not?'

The 'No,' was little more than a whisper.

'Oh Christ!'

'What am I to do, Violet? Help me?'

'I will, bab,' Violet said, giving her arm a squeeze. 'Every way I can.'

'Violet, you know I can't have this child,' Lizzie cried in panic.

'Hush,' Violet admonished. 'I know you're upset and no wonder, but unless you want the world to know, keep your voice down. Look, I'll get my thinking cap on and come around tonight. All right?'

'All right.'

But when Lizzie reached her door she found a letter from her daughter on the mat. She picked it up and pulled the blackout curtains and lit the gas, before removing her coat, and then she sat down in one of the armchairs and opened the envelope. Niamh's excitement sparked off the page, as in her childish hand she told Lizzie of her First Communion, which would be in early July, and which she was preparing for, and the outfit she was borrowing from her cousin her Uncle Oliver's little girl, who was just a year older than she was. It was the prettiest dress and veil and white shoes imaginable and could her mammy come home for it?

Lizzie stood up, folded her daughter's letter and stuck it behind the clock. She had to do something to end this pregnancy, she thought, as she paced the floor backwards and forwards. She knew there were places to go, she knew that, everyone knew, but no one spoke of it.

But she couldn't go to one of these people. She would be scared, for she knew of those that had died, bled to death after such a visit, and then it would be a mortal sin. Then she remembered Mrs Moriarty from the village shop, who'd lost her baby after a fall down the stairs.

She crossed to the stair door and opened it. The stairs were good and solid. Did she have the courage to throw herself from the landing onto them? Probably not, if there had been an alternative, but there was none. She mounted the stairs slowly and then stood on the landing and stared down.

She couldn't do this, it was madness! But then she thought of Niamh and her disappointment if her mother wasn't to make it to her first Communion.

She leant forward and then pulled back. Jesus, what was she doing? 'Get a grip,' she told herself firmly. 'It will take a couple of minutes and after that your troubles will be over.'

And then, before she could think any more about it, she jumped into the air. She automatically tried to save herself, grabbing out frantically, but there was nothing to hold on to, and she landed heavily on the stairs. She couldn't help the cry of pain escaping her as she went on bumping and banging down the stairs, and she bit her lip in an effort to stop herself screaming.

Violet and Barry plainly heard the commotion as Lizzie hurled herself from the landing and the cry of pain she let escape. Violet knew immediately what Lizzie had done and when she went in and saw the crumpled heap on the floor of the living room, she thought for a moment that Lizzie had killed herself. The relief when she moaned was immense.

In an instant, Violet was across the room. 'What've you done, you silly bugger?' she said gently, looking at Lizzie's face, devoid of colour, biting at her lip.

'Violet!' Now it was over she was glad to see her friend. 'Won't be long now, Violet. I've killed my baby.'

Holy Christ, she's done this on purpose, Violet

thought, and to Lizzie she said, 'Silly sod. You might have broken your neck.'

'Might as well have done if I can't get rid of this baby,' Lizzie told her. 'My life will be over anyway.'

'Stop that kind of talk!' Violet said sharply. 'Think of your kids.'

'Ah, yes, my kids,' Lizzie said. 'Like my wee daughter who wants me over for her First Communion in early July. She's written to ask me. The letter is behind the clock, and of course I'll be welcomed warmly with my belly full of the bastard child of a maniac. I had to bloody well do something.'

Violet's heart constricted in pity, but she said, 'All right. What's done is done and there could be a reaction to this night's work. But you can't stay here all night. Can you get up if I help you?'

'I don't know,' Lizzie said. 'My head's spinning because I banged it against the door.'

'Let's try,' Violet suggested, putting her arm through one of Lizzie's.

But when Lizzie tried to move she groaned with pain. 'Hush,' Violet cautioned. 'You'll have the yard in to see what's what.'

When Lizzie was eventually hauled to her feet, the room spun around her. 'Hold on,' Violet said, virtually dragging her across to the armchair before the fire where she lowered her thankfully. She knew Lizzie should be in bed, but she didn't know how that was to be achieved and so she filled a kettle and put it on the gas and then poked some life into the almost dead fire and shook more coal on. 'I'm going upstairs for a blanket,' she said. 'And I'm going to make up a hot, sweet cup of tea and put a drop of whisky in it. It's good for shock.'

'I'm not suffering from shock.'

'Course you are,' Violet stated. 'Anyone would be who'd fallen down the stairs top to bottom. Anyway, humour me. I bet you've had nowt to eat either?'

Lizzie shook her head, but slowly for she still felt incredibly dizzy.

'Well,' Violet said. 'When I've got you comfortable, I'll slip back home and bring you a bowl of stew.'

Later, at home, she said to Barry, 'I'll stay with Lizzie this evening because she's in a bad way. So if you want to slip out for a pint . . .'

'How bad is she then? She only had a fall, didn't she?'

'Yeah,' Violet said. 'But she cracked her head on the door and, well, I don't like the look of her. I'll feel happier if I stay with her this evening at least.'

But it wasn't the crack on the head that Violet wanted to stay for, but because she knew Lizzie would want someone with her when she began to miscarry.

Violet, in the armchair next to Lizzie, awoke with a jerk. She must have dozed off and she saw Lizzie also slept. She peered at the clock. Eleven o'clock, she thought, and Barry will be home in a minute. She couldn't justify staying with Lizzie all night, though she'd feel happier to do so because he knew nothing about the pregnancy.

She hesitated to wake Lizzie. She looked so peaceful. In the end, she raked up the fire as quietly as she could and banked it with slack before dousing the lights and popping back home, but she knew she'd sleep lightly and at any untoward noise from next door she would be round like a shot.

Lizzie awoke in the early hours and for a moment was disorientated. The room was in total darkness except for the tiny glow amongst the slack in the grate, and when she tried to move the pain was excruciating.

It all came back to her, the realisation that she was pregnant and the letter from Niamh that had spurred her to throw herself down the stairs, but the pains she would have welcomed, the drawing pains, had not happened yet. Surely to God they would. She closed her eyes and began to pray as earnestly as she had as a child.

The next morning, Violet came in, drew the blackout curtains, poked up the fire and surveyed Lizzie. 'Christ, lass, I bet you're black and blue.'

'That wouldn't matter a jot if it had achieved its objective,' Lizzie said wearily.

'No sign then?'

'None.'

'There is places. I mean, I know of people had babies took away, like.'

'Isn't it against the law?'

'Oh yeah,' Violet said. 'They don't advertise it, like, but people just get to know. It's risky, I know that much. It's not summat I could wholly recommend, like, but if you was desperate.'

'I am desperate, Violet, but abortion . . . well, it's a mortal sin.'

'Well, what about chucking yourself down the stairs?'

239

'That's different,' Lizzie said. 'It's more natural somehow.'

'Course it ain't!'

'To me it is.'

'So you won't consider an abortion then?'

'No.'

'Can't say I'm sorry,' Violet said, ''cos I know it's bloody dangerous.'

When Violet saw the state of Lizzie's body as she helped her dress, she gasped in shock, for she was a mass of bruises from head to toe, back and front. 'Got to hand it to you, girl,' Violet said. 'When you do a job, you do it right and proper.'

'No I don't,' Lizzie said fiercely.

'It may work yet.'

'And it may not. Then what will I do?'

'I don't know, but I'm sure we'll think of summat. As for your job, Christ, I can't see you getting back to the factory till after Easter. I mean, it's Tuesday now and Easter Sunday is this Sunday.'

'What will you tell them at work?'

'That you fell down the stairs. What else?'

'Thanks, Vi.'

'Think nothing of it, bab, and if Hitler attacks tonight let's hope it will be light and too far away for us to worry about it.'

Lizzie hoped so too, and fervently, especially when she tried to struggle down to the lavvy. Every step was agonising to her bruised and battered body and Minnie came out to see what the matter was with her. The news quickly flew around the court that Lizzie Gillespie had had a bad fall down the stairs – poor sod.

'Everything seems to happen to her,' Sadie observed.

'Aye,' Ada agreed. 'Ain't Lizzie one of the unluckiest buggers you've ever seen?'

'Certainly seems to get more of her fair share of trouble,' Minnie said. 'And that ankle was swollen up like a bloody balloon. Won't be able to walk on that for a few days I shouldn't think.'

'That's if it ain't broken,' Gloria said. 'I mean, didn't she tell you she weren't going to no hospital for an x-ray?'

'Yeah,' Minnie said, but she hated hospitals herself and went on, 'don't blame her really. Hospitals cost money, and anyroad, she can move her toes and that. It hurts, like, but she can do it. Don't reckon she could do that if the bloody thing was broke.'

'She should make sure,' Sadie insisted, 'and you should have told her that, Minnie. We can't all be running around after her.'

'Never notice you do much of that anyroad,' Minnie said. It was true, Sadie was always at the back of the queue when there was helping to be done, but she was furious at Minnie's accusation.

'What do you mean by that remark?' she demanded.

'You work it out,' Minnie said disparagingly. 'It ain't hard. 'Fraid I can't stop and help you, cos I'm popping up to see if Lizzie wants a hand, like.'

Minnie wasn't the only one to pop up either, though Sadie had gone into her house in offended silence and never went near. Lizzie was grateful, not only for her neighbours' invaluable practical help, but also for their company, which prevented her thinking too long and hard. Though Violet had always been her special friend,

241

these people had welcomed her from the day she moved into the yard and she counted them as friends too, and by God she knew she needed friends as never before.

Violet was glad they'd all rallied round Lizzie, especially with her at work all day. She would have expected it of them all and wasn't surprised that Sadie Miller hadn't put in an appearance. 'Wouldn't give you the skin off her rice pudding that one,' she commented to Lizzie later that evening.

She was glad to see the ghost of a smile playing about Lizzie's face at her words. 'But,' she warned, 'watch her, Lizzie, if she does come in. She's like a snake, nice as ninepence to you one minute, and then *wallop*! She socks you one between the eyes, spewing filth out of her gob! Don't, for God's sake, tell her owt.'

'I won't. I'm not mad altogether. Only you and I know the truth.'

'Yeah, I ain't even told Barry. I mean, he'd feel sorry for you and all. He saw the state of you that night and he'd not say a word sober, but I always find the more pints a man drinks, the looser his tongue gets, and I'd not risk to tell him and have it all over the neighbourhood by the morning and that cow of a mother-in-law getting wind of it.'

'Everyone will get wind of it unless I do something and soon.'

'I know, bab, I am working on it,' Violet said. 'Give me time, I'll think of summat.'

However, before Lizzie was able to think of anything, the sirens blasted out. 'Oh bloody hell,' Violet burst out. She read the fear in Lizzie's eyes and knew she'd never make it to any shelter and she said, 'We won't go yet, it might be miles away. Our Barry's down at the warden post tonight, so I hope it is, and I'll make us a cup of tea. Puts new heart in a body, tea!'

It was soon apparent that something more than tea was needed as the crumps and crashes got uncomfortably close. 'Come on, girl. Let's be having you,' Violet cried, slinging her shelter bag and Lizzie's over her shoulder to help Lizzie to her feet. 'We'll shelter on the stairs, like. It'll be better than nothing,' and she helped Lizzie over to the bottom of the stairs she'd flung herself from not that long ago. Then, taking some cushions from the chairs, they tried to make themselves as comfortable as they could, for no-one knew how long it would last.

The purpose-built shelters muffled noise more than the staircase and Lizzie heard the clamour all around them, the crashes and blasts of explosives and the answering sound of the ack-ack guns barking into the night. Smoke swirled in the air and seemed to lodge in her nose and the back of her throat and every bone in her body ached.

The German planes had a distinctive and intermittent engine noise, and each time Lizzie heard a number of them approaching and knew bombs would soon be hurtling down indiscriminately from the belly of those planes to land, her stomach would tighten in fear. She knew every minute could be her last and it could be Violet's too, that staunch friend who, without a murmur of complaint, shared the same danger.

The resultant crash of the explosives near at hand made both her and Violet jump and give little cries of

243

terror, and sometimes clutch each other, especially if it was close enough to shake the walls. The ack-ack guns would send up a volley and the planes would go away, but another wave would soon be overhead again, and another and another.

In the end you began to think you'd always been there. Lizzie felt as if her nerve-endings were jangling and exposed for all to see, for she was experiencing fear like the November and December raid had induced in her.

'Gets to you after a while, don't it?' Violet said suddenly. 'God, I feel as if my insides have gone to water.'

'I know what you mean,' Lizzie agreed. 'I feel the same. Only a fool would say they wasn't scared. Oh God Almighty, here they come again!'

Lizzie wasn't sure at what point in that terror-ridden night she'd thought it would be better if she didn't survive. Wouldn't it solve all her problems? The children would miss her, certainly, but they were happily settled with their grandparents now. And they still had their father, didn't they, and whatever his faults as a husband, he loved his son and daughter and they loved him. Everyone would be better off if she didn't survive this, she thought, as the reassuring 'All Clear' blared across the city.

Lizzie and Violet emerged from their makeshift shelter surprised they'd escaped unscathed and Violet crossed to the door and opened it.

Outside, dust and smoke was thick and stinking, but in the sky over Birmingham there was an orange glow and flames licked into the night sky. 'Dear Christ, there will be nothing left.'

'You're right there,' Ada said as she passed on her way from the shelter. 'One of the wardens was saying the city was ablaze from High Street and along New Street to the Midland Arcades.'

'God Almighty! Where's it all going to end?' Violet cried, but there was no answer to that.

CHAPTER THIRTEEN

The next day, Violet was back in Lizzie's house before half past nine, as the factory had been destroyed in the raid of the previous night, as well as much of the area surrounding it and a good proportion of the city centre.

'Well, what are they going to do? What are you going to do?' Lizzie asked, shocked.

'Well, I suppose they'll start again,' Violet said. 'I mean, what we did, well, it was important to the war effort, weren't it? But just now I don't know where they'll find new premises, cos there were so many places hit again last night and there won't be nowt till after Easter anyroad. But I did get a bit of news you might be interested in from Nancy. Remember, she was the one who put you wise about being up the spout in the first place?'

Lizzie gave a shudder. 'I'll never forget that moment, or that day,' she said.

'Well,' Violet told her. 'Nancy was telling me of a neighbour of hers wanted rid of a baby she was carrying. Course, I got my ear holes pinned back, like, and she said she used castor oil.'

'Castor oil?'

'Nancy says this woman swears by it. Shifts anything and everything out. She said this woman mixed castor oil with orange juice, like, to make it more – well it's bloody awful, ain't it, and you gotta have a fair bit.'

'How much is a fair bit?'

'Well, two bottles should do you, well, according to her, anyroad.'

'But Violet,' Lizzie protested, 'where am I going to find orange juice? I mean, when was the last time you saw orange juice? Unless you have a special ration book to get it from the Welfare for babies.'

'I dunno,' Violet had to admit. 'You'd have to have it neat, but anyroad, I thought it was a better plan than throwing yourself off the landing.'

'Maybe, but God, castor oil, Violet! And neat! Nothing to even try and mask the taste?'

'I know, but if it helps, like.'

Lizzie didn't have to think for long. She just had to consider the alternative and that was enough. She turned to Violet and said, 'You know I would walk across hot coals to rid myself of this child. Castor oil will be nothing.'

'We'll be best leaving it till after Easter, till you are fully fit and before we go back to work. That's if there is any work to go back to of course.'

'How will we know?'

'The bosses said they'll put a notice in all the Birmingham papers and for us to keep an eye out.'

'Might as well do it Monday then,' Lizzie said resignedly. 'Get it over with.'

'Yeah, that's a good day for me,' Violet said. 'Barry goes to see the Blues play on Monday afternoon, so he needn't know anything about it. See you later then, bab,' she went on, her voice sympathetic at Lizzie's woebegone face. 'Keep your pecker up.'

Barely had the door shut on Violet before it was opened again, and Lizzie had to suppress a sigh when she saw her mother-in-law on the doorstep. 'Am I to be told nothing?' Flo snapped, going straight into the attack. 'To be of no account? Nearly all the neighbours heard of the fall you had down the stairs, but I wasn't told.'

'It wasn't serious. I mean, I haven't even had the doctor in,' Lizzie protested. 'I just had bruises, that's all.'

Flo scanned the room, looking, thought Lizzie, for something else to criticise, and eventually said, 'Your step needs a good going over with a donkey stone. I noticed it on the way in, and have you seen the dust on that mantelshelf, and the state of the fireplace is a disgrace.'

'I have been at work, Flo.'

'Well, you shouldn't be. As a wife and mother, your place is in the home.' Lizzie knew Flo's views, for she'd expressed them often enough. As far as Flo was concerned, Lizzie was a married woman and a mother, and whether her children were with her or not, that meant she should be at home through the day and content to sit by her own fireside in the evening.

But this war could not be won on those terms. 'Flo,' Lizzie replied, 'we're at war. Our men, husbands, fathers and sons cannot fight without equipment. If women

248

don't make them, who will? Yes, I admit the money is useful, but so is doing my bit. Steve's doing his and I'm doing mine, and he approves of what I do.'

Flo couldn't argue with this and she didn't try. Instead, she said, though grudgingly, 'I'll get your rations in before I go if you like,' and Lizzie nodded. It would be helpful because it did hurt to walk far, and it would also get the woman out of her hair for a bit.

Later, when her mother-in-law had gone home, she said to Violet, 'She's the most aggravating woman. Even when she's supposed to be helping me, she's critical of everything . . . even when there is nothing to be critical of. God, what would she do to me if she knew what I'm carrying in my belly?'

'She's not going to know a damn thing about it,' Violet said vehemently. 'After Monday afternoon it will just be a bad memory.'

'Violet, I just can't swallow any more, I'll be sick.'

'No you won't,' Violet said, tipping the castor-oil bottle up. 'Look, you've nearly finished this bottle. Take a drink of water.'

'That doesn't help.'

'Take it anyway.'

Lizzie took a long drink from the cup beside her. 'Two more dessert spoons should do it,' Violet said cheerfully, 'and that's one bottle out of the way.'

'Isn't one bottle enough?'

'Maybe, but are you prepared to risk it? Nancy said two.'

'I can't.'

'You can. What's up with you? You once told me you'd walk over hot coals.'

'I'd rather.'

'Yeah? Well all you'd get then is scorched feet. This way there's a chance you'll get rid of that babby you're carrying. Now open your mouth, for God's sake. Let's get it over with.'

They got it over with, though Lizzie gagged more than a few times, and afterwards she lay back in the chair and closed her eyes. 'D'you want to lie down a bit?'

'Aye, I'd love to, but I know if I move I'll throw up,' Lizzie said wearily. 'My head feels as if it doesn't belong to me and my stomach is churning.'

Lizzie was concentrating on trying to stop herself from being sick, but knew she was losing the battle when the nausea continued to rise in her throat. 'Bowl, please, Violet,' she cried, and Violet ran for it and held her head while she vomited over and over. Fat lot of good that did, she thought. I bet if I vomited back all I took it will do no good at all.

Just a little later, Lizzie made one of her many trips to the lavatory, glad her bruises had begun to heal and her leg was less painful, for some of the calls were of the urgent type. Violet stayed with her. At one point she'd gone home to see to and serve Barry's tea, but she'd come back again, using the truthful excuse that Lizzie was far from well.

'Maybe it will happen tonight,' Violet said consolingly. 'Bang the wall if you need me. I'd stay with you, but I don't want Barry to get suspicious.'

'No, I'm fine,' Lizzie said. She felt far from fine, but

thought her friend had done enough. 'Really, you go now.'

'Try and eat something,' Violet advised. 'It might settle your stomach a bit.'

'I'll choke if I try to, Violet.'

'Ah, well, maybe you know best. Get some sleep if you can.'

But there was no sleep for Lizzie. She sat on the toilet nearly all evening and on into the night, often holding the bowl in front of her as the castor oil was expelling everything from both ends. She felt by eleven o'clock that she had nothing left inside her. Her throat was sore from retching and so was her stomach, and a throbbing had begun in her head; but there was no sign of miscarriage, no blood on her pants, no rush of water, no plug of mucus.

Next morning, Violet noted the blue smudging under Lizzie's red-rimmed eyes set in a face the colour of lint. 'Still nowt?'

Lizzie shook her head. 'My head's swimming and my stomach's aching, but not the way I'd like it to be,' she said.

'Could you eat a wee bit of toast or porridge?' Violet asked.

'Toast, maybe,' Lizzie said. 'But there's no reason to wait on me. I'm not an invalid.'

However, she found that the slice of toast she ate went straight through her, the same as the bowl of broth she attempted at dinner time. 'Surely to God no baby can go through this and still hang on,' she said, coming back into the house after yet another sojourn down the yard.

'Maybe it hasn't,' Violet said. 'I mean, maybe it is all over and you d'ain't seen owt. There's not much light in them lavvys and the shaded torches are worse than useless. Let's keep our fingers crossed that the castor oil has done its duty and skited the whole lot out of you.'

'I'll tell you what it has done,' Lizzie said. 'And that's got rid of the metallic taste, but I don't know if the cure isn't worse than the disease.'

'Christ, some people are never satisfied,' Violet said, and just then Ada gave the door a cursory knock and popped her head around it. 'Just thought you'd like to know, I met your mother-in-law on Bristol Street and she said she was coming this way'

Lizzie put her head in her hands and groaned. 'Oh God.'

'Quick,' Violet said. 'You get into bed. You're not up to dealing with that uppity bitch. I'll tell her you're sleeping, and if I can't keep her out of the bedroom keep your bloody eyes tight shut.'

Lizzie was glad to do that, but she felt Flo's eyes bore into her as she stood in the bedroom doorway complaining of the mess it was in and of the clothes littering the floor. Violet knew the haste and panic Lizzie would have been in to get into bed and could quite understand why her clothes were scattered, but that wasn't something she could share with Flo Gillespie.

With great determination she said not a word to Flo in Lizzie's defence, feeling it to be the safest option, but thought to herself that if Flo wasn't throttled by someone, and before too long, there was no justice in the world.

'What's the matter with her, anyroad?' Flo asked, looking at the waxen pallor of Lizzie's skin as she lay back on the pillows.

'She has diarrhoea and sickness,' Violet said. 'Summat she ate, probably.'

'Food poisoning,' Flo declared. 'Not cooking the food properly. Good job Steve isn't here. He doesn't think much of her cooking anyway, not a patch on his mom's, he's always saying, but he'd never expect it to actually make him ill.'

How does Lizzie keep her hands down by her sides and not put them round the scrawny woman's neck, Violet thought, or at least order her from the house.

'God, if it isn't one thing with that girl, it's summat else,' Flo went on. 'Christ, I've seen nothing like it. First she gets herself stabbed, and then, not content with that, she falls down the bloody stairs – and now this!'

Violet, anxious to get Flo out of the house, said, 'Look. There's no love lost between the two of us and I'll not pretend there is. But Lizzie could have an infection and there's no point in us both running the risk of catching it, is there? I mean, I live next door and it'll be easier for me to see to Lizzie.'

Flo could well see the woman's point, though it would probably be the first time. She had no wish to have that awful sickness and diarrhoea, not that she'd admit it. 'What about you – aren't you worried you'll catch it?'

Violet gave a shrug. 'Not really,' she said. 'If I do, I do. There's no work for either of us just yet anyway because the factory was hit the other night, so if me and Lizzie is going to be ill, this is the week to do it.'

'Well,' Flo said with a disdainful sniff, 'there seems little I can do here. I'll pop in tomorrow and see how she is.'

Violet came back up to the bedroom when she'd finally got rid of Flo and Lizzie heaved herself out of bed and began to dress. 'It isn't going to work, is it?' she said to Violet.

'Don't look like it,' Violet had to admit.

'All that castor oil,' Lizzie groaned. 'Oh God, Violet, I feel so bloody ill, and I wouldn't care, wouldn't care about any of it if the damned stuff had just worked.'

'I know, bab, I know,' Violet said, putting her arms around her weeping friend.

By Monday, 21st April, the munitions factory had found a new site to accommodate the workers. It was on the Tyburn Road, not far from Fort Dunlop, and because Lizzie didn't know what else to do, she went with Violet to catch the tram outside Lewis's department store. They travelled up Lichfield Road, past the fire station and through Aston, passing the big green clock at Aston Cross and Ansell's Brewery, then on to Salford Bridge, over the network of canals that met there, before turning right into Tyburn Rd.

This road had once been full of little workshops backing on to the canal, but from the tram they could see the gaping holes and piles of rubble and knew that this area too had seen plenty of enemy action. But then, haven't we all? Lizzie thought, for though the raids hadn't been as ferocious as the one on the 9th April, they were still raids most nights and it still played havoc with your sleep patterns. She was feeling decidedly jaded.

It was good, though, to see most of the women had also come to the new place when they turned in the gates, and they greeted each other warmly. But although Lizzie tried to act as naturally as possible, she knew she was on borrowed time. Eventually a decision would have to be made and all she was doing was postponing it. The worry of it pressed each day on her mind and heart, occupied each waking minute and many of those spent sleeping, where it portrayed itself in nightmares.

Each morning when the alarm would ring, Lizzie would heave herself from the bed and onto her knees where she'd plead and beg the Almighty to deliver her from this shame; and it was what she asked for too before she slept. She began a novena and had a Mass said. Steve's family and even the priest thought it was for Steve, but Lizzie had done a deal with God. Whatever the priest thought, or even what he said, didn't matter: God knew what she was about.

She seldom talked to Violet about it, for what could Violet do? And of course, she could talk to no one else, and so she coped alone and remained terribly frightened, taking each day at a time.

And then one balmy evening in mid-May, when Lizzie was writing a letter to Niamh to go with the card for her birthday, Violet came in the door to say, 'Lizzie, I have heard of summat else.'

Lizzie just looked at her. 'To get rid of the babby, like?' She suppressed the hope that rose inside her. Nothing had worked so far, so why should this be any different. 'What?'

'Well,' Violet said. 'I don't know much about it, like, and I'd have to make enquiries, but I can be discreet when I want to be. It's these tablets, and you take them and have a bottle of gin and sit in a hot bath and bingo. Only,' she added, 'it only works if you are three months or under. How far on are you?'

'Going on fifteen weeks,' Lizzie said, 'so it probably wouldn't work, but anyway, I couldn't do it.'

'Why not?'

'Violet,' Lizzie said, 'I have no feelings for this child I am carrying, but nothing is its fault. I've taken cod-liver oil and thrown myself down the stairs to no avail. But tablets . . . I've thought long and hard about this and I've decided now that the only good thing I can do for this child is to hide away somewhere until it is born and then let it go to someone who will give it a good and loving home. What if I took something that damaged it in some way? No one would want it then and it would spend its life in some institution, and I would feel guilty for the rest of mine.'

Violet thought about Lizzie's words and could see her reasoning. 'But how long are you going to leave it?' she said, 'because though there is nowt yet, you'll be showing soon. And where're you going to go, anyroad?'

'Back to Ireland,' Lizzie replied.

'Is that the only option?'

'All I can think of,' Lizzie told her resignedly. 'What would Flo do if she got to know? And Steve would be told her version of it posthaste. I can't risk that.'

Violet knew that Flo and Steve wouldn't be the only ones to judge and castigate Lizzie. Because she didn't mention the rape after the attack, few would believe she was raped at all, but she didn't share these thoughts. She just put her arms around Lizzie and held her tight. 'If anyone in the whole bleeding world will believe you, surely to God it will be your mother?' she said at last.

Lizzie doubted it. Her mother wouldn't hear the words of any sort of explanation. She'd see only the shame of it, the disgrace, the fact that she'd be snubbed shopping in Ballintra, and ostracised at St Bridget's. The whole family, including her own two wee children, would become social lepers. She knew that a girl may as well commit suicide as take that news home to her mother in Ireland. However, she didn't think there was any alternative for her.

'There's places women can go away to and stay until they have their babies,' she said, 'and then the nuns find homes for them. I mean, I don't know where they are or anything, but everyone knows about them. I heard of a girl like that once. Her parents said she'd gone to her auntie's in England, but there had never been talk of any auntie before, no letters or anything, and no one from England had ever come to visit, so people drew their own conclusions and a few months later the girl was back.'

'Well at least they'll not know or suspect that of you here,' Violet said, 'because it's natural for you to go to Ireland to see your kids and then come back again.'

'Aye,' Lizzie said, and gave a grim little smile. 'And Niamh will be pleased at least. I haven't really answered her letter properly yet. I've just made vague promises, you know. But I can tell her I'm coming home for a bit in this latest letter. But not just yet. I'm going to hang on as long as possible, because I am terrified of facing my mother. And these places are run by nuns, and nuns are . . . well, they're not exactly angels of mercy, you know.'

'At least stay a little longer,' Violet said. 'You're so blooming thin there ain't even the slightest bulge yet. So, when you find out about these places, what you've got to remember is however bad they are, you will only be there for a few months and anyone can stand that. Have the baby, leave it with the nuns for adoption, and come back here and pick up on your life again: and Bob's your uncle and no one's any the wiser. But for God's sake be careful. Don't leave it so long that someone will jump to it before you can get yourself away.'

'I know, Violet. I won't, don't worry.'

'That's it, girl,' Violet said encouragingly, 'and when it's all over, I'll be waiting here for you. Feed Flo some line like you're sick or summat and going home for a rest, and tell the factory the same and any who ask. Give your notice in properly, because you don't want anyone getting suspicious and poking about in your business, especially not now.'

Lizzie knew Violet spoke sense. She must handle this just as if she was really going home for a wee holiday. She wondered how big she would be by the time of Niamh's First Communion. She'd be five months pregnant, but maybe with her physique she'd get away with it, and she remembered how the doctor used to laugh when she was expecting the other two and ask if there really was a baby there at all. 'Please God,' she implored. 'Let this one be the same.'

And when the child was born it would go to a good, respectable, childless couple who would give it all the love, attention and time that it needed. Then she really could put the events of that terrifying night in February behind her and look forward at last.

Towards the middle of June, one of Lizzie's workmates who often worked alongside her said, 'Hey, Lizzie, you must be the only one here that's putting on weight.'

Lizzie paled and bent her head so it should not be seen as she said, 'What are you talking about?'

'Pretty obvious, ain't it. I mean, there ain't much to you and never has been, but there's more of you than there was, that's all. While the rest of us are half-starved on the bleeding rations you seem to be thriving on yours.'

'It was bound to come sooner or later,' Violet said on the way home. 'Pregnancy is one thing you can't hide, though you've managed much longer than many could. But to dally any longer would be plain stupid.'

Lizzie knew that too. 'I'll give my notice in tomorrow and then write to mammy and make the arrangements,' she promised. 'I'll write to Steve too, though I know he'll have no objection.'

Lizzie's boss had plenty of objections, though. He liked Lizzie and thought her a good worker. 'Go home for a while, see your kids, watch the young one make her Communion or whatever and I'll hold your job.'

'It's very kind of you.'

'Kind, be damned. It's myself I'm thinking of as well.'

'I don't know how long I'll be away.'

'You could send me word?'

'No, really, I think it's best if I just leave,' Lizzie said, and added untruthfully, 'My doctor recommended me to have a break; my nerves are bad.'

'Hmph! The very devil, nerves,' the boss conceded. 'But I must say, my girl, you show no sign of it. You're positively blooming. In fact, I wish half the factory looked so healthy.'

And Lizzie did look healthy. Her skin was clear, her cheeks tinged with pink from the early summer sun and her hair shone. Inside herself, a solid lump of panic, fear and dread had settled. It sometimes seemed to fill Lizzie's throat so she didn't feel hungry, or it would attach itself to her raw nerve-ends so she was nervous and jumpy.

No one could see inside, however, but most women she worked with could understand how she would miss her children. Many of the children in the area who'd been evacuated in the first rush on 1st September had been brought back by Christmas, though more were evacuated a second time after the severity of the November raids the following year. 'I know they went to strangers, like,' one girl said to Lizzie, 'but they're all right, with good people and not that far away really, means I can see them of a weekend, like. Must be awful for you to take them over to Ireland and not clap eyes on them for six months. I don't blame you going to see them.'

Flo blamed her, but then hadn't Lizzie expected that? When had the woman ever approved of anything she'd ever done?

'What about the house?'

Lizzie longed to retort. 'What about the house? Hitler could deprive us of it at any time?' But this time Flo had a point, because empty houses could soon be occupied by squatters and they would be the devil's own to shift when she came back. So she controlled the anger that this woman's malevolent stance and voice evoked in her and said, 'Maybe Neil would take it on for a bit?'

'Who'd see to him?'

God, the woman hardly did a hand's turn for the man now. And he was a man, well able, surely to God, to see to himself. 'Well, doesn't he get his breakfast and dinner out now?' she said. 'He could come to you for his evening meal if he wanted, but it would be someone in the house and he could take over the rent, like.'

And while Flo was ruminating over Lizzie's words and trying to find fault with them, she added, 'Steve was all for me going over and checking that the children are all right.'

Flo was silent and so Lizzie knew Steve had written in the same vein to her. When Flo did eventually speak, it was to say, 'How long do you intend to stay?'

'I don't know yet,' Lizzie said evasively. 'A few months.'

'A few months!' Flo shrieked.

'Aye, maybe. I'll have to see how things pan out.'

'How things pan out,' Flo repeated with scorn. 'Things have panned out, my girl, and let me tell you, your place is here, waiting for your man, with or without your children. A couple of weeks is all the time you need.'

Lizzie lifted her head, her eyes flashed fire, but still she controlled herself. 'Surely,' she said, 'I am the judge of that.'

'We'll see about that, girl. See what our Steve thinks.'

Lizzie knew what Steve would think, for he'd told her clearly enough, so Flo could go and drown herself, and she went on with the preparations for the journey. By Monday, 30th June she was ready, tickets bought, letters written, welcome assured. Violet uncharacteristically kissed Lizzie goodbye with tears in her own eyes. She was worried by the unfathomable sadness Lizzie seemed to carry around with her, which deepened as the day of departure drew near. She had a near-desolate look in her eyes and Violet was very anxious about the reception she would have when she told her parents the real reason that she was back home.

If Lizzie could have allowed herself to talk of it she would have said Violet's apprehensions were nothing compared to her own. But she couldn't talk about it, not without breaking down and crying her eyes out and what earthly good would that be, for however she felt there was no alternative plan.

By the time the train pulled in at Donegal Station, Lizzie felt sick with fear; but as she stepped onto the platform she saw her two children running towards her with cries of, 'Mammy'. She put down her cases and crouched with her arms held wide and was nearly knocked on her back as Tom cannoned into her, while Niamh approached her more gently but just as eagerly. Lizzie hugged them both tight, realising afresh how she had missed them, and she felt a lump in her throat.

Johnnie came after the children, and when they eventually let her go he too embraced her. 'Ah, Lizzie, the weans aren't the only ones to have missed you,' he said. 'Even Mammy, never one to show her feelings overmuch, is like a dog with two tails.'

Lizzie didn't answer, for every word Johnnie said was like a hammer blow. The more her mother looked forward to her coming home, the greater her disappointment would be when Lizzie told her what she'd come home to tell her.

Johnnie didn't notice Lizzie's silence then, for the children were chattering away and he was busy stowing Lizzie's luggage in the cart. But later, with the children drowsily quiet, for it was late for them, the silence stretched out between Johnnie and Lizzie and eventually Johnnie said, 'Are you all right, Liz? I mean, are you just tired, or is there something wrong, for I never remember seeing you this quiet before?'

How Lizzie longed to tell him, this brother of hers who she knew would never doubt a word she said and would help and support her in anything she wanted to do. He would listen and not interrupt as the horse clip clopped along the quiet country road, and if she got upset in the telling he would rein the horse in and take Lizzie in his arms. But Lizzie's children were in the cart and they must never know of that night, and really she knew her mother had to be the first to be told of it. So she said, 'No, Johnnie, there's nothing wrong. I'm just tired.'

Johnnie looked at her strangely, but said nothing, and Lizzie forced a laugh. 'Anyway,' she said, 'you are a fine one to talk, for you have scarcely opened your mouth either. Don't you go worrying your head about me, for I'll be as right as rain after a good night's sleep.'

As the cart clattered across the cobbled yard of the farmhouse, the children were roused from their semi-slumber and Tom leapt from the cart before it had stopped, so careless in his excitement he almost fell under the wheels, earning him a reprimand from his uncle. But nothing could dim his excitement that day and he looked not the slightest bit abashed.

'Come on now,' Johnnie said to Niamh as he unloaded the luggage. 'Catch up your mammy's bag and go and ask your Granny has she the kettle on.'

Niamh caught the bag Johnnie threw and ran across the cobbled yard, shouting, 'Granny, Granny, Mammy's here.'

Johnnie grinned at Lizzie. 'She'd have to be deaf not to know already,' he said, and added, more gently, 'Go in now and rest yourself,' and Lizzie followed her daughter with Tom hanging on to her hand for grim death.

She stood at the farmhouse door for a moment and drank in the familiarity of it all. Inside, right beside the door on a stool was the bucket of water from the well. Beside it was a scrubbed wooden table with chairs and stools tucked beneath it, and in front of the small lace-trimmed window was the settle, which could be opened up if a spare bed was needed, only the wooden seat was almost hidden by bright cushions. Before the hearth was set a small settee and a chair and a couple of creepie stools made of bog oak. Above the glowing peat was hung a simmering pot and the smell was making Lizzie's mouth water. To one side of the fireplace was the press holding all the everyday delft, and to the other side was the bed for Lizzie's parents, surrounded by curtains for privacy.

Against the far wall was the sideboard and wooden bin where the oaten meal was stored, but pride of place beside the door that led to the first bedroom was the dresser. Polished to a high shine, it held the best delft – the willow-pattern dinner-set plates and dishes were displayed and cups hung on the hooks, and she remembered sitting as a child before the fire, the firelight and lamps catching the delft and making it sparkle.

Her mother turned from the press, her arms full of dishes, her dancing granddaughter before her, and smiled at Lizzie as Johnnie came in after her with the case and caused her to step into the room. 'Hallo, Mammy.'

Catherine put the dishes on the table and put her arms about her child. 'Welcome home, Lizzie,' she said. 'I'll rest easier in my bed, knowing you are here and safe, for a wee while at least.' She held her daughter away from her for a moment. 'You look well,' she continued, 'And I'm glad to see you have gained weight, for while it might be fashionable to be thin, you were too skinny for my liking. You look good now, you carry the weight well, so you do. Come on up to the table now and I'll endeavour to keep you well-fed at least.'

And then, turning to her son, she said, 'Will you go out to the byre and see if your father is finished with the milking? I've kept the water hot for his wash, so.'

Johnnie turned and went out, and Lizzie, too choked

to speak, helped her mother lay the table. She knew she had to tell her things that would wipe the delight from her face, and she trembled, fearful of her reaction and guilty for bringing shame to her door.

But she decided she'd say nothing yet awhile, for the urgency had gone now that she was here. For a few days at least she would bask in her parents' approval, be the feted daughter home at last, and later, before the fire, the children tucked into their bed, she talked and laughed with her parents and Johnnie as if she hadn't a care in the world.

Eventually she had to seek her bed, and she was moved when her father put his hands on her shoulders as she stood at the threshold to the bedroom and said, 'It's good to have you home, cutie dear.' Tears stung Lizzie's eyes as she kissed her father's creased cheek, for she couldn't have spoken without breaking down. She went into the room, undressed and got into bed beside the sleeping Niamh, curling against her, taking comfort from her warm little body, and tried to sleep.

CHAPTER FOURTEEN

For a week, Lizzie said nothing. She visited all her brothers and sisters and their families and she and Tressa spent time together. Lizzie wondered if she should tell her cousin. Once, she wouldn't even have had to think about it, but that Tressa was gone, swallowed up in the demands and needs of her children, so that she seemed to have no time or energy for anything else.

Anyway, Lizzie thought Tressa may not need to know anything and maybe it wouldn't be wise, for if she was to tell her mother, Margaret could always let it slip in the shop as she served the customers. Tressa was always saying her mother liked nothing better than a good gossip. Lizzie knew she was right, for though she liked her Aunt Margaret, everyone knew she could never be trusted to keep anything quiet for long. No, Lizzie decided, it was better that Tressa too was kept in ignorance.

Lizzie enjoyed her time with her children and the weather was kind to them. Once Niamh had come home from school, Lizzie would often take them down to the shore where the big Atlantic rollers cascaded onto the beach. It delighted the children, and they all leapt over the waves, squealing at the cold of the water slapping at their legs. They liked the feel of sand between their toes as they walked or they'd kneel to build big sandcastles or perhaps clamber over the rocks and search the rock pools for anything interesting, before settling down to the picnic tea Lizzie had made up for them. The children were so happy she was there, for neither of them had realised how much they had missed her, and Lizzie treasured every day.

After Mass on Sunday, Father Brady spoke welcoming Lizzie and he talked kindly to the children and made them laugh. Lizzie had decided that morning at Mass that the time had come to tell her mother, for she could see changes in her body and she wanted to tell her before Catherine tumbled to it herself.

Later that evening, she listened to the children's prayers before bed and asked Niamh the questions in the catechism that she needed to know before she could take Communion. 'It's just a week now, Mammy, I can hardly wait,' Niamh said.

Lizzie remembered her own excitement. Niamh's dress hung in the wardrobe, protected by the thin plastic sheets either side of it, and the white sandals and socks, brand-new, stood at the back, ready for the child to wear the following Sunday.

'I'm glad you're going to be here, Mammy,' Niamh went on. 'When I wrote and asked, Granny said you mightn't be let, now you're working an' all.'

'Oh, I told them,' Lizzie assured her daughter. 'I

said my wee girl is taking her First Communion and I had to be there and was taking no nonsense, so don't you worry your head.'

Niamh giggled and said, 'I love you, Mammy.'

'And I you, pet,' Lizzie said. 'Lie down now and go to sleep or you'll have bags beneath your eyes and be a sight by next Sunday.' And she bent and kissed her small daughter, turned down the lamp and left the room.

That evening, Lizzie waited till both her children were in bed, Johnnie out on business of his own and her father checking the stock, before attempting to speak to her mother. She knew her father would be quite a while. On fine nights like this he was in no hurry to come in; he'd sit on a wall for a while and have a smoke of his pipe, and since Lizzie had been home he'd tended to linger longer, giving the two women time to talk, Lizzie presumed.

That evening she was glad of it. Catherine had made tea and Lizzie took it and they sat together before the fire. Lizzie's heart thumped against her ribs and her mouth was so dry she took a gulp of tea, scalding though it was.

She licked her lips, and, doubting things would ever be the same between them after this, she took a deep breath and said, 'You know you noticed I'd put weight on, Mammy?'

'Aye, and it suits you. I told you that too.'

'Aye, Mammy, but d'you see, there's a reason for it. I'm . . . I'm pregnant, Mammy.'

'Ah, that's it,' Catherine said. 'I knew there was

something a sort of bloom about you, but I never thought. And God knows, I hardly think it very sensible, the way you're placed with Steve away and you in the middle of war . . . but there, I suppose we must be grateful for what God sends. You didn't tell me Steve had leave?'

'He hasn't had any leave.'

She saw her mother's eyes widen and then, as the realisation of her words sank in, she saw her mouth drop open in shock. Her hands, holding the cup, were shaking so badly that she was in danger of spilling the tea all over herself. Lizzie put her own cup on the hearth and took her mother's cup from her and knelt on the rug before her and took hold of her hands. 'Mammy, I have to tell you something now, something awful and terrible that happened to me, and I swear to God on my own children's lives that every word passing my lips will be the truth.'

She saw the hard mask fix on her mother's face, the mask she'd learnt to dread as a child, and she felt her heart sink. She told her first of life in the blackout. She'd spoken of this before on her holidays home the previous summer, and the time she'd brought the children in the autumn, but in passing only. Now she endeavoured to get her mother to see the horror of it all.

'It's dense, Mammy, so that you can almost touch it. Sometimes there is a moon and twinkling stars, but these are often obscured by clouds and the smoke-riddled air that many a time turns to swirling, stinking fog that is smelt rather than seen. That's how it was that night. I had a torch, but the batteries had given out and it was the time also that Violet was ill, so I was on my own coming home, and a lonely, cold journey it was, for no trams were running because of the fog.

'When I got down the entry and was nearly at the house, I was so relieved, and then suddenly there was a shape before me. I wasn't alarmed, that sort of thing happens often in the blackout, and I apologised and made some comment.

'There was no reply. Whoever it was had no time for pleasantries. He grabbed me, a hand around my mouth so that I could make no sound. I tried to struggle, though, and then I felt an agonising pain in my side and I fell to the ground. I remember no more. He must have dashed my head on the cobbles, the doctor said, though I have no recollection of it. Whoever it was and for reasons known only to himself, he had stabbed me in the stomach. The doctor said the coat saved my life.

'The next thing I remember is waking up in Violet's. She'd tripped over me in the yard and she'd found my knickers lying beside me and put them into her pocket.'

'You have no idea who did this?' Catherine said, scarcely able to believe it.

'None,' Lizzie said. 'The police were called. They had to be, for the doctor insisted. He said they couldn't have a madman like that loose in the blackout. After the attack, no women went out alone. A lot of women at the factory were collected by any men folk they had left at home and there were more police drafted into the area.'

'But he was never found?'

'No, and as far as I know he attacked no one else, though he could of course have been killed in one of the raids.'

'But if he just attacked you, it must have been someone you knew.'

'Mammy, I wouldn't know. I could see nothing.'

'You must have encouraged him.'

'In that dark and black night? Encourage him to stab me?'

'Not then,' Catherine said, 'but I've heard of the lax morals in England. Women enjoying themselves with the men away.'

'Mammy, I never go over the doorstep except to work or Mass or to Violet's next door.'

'I don't understand.'

'No more do I, Mammy, and the police too were baffled.'

'And this man . . . You let him . . . ?'

'Let's get this straight, Mammy,' Lizzie said angrily. 'I didn't let anyone do anything. I wasn't aware of any of it. I was unconscious and bleeding. I had no idea what he had done and have no recollection of it.'

'Well, you know now all right!' Catherine snapped. 'How far on are you?'

'Nearly five months.'

'Oh Holy Mother of God,' Catherine wailed. 'I can't believe you've done this. Brought this shame to our door.'

'I know, and I am sorry,' Lizzie said. 'Truly I am, but Mammy, it wasn't of my making. Surely you can see that?'

'What I see, girl, is a woman with a swollen belly and her husband overseas this long while. We won't be able to hold our heads up. We'll be dragged through the mud.'

'What could I do about it, Mammy?' Lizzie asked. 'Just tell me that?'

'You have no right to demand answers of me, and don't you forget it,' Catherine said, her worry turning to anger. 'Why were you attacked and none other? I think there's something here you're not telling me?'

'Mammy, I swear to you,' Lizzie pleaded. 'Please listen? I want nothing to do with this child, begat of violence. Do you know of a place I can go to have the child and afterwards leave it with the nuns?'

'So you can forget all about it and go on with your life?'

Lizzie sighed. 'Well,' she said, 'what is the alternative, Mammy? And in your anger over the condition I'm in now, remember what I told you first. The man nearly killed me. He had a damned good try.'

'I remember all you've said. And I know this much,' Catherine continued, 'I'll never be told the truth if I ask from now till doomsday.'

She sighed heavily. 'I will discuss these things with your father and we'll have to have a word with the priest.'

'Shall I have speak to daddy?'

'You will not,' Catherine said. 'You've said enough for one day anyway. You keep your mouth shut. I'll speak with your father. Get yourself into the room before he comes in.'

* * *

Next morning, Seamus could hardly bear to look at Lizzie and spoke not at all. Her mother told her in clipped tones that her father would take Niamh up to the school in Ballintra that morning and talk with the priest, while Johnnie would look after Tom until the discussions were over.

Lizzie had known Father Brady all her life. He'd christened her, christened them all at St Bridget's in Ballintra and later was a regular visitor to the county school. He'd heard her first confession, administered Holy Communion and was with her when she was confirmed by the Bishop at the abbey in Donegal town. He was a regular visitor to her parents' home and often stayed for a few words with them all after Mass, and she had always counted the man as friendly and kind. She would have said he liked her. He certainly had when she was small.

But the man who strode down the lane with her father later that morning bore no relation to the priest she'd known for years. The grim expression on his face and the very stance of him made him appear a stranger to her.

Johnnie spotted the men and said, 'I'm away then, Mammy.'

'Aye, son.'

'Come on, Tom,' Johnnie said to his small nephew.

Tom was by his uncle's side in a minute. 'Where are we going?'

'To Owen's,' Johnnie answered. 'He needs me to give a hand with something, and I thought you might want to come along and play with your cousin Chris.'

'Oh yeah.'

'Put on your jacket then. For all the day's fine now, we might be away a long time and it could turn colder before we come home.'

Tom did as he was bid and Catherine scurried about buttoning him into his jacket, despite his protests, and readied a wee bottle of rhubarb preserve, for Owen's wife was partial to it.

Johnnie took the opportunity to sidle up to his sister. 'Sorry for your trouble, Lizzie,' he said.

'Johnnie . . .'

'Hush, don't let Mammy hear. The way I was told, I think you're more of a victim than sinner. Remember that when it's over.'

'Aye. Aye, I will.'

He turned from her as if a word had never passed between them, and said to Tom, 'Are you ready yet?'

'Course.'

'Well, come on. What are we waiting for?'

Tom shrugged his shoulders. 'I dunno,' he said, and Johnnie laughed. Even Lizzie, with emotions running ragged around her body, smiled at her small son.

'Are you not giving Mammy and Granny a kiss?'

Tom gave a sigh, anxious to be gone, and the hug and kiss he gave Lizzie were perfunctory. Then he was across the room after his uncle, passing the priest in the doorway. He hadn't seen the priest coming down the lane, but because it wasn't unusual for the priest to call, he smiled and said, 'Hallo, Father.'

'Hallo, Tom,' the priest answered heartily. 'Where are you bound for?'

'Uncle Owen's, Father,' Tom said.

The priest's eyes met those of Catherine's above the

child and he nodded his head. But to Tom he said, 'Be a good boy for your uncle now and enjoy yourself.'

'Aye, I will, Father,' Tom called. 'Bye, Father.'

Lizzie watched her young son almost scampering up the lane holding on to his uncle's hand, and heard his high-pitched voice rising into the summer air as Catherine turned to greet the priest. 'I've got the pot boiling for a drink, Father.'

Lizzie was silent and desperately afraid, a queer weakness had affected her limbs since she'd seen the look pass between the priest and her mother. It had also affected her mouth and she seemed unable to speak.

But the priest spoke to her. 'Come, Elizabeth. Sit yourself down. You and I need to have a little chat.'

Elizabeth, Lizzie thought. I've not been called that since my school days. She forced her legs to obey her, to move forward, and she crossed the room like a zombie. The priest had a chair pulled out for her.

She was aware of her father standing behind her motionless. Her mother was busying herself at the hearth as the priest said sternly, 'Your father's been to see me with shocking news, Elizabeth, absolutely disgraceful news. He says you are with child.'

Lizzie had never noticed how small the priest's brown eyes were, or how cold. And he'd stated the bare facts only. She wondered what he'd been told. She glanced over at her mother and wondered if she'd even told her father the whole truth.

Maybe not, but she'd put the priest right now, and maybe her father too.

'Father, in early February I was attacked. I was

stabbed and my head smashed against a wall and I lost consciousness.'

The priest lifted his hand. 'I understand that is what you want your parents to believe.'

'It's what happened, Father.'

Lizzie didn't imagine the look that came over the priest nor the curl of the lip. Incensed, she leapt to her feet. 'I'll show you, Father,' she cried, and she ran to the room to fetch her coat. 'I brought it especially to show you.'

By the time she returned, her mother had put two earthenware mugs of orange-coloured tea on the table and some buttered oaten cake and barn brack and the priest was helping himself. 'Delicious, Catherine,' he said as he finished the slice of barn brack and licked the butter from his fingers. 'The sign of a good woman, eh, Seamus?'

'Aye, Father. I've a good woman and I try to be a good husband and father. That's why I can't understand this trouble brought to my door.'

'Daddy, I couldn't help it. Will you look, Father? The place where the knife went in has been darned, but you can see it clearly.'

But the darn had been expertly fixed and the fibres had begun knitting together. The priest gave a wry smile. 'Such a mark could have been made by many things. But, d'you see, Lizzie, this changes nothing. The result is the same. You are having a baby, and though you are married this child is not and cannot be your husband's. Your mother says you want nothing to do with it after it's born?'

'No, nothing,' Lizzie said dejectedly, knowing it was

useless to protest any more. If she tried to show them the scar the knife had left, the priest would probably be shocked at her exposing herself in such a way. And the cut in the coat could have been caused by anything. None of them would listen, they weren't interested enough to listen, and in a way the priest was right. At the end of the day, the way the child was conceived was immaterial.

'I know of a place the other side of Sligo,' the priest went on. 'Thank God, this is a rare occurrence, but I have had occasions to use this home in the past. It is run by the Sisters of Charity and when the woman or girl is delivered of the child, a good Catholic home is found for it. This is presumably what you want?'

'Yes, Father.'

'Well then, Elizabeth, if you will collect your things.'

'My things, Father? Surely you don't intend me to go now?'

'Aye.'

'No, no, I can't do that,' Lizzie said. 'I can't, d'you see. I . . . I mean . . . It's Niamh, she is taking her First Communion in just a few days now. She wants me here. I've heard her catechism every night since I arrived.'

'Surely you are not suggesting sullying your wee daughter's special day by attending it in such a sinful condition.'

'What exactly are you saying, Father?' Lizzie was aware of a feeling of dread stealing over her.

'What I am saying, Elizabeth,' the priest said sternly, 'is that there is no way you will be allowed into the

278

church to see your daughter make her First Holy Communion. And I might say I am astounded that you seem determined on this course of action and that you are not bowing your head in shame.'

'You can't prevent me from attending chapel.'

'Believe me, Elizabeth, I can, 'the priest said, his voice rising in anger at Lizzie's defiant tone. 'And I will.'

Seamus stood looking at Lizzie as if he hated her, but surely her mother would understand and back her up. It was only a few more days, for pity's sake. 'Mammy?' she said in appeal.

'Will you not listen to the priest, Lizzie?' Catherine said sharply.

'Come, come, Elizabeth,' the priest said impatiently. 'We've wasted enough time.'

And then Lizzie saw what the Church was capable of and knew she had no power to stand against it, and knew too that neither of her parents would put out a hand to help her. Yet she tried once more. 'Father, please? I have done no wrong.'

'The state of you belies that, Elizabeth.'

'But, it wasn't my fault.'

'Even if that were true,' the priest said, and by his very tone Lizzie knew he didn't believe she'd had no hand in it, that perhaps she'd even welcomed it, invited another man's attentions. Christ Almighty!

'My dear Elizabeth, would you risk bringing further shame upon your parents? You say you have done no wrong. What wrong have they done, pray, that you must insist on this course of action? By your own admission this distressing incident happened in February. Next week is the second week in July. You are five months pregnant. Any at that ceremony could guess, and if then you disappeared suddenly they would put two and two together.'

Even in the midst of her confusion and distress, Lizzie realised that a lot of what the priest said was right. Seen sideways in certain clothes it was noticeable; she'd checked in the dressing-table mirror in the room.

'I do see all you say,' she said to the priest. 'But surely I haven't got to go right now? I must at least say goodbye to my children. Please, Father, you can see that, can't you?'

'What I see,' the priest said coldly, 'is a defiant and shameless girl, who even now is making demands. This is not your decision alone, Elizabeth. I have telephoned the nuns and they are expecting you and I am giving up my very valuable time to drive you there. We must go now and speedily, for it is a fair distance away.'

Lizzie took a gulp of tea. This couldn't be happening to her; she was not to be shunted away in the priest's car without a word of explanation to her children. She remembered how happy they were to see her and she felt tears sting her eyes.

'Both children will be told your mother-in-law is ill and you had to return home, and that's what we will tell any others that ask. They are but children and will get over any disappointment.'

'People will not believe that. The postmistress knows I've had no letters or telegrams.'

'Yes,' Father Brady said. 'That's why I will say I received a call from the hospital and came straight down to fetch you. Then, if any have spotted my car at the head of the lane, it is explained.'

'You've thought it all out,' Lizzie said bitterly.

'Someone had to, girl, when you drop us in the shit,' Seamus snapped. 'Beg your pardon, Father. Will there be any charge for this place?'

'No, Seamus,' Father Brady said. 'The nuns see to it all out of the goodness of their hearts and as a way of serving God. The place was set up in memory of Mary Magdalene, who was turned from a life of prostitution by our Good Shepherd himself. The girls are also encouraged to work while they are there, for isn't it true that the devil makes work for idle hands?'

'Aye, that's true enough, Father.'

'Lizzie's no stranger to work at least,' Catherine said with a sigh. 'What manner of work is it, Father?'

'Well, as I understand it, they keep the place clean and help cook the meals, and then they take in laundry from the places around and the convent is paid for that, and that pays for the girls' keep, you see? In fact, it is known as a Magdalene Laundry.'

To Catherine and Seamus the place sounded ideal, and in time this whole ordeal would be just an awful memory. However, Lizzie didn't seem to see it that way. She sat in her seat stunned, making no effort to move, and suddenly Seamus was so angry with her, the cause of potential shame on him, on the whole family, that he had the urge to shake her till her bones rattled. He was mindful of the priest, however, and he just growled out, 'Go on, Lizzie, will you, for Christ's sake. Get your things gathered up and out of my sight, before I forget myself altogether and take my belt off to you, big as you are.'

Lizzie turned and looked at her father as she got to

her feet and saw how he was struggling to restrain the anger sparking from his dark eyes, and she shivered.

She turned her gaze to her mother and said, 'Can I come back, Mammy?'

'Not at all, child. You go back to England when you're out of that place. People will wonder if you come back here. Come back next summer.'

'Next summer?' Lizzie cried. 'I'm not to see the children for a whole year?'

'Think yourself lucky we're allowing you back at all,' Seamus said. 'Some people would disown their daughters totally.'

'Catherine,' the priest added, 'time is pressing. Could you make up some refreshments for the journey?'

'Oh, certainly, Father, no problem,' Catherine said, and Lizzie knew she'd lost – lost everything – and she went into her room.

Her belongings were few, for most things were tight on her now, and she was back in a few minutes. 'Well, bye then,' she said bleakly.

She would have welcomed a hug or kiss, an assurance that she'd always have a place there, but she got none of these. Her father just gave a grunt and Catherine said, 'Be a good girl now, Lizzie,' and Lizzie gave a nod as she followed the priest out of the door and up the lane.

Sometime during that long journey down the country way past Sligo, Lizzie and Father Brady must have talked, but all Lizzie's memories of the journey were wiped out when she saw the grim, grey building in front of them surrounded by a high brick wall and knew they were heading straight for it.

Her knees began to tremble and she turned panicky eyes on the priest. 'Oh, Father.'

'Easy, Elizabeth, easy now,' the priest said as they drove in through the wrought-iron gates, which he explained had been left open for him. 'It's the only way and it's only for a wee while.'

Of course it was. A few months was all. Lizzie forced herself to take deep breaths, to try and calm herself as the priest got out to close the gates again, but the high wall surrounding the whole place didn't help her feel at ease. It was ten or maybe twelve-foot high. Too high to climb over anyway, and later Lizzie was to hear about the shards of broken glass that were mortared into the top of it.

The priest pulled the car to a halt on the gravel path. There were five grey steps to the front door made of solid wood, reinforced with steel bands, with the words 'St Agnes's Convent' on a brass plaque above it. A nun opened the door and Lizzie blinked, for she hadn't been aware the priest had rung the bell. 'Come in, Father. Sister Jude is waiting for you.'

She made no greeting to Lizzie, but led the way down a long, wide corridor, the floor patterned in squares of black and white. Every day, every floor was scrubbed on hands and knees and then mopped dry, and Lizzie was to have her share of it, but the girls at that time of day were all working in the laundry to the back of the building.

They were brought to a halt before a door with 'Sister Jude' on yet another brass plaque screwed to the front of it. 'Wait here,' the nun said curtly to Lizzie, and then she gave a knock and at the answering call put her head around the door and said, 'Father Brady.' Then she smiled at him and opened the door wide. 'Go in, Father.'

Father Brady had carried Lizzie's case in from the car and he said now, 'Shall I leave this with Elizabeth?'

'What's in it?'

'Clothes, I imagine. Bits and pieces.'

'She has no need of clothes,' the nun said, casting an eye over Lizzie as if she was a slug she'd just found beneath a stone. 'All is provided. I'll take them, Father.'

The priest handed the case over and the nun went off with it and the priest entered the room. With the door closed behind him, Lizzie felt very isolated. She wondered where all the other girls and women were. Surely she wasn't the only one there, in that great mausoleum of a place. Her boss at the munitions works in Birmingham always said women never stopped talking; like chattering magpies, he'd said they were. But here there was a grim, forbidding silence.

And then, suddenly, the door was opened and the priest said, 'You can go in.' He pressed Lizzie's arm as he passed. 'Be a good girl now.'

Lizzie didn't want him to go, though he'd brought her here, for he was her link from home. 'Father, can you stay?'

'It would serve no purpose, child,' the priest said, shaking his head. 'Go on now. Don't keep the good sister waiting.'

It took all Lizzie's courage to step into that room, close the door and face the nun across the desk. Her skin was the colour of putty with eyes of hardened steel that glistened with malice, and she had a long, beaked nose and a mean, cruel mouth.

'So you are Elizabeth Gillespie, and you are a married woman who can't keep her legs together, even though your husband is risking his life daily? You have let down your entire family, your parents, brothers and sisters, and even your own two wee children. You are a sinner, Elizabeth Gillespie, and I hope you are aware of it?'

Something snapped in Lizzie, the shock of it, her parents' reaction, the way the blame was laid at her door, and the mention of the two wee children she'd seen for such a short time, especially Niamh away at school all day.

She leapt across the room and shrieked into the face of the startled nun, 'I'm no sinner, you mean-faced bugger. I know full well who the sinner is in this, the foul monster who attacked and raped me. He's the sinner.'

The power of the first slap across her cheek caused her head to spin; the second to the other cheek sent her reeling into the bookcase dislodging the books.

At the commotion two nuns rushed in. One held Lizzie's arms tightly and the other rushed across to ask, 'Are you all right, Sister Jude?'

'Perfectly,' the nun said in clipped tones. 'But our new guest needs a lesson in manners. Fetch me the birch cane.' Lizzie had felt the strength of the nun's arms in the slaps she'd administered and she expected the caning to hurt. There was nothing to be done by resisting, except to enrage Sister Jude further, so she pulled up her dress as the nuns directed.

Out of the corner of her eye she saw the cane raised and the nun's arm flexed, her face contorted. She braced herself as it whistled through the air, but couldn't prevent the gasp that escaped her as the cane sliced through her cotton knickers. No more, she vowed, clenching her teeth. She will never make me cry out again.

The power of the next stroke of the cane caused her body to bounce, and the next, and by the time the nun struck her for the fourth time she swayed on her feet and saw black spots before her eyes. She was terrified she would faint, that she would show weakness before this woman, this heinous excuse for a human being that was trying to beat her into submission.

She bore the next two strokes valiantly, fighting with waves of sickness, and although the pain was extreme she made no sound.

The nun seemed disappointed. 'Take her away to the bathroom, Sister Maria,' she said, 'and cut nearly every hair from her head.'

Lizzie turned and looked at her in shocked disbelief and the nun smiled. 'Oh yes, Elizabeth Gillespie, there is no place for vanity here. Your hair will be shorn, and because you are a sinner you cannot be called the same name as the mother of St John the Baptist. We have other names here. Yours will be Pansy. Do I make myself clear?'

Lizzie couldn't believe what she was hearing. This place was surely worse than prison, and like a prison there was no way out and they were ruled over by these malicious, oppressed women that went under the name of nuns. Well, they'd not break her, but for now she'd put up with it.

A prod in the back told her the nun expected an answer. You wouldn't know what to do in this place that you wouldn't be beaten for. 'Yes, Sister Jude.'

It hurt to walk; it hurt to stand. Her bottom was stinging like she'd sat on a red-hot griddle, but she forced herself to walk with her head held high and her back straight and followed Sister Maria without wincing or faltering, when really she wanted to lie down in a corner and weep.

'Now, I'm Sister Maria and this is Sister Clement,' the nun said to Lizzie when they reached the bathroom. 'Sister Clement will run the bath while I cut off this hair.' She ran her finger through it as she spoke and Lizzie did nothing, she didn't push her hand away or even toss her head back, though her nerves seemed stretched to breaking point to prevent her doing these things. She didn't want to show these vindictive women she cared what they did to her.

She sat on the chair indicated, unable to help wincing when her bottom made contact with the hard board, and this seemed to amuse both nuns who watched the dark brown curls and waves toss down to the floor. The only sound was the water gushing into the bath, filling the room with steam, and the nun's voice in her ear as she hacked roughly at her hair, muttering about vanity and the sin of pride.

Lizzie felt sick as she looked at the beautiful curls and waves. In a way, the nun was right, she was proud of her hair. It was her shining glory and she kept it in good condition. She wanted to weep, but she wouldn't. That's what they'd like, these nuns. She told herself to get it in perspective. After all, set against what was in her belly, what did the loss of her hair matter compared to having this child and being able to walk away without it, to go back to Birmingham? Life with Steve would be a bed of roses after this, she thought. After the war she'd have her children back too, and no one would be any the wiser.

The nun put down the scissors and went over her head again with clippers, and then when she stopped she snatched up a mirror. 'Look at yourself, slut,' she commanded. 'See if your fancy man would look at you now.'

Looking back at Lizzie was a white-faced woman with pain-filled, confused eyes and blue lines of strain pulling at her mouth and running down each side of her nose, and the whole lot topped with little more than fuzz on her head.

'Well?'

Lizzie had been so shocked at her appearance she'd forgotten the question. 'Are you a simpleton?' the nun said.

'No, no, Sister.'

'Well then, I asked you will your fancy man look twice at you now?'

It was useless to protest that there was no fancy man. 'No, Sister.'

'He took what he wanted and cast you aside, and you, you dirty slut, allowed him to.'

I didn't. I didn't. Lizzie longed to cry.

'Well, for your moments of stolen sinful pleasure, you must pay dearly,' the nun said. 'It is penance offered up to the good Lord. Pour some disinfectant in the bath, all whores need that,' she directed the other nun, and then she said to Lizzie, 'Remove your clothes.'

Lizzie didn't want to strip before these women. They were strangers to her, however holy they purported to be, and it didn't seem at all right. But already she'd felt the reaction to a disobeyed order here and she pulled her clothes off quickly, and then, almost automatically, wrapped her arms around her body, which was bent over in an effort to cover herself. 'Stand up straight.'

Lizzie couldn't believe she'd heard right. 'Are you deaf, dear Pansy?' Sister Maria asked sarcastically.

'No, Sister.'

'Then stand up!' The bark wouldn't have been out of place in the parade ground and Lizzie jumped and slowly she uncurled herself. 'Arms by your sides.'

She felt vulnerable and helpless and she kept her head lowered in shame as the nun came up close to her. Sister Clement was at her back, although Lizzie wasn't aware of it until she spoke. 'She has a fine pattern on her bum,' she said, 'and it's a big enough bum too.'

'She had to be reminded of her manners,' Sister Maria said. 'Five minutes here and shrieking at Sister Jude. It wasn't to be borne.'

'No indeed.'

Lizzie felt as if her nerves were pulled tight. She wanted to turn and face the nun who prowled at her back, but then that would leave her exposed at the front and Sister Maria was there. Any minute she expected to feel the nuns hands on her bottom, which felt as if it were on fire, feel her fingers tracing the marks of the cane. She knew she'd scream if the nun

289

did that and damn the consequences, for she wouldn't be able to help herself.

But the nun said nothing and didn't touch any part of Lizzie's body, though she was close enough for Lizzie to feel the nun's breath on her skin. With her ears on high alert for any movement Sister Clement might make, she watched Sister Maria as she paraded in front of her. 'You have a fine body. Do you think so. Pansy?'

Now what response should she make to that, Lizzie wondered? 'Yes, Sister,' seemed safest.

'Soon it will be swollen with the child inside you.'

'Yes, Sister.' God, thought Lizzie, where was all this leading?

Suddenly, and without warning, Sister Maria flicked at both her nipples. Lizzie couldn't help the gasp of pain, nor moving her arms to enfold her throbbing breasts. 'Put your arms down,' Sister Maria hissed. 'I'll not have you standing there sticking your breasts out like that. No shame in you at all. Get into that bath and scrub yourself.'

Lizzie was glad to slide under the water away from the eyes of the nuns, and though it hurt her to sit and the disinfectant stung the open sores on her bottom, the water was soothing on her smarting nipples. She scrubbed herself from head to foot with the hard cake of soap and flannel she was handed, even pouring water over the stubble on her head.

Sister Clement handed her a coarse towel and she stepped from the bath and began to dry herself. Sister Maria came in with a handful of clothes. The first was a wide strip of calico, which Sister Maria wound around her breasts so tightly she wondered if she'd be able to breathe. She fastened this to the side with a knot and it effectively squeezed Lizzie's breasts almost flat, though they ached in protest. This was covered by a shapeless smock that hung over Lizzie's narrow shoulders and a pair of knickers so large a knot had to be tied in the waistband. An elastic band with suspenders dangling from it held up thick stockings, and instead of shoes she wore boots. A shapeless cotton hat that Sister Clement shoved onto her head and secured with kirby grips completed the hideous outfit.

Lizzie didn't need the mirror to know she looked dreadful. She felt dreadful, but no matter, she told herself. She supposed it was all part of the penance, and in a few months it would all be over. No one would see her except those in the same boat.

'Now,' Sister Maria said, 'you've missed your lunch and have a fine long afternoon before you, and as we don't believe in idleness here I will take you along to the laundry.'

Lizzie thought this needed no response and she followed the nun to the back of the building.

CHAPTER FIFTEEN

Lizzie never forgot her first sight of the Magdalene Laundry. As soon as Sister Maria opened the door, the moist heat hit her and she stood at the top of the steps and stared. The very air was clammy, steam rose in the air and it smelt of soap and soda.

To one side, three boilers bubbled away. Two had their lids open and girls were pulling clothes from the boiler with wooden tongs into poss tubs, while other girls were standing by deep stone sinks or galvanised baths, scrubbing at articles of clothing with carbolic soap and washboards. Others were scrubbing at sinks full of foaming suds, or rinsing articles and mangling them, and three girls at the other side were ironing the overflowing baskets of clothes with heavy irons that hissed with steam.

All the girls, Lizzie noticed, were clothed as she was, and each one had a sheen of sweat on their faces. It didn't surprise her, for even as she stood there beads of sweat stood out on her forehead, but what did surprise her was that not one girl's head was turned in her direction.

A prod in the back brought her back to the present and nearly toppled her down the steps. 'What are you gawping at? Think this is a rest home? Got to watch this one, Sister Carmel. She's a born slacker, I'd say.'

The older nun's face was very wrinkled, but her eyes were bright with malice and she surveyed Lizzie disdainfully. 'My name is Sister Carmel,' she said, 'and I am in charge of the laundry; and believe me, there is no slacking of any description tolerated here. Do you understand that, my dear?'

'Yes, Sister.'

'Well now, what name have you been given? It would begin with a P, I think.'

'Yes, Sister,' Lizzie said again. 'Pansy, Sister.'

The nun tittered. 'Well, I hope you're stronger than that wee flower,' she said, 'for you'll need strength and stamina here.'

'I'll leave you to it, Sister.'

'Aye, Sister Maria. I'll see to her, never fear,' the nun said, steering Lizzie towards the boiler. 'Now, you see what these girls are doing? You take the clothes from the boiler and pound them with the poss stick and then pass them over to the sinks to be washed and rinsed. Can you do that?'

'Aye. Yes, Sister.'

It was what Lizzie did anyway, although now, with the children away, her washing wasn't an enormous job, but this she found was back-breaking work. When she had no more clothes left in the boiler, she had to empty it, wash it out, fill it up from the tap, bucket by bucket, put in the soap suds and light the gas for the next load of washing. And then she rubbed her knuckles raw on a washboard while she waited for the water to heat.

But hardest of all was the lack of any form of human kindness. The girls barely looked at each other and never spoke. The nun, Sister Carmel, would sit at her embroidery, head lowered. Lizzie knew without being told that talking was forbidden here and also that the nun would hear a pin drop at fifty yards, and even a whisper wouldn't get past her.

Suddenly, the nun gave a sigh, consulted her watch and began the rosary. Lizzie thought how comforting it was to hear a human voice even raised in prayer and the litany at least gave her a rhythm to work with.

Barely had the rosary finished before the bell went. There was no sound, not even an isolated sigh, and yet Lizzie felt the tension ease. Without a word, girls emptied boilers and poss tubs, drained sinks, hung damp washing in lines criss-crossing the room, wiped down mangles, folded dry, ironed washing and put it into baskets and lined up at the door behind Sister Carmel.

She surveyed the room, and as it was obviously to her satisfaction she led the way from the laundry down the corridor. Lizzie's stomach rumbled. She'd eaten little since the few spoonfuls of porridge she'd managed this morning, for though her mother had packed a more than adequate picnic to sustain her and the priest on the journey here, she'd been too nervous to eat. And she knew as they filed into the room and stood behind the benches before the black refectory table that she'd been right to feel nervous, for this place was worse than anything in her wildest dreams.

Before she sat down, Lizzie caught a glimpse of the nun's tea behind the carved screen, plates of assorted sandwiches, crumpets dripping with butter, slices of fruitcake and a tray of other fancies. They were waited on by older women, dressed in the same garb as the girls wore, but they had nothing covering their heads, their hair wasn't shorn and they wore shoes not boots.

The sight of those middle-aged, nearly old women threw Lizzie into a panic. Dear Christ, what were they doing in such a place? Whatever they'd done had to have been years before.

She sat down carefully but still had to bite her lip to prevent the gasp of pain escaping. She saw the girl sitting beside her look up, and though she spoke not a word her eyes were full of sympathy and Lizzie knew she wouldn't have been the only one in this company of women to be beaten in that way.

Their tea was jam sandwiches, the jam merely smeared across the bread, and a pot of weak tea with little milk and no sugar. Lizzie was used to meagre fare, for rationing had begun to bite and didn't allow for luxury, but she'd seldom got up from a meal almost as hungry as when she'd sat down to it.

After tea there were prayers, the rosary said together, and then it was bedtime, in a bleak dormitory room where she was assigned one of the basic wooden beds. They were set in two rows down either side of the room, a chair beside each bed to take the clothes and a voluminous nightdress tucked underneath the pillow.

The sheets were clean enough, Lizzie thought, stripping back the bed to get into it, but though you'd hardly need blankets in this weather, she hoped there were more for the bitter winter nights. But, she reminded herself, she'd hardly be here for them: the baby would be born in November, before the winter really set in, and she'd be gone from this Godawful place as soon as she was able.

Almost as soon as the light was out and the door banged shut and locked, the girl in the next bed whispered, 'What's your real name?'

It was the first time any of the girls had spoken. It was like living amongst deaf mutes, and Lizzie whispered back, 'Lizzie, but they've christened me Pansy.'

'Aye, I know, I'm the same. They go down the alphabet and when they get to Z they start again I suppose. My name is Celia, but they call me Hetty.'

'Well, I'm P, which means there should be sixteen girls here, but I can only make it twelve,' Lizzie whispered back, for she'd counted them all as they came to bed.

'Aye,' Celia said, and added wistfully, 'Two got out. Babs had an uncle and Gladys a father to speak for them.'

'What d'you mean, "got out"?'

'You are having a baby?'

'Aye, of course. Why else would I be here?'

'Jesus, there's a hundred and one reasons why they put a girl in a place like this. I think sometimes it's because they don't like the look of her. Edna was in here because they thought she was in moral danger. Her mother, a widow woman, playing fast and loose they said.'

'Was she?'

'Edna says not, but who cares. And whether her

mother was free and easy with her favours or not, why stick Edna in a place like this. And she'll be here for years. No father to speak for her, and if her mother is considered immoral she won't be released into her care, so . . .'

'For years! You mean . . . ?'

'You think you'll have the child, hand it to the nuns and walk out of here?'

'Aye.'

'You'll be lucky,' Celia said. 'Mind you, that's what we all thought when we came here first. Didn't you see the old lags fawning around the nuns while we were at tea?'

'Aye.'

'Watch them,' Celia warned. 'They are more vicious and vindictive than some of the nuns at times and they carry tales. They seldom come into the laundry, they see to the nuns' things and clean their living quarters and that, and sleep four to a room. Most have lived here all their lives. It's the only life they know now.'

'But why?'

'You can't get out of here unless you have someone to speak for you,' Celia said, 'and this person should preferably be male.'

'You can't hold grown women prisoner.'

'They can do as they please in this place,' Celia said grimly. 'I think the old people would be afraid to leave now, and so they are in a privileged position.'

'What happens if you just run away?'

'How? Fly over the wall? And even if you managed that where would you run to? One girl tried it. She smuggled herself into the laundry van, but the Guards hunted her down and she was beaten so severely that she was in the infirmary almost a week.'

It sounded incredible to Lizzie. 'They cannot keep me here,' she said fiercely. 'I'm a married woman.'

'Ssh, I wouldn't trust those at the far end. If they go blabbing to the nuns we're in trouble, so keep your voice down.'

'All right . . . but surely they can't.'

'There's not a bloody thing the likes of us can do about any of this. You have to have someone respectable working for you from the outside. What about your husband?'

'Hardly. The child isn't his, he knows nothing about it.'

'Tricky one, eh.'

'It wasn't my fault.'

'I don't care whether it was or wasn't. After this place I'm judging no one.'

But Lizzie had to make it clear. 'I was raped.'

'So was Olga, and by her brother,' Celia said, and added bitterly, 'so he's not going to come hammering on the door for her, is he? She says if he does she'd kill him, even if she has to wait a lifetime to do it. Her little boy was taken away two weeks ago. Sometimes she still cries in her sleep.'

'Well, I won't be doing that,' Lizzie said. 'I don't know who raped me. There was a blackout, you see, in England, and the night was as dark as pitch and he was waiting for me. He stuck a knife in me and knocked me unconscious before anything else. I remember nothing of the rape, and the doctor said if I hadn't been wearing my thick winter coat I'd have died.'

'God,' Celia breathed. 'The more I hear, the more I'm sure men are bastards. My fellow and I were to be married and so I let him, you know, just the once. Next thing I'm pregnant. He's real quiet when I tell him. He says he'll sort something out, but I don't hear from him for a few days and so I call round and he's hightailed it to England. The family claim they have no address. My father brought me here. He said I am no longer his daughter and I have no family but this. Christ, this is Hell on earth, this place.'

There was a catch in Celia's voice and Lizzie felt a lump in her own throat. 'How old are you, Celia?'

'Seventeen,' Celia said, 'and sometimes I think you know life isn't worth living. I suppose that's how Candy felt.'

'You mean she killed herself?'

'We're not supposed to know. She crawled out of the skylight in the laundry roof and threw herself onto the cobbled yard.'

'God, it's a mortal sin.'

'Yeah, well, Hell can't be worse than this place,' Celia hissed fiercely. 'They'd left Candy's baby with her four months. She fed her, changed her, cuddled her and loved her, and when they took her away she went mad. They had to lock her in one of their cells for the night. She thought they were coming from the asylum. They might have been. It's what happens when you show normal bloody emotions in this place.'

'And then,' she added, 'there was Jane, died of the flu.'

'Flu?'

'Aye,' Celia said. 'They don't believe in calling the

doctor out to us sinners, and the untreated flu led to pneumonia. Her parents came and took the body for burial in their own parish graveyard and that doesn't always happen. But you said you're married. Have you already got kids then?'

'Aye. Tom's going on for five and Niamh is just seven.'

'Did you have any trouble?'

'Not especially.'

'You'll probably do all right here then.'

'Are you expecting?'

'I was, I gave birth four weeks ago. It was bloody awful, I tore and bled like a stuck pig. I thought I would bleed to death, but it healed eventually.'

'And your baby?'

'A wee boy, a bit premature, three weeks early, and they had to take him straight away because I refused to feed him.'

'Why?'

'Because I didn't want to love him like Candy did,' Celia said. 'He looked so wee in the cot, so delicate, and I ached to lift him up, put him to my breast, and they throbbed and leaked all over my nightdress when he cried. The nuns shouted and Sister Jude slapped me. They even tried coaxing, but I wouldn't budge.

'Lizzie, I wouldn't wish a day in this hellhole on my worst enemy; how then could I wish it for my precious child. It was better he got right away than be poisoned by the fetid, malicious air of this place.'

'Did it hurt to give him up?'

'Oh God! You've no idea. I couldn't eat, couldn't sleep; I cried for days, but alone, never in front of those old crones. I've seen girls ridiculed who've done that and I really think I'd have attacked any who ridiculed me. That would have cooked my goose right and proper.'

Lizzie was so shocked by all she'd heard she could barely take it in. She had no idea these places existed and she knew few would believe it. Would she have believed it if she hadn't seen it herself? Probably not! And no one outside these walls got to know because it all hinged on secrecy.

'Where does all the laundry come from anyway?' Lizzie said. 'I've been thinking about it all day.'

'The town. We do all the washing for them,' Celia told her. 'Two men deliver dirty washing on Tuesdays and Fridays and take the laundered stuff back. And when they do, I'm warning you now, Lizzie, don't look at the men, not that they're worth a second glance anyway, if you know what I mean. They may speak to you, ridicule you, call you names or look at you as if you've crawled from under a stone; and whatever they say or do, keep your head down, don't look at them and definitely don't speak. The nuns might be about, but even if they are not in the yard with you they'll not be far away, and it seems the men can say what they like, but should one of us reply . . . God, one girl was beaten black and blue because they said she was flirting with the men. As if you'd flirt with men who call you fucking whores or sodding trollops, or who ask if you are gagging for it and offer to give you a poke to put you out of your misery.'

'I can hardly believe men would say such things, and to a woman.'

'We're not women, Lizzie, we are all whores and hookers and sinners, the dregs of society and not worthy of respect or even common courtesy,' Celia replied. 'And they pay Sister Jude for the laundry done, but we never see a penny piece of it.'

'Where does it go?'

'To the black babies in Africa,' Celia said. 'I've heard Father Conroy say Sister Jude is a credit. He said she collects more in months than many convents twice the size. Of course she bloody does. Those black babies are kept by our red-raw, chapped hands, our aching backs and the sweat running from us.'

'It's incredible,' Lizzie breathed.

'What is?'

'Everything.'

'I don't think for one minute that this is just one on its own. I think places like this are peppered all over the country,' Celia said. 'I think it's out of sight, out of mind. You better believe it, Lizzie, we are the forgotten women of Ireland.'

Lizzie lay wide awake for a long time after Celia's even breathing told her the other girl was asleep. She'd told her much that night, much that had shocked her to the core. 'Forgotten women of Ireland' sounded desperate altogether.

She'd make sure she wasn't forgotten, she thought. She'd write to her mother, to Violet. She had no paper and no stamps, but if the nuns would loan her enough for one letter, her mother or Violet would surely send her the makings for any number of letters. Surely to God she couldn't be just wiped from their lives like that?

And the first thing she must do tomorrow would be to send a wee card to her daughter for her First Communion Day. Even the nuns would countenance that, surely to God.

With the decision made she tried to sleep, but instead she tossed and turned on the hard, lumpy mattress and eventually slept as the sun was preparing to rise.

'A card, Pansy?' Sister Jude asked, as if she'd never heard of such a thing before. She was smiling but it was not a warm smile. It was as if she was laughing at her.

But Lizzie had no intention of giving in. She'd asked to see Sister Jude as soon as she rose, heavy-eyed and sluggishly tired after her disturbed night, and had asked again after Mass and yet again at breakfast, which was lumpy porridge and tea, and eventually she was given permission.

'Yes, Sister, a card. Niamh is taking her First Communion on Sunday. And with me not being there and all, I just wondered . . .'

'I know all about your daughter's First Communion,' Sister Jude snapped. 'Pity you didn't remember it when you opened your legs for some man. I understood it was the occasion of your daughter's Communion that caused Father Brady to move you speedily from the home.'

'It was, Sister, but . . .'

'Lest you contaminate her day, displaying your sin for all to see, your parents bereft with shame.'

'Just a card. Sister, that's all,' Lizzie cried desperately. 'Please.'

'And just where do people think you have vanished to all of a sudden?'

'Back to England, to tend my sick mother-in-law.'

'So wouldn't it strike the postmistress as odd if your family get a letter from you with a Sligo postmark?'

Lizzie hadn't thought of that and knew what the nun said was right. The postmistress knew everything about everybody. She knew Lizzie's writing too, because she'd written weekly letters home to her mother since she'd first gone to England, and she'd be suspicious about letters from her coming from Sligo and would make it her business to tell everybody.

Sister Jude saw the slump of Lizzie's shoulders and hid her smile of triumph. 'I'm glad you see that it would be impossible, Pansy,' she said. 'While you are in here, it is far better that you forget all about your family. I'm sure they would prefer it that way.'

And Lizzie remembered her father's hard eyes and stern face and her mother's extreme nervousness and the anxiety of them both for her to be gone from the place, and how she went without the smallest gesture of affection, and knew the nun was right. 'Return to your duties now, Pansy,' Sister Jude said, and Lizzie turned and left the room because there was nothing else she could do.

But there were people who hadn't forgotten Lizzie. Niamh had cried bitterly when she was told that evening after school that her Mammy had had to go back to England and wouldn't be there for her Communion. 'She promised,' she said through her tears. 'She came specially.'

'She had to go back, I've told you. Her mother-in-law was ill.'

'She don't even like Granny,' Niamh complained. 'She told me. No one likes her much. She's horrid.'

'That will do, Niamh!' Catherine had snapped. 'That's a dreadful thing to say, and what's liking a person or not got to do with it? If a person is ill, they're ill and need to be seen to, and that's that.'

Tom had been unnerved by his sister's tears, for she seldom cried, and his own voice was wobbly when he said, 'She never even said goodbye to me.'

'You were away at Uncle Owen's, sure. You said goodbye when you left.'

'Not a proper goodbye,' Tom said. 'Couldn't someone have come and got me?'

'Everyone was busy,' Catherine replied. 'Anyway, it's no good going on about it, it's done. Your mammy's gone and that's that.'

'She'll probably send us a long letter explaining it, won't she?' Niamh asked her grandmother.

Catherine didn't meet the child's eyes. 'I don't know, child,' she said. 'Have you no homework to do, for I'll want the table to dish up the food shortly?'

'I've only got reading.'

'Well, go through your catechism.'

'I know it.'

'You can't be too sure of it. Read it through again and I'll test you when we've eaten.'

Niamh had sighed. When her grandmother spoke with that snap in her voice it was best to say nothing. But she knew what she'd do as soon as she could: she'd write a letter to her mammy and ask her why she'd left like that and she'd do it without her grandmother being aware of it. If she saved a little of her pocket money she could buy a stamp on her way to school and she'd use the page from her copy book to write it. She knew her grandmother kept envelopes in the drawer of the dresser.

She felt better when she'd made that decision because she loved her mammy. It had been grand to see her. She hadn't realised how much she had missed her until she'd arrived. As for Tom, she knew he'd been fizzing with excitement for days, and that night when she'd gone to bed she heard him crying in the bed he shared with Uncle Johnnie in the far room.

Johnnie wouldn't be in bed for hours yet, Niamh thought, and she plodded across the floor and, slipping in beside her brother, she put her arms tight around him. There was no need for words.

Later, Johnnie, who'd been upset by the children's obvious distress, saw them fast asleep curled together in bed and hadn't the heart to disturb them, so he slept in Niamh's bed instead that night.

Tressa called around on Thursday morning as she hadn't seen Lizzie since Sunday.

'She's away back to England,' Catherine said in answer to her query. She didn't know how much Tressa knew and had no intention of asking her, and anyway the story had to be stuck to for all outside the immediate family.

'England!' Tressa repeated.

'Aye.'

'Before the child's Communion? Without saying goodbye?'

'She hadn't the time,' Catherine said. 'The call came through to the priest. Her mother-in-law was ill. She had to go home urgently and see to her.'

Tressa's eyes narrowed. See to her mother-in-law my eyes, she thought. God, if the woman was on fire in the gutter Lizzie wouldn't spit on her. If the woman was too sick to leave her bed to come around and berate Lizzie for each and every mortal thing, she'd be more likely to dance a jig in the yard.

Funny do altogether, to be whisked away only days before her own child's big day. Maybe, Tressa thought, she'd send a letter of explanation later. She'd have to, because there was more to this than met the eye and yet she knew she would get no more out of her Aunt Catherine. She could be as close as a clam when she had the mind and so she left it there. When Lizzie wrote she was sure she'd hear the whole story.

Violet had no knowledge of life in a small Irish village. Lizzie had written to her when she'd been in Ireland a few days. She'd told her how good it was to be home and how excited the children were to see her and how they'd grown and blossomed. She spoke of the hills and the sea and the fine time she was having with Tressa and her family and visiting old friends. Just one line said she intended telling her mother after the weekend, when she'd been home a week, and Violet had waited for her to tell her the outcome and there had been silence.

It wasn't like Lizzie. She must know Violet would

be concerned and interested. She'd wait a couple of days and write and see what was happening. Barry said she was probably having such a good time over there she'd not taken time to write, but he didn't know the secret she carried. 'I know you like her an' all, ducks,' he said. 'I'm pretty fond of her myself, tell the truth, but if I was her and got the offer I would stay in Ireland. I mean, she misses them nippers shocking, don't she?'

Violet had to admit she did, and maybe she would stay now she'd gone home, and she could when she'd had that bastard's baby and given it away. Violet would miss her, God knows, but she could see the point of it, and perhaps it was for the best.

'You could be right, Barry,' she told her husband. 'But if she hasn't written by, say, Monday or Tuesday of next week, I'll write and ask her what's what.'

'Don't blame you, old girl,' Barry said. 'You need to know one way or the other.'

Lizzie tossed and turned on Saturday night and when she did drop into a fitful sleep, she dreamt she saw St Bridget's bedecked with flowers, her daughter in the white communion dress full of frills and lace, the veil held in place by a comb covered with white satin and decorated with rosebuds. She was in a row of girls, all similarly dressed. Across the aisle were the boys in their grey shorts and white shirts with a satin sash draped across their shoulders. They were scrubbed cleaner than they'd ever been and any stray curls or unruly locks of hair were subdued by Brylcreem.

The church was crammed full of relations belonging

to the children. There were mothers, fathers, uncles, aunts, grandparents ... but it was the hurt look on her daughter's uncomprehending face that jerked Lizzie awake and caused her to run to the bathroom adjoining the dormitory and vomit into the bowl.

'What is it?' Celia said, standing in the doorway. 'Bit late in the day for morning sickness?'

What was the point of telling her? There was no point in complaining in this place, so she shrugged. 'Don't know. Could be anything.'

'You all right now?'

Lizzie was far from all right and the bad taste stayed in her mouth all day. Being Sunday, there was no cleaning and laundry work. Instead, the girls sat in two circles, with a nun and older woman or two in each circle to ensure there would be no inane chatter between them and who read passages out of the bible while the girls hemmed sheets and darned holes in clothes and stockings.

Lizzie would have preferred work where she wouldn't have had time to think or brood, for the constant thoughts of her children, particularly Niamh that day, could bring tears to her eyes. She was careful not to let anyone see this for she'd have hated the nuns to have something to mock, and she knew that if she wanted to survive this, she had to get a grip on herself.

Every morning at five o'clock, the girls were roused. Sleepy-eyed, they dressed beneath their nightdresses and filed down to Mass in the chapel. After Mass there was breakfast and after breakfast there were prayers. They began work at seven.

Some girls were assigned to the kitchens and some for cleaning duties, but most went to the laundry where they worked until twelve o'clock when they had their dinner. The regime was harsh and the work hard, but if the nuns had ever spoken kindly, smiled, allowed the girls to talk a little, it would have been more bearable.

Here, if you saw a nun smile it was because someone was going to catch it or be made fun of. And if they were, you had to stay silent, for to try to support the person brought worse punishment down on your own head. You learnt to keep your head lowered and look out just for yourself, knowing that one day it would be your turn to be mocked, ridiculed or beaten, and no one would come to your aid either.

Saturday night was bath time and a time for Sister Maria and Sister Clement to have fun at the girls' expense. They mocked their bodies and compared and laughed at them and often made them run on the spot, noting whose breasts bounced the more or whose bottom was more wobbly. For Millie and Cora, who looked as if they were ready to deliver any day, you could see this running and jumping up and down was causing them severe discomfort, but Lizzie didn't say anything and neither did anyone else. Lizzie supposed the heavy work in the laundry didn't help either, but no allowance was made here for pregnancy, and Lizzie knew her time would come when the baby would lie heavy on her and everything would be an effort and she would have to cope as these girls did.

CHAPTER SIXTEEN

The following Friday, two letters arrived at the farm-house for Lizzie. 'Put them in the fire,' Seamus said gruffly. 'Burn them.'

'We can't do that,' Johnnie said.

'Hush, we don't want the weans to know,' Catherine cautioned both men.

'Well,' Seamus challenged his son, but in a lower voice, 'what would you have us do, send them along to her?'

'Aye, maybe we should. We can't just ignore them.'

'Why not?' Seamus growled.

'Look,' Johnnie said. 'If you want to pretend Lizzie doesn't exist that's fine. I personally think you're wrong, but I'll live with your decision. But other people won't know this and maybe it will be suspicious to them if they receive no reply to the letters they send. We should at least open them and see who they're from.'

Seamus looked across at Catherine and she shrugged. 'Johnnie has a point, but not now. We'll open them when the weans are out the way, especially Niamh, she's too knowing altogether.'

Niamh was too knowing, and needed to find out why her mother hadn't been there at her First Communion as she had promised she would be. Wasn't there someone else who could have looked after her other granny for a few days? It wasn't much to ask. But she knew she'd get no answer to these questions if she were to ask her granny, and not even her Uncle Johnnie seemed to want to talk and speculate about her mammy like he used to before.

So, unknown to any of them, she had written to their house at home. She didn't know if her mother was there or at her grandmother's house, but she worked out that her mother would have to go home sometimes, and so she said as she came into the room dressed for school, 'Any letters?'

Catherine thanked God she'd thought to put the letters behind the clock on the mantelpiece. She knew what Niamh meant. She wanted a letter from her mother, for previously Lizzie had written every week. How would she explain an absence of letters? She didn't know. Having a woman disappear for a few months was a hard thing to do when that woman had a family and friends who cared about her.

But Niamh deserved an answer. She'd been upset at her mother's absence on Sunday but had bravely held back the tears, and this would be another blow to her. 'No,' she said, but gently. 'No letters.'

'She's had time to write by now.'

'Maybe she's busy.'

'Huh.'

'Don't sulk, Niamh, it's a bad habit.'

But Niamh wasn't really sulking, she was hurt. She'd

begged her mammy to write quickly. She'd told her all about her First Communion. You'd think she'd find time to write a few lines.

Catherine watched her grandchildren surreptitiously, the outspoken Niamh and the more introverted Tom, and knew both children were suffering in their own way. Whether or not Lizzie had sinned was a matter of opinion, but what wasn't in doubt was the children's innocence. They were affected too, and she knew that whatever she did, it wouldn't make it any better for them.

Later that morning, with Niamh on her way to school and Tom in the fields with his uncle, Catherine opened the envelopes.

One of the letters was from Violet. She told her of the happenings in the street and said her description of Ireland sounded lovely and that maybe she'd make the trip herself someday and urged Lizzie to tell her all the news.

Catherine knew what Violet meant by 'all the news'. The woman had been a good friend of Lizzie's for years, and if she'd confided in anyone it would be Violet. Lizzie herself had said it was Violet who found her collapsed in the yard after the attack. She could take a bet Violet knew everything.

The other letter was from Lizzie's mother-in-law.

Lizzie,
Just what are you playing at? All I've had from you is a note to say you'd arrived in Ireland safely. I never doubted it, and since then there has been

nothing. No letter and no indication of how long you'll stay. Steve hasn't had a letter either and I think it's very remiss of you not to write to him when you think of what he faces daily. Of course, you always did think of yourself first, so I shouldn't be surprised.

We can't hold this house for you forever. How would it be if Steve came home from the war to find no home at all to welcome him? You were happy enough to run when the going got tough and leave the rest of us to cope with the rationing and blackout and the constant threat of bombs, while you live the life of Riley over there. And I know that at first Steve was fine about you going home for a while, that just shows you the type of man he is, but he thought of you going over for a wee rest, not languishing there for weeks on end. After all, you have been there over two weeks, long enough to get over anything that ails you I would think. Surely you will be thinking of coming back any day now.

Steve will be writing to you about this I'm sure, when I point it out about the house and everything . . .

The censuring letter went on in a similar vein, talking about people and places Catherine didn't know and taking every opportunity to complain about or denigrate Lizzie. Lizzie hadn't complained much about her mother-in-law and Catherine had to admit she generally complained about little. This woman was a cow of the first order and she detested Catherline's daughter, that much was obvious. But, that being so, she would grasp any opportunity to shame Lizzie, and if her family were caught in the fallout she'd lose no sleep over it.

This woman's suspicions had to be allayed at all costs. And yet Catherine didn't know what could be done. She put the letters back behind the clock. She'd ask Seamus and Johnnie if they had any ideas, although she knew this would probably have to wait until evening when the children were in bed and the chores done.

She knew Seamus wouldn't want to discuss it at all at any time. He was so embarrassed by the whole episode anyway that he even found it hard to say Lizzie's name. Whatever she'd claimed had happened, the outcome was she was having a bastard child, the thing a father dreads his daughter saying, and he wanted nothing to do with her till the child was born and sent away somewhere. Then he might feel differently about it, but for now . . .

'But, Seamus, what are we to do?' she asked that night, as he sat smoking his pipe before the fire as if she hadn't spoken.

'Do what you want. Just don't concern me over it.'

'Come on, Daddy,' Johnnie said. 'We can't pretend this isn't happening.'

'I can do as I please in my own house,' Seamus said, his voice rising in anger.

'Hush,' Catherine said, glancing at the bedroom door. 'You'll have the weans awake.'

'Aye, well, for a man to be told what to do by a mere lad.'

'I'm not a lad, Daddy,' Johnnie said, enraged. 'My

315

opinion is as valid as yours, and I say this attitude will not help.'

'Let's not argue about it now,' Catherine pleaded. 'Let's leave it a few days and think it over. A decision has not got to be made tonight.'

Johnnie shook his head. He knew his parents ran the risk of the whole thing blowing up in their faces. But what could he do? Very little, and he took himself off to bed where he found Tom curled up in a defensive ball in the middle of it. He stroked the little lad's hair gently and he stirred in his sleep. Johnnie slid in beside him and lay wide awake for hours, though his eyes smarted with tiredness, and worried over the letters and what to do about them.

In the convent, where the only hint that you were still a member of the human race was a glimpse of sky, or occasionally, when pegging the laundry out in the garden, smelling the fresh air while carefully guarded by one of the nuns, days had no meaning. One slid into the other effortlessly, punctuated only by Sundays.

When Celia told Lizzie some girls stayed for years and some never got out at all, she began to score her hobnailed boots on the underside of the wooden palette she slept on: six notches for the days of the week and a long line through them for Sunday. So she knew she was in her third week when Millie had her first pains. 'Is it the baby?' Lizzie asked, going over to the girl's bed when she heard the groans. 'The bedroom door is locked until morning.'

'That's all right,' Millie panted, breathless with pain. 'I'll not want the nuns to know yet awhile.'

'You're right,' another agreed. 'Hang on as long as you can,' and in explanation went on to Lizzie, 'They just use it as an excuse to point out what a sinner you are. There is no attempt to make it easier for you. Pain's good for the soul, they say.'

'Pity they don't suffer a lorry-load of it then,' put in a girl called Freda. 'For their souls must be as black as pitch keeping us cooped up like this.'

'Ah,' said a girl named Dot, 'but they'd have to do the monkey business first.'

'D'you think they don't want to?'

'Aye, that's what's the matter with them.'

'Maybe the priest would do the necessary.'

'He'd be delighted, the dirty old bastard,' a girl said with feeling. 'He'd like to do it with the lot of us, if he had the bottle.'

Lizzie was shocked at such talk about a priest. She resented Father Brady for whisking her away from her home the way he had, but this was dirty talk, and about a man of God.

The lights were turned on so that they could see Millie properly and Celia caught sight of Lizzie's face. 'Oh, our little Pansy is disgusted with us, so she is. She thinks we're making all this up. She pressed her face close to Lizzie's and said, 'I tell you, you might get your eyes opened yet. Wait till he asks you to wait behind sometime in the sacristy.'

'What does he do?'

'You'll find out, and I wouldn't spoil it for you by telling you.'

Some of the girls laughed nervously, while others wore a mask of misery, and Lizzie wondered what other horrors were in store for her in that place.

But there was little time to worry about it now, for Millie's contractions had become stronger and closer together and she clasped the hands of the girls closest to her, her nails scoring into them when the peak of the contraction was reached, and she writhed in the bed and moaned. Cora watched her, knowing in a few days, maybe a week, it would be her turn.

Lizzie remembered the old midwife she had helping her when Niamh was born who'd told her the pain of childbirth was forgotten when the child is in your arms. She'd been in agony and hadn't believed a word of it. However, she'd found it to be true. It had faded from her mind as she looked at the perfect little person she'd helped create, and when the baby's rooting mouth found Lizzie's nipple she'd felt utter contentment.

But none at the convent would have that consolation, including her, but she'd had two children already so maybe she'd find it a little easier. For these girls it would be hard and painful and the last thing any woman in labour wants is being berated when they are at their most vulnerable.

All through the long night, the girls took turns to stay with Millie, holding her hand, soothing her, one using the flannel from the bathroom to wipe her gleaming face, and when the bell eventually shrilled out and the girls reluctantly left Millie and began to dress by their beds, Celia said to Lizzie, 'That's the last kind word or kind act she will know.'

And it seemed she was right. Certainly, Sister Mary, who was in charge of the dormitory, was totally lacking in any compassion. 'Get up,' she said to the pain-ravaged girl. 'Stop making such a fuss and go down to the infirmary.'

Too scared to disobey, Millie swung her legs over the bed and tried to stand on them. She'd gone two paces when a pain doubled her over and she felt the whoosh as her waters gushed from her.

The nun was outraged. 'Look at the mess, and all over the floor,' she railed at the girl who'd collapsed in a heap onto the wet floor. 'Two of you stay behind and clean this up and two more might as well help the girl down to the infirmary.'

Lizzie and Celia were the two chosen to clean the bedroom, and as they collected mops and buckets from the store cupboard, Lizzie whispered, 'Is it right what you said about Father Conroy last night?'

'Aye.'

'But what does he do?'

'I told you, you'll find out,' Celia said. 'But whatever he does, never say a word about it and don't complain.'

'Why not?' Lizzie said. 'If he should behave improperly . . .'

'Listen to me,' Celia hissed. 'This isn't the real world here and normal rules don't apply. This is a world of priests and nuns and filth and depravity. It's a world where power over others is the most important thing. The minute you walk in here, you lose any basic rights you might have had or thought you had. We had a girl in here once who complained and she was taken away one night and we never heard of her again.' Celia gave a sudden shiver and said, 'I don't think I'll ever forget her screams.'

'But where did she go?'

Celia shrugged. 'People said to the asylum. Wherever she went, I imagine it was worse than this place. By Christ, just think of that and don't let the same thing happen to you.'

There was no doubting Celia's words, no doubting the passion or sincerity, and it chilled Lizzie to the marrow. She still believed in God, though. What these people did was not in the name of Jesus. He was a God of Love, surely, and didn't he forgive sinners – even Mary Magdalene – and what of the prostitute the town people had wanted to stone.

Did they ever think of that, she wondered, or were they so puffed up with the idea of their own importance that they thought all their actions justified? They were more malicious and vicious than anyone she'd ever had dealings with, and that included her mother-in-law By God, she was just an apprentice trouble-maker when you measured her up against these nuns.

'Help me, Father,' Lizzie prayed earnestly in her bed that night. 'You are the only one who can, for here we have no rights at all, as Celia pointed out. Protect me, Jesus, from this priest.' But she didn't feel comforted and wondered for the first time if there was a God, and if he was prepared to listen to her if he did exist, and her dreams when she eventually dropped off were punctuated with terrifying nightmares.

The next day, they found out Millie had had a baby boy. There was no joyful announcement, no congratulations, just the bold statement that Millie was well and would be joining them in the dormitory in a few days. 'Bully for Millie,' Celia whispered in Lizzie's ear as they sat in the refectory having breakfast. 'I bet she can hardly wait.'

Aye, I bet, Lizzie thought, but she said nothing for Celia's words, soft as they were, had brought the nun's head swinging round to scrutinise them, although she wasn't sure where the sound had come from. Lizzie had learnt that in the convent it was safer to keep your head lowered. If you were forced to lift it, if they demanded it, you fixed your gaze on a point above their head and you kept it there. So now she studied her feet on the polished floor.

Eventually, the nun, rapped out, 'Now we will say Grace, to thank the Good Lord for his bounty,' and though Lizzie mumbled the prayer she couldn't help feeling she'd be a lot more thankful if she'd had the rashers and eggs that she'd seen carried behind the nun's screen, and the smell of bacon rose in the air, tantalising them as they ate their lumpy porridge.

Five days later, Cora announced she'd begun her labour by collapsing in the laundry room just after they began work. Millie hadn't returned as she was still lying in, and Cora was taken to an adjoining room. By teatime, Cora's screams could be heard reverberating off the walls. 'They'll kill her, behaving like that,' Celia hissed as she and Lizzie worked the mangle together. 'They're not above giving you a slap if you make a fuss.'

Slap or not, the screams went on, even in the chapel, though it was fainter there. By bedtime, Cora was crying for her mother, the Blessed Virgin, the Living God, and tears for the girl so filled Lizzie's eyes she could hardly see what she ate, and the lump in her throat made it hard to swallow and her stomach was tied in knots. Others besides herself looked equally miserable. No one said a word then, but later in the dormitory, with the door locked and bolted, Freda said, 'She was terrified anyway and small wonder in this place. I mean, it's a frightening enough thing if you have your man by your side and a neighbour woman in attendance who has done it many times before, knows what she's doing and is doing all she can to help you.'

'Aye, and you know she'll have a doctor look at you if she's at all worried.'

'Do you have no doctor at all?' Lizzie asked.

'There's one in the village,' Celia said. 'You'd have to be on death's door to see one, and I mean it literally.'

'Aye, Sister Clement trained as a nurse. They think what she can do is enough and that only basic medical intervention is suitable for ones such as us.'

'Aye, and when did she train? The year dot, I bet'.

'God knows. It's a wonder she doesn't prescribe leeches for everyone, whatever ails them,' Celia said.

'Christ, will you be quiet and stop giving them ideas.'

'Still, I'm sorry for Cora,' Lizzie put in. 'The screams were getting to me.'

'They were getting to us all,' said Dilly from the far bed. 'And I'm not being heartless when I say I'm glad we can't hear her any more.'

Lizzie felt the same. The attic room the girls shared was just two far away from the infirmary. The nuns' quarters weren't, but she guessed they wouldn't be disturbed by anything or anyone.

The girls knew they could do nothing, and

eventually, one by one, they fell asleep and the room grew silent.

Lizzie was awoken by the noise of car tyres crunching on the gravel path outside. It took her a while to ascertain what had woken her and then she got up and ran to the window. There was already a cluster of girls there and others came vying for a space. Celia was one of the ones with her nose pressed to the pane. 'It's the doctor,' she said in ominous tones. 'The bloody nuns have called the doctor.'

'Jesus, she must be in a bad way.'

Lizzie felt sick. She thought of the young girl below in the throes of labour, sick enough to need the services of a doctor and yet no one to give her a kind word or gesture.

The doctor stayed a long time. Lizzie had no idea how long, though she heard his car drive away. Some had fallen asleep by then, for she heard their even breathing, and she thought others might be listening as she was, unable to drop off.

She was still wide-eyed when she heard Sister Mary's tread on the attic stairs and the key turned in the lock The nun turned on the light and all the girls stirred and those already awake turned to stare at her. Lizzie was surprised that she wasn't barking at them to be out of bed and quick about it, and she felt as if ice had trickled down her spine at the look on the nun's face.

Her voice was surprisingly gentle as she said, 'Cora passed away early this morning.'

'Passed away! She was having a baby. Women don't die in childbirth these days.'

It was Celia's voice and Lizzie bit her lip in trepidation for the young girl, but the nun just shook her head sadly. 'Some do, Hetty. They do indeed, but I understand you are shocked and maybe upset so I will forgive your little outburst. Mass this morning will be dedicated to Cora, so get up and dress quickly and quietly in respect for the poor dead girl.'

'Poor dead girl!' Lizzie wanted to cry. 'You never thought her poor while she was alive. What respect did you show her then?' But what would she achieve by throwing this in the nun's face. She might get away with it, it might again be put down to shock, but it would change nothing.

Two new girls joined them that afternoon. Both were incredibly young and frightened witless and Lizzie knew they'd have to wait for nightfall or beyond to find out anything about them. They were told their names – Rosie and Queenie – by Sister Carmel before they were set before a sink full of suds, soda water and a washboard.

That night, Lizzie was woken by the sound of muffled crying. She sat up in the dark and looked around her. As she'd thought, it was the two new girls both further up the room by the window, in the beds once occupied by Millie and Cora. Lizzie wondered if she should cross the room and say something.

Say what? said a wee voice inside her. Say everything is fine when it blatantly isn't? Say they'll get used to this harsh regime when they shouldn't have to? Say they don't have to stay in here forever when they might have been disowned by their families and be totally destitute?

No, she decided, there was nothing to be gained by trying to talk to the distressed girls. They'd have to get over it like so many others before them, and she turned over and closed her eyes.

The next day their swollen eyes bore evidence to the hours they'd spent weeping, and they were reluctant to rise from their beds. Lizzie's conscience smote her, but she reminded herself that any assurances she gave them would hardly make them feel better.

But what she could do was prevent them being beaten that morning. 'Get up,' she hissed at the pair of them, 'before Sister Mary comes back. You'll get the cane across your backside if you're not ready for Mass.'

Wearily, the two girls clambered from their beds and Rosie began taking off her nightie. 'No,' Lizzie said. 'You must dress and undress under your nightie. You only strip off when the nuns tell you to. At other times, nakedness is to be frowned on.'

Rosie had never dressed covered by a nightie before, and Lizzie, who was ready, helped her, catching a glimpse of the mound of her bulging stomach before the smock dress covered it. 'How far are you?' she whispered.

'Six months,' Rosie said. 'I've been a prisoner in my bedroom for two months till my father heard of this place. He beat me black and blue when I told him. He wanted the name of the father – and I told him too, for all the good it did. The man was married. You wouldn't have thought it when he was courting me, buying flowers, taking me out. Never said a word of his wife then. I loved the very bones of him, and when

325

I let him . . . you know, he said I'd be safe, he'd make sure. When I told him I was expecting he was a different man altogether, told me I was a stupid little trollop and I needn't think he'd marry me, for he already had a wife and three weans.'

She looked at Lizzie, her large and very beautiful blue eyes still brimming with tears, and went on, 'I told Daddy all this and he went off to see the man. He told Daddy I was mad for it, that I trailed him in the town, that I offered myself freely, that I was more than willing. The truth was I put up with it to please him, for I never took enjoyment out of it, but Daddy believed him. I really thought he was going to kill me. In the end, Mammy stopped him, not for my sake but in case I should miscarry. But I can't understand why he believed a man he'd just met, over me that he'd reared for years.'

Lizzie didn't know either. It was just the way of things. Didn't her own parents doubt her tale? She patted the girl's arm and said, 'They'll likely get over it.' She didn't believe it, but the girl might for now. She'd come to the realisation that she was stuck in this place indefinitely in her own time, but now she was hurt and disillusioned and both were feelings the nuns would play on if they were aware of them.

'Look,' she said to the two girls, 'a word of warning to the both of you: don't let the nuns know how upset you are and try not to cry in front of them. They'll see it as a sign of weakness, and, like all bullies, hone in on it.'

The girls were dressed just in time and Lizzie, her eyes attuned to the rustle of the nun's approach, was beside her bed before Sister Mary entered the room, grateful to Celia, who'd tidied her bed when she saw her helping the new girls.

Cora's funeral was three days later on, Monday, 4th August, in the little chapel. Lizzie thought she had got over being shocked or surprised at anything that went on at the convent, but this time the fact that no member of Cora's family attended the funeral shook her to the core. All that said goodbye to the young girl and her dead baby placed beside her in the coffin were the nuns and girls she'd been sent to live amongst.

Somewhere in Ireland, that child, for she was little more, had been born to a family and raised, possibly with siblings; and because that child had sinned, even though it might not have been her fault at all, she was cast out. Not even in death could she be accepted back into the family, and Lizzie knew she'd be buried in the small graveyard behind the chapel, like plenty more.

'They're probably pleased,' Celia said bitterly as they stood clustered by the grave. 'The dead tell no tales. Now there's no child who might one day take a notion to search for his mother. Dead and gone and out of the way is best, and no need for any of them to make the journey to see her laid to rest as if she was a valued family member.'

'Don't, Celia,' Lizzie cautioned, for she heard the break in the girl's voice and the rise of it in her distress. Any minute she would bring the nuns' attention upon her. If she was taken for punishment, in the mood she was in, she could say anything and that could be disastrous.

'I'm all right,' Celia said, taking a grip on herself. 'I thought I couldn't be hurt further, but I know if I had died giving birth to my wee boy, no one belonging to me from my home in West Meath would have shed a tear or travelled to my funeral. God, sometimes I don't think I can stand this place a minute longer.'

'Please, Celia, please be quiet.'

Even as she pleaded, Sister Maria grasped both Lizzie and Celia by their collars. 'Talking when they should have been praying for the poor dead girl's soul,' she informed Sister Jude once they were in the nun's office.

'Pansy wasn't talking,' Celia burst out. 'I was talking. She was trying to get me to stop.'

'I didn't ask you to speak.'

'I don't care,' Celia shouted. 'I don't care about any of you, can't you see? You're repressed, wizened-up old women – dried up inside with hate and evilness.'

Lizzie had the urge to clasp her hand over Celia's mouth, to stop the words that she could see were infuriating Sister Jude. She saw it by the flush of her face, the spittle forming on her lips, and the tic beating in her temple. 'Sister Maria,' she bawled, and the nun, who must have been hovering outside, popped her head around the door. 'Take Hetty into the office of the infirmary,' she said. 'She's overwrought. I'll deal with her later.'

But Celia wouldn't go quietly. She kicked and screamed and hurled abuse, and in the end Sister Clement and Sister Carmel had to be called to almost carry the struggling girl, whose voice could be heard still, but became fainter and fainter.

Sister Jude turned her attention to Lizzie. 'Hetty said

you tried to stop her speaking. What was she saying?'

Lizzie had the urge to sink on her knees and plead for leniency for Celia, for she knew what their ways of dealing with people were, but she also knew it wouldn't help and might make things worse. So she said, 'It wasn't anything, Sister, I mean nothing particular. She was upset over Cora, the fact that none of her people came to her funeral an' all. She wasn't herself when she said those things to you.'

'I'll be the judge of that,' the nun snapped. 'As for being upset, don't you girls realise most of your families want nothing more to do with you. If we didn't take you in and feed and clothe you, you would starve to death in the gutter, for no one else is wanting to take on that responsibility.'

'No, Sister.'

'So what should you have done when Hetty spoke?'

'Told one of the Sisters.'

'I'm glad you know,' said Sister Jude. 'Maybe this will help you remember promptly in future. Lift up your dress.'

It was not quite as painful as last time, and yet Lizzie was so worried about Celia the strokes seemed to matter less.

Celia didn't appear again that day, nor the next. When Lizzie asked Sister Mary she said she was in the infirmary because she wasn't well.

It was a Saturday, four days later, before Celia entered the laundry again, and Lizzie noticed she moved stiffly and painfully and the marks of grazes and bruises were on her face, and both her eyes were discoloured. Lizzie's eyes were sympathetic, but Celia muttered under the cover of folding clothes, 'Don't worry, they tried to punch and kick the shit out of me, but they didn't succeed and it was worth it to say what I did. I'm just sorry you got it. How many?'

'Six.'

'Oh God.'

'It's all right.'

Sister Maria came in the door at that moment and scanned the room. On catching sight of Lizzie, she went across to Sister Carmel and whispered something to her, and the nun looked up and straight at Lizzie. 'You are to go to Sister Jude's office, Pansy.'

Lizzie stared at her. She'd never gone in the woman's office without trembling, and with reason, for it usually resulted in at least a severe rebuke or a caning. For the life of her she couldn't think of anything she'd done to warrant being sent for. 'Me, Sister?'

'Yes, you. Would I have said you if I meant someone else?' Sister Carmel said. 'Go along quickly. Don't keep Sister Jude waiting.'

Lizzie's heart was thumping and her hands suddenly so clammy she had to run them down the front of her skirt, as she followed the nun up the steps and down the long corridor, wondering what now was in store for her.

Sister Maria knocked at the door and on the curt command to, 'Come in,' she swung the door wide for Lizzie to go in, but didn't attempt to enter herself. And so, tentatively, Lizzie approached the desk, which she could see from the door.

As she went into the room, she knew there was a person to the side of the nun that she'd caught sight

330

of out of the corner of her eye, and that it was a man. She knew she mustn't look at him or acknowledge him in any way, unless given leave to do so, and so she kept her head down.

But the man spoke. 'Lizzie?'

It was said almost hesitantly, for Johnnie couldn't be sure that this stumbling person with the swollen belly, dressed in hideous clothes, was the sister he'd come to seek.

But at the one word he spoke, Lizzie swung her head around and her lacklustre eyes were suddenly alight with joy. Nothing, no nun on earth, could have stopped the cry of relief and pleasure, nor the way she bounded across the room and threw her arms around Johnnie's neck, so that he was nearly overbalanced. 'Johnnie. Oh, thank God. Thank God!'

'This is highly irregular,' Sister Jude said. 'We don't encourage visitors, but in view of the circumstances.'

What circumstances? Sudden fear gripped Lizzie. Surely some calamity had happened. 'What is it?' she said. 'Is something the matter with the children? Mammy? Daddy?'

'No, nothing like that,' Johnnie assured her. 'They're all grand.' But he was thinking, by Christ, what have these monsters done to my beautiful sister? 'We need somewhere quiet to talk,' he went on. 'Sister Jude has been kind enough to let us stay in the office.'

Lizzie continued to stare at him. She wanted to touch him, convince herself he was real. She listened to his words: ordinary, everyday words from a person outside these prison walls. She didn't know whether she'd pay for this later and didn't care either. 'All right,

Johnnie,' she said. She'd have said all right to anything he suggested.

She was hardly aware of the nun, muttering, 'I'll leave you now, then,' or of her leaving the room. Then Johnnie took hold of her hand and sat her on one of the chairs set before the desk, while he stayed on the one beside her.

'Almighty Christ, Lizzie,' he said. 'When it's all over, I'll make it up to you, I promise. But, for now, we've hit a few problems.' For a brief moment he remembered the fight he had had to get so far and he sighed, for it had been well worth it.

CHAPTER SEVENTEEN

'What is it?' Lizzie demanded of Johnnie. 'Glad though I am to see you, I feel only a major event would bring you here, and yet you say everyone is fine at home.'

'They are,' Johnnie said. 'I've come because of the letters.'

'Letters?'

'People can't just disappear off the face of the earth,' Johnnie said. 'Not even for a few months, no matter what Mammy and Daddy may think. There are a number of people asking about you. I'm afraid we opened the letters. You'll see the first one's from your mother-in-law, and there's one from your neighbour from three weeks ago. Since then, we've had another two from your neighbour, and you'll see that inside the first one there are two letters from Niamh.'

'Niamh wrote?' Lizzie said.

'Aye, and in secret,' Johnnie said. 'We knew nothing about it.'

Lizzie opened up her daughter's letters. In the first one her child's confusion and hurt could be almost lifted from the page.

*I was upset that you weren't there to see me
make my First Holy Communion, when you'd
come home spesahlly for it and you promised.*

*Granny told us you had to go home because
our other Granny was ill and I felt sorry for you
then, because it must be horrible looking after
someone you don't like very much . . .*

The tears squeezed from Lizzie's eyes, so that she was
unable to read any more for a while. She imagined her
daughter's sadness and realised she'd put it there, whether
it was inadvertently or not, and her heart ached.

In the next letter, she was more angry than hurt:

*Why didn't you answer my letter? I waited and
waited. Granny said you're busy, but no one can
be that busy. Please write to me, Mammy. I miss
you so much . . .*

'Oh dear God!' Lizzie said, and put her head in her
hands.

'There's more, sis,' Johnnie said. 'In the next one
she wrote to Violet to find out what was up with you.
See, Mammy and Daddy foresaw none of this. They
can be grateful that the postman passed all post to
Violet, knowing the house was empty.'

'It wasn't. I mean, Steve's brother Neil is supposed
to be living there.'

'Well, if he had been, and had opened Niamh's letters, it would have really set the cat amongst the
pigeons,' Johnnie replied.

But on opening Flo's letter, Lizzie knew why Neil hadn't been at the house, because, amongst the vitriolic abuse, she read that:

Neil has received his call-up papers. Another son to worry about not that you will have the slightest idea what that feels like.

'Now that Steve's brother has been called up there may not be a house for me to return to in the end anyway,' Lizzie told Johnnie,

'Why?'

'They'll not hold a house with no rent coming in,' Lizzie said. 'The point was, none of the women were going to tell the landlord the house was empty, and I never saw him anyway. As I was working, Violet and I always left our rent money with one of the neighbours.'

'That's all sorted,' Johnnie said. 'I didn't know the arrangements you had made with Steve's brother, but I knew rent had to be paid on a property, and so I wrote to that friend of yours, Violet. I knew she'd know everything because you always mentioned her so much in the letters you wrote home. She told me she has been leaving your rent and hers with someone called Minnie, and she is going to continue to do that, only now I am going to reimburse her.'

Lizzie was flabbergasted by the resourcefulness of her brother. 'Johnnie, you are amazing!'

'You have to have something to return to,' Johnnie said simply, 'and Violet played her part in this too, and now that's sorted I think you had better read the rest of the letters.'

There were two letters from Steve, the first mildly annoyed that she hadn't written to him for weeks and the second furiously angry.

You seem to have forgotten your duty as a wife, residing as you are in the bosom of your family in Ireland, while I am living daily with mud and blood, death and destruction, without as much as a wee note to say I'm even in your thoughts.

I think it's now time for you to come home. You've dallied there quite long enough and your place is in Birmingham, looking after the house. With Neil called up, there's no one to see to it. I expect your immediate return. It isn't as if there's any danger from bombs any more. Mom says it's as safe as houses.

'He was all for me to come here,' Lizzie said. 'And now he wants me home. Flo put him up to it.'

'Maybe, but it's a long time with no letters or contact of any kind.'

'What could I do?' Lizzie cried. 'I wanted to send Niamh a card for her First Holy Communion and Sister Jude took pleasure in telling me the postmistress would think it funny to get a letter from Sligo.'

'Thank God that in a city like Birmingham no one would care where a letter came from.'

'Yes, but . . .'

'Look, Lizzie, we've had weeks to think of a plan,' Johnnie said. 'Or at least I have, because for the first fortnight or so, the time the first letters arrived, Mammy and Daddy refused to see there was a problem at all,

336

never mind think up a solution. They're hell-bent on keeping your pregnancy a secret, and couldn't see that if something wasn't done it was going to be blown wide apart.'

'Johnnie, d'you believe the account of what happened to me?'

'With all my heart and soul.'

'Why? I know Mammy and Daddy doubt me, and Father Brady. And as for them here . . .'

'You are my big sister, Lizzie, and I've never known you tell a lie for one thing,' Johnnie said simply. 'Tressa believes you too. She collared me one day and asked me point blank where you were and I told her. She'd written to the house and got no reply and was worried stiff. She was surprised you didn't tell her everything when you arrived, but I told her you thought Mammy ought to be the first to know and that after you did that you were lifted from the house faster than the speed of light. Anyway, she knows now, so maybe you can write a wee note to her too.

'As for the nuns, it wouldn't suit their purpose to believe you, and when all is said and done they hardly know you. They're all colluding anyway. I had to almost threaten the priest before he'd give me the address of this place. Mind you, I'm not surprised. I wouldn't want to be running coach tours out to this bloody prison, would you?'

'Oh Johnnie,' Lizzie said. 'I can't remember when I last smiled.'

'Well, all that will change, I promise,' Johnnie said. 'But for now I have with me paper, stamps and envelopes. I want you to write to Niamh and wee Tom.

Tell them you've been ill, caught whatever Flo was supposed to have.'

'But Johnnie.'

'"But Johnnie" nothing. I haven't been idle since you've been here. When I wrote to Violet I told how things were and she's agreed to post the letters to the children from there. You can write to her too, and tell her everything so far. She seems a good friend.'

'The best,' Lizzie said. 'Oh, Johnnie, you're so good to me. It's grand to have you here, like Christmas, but have you a magic formula for Steve and his mother?'

'The only magic formula for that Flo is a tight gag around her mouth and her hands tied behind her back so that she can't write or spew abuse at anyone,' Johnnie said. 'But since we can't do that, this is what I would suggest. Stick with the illness. Say you were sick and then say that Mammy finds it hard coping with the two weans now that school has broken up for the summer and you feel you should stay and give her a hand and spend some time with the children too, especially as Tom is starting school in Ballintra in September. Say you'll be home when you've settled him in. I'll post those from home.'

'D'you think it will work?'

'It's better than doing nothing,' Johnnie said. 'As for Steve, unless he has leave, and let's pray to God he doesn't, he can't check for himself and I don't think his mother will. So all they can do is write and make demands and castigate you, and judging by the general tone of your mother-in-law's letters, you're well used to that.'

'Oh, I am,' Lizzie said. 'You're right of course. It is

far better than saying nothing. And Johnnie, will you come again?'

'Aye,' Johnnie said. 'This will be ongoing now, for I'll have to bring you the replies. I think it would be better if I come every fortnight until you've had the baby and can come out of this place.'

'Oh, Johnnie, you don't know what this means to me.'

'Don't cry. Please, Lizzie, don't.'

'I'm crying because I'm happy,' Lizzie said. 'Happy and relieved.'

As Johnnie put an arm around his sister he dislodged the cap, and when he saw the front of her hair was shorn he pulled out the kirby grips and removed the rest of it gently. Then he just stared at the brown stubble, appalled.

'Why?' he said simply.

Lizzie tossed her head and replaced the hat, knowing she'd be in trouble if she was spotted without it, 'There's no place for vanity here,' she said. 'That's what they say.'

'God! It's inhuman!'

Lizzie was tempted then to tell him everything, but she resisted. What could he do but fret, and if he spoke out about it and made waves while she was still here, things might be worse for her. If, for example, she was spirited away into some asylum, maybe even the influence of a brother wouldn't be enough to effect her release, and that didn't bear thinking about. So she shrugged as nonchalantly as she could and said, 'You get used to it after a while, and every one of us is the same.'

'Oh God, Lizzie,' Johnnie said. 'I'm sure Daddy and Mammy didn't know it would be like this.'

But even as Johnnie spoke the words, he doubted it would have made any difference to the outcome if they had known. The secrecy, to protect their self-respect and standing in the community, seemed to be all they cared about. In their heart of hearts, Johnnie knew they blamed Lizzie, even if they believed her; and he thought his mammy did believe her, but she still blamed her, as if she could help a violent attack and rape. 'Don't worry,' he assured Lizzie, 'I'll come for you when it's over.'

'I can't go home. Daddy and Mammy won't let me,' Lizzie said.

Johnnie hadn't known this, but Lizzie went on, 'I don't mind. Well, I'd like to see the children, especially as I'll want nothing to do with this child. I'll go back to Birmingham to the house and Steve, if he survives this war.'

'Write your letters now.' Johnnie said, giving her arm a squeeze. 'I'll go outside and walk around a wee while. This place is making me feel claustrophobic.'

Lizzie watched him go, this youngest brother, the one she'd helped rear, the one she'd played with and protected as well as she was able, and her heart was full of love for him; love and gratitude.

When Lizzie returned to the laundry she was the subject of speculation – silent of course, but many had glimpsed Johnnie walking the grounds as they worked in the laundry, the doors open because of the heat, or took washing in and hung out more. Celia mouthed to Lizzie as they worked at the sink. 'Who?'

Lizzie glanced across at Sister Carmel, but she was bent over some intricate embroidery and she mouthed back, 'My brother.'

She saw the look of envy flood over Celia's face and could well understand it, for Celia had no brother taking any sort of interest in her.

And Johnnie's influence went further. That night, being Saturday, was bath time, and as usual as they filed before the nuns naked to have their hair cropped. Sister Maria said almost mockingly, 'Your brother has asked for your hair not to be cut any more. He is to take charge of you afterwards and says it will be difficult for you to take up the threads of life again marked in such a way.'

Her lip curled, and Lizzie knew that she didn't think any of these girls should ever be forgiven for whatever reason they were in this place; that they should never have a chance to start to live in the world again as if they were part of the human race. But she was to have that chance, and just the fact that her hair was no longer to be clipped close to her scalp gave her an absurd lift. She was still three months from the birth: three months when she would see Johnnie regularly and her hair would grow again and would curl and shine like a beacon towards her freedom.

Yet she knew in all other ways she had to continue to toe the line. Johnnie could do little to alter the day-to-day regime, and if she were to complain at all and he was to tell Sister Jude, it might be worse for her afterwards. Anyway, she didn't want to spoil his visits by carping and moaning about things he could do nothing about. She would ask about news from the farmhouse and about the children and her parents and Tressa.

The second time he came, as he spoke of these things, tears ran down Lizzie's face. Not for herself, for she knew in that moment she was possibly the most privileged woman in that whole convent, but she cried for the other girls, trapped and hopeless, those with no future at all. Johnnie seemed to understand her need to cry and he didn't urge her to stop, but clasped her tight in his arms until she was calmer.

The letters became easier to write, though Flo still grumbled. Steve, once it was explained to nim, could see that Lizzie would miss the children and quite understood that the two at home all day could be a handful for Lizzie's mother. If the situations had been reversed, much as he loved her, he couldn't see his mother taking full control of two boisterous children. It was odd to think of wee Tom nearly old enough to go to school. It would all be strange to him, Steve guessed, and he'd want one of his own there beside him. He wrote and told Lizzie to stay where she was for the time being.

His understanding made Lizzie feel worse in a way. It wasn't her fault, she knew, but she had betrayed Steve. He was her husband and yet she carried another man's seed in her womb. 'I'll make it up to him when this is all over,' she promised herself. 'I'll be a model wife. I'll not complain if he drinks too much or even if he stays out all night a time or two. It will probably take me a lifetime to make it up to him.'

The children's letters she found easier to write. She told them about life in Birmingham, relying on memory and the snippets Violet spoke about, and tried to make them funny. Niamh's replies often reduced her to tears, and also the kisses Tom made on the bottom of the letters. She longed to see them and hold them and was heart-sore that it would be some time before she could do that.

By September, Johnnie had made three visits. After each one, always on Saturdays, the nuns taunted and mocked her, but their scorn didn't touch her, for Johnnie, a real-life flesh-and-blood brother, would hold her tight and kiss her cheek as he left. 'I wish I had a brother like him,' Celia had said more than once, 'or an uncle. Anyone to take an interest in me.'

'I'm sorry, Celia,' Lizzie said, and she was sorry. 'I wish I could help.'

'Och, I know you do, and I know too you can do nothing. Jesus Christ, you have troubles enough of your own. Don't worry about me, I'll be grand.'

But it was hard not to worry when later Lizzie would often hear the muffled sniffles coming from Celia's bed and know she was crying. She didn't get out to comfort her, for Celia had no need of sympathetic words or pats on the back; she wanted a way out of that hell-hole and Lizzie was unable to help her there.

But despite Johnnie's visits, as her pregnancy progressed she was finding the work hard-going, especially as the heat was prodigious. So one day, just after Johnnie's visit and just before the bell for tea when she was asked to take the vestments across to the sacristy, she was glad to be out of the heat and steam of the laundry, even for a short time. Celia was going with her and as they walked along the corridors, their arms laden with vestments, Celia said, 'God, my clothes are sticking to me.'

'And mine. I'll be glad of the bath tonight.'

'The bath's all right. It's the nuns, poking and prodding and making fun of us, I can't stand.'

'Aye, and if you cry like Queenie did last week, it's worse for you.'

'Aye. Still, it can't stay as hot as this for too much longer. It's September now, it's got to cool down eventually.'

'Then we'll be complaining of the cold, no doubt. We're never satisfied,' Celia said, and then went on, 'Everything all right at home?'

'Aye, so Johnnie says. Tom starts school next week, and I've told him in the letter I'll be thinking of him. Mammy has bought him the copy books and jotters an' all, and he's had new clothes and a brand-new pair of boots now he's almost a schoolboy.'

There was a catch in Lizzie's voice and Celia said gently, 'You'll see them before too long, Lizzie, and you can make it up to them.'

Lizzie struggled to control herself. She knew this day would come with Tom, so why was she making such a fuss? Hadn't she the best outlook of anyone there? And here she was accepting sympathy from Celia, who'd change places with her tomorrow. 'I know that,' she told her. 'It was a momentary pang, that's all.'

'Atta girl,' Celia said, and they laughed together, but gently, lest any of the nuns hear.

Father Conroy was in the sacristy writing something at the desk and surprised both girls. 'I'm sorry, Father,' Celia said. 'We've brought over the vestments. Sorry to disturb you.'

The priest looked up. He barely saw Celia. His eyes were drawn to Lizzie. The curls had now grown a little and wouldn't fit snugly into her cap. Tendrils framed her face and these were set aglow by the slanting September sunlight coming through the window.

The priest watched the girls as they busied about the small room, hanging some garments and folding others into drawers in the chest, and he felt his innards grip him so tight he bit his lip to prevent a cry escaping him.

She looked, he thought, like one of the cherubs, and yet she was alive with sin. It must be writhing inside her, for she was a harlot and whore or she'd not be in this place. One who enjoyed sex and gave herself freely to men, any man. Oh, they came with their stories of innocence, of rape and all, but he knew what these women were, flaunting themselves, even before him, a priest.

He felt a stirring in his loins that he'd fought and prayed to control for months, but this girl was so affecting that he could feel his penis getting harder by the minute. The two girls had finished. He could let them go, and no one would be any the wiser. He'd cope. God, he'd done it before. But at the door the girl smiled at him and he knew he was lost.

He got up from the desk. 'Go on now,' he said to Celia, 'but not you, my dear.' And he put his hand on Lizzie's arm as he spoke. 'It's time you and I had a little chat.'

Until then, Lizzie had had no feeling of alarm. She didn't disbelieve the things Celia had said about the priest, but he'd done or said nothing untoward to her and so she'd pushed it to the back of her mind and thought, in a way, her advanced pregnancy protected her.

She saw the priest's brow glisten with sweat and the fingers holding her arm tremble slightly.

Her startled eyes met those of Celia's. 'You poor sod,' Celia's eyes said, almost as if she had spoken the words, and the roof of Lizzie's mouth felt suddenly very dry.

Celia closed the door behind her and the priest released his hold. Lizzie told herself to act normally. 'What is it, Father?' she asked, and her dry mouth made her voice husky. 'What do you want?'

The priest was mesmerised. First the smile and then the husky voice. The girl was coming on to him, gagging for it most likely. And Lizzie saw the look on the priest's face and every nerve in her body urged her to run from the place, whatever the consequences later. But, as if the priest knew of her intention, he was in front of her, blocking her way to the door. He turned the key in the lock and smiled. 'Sit down, sit down,' he urged, and Lizzie, not knowing what else to do, sat on the edge of her seat and the priest sat opposite her, the other side of the desk. He mopped his face with a large handkerchief and tried to control his breathing.

'What do I want, you ask?' he said. 'It's what anyone wants, what you want too, for you've shown me as much.'

'I don't know what you're talking about, Father.'

'You do know what I am talking about,' the priest said contemptuously. 'Don't play the innocent with me. You are a whore, up for it at any time, night or day.'

The priest looked at her and thought it sacrilegious to look so soulful when she was so sinful. Girls such as this one needed no consideration, no respect, for they had none for themselves.

'No, Father.'

'What do you mean, no?'

'I'm not like that, Father.'

'What sort of girl are you then?' the priest said mockingly. 'One who's pregnant, but wears a wedding ring. Did your husband send you here?'

'No, Father. We lived in England then and he's in the army overseas.'

'And you opened your legs for another,' the priest said, his breath coming in short pants. 'How many men? Did they pay well?'

'No, Father.'

'Oh, you gave it them free, did you?'

'No, Father.' With horror, Lizzie saw the priest's hands were between his legs, rubbing himself, and her mouth filled with sour-tasting saliva. She must make the priest see what sort of woman she was. She must stop this nonsense.

But the priest had seen the disgust on her face and it had enraged him. What right had she to look at him, a man of God, in that way?

'Father, it was dark,' she said. 'There's a blackout in England and in this pitch blackness I was attacked on my way home from work.'

'D'ya expect anyone to believe that?'

Lizzie gave a sigh. Despite herself and her trepidation of the position she was in, the fact that she'd told the truth and that pervert was working himself up over it inflamed her. 'D'you know, Father, in this place I don't, for all it's the truth, that I'd swear on my mother's life. Here they bend the truth for their own ends.'

'You are a harlot! A whore!'

'I am not, Father.' Even in her anger, Lizzie quailed. What was she doing, answering back to a priest? Sister Jude would kill her for this.

Father Conroy saw the fear flit across Lizzie's face and he smiled, and the maliciousness that Lizzie read in that smile made her stomach turn over. 'I'll tell you how you earned your money,' he said, and she saw the lust in his eyes and his hands worked faster. 'You lay down and let men have their way with you. His voice was now punctuated with pants. 'If you were attacked at all, it was because you wouldn't give the man what you'd promised him.'

'No, Father, no. Jesus Christ!' Lizzie had risen to her feet. 'Please, please let me go, Father.'

The priest's face was crimson, she noted, his voice guttural as he said, 'I know how it was. I know how you girls are, parading yourself, selling your bodies, craving sex.'

'I'm not, I wouldn't. Dear Christ, believe me, Father,' Lizzie cried, leaping towards the door. 'I can't stay here. It's wrong. Sister Carmel will . . .'

'The other girl will have told her I have need of you,' the priest said, as he came from behind the desk and began to approach her. 'And by Christ I have. Do you know what you have done to me, girl?'

Lizzie began backing away from him, until her knees connected with the chair and she sat on it and watched the priest approach her, soutane lifted, so she saw his penis hard and erect before her. 'You're a mass of sin, if you can work a man like me into such a state. Well now you'll pay for it, you whoring temptress. Take it in your hands.'

'Oh God Almighty, I can't, Father, really I can't,' Lizzie cried, and tried to screw herself further into the chair.

The priest reached out, plucked the hat from her head and grabbed a mass of Lizzie's curls, and then jerked her towards him with such force she fell onto her knees, inches from the vile thing the priest was pushing at her. 'Take it,' the priest thundered. 'Or by Christ I'll beat you black and blue.'

Lizzie knew the man meant it, and in the state he was in he could easily kill her. Then the nuns would name some disease that she'd died from and that would be that, and so she took the pulsating organ with hands that shook.

For all her married state, Lizzie had never held or seen a man's penis. Steve wasn't into the niceties of the act. A wife's duty was to submit to her husband when he wanted sex, and lie passive beneath him while he took his pleasure. Lizzie accepted it as part of marriage, pleased when she enjoyed it, and took the other assaults on her body without complaint.

But now, for the first time, she held a man's penis, and felt it pulsating as the blood pumped through it. She saw the testicles hanging like two wizened sacks and the mass of brown curly hair, and felt nausea and revulsion course through her.

'Put it in your mouth.'

Lizzie stared at the priest, unable to believe she'd heard right. He couldn't mean that. God Almighty!

'Your mouth,' he screeched.

She shook her head. 'I couldn't, Father. Please don't ask me.'

'I don't ask you, whore, I'm telling you,' the priest said. 'I know you're gagging for it.'

Lizzie was unable to make a reply, for suddenly the priest's hands were either side of her head, crushing her ears, and he began pushing her head down. Her mouth was fixed open as she'd tried to speak, and now she couldn't even cry out a warning as she felt sickness rise in her when the penis was just an inch or so from her lips. She tried to move her head, but it was held fast in his hands like a vice, and the priest had his eyes closed and he was groaning. Suddenly, she could hold the nausea no longer, and she vomited over him, his soutane, her hands and down her dress.

Fury like he'd never felt before pounded through the priest's body. He caught Lizzie under the chin, as he lifted his foot and kicked her with such fury she hit the wall with a sickening thud and slithered to a heap on the floor.

Father Conroy looked at the girl slumped against the wall and her pallor and stillness terrified the life out of him. He cleaned himself off as well as he could and wiped the vomit from her hands with his handkerchief before feeling for her pulse, relieved to find one. He noted blood dripping down her front from the cut on her chin and seeping into her curls from the one at the back of her head.

He arranged her inert body in front of the desk and went for Sister Jude. He didn't know if she believed his explanation of how Lizzie sustained her injuries, but he didn't really care. She'd never betray him and just nodded sagely when he explained how the girl had stumbled and caught her chin on the desk before falling to the floor and banging her head. 'We must take her into the infirmary,' Sister Jude said, 'before we decide what to do.' She thought the girl might be roused as she was carried on a stretcher, but there was no reaction, and as they laid her on one of the beds she said, 'I think we must fetch the doctor.'

'Do you think that's necessary?' Sister Benedict said. 'I'm sure I can cope. Sister Maria can help.'

Father Conroy, who'd followed, was thoroughly alarmed. 'What happens within these walls is sacrosanct, but outsiders ask awkward questions. Doesn't she just want a wee sleep and she'll be as right as rain?'

'Maybe, aye. But what if she needs more than that?' Sister Jude said. 'Remember, this one has a brother who's concerned for her and comes to see her every fortnight. He might make trouble.'

Father Conroy knew he might. He'd caught sight of the young man himself and so he bowed to the inevitable. 'Maybe,' he said to Sister Benedict, 'you could take off her soiled clothes and put her in a night-dress before the doctor sees her.'

Doctor Murray was very worried about Lizzie and not at all convinced by the explanation of how she came by her injuries. He examined her gently all over and then asked for help to turn her over so he could see if there was further damage and he whistled at the extent of the bruising on her back. He didn't like the set-up here at all. He hadn't liked it the last time he was here, when he lost the girl and baby in childbirth because they'd left it too late to call him in.

He knew Sister Jude ran this place and so he spoke to her. 'She's a sick girl, Sister,' he said. 'I'll not beat about the bush. I don't know what goes on in this establishment and maybe you have reason to behave as you do. But now this young woman is my patient and you ignore what I say at your peril, for if anything happens to her through neglect, I'll hold you responsible.'

'Are you threatening me?'

The doctor gave a grim laugh. 'You give it whatever name suits. I'd call it more in the nature of a warning. The cuts beneath her chin and on her head will not close on their own and she's lost enough blood already. She is deeply concussed and in shock and I wouldn't be at all surprised if she doesn't go into premature labour.'

'Now.' he said, when he'd finished stitching and dressing the wound, 'someone must stay with her night and day until she regains consciousness. When she does, phone me, I will need to test for brain damage. If she shows signs she is going to lose the baby, conscious or not, again send for me.

'Once conscious she will need bed rest for a week, more maybe. In fact, I'll tell you when she can get up. Her bottom teeth were loosened by the blow to her jaw, but they'll probably bed back in the gum and so nourishing broths will probably be best at first.'

'It was no blow,' Sister Jude said. 'It was . . .'

'It was a blow, Sister. She wouldn't have sustained an injury like that smacking it on the table, and from the shape of the wound I would say a toecap did it.'

'I assure you . . .'

'I'm a medical man, Sister,' Doctor Murray said. 'I've attended accidents before and seen the result of a kick. And if she then banged the back of head on the floor, she'd have had to turn a somersault before she fell. Quite a feat, don't you think?'

'I think your manner offensive.'

'My manner, you say? I feel what happened to that young woman was offensive. Be careful, Sister. I'm not one of your wayward girls to be cowed and frightened half to death, and once through that door a few words dropped in the right ears would mean, at the very least, you'd have to answer very difficult questions.'

'Really, Doctor . . .'

'Really, Sister,' Doctor Murray cut in. 'I've stitched and dressed both wounds, they won't need touching yet awhile, and though I've left more salve she shouldn't need it again until tomorrow and I will administer it myself when I call. I'll see myself out. Good day to you.'

Sister Jude sat back in her chair, stunned. For the first time in her life that she could remember, she was lost for words. Completely nonplussed. Damn the girl, she thought. And damn the doctor too. But she didn't give voice to these thoughts.

CHAPTER EIGHTEEN

Muzzy unformed memories swirled in Lizzie's brain, as if they were shrouded in grey mist. She was aware of pain and discomfort, and her eyes felt heavy when she tried to lift the lids, but when she eventually peeled them open she snapped them shut again at the glaring whiteness of everything.

Slowly she again opened them just a little and gazed about her. She knew she was in the infirmary and wondered why. The slight movement had been spotted, and the next moment a shape loomed above her. As her eyes focused, she recognised Sister Benedict. 'So, you're awake at last.'

Lizzie felt she had to make no reply to that comment, so she asked instead, 'What happened?'

'You had a wee fall.'

'A wee fall!' Lizzie repeated. She tried to cast her mind back, despite her head throbbing in protest.

'How are you feeling?'

Never in the months she'd been in the convent had a nun asked her how she was feeling. It gave Lizzie quite a jolt. And, really, how did she feel? Awful! Bloody awful! Everywhere ached, even her face and her jaw-bone and her head thumped. Should she say? Would the nun care? She decided to say nothing about how she felt, but again she asked, 'The fall, where was it?'

'In the sacristy.'

The sacristy! That word produced a window through the fog. The sacristy and her and Celia, their arms full of vestments going in there, thinking it empty and finding Father Conroy still there.

And at the remembrance of the priest, Lizzie's skin began to crawl, for the memories now crowded inside her. She remembered being forced to hold the throbbing penis of that perverted excuse for a man of God, and then her head being pressed down so that her mouth, held open, would take it between her lips. And if I had, she thought now fiercely, I'd have bitten the bloody thing off and taken pleasure in it.

She wanted to fling this at the nun looking at her now in consternation, tell her the manner of priest they served and sought to please, but Celia's warning to say nothing stilled her tongue. But, by Christ, why should he get away with it?

Nevertheless, she knew he would, like the pervert who raped her. She lifted her hand and tentatively touched her jaw and felt the dressing there, and then her probing hands touched the bandage encircling her head.

'You caught your chin on the desk as you fell and then gave your head quite a crack,' the nun said.

Lizzie remembered the priest's red face suffused with rage as she vomited all over him. She didn't see the boot, but she'd felt the crack of impact that set her

355

against the wall with such violence she lost consciousness. 'A fall,' she repeated ironically. 'Is that the name they put upon it these days?'

She saw Sister Benedict's face flush. Was it embarrassment, or shame, or guilt? She wasn't sure, nor was she sure how much the nuns were aware of. She might never know, but it wouldn't matter really because she knew they'd stick to their story, and if she was to voice hers and continue to voice it she'd be speedily whipped away to a place where no one would listen. Who would take notice of the ramblings of a mad woman incarcerated in the asylum?

And so she met the nun's look levelly, but said nothing. And the nun said, with a hint of satisfaction, 'Some of your hair had to be shaved for the doctor to stitch the cut. You will have to explain to your brother.'

'The doctor? They called the doctor?'

'Oh aye,' Sister Benedict said, and gave a sniff of disapproval and went on, 'He was very worried about you. Gave specific instructions. You have been in that unconscious state over thirty-six hours, for it's Monday morning now.'

'Monday morning?' Lizzie wondered if her mind was affected. She seemed only able to repeat what the nun said.

And now Sister Benedict bobbed her head and went on. 'Aye, thirty-six hours. The man himself will be along shortly. Glad to see you so recovered, I imagine. Now, do you want a nice bowl of nourishing broth?'

'Nourishing broth?' There she went again, but nourishing broth was not on the menu for the sinful inmates of that place. She wasn't hungry, and yet it might be a while before anything else was offered, and she'd like to see their bowl of nourishing broth.

But when it came, on a tray carried by Celia, which made Lizzie's eyes light up, it was thick and rich and filled with meat and vegetables. 'Leave the tray and return to your duties,' Sister Benedict said curtly, and to Lizzie she said, 'You'll be all right on your own? I need to pop along to the nursery.'

'Aye,' Lizzie said, but barely had the door closed behind the nun when Celia, putting the bowl of broth down on the locker beside Lizzie, said, 'What did that bastard do to you?'

And Lizzie told her, just as it was, and noted that Celia didn't seem even mildly surprised.

'You too?' she asked, and Celia nodded miserably.

'It happened three times to me.'

'Oh, Celia!'

'I never thought of vomiting over him, though.'

'I couldn't help that.'

'He very nearly killed you,' Celia said. 'I heard the doctor giving out to Sister Jude when I was clearing the hall outside the room. We were all hugging ourselves with delight, though I was real worried about you.'

'I'm all right,' Lizzie assured her. 'Though a bit sore still, and I'm not at all hungry, so you eat that broth.'

She saw the longing on Celia's face and yet she shook her head. 'I can't.'

'Course you can, I don't want it.'

'Are you sure?'

'Positive, and eat it quick before the old harridan comes back.'

Celia needed no further urging and Lizzie smiled at the look of pleasure on Celia's face as she emptied the bowl in seconds. 'Oh God, I'm full for the first time in months and warm inside. Oh, Lizzie, thanks. That was terrific.'

'Good,' Lizzie said with satisfaction. 'Leave the tray, or they'll know you stopped too long.'

'You're right,' Celia said. 'But I'll be back if I can. Most of the girls know we're friends, so they'll let me come if there is ever a choice in it.'

'Well, go now in case Sister Benedict comes,' Lizzie said, 'for if she imagines we are friends I'll never see you in here again, and she'll find ways of making our lives more miserable than ever.'

Celia saw the wisdom of Lizzie's words and she hadn't been gone that long when Sister Benedict came back and was pleased to see the bowl empty. 'Soon have you strong and healthy again,' she said, 'with food like that. Now, I'll let the doctor in. He arrived some minutes ago.'

Lizzie had never seen Doctor Murray before, though she'd glimpsed him through the gloom when he'd come in to attend to Cora. She found him kind and gentle, and he asked her questions and held up cards for her to describe and looked into her eyes with a special instrument. He was able to say with a smile that there was no sign of any brain damage. Sister Benedict left them alone in the end and the doctor, as he examined her physical condition, asked, 'How did this happen?'

'Did they not tell you? I had a fall.'

'They told me,' the doctor said grimly. 'Now I want you to tell me who kicked you in the face?'

'No one kicked me . . .'

'Give me some credit.'

'Then give me some consideration,' Lizzie retorted. 'What you want me to say could sign my death warrant, or as near as in this place. My friend said normal rules don't apply here and she's so bloody right. Until I'm well away, from here, with the stink of it washed from my body, I'll tell not a soul about what happened in that sacristy. I fell, and we'll leave it so.'

The doctor, though shocked by Lizzie's outburst, was perturbed enough to protest. 'No one should get away with kicking you.'

'Ah God,' Lizzie said with feeling. 'If that was all it was! Look, Doctor, I know the townfolk think of us as whores and harlots inside this place, but I'll tell you how I came to be here and I'm not the only one by any means.'

And Doctor Murray listened to a tale so horrifying he might have doubted it if he hadn't seen the pain reflected in Lizzie's eyes as she repeated and relived it. He imagined her panic as she realised she was pregnant, and could even see her parents' desire to hide her away someplace till it was over; but this place . . . God, the whole ethos of it sickened him.

If there was the slightest doubt lingering, that was dispelled when he saw the scar running down Lizzie's abdomen as he gently examined her there too. 'Any pains?'

'Plenty, but not labour pains,' Lizzie said. Funny that although she'd wanted to get rid of the baby for so long, now she wanted the child to live, to have a crack at life. 'My dearest wish now,' Lizzie said, 'is for my baby to go to a good and loving home and have the chance of a happy life.'

'You'll leave it here with the nuns then?' the doctor asked.

'There is no alternative,' Lizzie answered. 'How could I take to a child born of a brutal rape, and even if I could, how could I do that to my husband, expect him to raise a bastard child. He might think I was playing fast and loose while he was away fighting. This is best for the child, for everyone. The nuns will keep it in the nursery and it will go to a Catholic and childless couple.' She gave a small sigh and went on, 'They probably have parents lined up already.'

The doctor, looking at Lizzie's wistful face, thought it might not be as easy as she thought to give up her child, but there was nothing to be gained by going down that route, so he said instead, 'And then what?'

'Then I go back to Birmingham.'

'And take up your life again?'

'Aye. What would you have me do?'

The doctor shook his head helplessly. He had no answers, he just felt bad that such a young woman should have to shoulder the anguish and stress all by herself, especially when she was totally blameless.

However, anything he might have said was cut off by the entrance of the nun. 'The teeth are bedding down nicely,' he told her, 'so from tomorrow, she can have something more solid than broth. Good red meat, cheese, eggs and milk should build her up. And she should have about ten days' bed rest. I'll be in Thursday of next week to remove the stitches, and by then she should be able to get up.'

'Yes, Doctor.'

'There is no sign of her going into labour prematurely either,' he said, 'and she would have done by now, I think, so that is at least one problem we haven't to deal with.'

'No, Doctor,' Sister Benedict said, and she led the doctor out of the infirmary. Lizzie leant back and shut her eyes.

For ten days, Lizzie languished in bed, even glad of the altar cloths she was brought to embroider, for time hung heavy. Celia came most times with her tray and shared Lizzie's food if they were left alone long enough. They also shared many confidences and fears about the future and grew closer than ever, and Lizzie was worried over what would happen to Celia when she went away with Johnnie. A plan began to formulate in her mind, but for it to succeed she needed the help of the doctor and her brother.

Johnnie was expected on Saturday, but first the doctor would come to remove her stitches, and once that was done she would be back in the fray. As soon as Sister Benedict left the room, Lizzie, knowing she'd probably not have the opportunity to speak to the doctor alone again, told him that when she left she wanted to smuggle another girl called Celia out with her.

He stared at her as if he couldn't believe his ears. 'D'you know what you're risking, for the girl at least?'

'D'you know what the alternative is?' Lizzie snapped back. 'You're not stupid. You know the set-up here.'

'But . . . Oh, God Almighty,' the doctor cried in

horror, for he couldn't see how this planned escape could be achieved. 'What will you do if the nuns get wind of it?' he asked. 'If they should catch you?'

'Then we may as well be dead,' Lizzie said. 'But I'm prepared to risk it.'

'What about the other girl, this Celia?'

'Listen, Doctor,' Lizzie said earnestly. 'If Celia doesn't get out soon, you might be called back here in a short while to declare the girl clinically insane and have her committed to an asylum. She really is that close to the edge, and there is no hope that any family member will ever come for her. They have totally disowned her, every one of them. It is as if she never existed.'

'That's appalling!'

'In the real world it may be,' Lizzie said. 'Here it is surprisingly common. Look, I once said that I'll not talk about what goes on here until I'm well away from it, and I won't go back on that, but you must believe me that this place is Hell on earth. All the girls suffer and I am sorry for them, desperately sorry, but I can't smuggle them all out; and Celia ... well, she's my friend. I feel sort of responsible for her and I am seriously worried that she will go under if I don't do something.'

The doctor still hesitated and Lizzie said impatiently, 'We haven't much time. Sister Benedict could be back at any moment and it's not even going to involve you. I'm only asking that whenever the child is born you give some excuse that I'm not ready to leave until it coincides with the laundry van that comes on Friday. I know my brother would find a Friday easier than a Tuesday, and the van comes at about half past ten.'

'And if I refuse?'

'Then you're not the man I took you to be, and I'll bid you good day and hope you sleep easy in your bed tonight,' Lizzie replied testily.

The doctor laughed, but checked his mirth lest the nuns heard. 'I've got to hand it to you, Lizzie, you have a way with you. But have you thought I might have nothing to do with your baby's birth? It isn't their normal procedure to contact the doctor.'

'They'll call you if you say they must,' Lizzie said emphatically. 'They're scared stiff of you. Celia heard what you said the time you wiped the floor with Sister Jude and their reaction afterwards. It gave the girls some lighter moments even thinking of it.'

'So, if I go and lay the law down and say I must be called for the birth, then I will be.'

'Aye, I'd say so, and I'll feel happier too.'

'Then, madam, it shall be done,' the doctor said with a mock salute, but despite his bantering manner he was a worried man. Lizzie had coerced a promise from him, and if the whole plan should go wrong then God help those two young women. He didn't know the full extent of the horrors of that place, but what he had seen reflected in Lizzie's eyes and the fall that was no fall at all told him enough.

Lizzie smiled at him. 'See you then,' she said. She was sorry to see the doctor go, sorry that she would soon be back to sternness and forbidding silence.

Not five minutes after the doctor had left, Lizzie was back in the laundry, and it was well she had the doctor's promise to sustain her, for Sister Carmel took great pleasure in taunting and goading her at every turn. She was given the job of heaving the bedding from the boilers to the poss tub to be pounded with the dolly, and then to the sinks where stubborn stains would be rubbed with the washboard, and then on to the rinsing sinks.

It was one of the most strenuous jobs, for the sheets weighed heavy, but when another girl suggested taking her place, Sister Carmel refused. She'd looked over the glasses she had perched on her nose and knew she'd be glad to see the back of Lizzie Gillespie. She was a troublemaker, and look now at the fuss made of her over a wee fall. Well, she needn't think she was having an easy ride here. 'Isn't Lizzie Gillespie just back from nearly a fortnight's bed rest and over nothing at all, waited on hand and foot and special food prepared? If you ask me, she's more able for the work than any of you.'

Lizzie flashed a smile of gratitude at the girl who'd risked censure to ask, and bent to the task. Before too long she felt the strain on her neck muscles and her back began to ache so badly that pains shot down both her legs.

When Johnnie arrived the following Saturday she was glad to sit down on the chair in Sister Jude's office where she told Johnnie of the fall she had had and showed him the scar under her chin and the shaved part of her head, which her hair was beginning to cover nicely. Lizzie made great play of the fact of how ungainly a woman could be when she was expecting, and how light-headed they often are, to allay any suspicions he might have.

It was later, with the letters written, that Lizzie said, 'When it's over, Johnnie, what happens?'

'I'm to come for you,' Johnnie said. 'I'll have the loan of the car again and I'm to take you straight to the docks at Dun Laoghaire and set you on a ferry.'

Lizzie nodded slowly and then said, 'I want to take Celia out with me.'

'Are you mad?'

'She has no one to speak for her. And she is my friend.'

'And what manner of girl is she, to be here?' Johnnie said.

'Don't turn your nose up like that, Johnnie,' Lizzie said sharply. 'Don't judge on rumour or say-so. Celia lived with her family on a farm in West Meath and was engaged to a fellow. He said it was what engaged people did and she gave in, just the once. As soon as he heard of her pregnancy, he's off to England, no engagement and seemingly no address. Her family disowned her. She had a little boy and gave him away. Now she's set here for life.'

Johnnie bit his lip. Her life sounded harsh, but she wasn't his problem. 'I still don't . . .'

'Please, Johnnie, I've never asked anything of you before,' Lizzie said.

'But how is it to be done? I can hardly bundle the two of you into the car and wave a cheery farewell to the nuns.'

'No, look,' Lizzie said. 'I have a plan. I've had nothing else to do most of the time but plan Celia's escape. The laundry van comes here every Tuesday and Friday about ten o'clock, full of the town's dirty washing. We have first to unload the dirty washing and put it into the laundry and then load the clean washing in the van. It takes time, for there is a lot of it and all the girls are in and out of the door and it is the only time a girl would have a chance to slip away unnoticed, especially as when we have finished, the men lock up the van and Sister Carmel takes them up to pay Sister Jude.'

'So, why hasn't anyone tried escaping before now?'

'They have,' Lizzie said. 'A girl hid in the van, but she was soon hunted down in the town and brought back and whipped. The men keep a weather eye on it now, so that that trick can never be tried again. And even if you were to get out of the convent building, where could you go? The gates are locked and you'd never climb that wall.'

'And you'd stick out like a sore thumb,' Johnnie said. 'You must see, Lizzie, that this is madness. Sheer madness!'

Lizzie sighed in exasperation. 'Please, Johnnie,' she pleaded. 'You must help. There is no one else I can turn to. When you come to fetch me, you'll be bringing a case full of clothes, right?'

'Aye.'

'Well, there is bound to be something suitable for Celia to change into later,' Lizzie said. 'And she'll need a scarf or something for her head, until we are well away from here anyway. You turn up to fetch me when the laundry van is here and Celia will be able to slip off in the confusion, climb into the back of the car and cover herself with the blanket.'

Johnnie surveyed his sister. She'd thought it out carefully and it could just work. But did he want to get involved in this? No, he bloody didn't. Yet how could he do that to Lizzie? It obviously mattered so much and she'd been let down at every turn so far.

He sighed and said. 'Okay, Lizzie, say I do agree to this crazy plan. If it succeeds, and to my way of thinking it's a bloody big if, what do I do with Celia when I get her away from this place?'

'Nothing,' Lizzie replied. 'For nowhere in Ireland is safe. She'll come to Birmingham with me.'

'What of Steve and Flo?'

'What of them?' Lizzie said recklessly. 'I'm past caring about Flo and I'll tell Steve she's a workmate who has been bombed out. He'll swallow that. Jobs were ten-a-penny when I left and she'll soon be independent. She's that kind of girl.'

Johnnie had got to his feet and was pacing the room, running his hands through his hair distractedly. 'I just don't know, Lizzie. I mean, what if you're ready to leave before the day the laundry vans arrive?'

'I won't be. The doctor is going to help and when the baby is born he will tell the nuns when I can be expected to leave the infirmary.'

'And if he breaks his word?'

'He won't,' Lizzie said confidently. 'He has no time for the nuns, and that's not so much what he says, but the way he speaks to them and looks at them. As for Celia . . . she's not yet eighteen, Johnnie.' She touched his arm. 'Please, do this one thing for me?'

Johnnie looked at his sister, banished from her home and separated from her children for an incident she was no willing partner to. And now she had to give birth to the child and see it given away to someone else, and he knew he had to help her in this one thing.

'All right.'
'Do I have your word?'
'You have my word.'
'Oh, thank God.'

It was hard in that accursed place to find anywhere a person could talk, let alone talk privately where no one might eavesdrop, for to give the plan any chance of working at all, secrecy was essential.

Lizzie was like a cat on hot bricks, but she had to wait until she was sent with Celia and two others for kitchen duties. There, with the nun called away and the others girls the far side of the room, Lizzie told Celia, quietly covering her words with the clatter of the pots, plates and dishes they were washing.

It was even harder for Celia to listen to this fantastic, magnificent and yet terrifying plan in silence. 'So, have you got it?' Lizzie whispered urgently.

'The doctor is to say you are not fit to leave until a Friday morning after the birth, and Johnnie is to come the same time as the laundry van and I am to slip away and hide in Johnnie's car,' Celia whispered back.

'D'you think you can do it? That it will work?'

'God knows,' Celia said. 'I know I can't not do it though. It's my one chance to get out of this hellhole and I am going to grasp it with both hands.'

Celia wasn't a fool and she knew it was risky. She also knew the arrival of the laundry van was the only time that she could slip away unobserved, for with the loading and unloading it was hard to keep tabs on everyone. As long as Johnnie was on time and he parked close to the hedge on the gravel path before the door,

368

it might just work, especially as Lizzie said there would be a bag of clothes for her and something to cover her up with.

'Oh sweet Jesus,' she said. 'I can scarce believe it.'

'Well you'd better start believing it,' Lizzie said, her face aglow, 'because it is going to happen.'

'I'll never forget you for this,' Celia said solemnly. 'Not as long as there is breath in my body.'

The girls at the convent were not encouraged to touch each other, but Celia threw her arms around Lizzie and kissed her cheek. The other two girls looked at them askance and then averted their eyes quickly, and Lizzie warned Celia in a shaky voice, 'Don't let them see you looking happy. They'll want to know the reason for it.'

Celia knew Lizzie was right and yet it was hard to assume a serious, ever-sorrowful face with a heart full of joy. Oh, for Lizzie to have such a brother! Yet she knew the path to freedom was strewn with thorns, and if she was to be found or brought back then it would be God alone who would help her. She might not be kept in the convent at all: the asylum was host to the girls who couldn't or wouldn't conform.

But then, she thought, what were the odds? If she didn't take this chance offered out to her because she was afraid, it would never come again, of that she was certain. Then she was condemning herself to a living death. The thought of spending the rest of her years here was one that would surely send her clean mad. Then she'd be knocking on the doors of the asylum herself, asking to be let in.

*　　*　　*

The strenuous work at the laundry went on and each day it got harder for Lizzie. She was in more and more discomfort, but she wouldn't complain. She'd bite her lip and go on. Never would she let those malicious cows know they were getting to her. Celia often heard Lizzie crying with the cramping spasms in her back and legs, even though she tried to muffle the sobs in a pillow, and in the laundry her face was often blanched with the unrelenting pain that was also reflected in her eyes. She hoped to God Lizzie wasn't doing herself harm.

Johnnie too saw how exhausted she looked when he called the following fortnight, but when he asked her if she was doing too much, she laughed. She had the urge to take his dear head between her hands and tell him what she did each day, but she resisted. She didn't want him to rock the boat now. Time enough to tell him when she was well-away from this place and free. 'I'm grand,' she told him. 'The last few weeks are like this for everyone.'

Johnnie took her word for it, and why wouldn't he? 'Not long now, anyway,' he said. 'Soon it will be all over for you. An end to the nightmare and time to look forward.'

'Aye,' Lizzie agreed, 'and it can't come soon enough for me.'

Lizzie's pains began on Thursday, 7th November, when she was working in the laundry. The girl beside her saw her give a grimace as she lifted the heavy tongs. She said nothing, but her two eyebrows went up questioningly and she nodded her head towards Sister Carmel bent over her embroidery.

Lizzie shook her head vehemently. She would let the nuns know only when she had to. She could well do without them telling her how sinful she was and how the pain was purging her soul.

She had pains all morning. They were niggling ones at first, just a bit stronger than she'd experienced every month. She toyed with her dinner, unable to eat the tasteless thin broth let alone the slice of stale bread, and she saw many girls look at her as if they couldn't believe it, for they were too hungry to be choosy. Surreptitiously, Lizzie passed her bowl and plate to the girl next to her. If she hadn't, the nuns would have gone on about wasting good food when the poor wee heathens in Africa were starving, and she couldn't have borne that.

By the afternoon the pains had worsened, and now, in the last hour or so, they'd become almost unbearable. But still Lizzie hung on. The small groans she couldn't help were covered by the noise in the laundry: the bubbling water, the creak of the mangle and hiss of the irons.

It was as they were told to tidy the laundry ready for tea that she suddenly experienced a pain that caused her to crouch with her arm wrapped around her stomach.

Celia, who'd been watching Lizzie for hours, put up her hand. 'Sister, Pansy is . . .'

She didn't have to say any more, for blood was running from Lizzie when she tried to stand, dripping in steady drops onto the floor.

'Almighty God!' Sister Carmel cried. 'Get her to the infirmary and quickly, and someone clean up this mess.'

Celia leapt forward, her arm around her friend, and with Queenie on the other side they almost carried Lizzie, who was letting out whimpers of pain.

She'd had children before and thought she'd have an easier time of it, but the pains went on hour after hour. They were so excruciating she couldn't help crying out with them, and the nuns took no notice when Lizzie asked for the doctor. 'You need no doctor,' Sister Benedict told her sharply when she screamed out. 'Don't be making such a fuss. You know what you are about; you knew this day would come. Pain is good for the soul. Bear it bravely.'

There were more words in the same vein as the night wore on, and by then Lizzie was too exhausted to make any sort of reply.

The minutes ticked into hours and Lizzie screamed and writhed on the bed. She felt as if she was being torn in two. The others were never like this. 'Get the doctor,' she begged. 'I'm in agony. Something is wrong. Please, for God's sake, get the doctor.'

'We don't need to bother the doctor.'

'Get the doctor, you bloody vixen.'

The slap took Lizzie unawares and yet she barely felt it as she was in the throes of a massive contraction; but when it eased a little she looked straight at Sister Benedict. Lizzie's face was lined with pain and her eyes were glazing over, and yet her voice, punctuated by pants, was definite enough. 'If anything happens to me, questions will be asked. Both the doctor and my brother won't rest.'

Sister Benedict knew Lizzie was right. There were

people who cared about Pansy. Most families were too glad to rid themselves of their pregnant daughters and had no wish to hear anything about them once they'd gone into the convent to get rid of their 'little problem', but this one . . .

She came back from the phone and told Lizzie with great satisfaction that the doctor was out on call. 'The housekeeper was none to happy about being roused,' she said, 'especially when the call came from here. Most decent people think the doctor shouldn't have to treat girls so full of sin and badness. Anyway, she said she has no intention of waiting up, but she'll leave a note. Whether he sees it when he comes in or not is another matter entirely.'

That's when Lizzie knew she would die. Die like Cora, and the child with her. Tom and Niamh would be motherless and Celia would stay in the convent forever, but her troubles would be over. She didn't fear death any more, she longed for it. She'd embrace anything to make this unbearable pain stop.

She was semi-conscious when the doctor came, and seeing the state of her he berated the nuns.

'We called you,' Sister Benedict said in defence.

'Not in time you didn't. Almighty Christ, she didn't get into this state in an hour or two. Get me water quickly, I must see what the problem is.'

He thought he was too late, that this one too would slip through his fingers, and he knew if she did he'd expose this place, even if by doing so he jeopardised his own position.

A swift examination revealed the problem. 'The baby is breach,' he said. 'Too late to turn it and both mother and child are totally exhausted. She's too narrow to give birth, I'll have to make a cut.'

He poured chloroform that he'd got from his bag onto a cloth he put over Lizzie's face, and she drifted blissfully to sleep while the doctor went to work.

There was a sudden silence in the room and Sister Benedict and Sister Maria, who'd been sent to assist, were looking with ill-concealed contempt at the child that the doctor had removed from Lizzie.

And he was regarding it with pity. The poor, bloody little scrap. Yet another cross to load on the narrow shoulders of Lizzie Gillespie. Almighty Christ! Maybe it would be better to let the child drift away. She'd get over it in time, know in the end it was for the best; and she'd never know the truth, she hadn't come around yet. The child had let out no cry and he knew, could see, her nostrils and mouth were coated with mucus. All he had to do was nothing.

He watched the arms and legs twitching desperately, and beside him he heard Sister Benedict give a sigh of satisfaction as she said, 'Blessed relief!' He was suddenly engulfed with shame. He was a doctor, for God's sake, committed to saving life, and he was proposing to let a small and vulnerable baby die for no better reason than he thought it would be kinder that way.

'Get me some water and quickly,' he commanded as he bent over the child and began to softly massage the baby's chest. When the water came he dampened a soft muslin cloth and began to wipe away the mucus that had begun to crust under the child's nostrils and around the lips. The child gave a gasp and the limbs threshed more vigorously as newborn wails filled the room. The doctor wrapped the baby in a blanket and lifted her into his arms and smiled, a smile that wasn't returned by the scowling and obviously disapproving nuns.

He was suddenly aware that Lizzie was haemorrhaging, the blood pumping from her in a scarlet stream. 'Take the child,' he said to Sister Benedict, holding her out. 'I must see to the mother, for we're not out of the woods yet.'

'I'll not touch that,' Sister Benedict said. 'None of us will. Put it in the crib beside the bed.'

There was no time to argue. Lizzie was in distress, and if he was to save her then speed was essential. And so the doctor tenderly laid the child in the crib and bent over the bed again.

CHAPTER NINETEEN

Later that same morning, Johnnie was chopping wood in the barn when he saw the car stop at the head of the lane and he peered through the rain-laden gloom to see who it was.

The car was a taxi, he realised, and when the nun alighted from it, he recognised her as the head nun at the Godawful place Lizzie was at. He knew only something of mammoth proportions would have brought her here and the blood turned to ice in his veins. Had something happened to his sister and without one of her own beside her? Ah Jesus! He left the axe stuck into the chopping block and went into the kitchen to prepare his mother.

It smelt sweet and hot inside, for Catherine had been having a big bake and the things were cooling on trays on the table. 'Mammy,' he said. 'There's a nun coming down the lane.'

'A nun!'

'From that place, you know, where Lizzie . . .'

'Oh Holy Mother of God.' Catherine turned anguished eyes to her son and he put his arm around her. 'Let's see what she has to say,' he said, though his own heart was filled with dread.

And that's how they were when Seamus brought Sister Jude inside. Catherine continued to stand and stare at her. It was as if she had turned to stone. 'You don't know me,' the nun said to Catherine, 'though I've met your son,' and at this she inclined her head to Johnnie. 'My name is Sister Jude and I am in charge of St Agnes's Convent, where your daughter is. I have something of importance to say to you and something that could not wait.'

Catherine's insides had turned to water. 'Is Lizzie all right, Sister?' she cried. 'Has anything happened to her?'

'Your daughter is perfectly well,' the nun said with a curl of her lip. 'In the early hours of this morning she gave birth to a baby girl. Pansy had to undergo an operation and she is still a little weak, for the birth was a difficult one, but she is out of danger now, the doctor said.'

'Oh, thank God,' Catherine said, and Johnnie let out the breath he hadn't been aware he'd been holding.

Seamus said, 'Beg your pardon, Sister, but just who the Hell is Pansy?'

'I told you, Daddy,' Johnnie said. 'They give them all different names. Sister Jude means Lizzie.'

'Then I don't understand at all,' Seamus said. 'I thought when you put a girl in one of those places you didn't hear from them again till it was over, and the child was never mentioned, given up for adoption. I don't wish to be rude, Sister, but I have no wish to know anything of the child. It will have nothing to do with us, after all.'

'If the situation was normal, it wouldn't, you may be assured,' Sister Jude said.

Catherine, now assured by the visitor that her daughter was all right, busied herself at the hearth as Seamus began, 'Then what . . . ?'

'Let the good woman make herself comfortable, Seamus, and I'm sure she'll tell us all,' Catherine said. 'Will you come up to the fire, Sister, for it's a raw day outside and I'll brew tea in a jiffy to have with barn brack and scones.'

Sister Jude sat down before the fire with Seamus opposite her before answering. 'I wish to know what arrangements you have for your daughter and the child?'

'Johnnie here will fetch her when it's time for her to leave and take her to the boat to return to Birmingham,' Seamus said.

'And the child?'

'But that's . . . I understood you dealt with the babies?' Catherine said, handing the nun a cup of tea, which she accepted thankfully.

'We do in the majority of cases.'

'Well, why is this different?'

'Mrs Clooney, our babies are adopted by childless Catholic couples, but no one will want Pansy's baby.'

'Why? Is it deformed, handicapped in some way?'

'Deformed, no. Handicapped, certainly.' The nun took a sip of the tea before saying, 'Your daughter, Mrs Clooney, has given birth to a black baby.'

The shock was almost tangible. Every eye was on the nun, but no one could speak. They seemed incapable of uttering a word. 'I see you are as stupefied as we all were and are. We have never had such a thing happen in all my years at the convent. It is an abomination. No one will want it.

'I think you will agree there will be no nice, loving home for Pansy's baby, and the child will probably reside in one of the country's orphanages, if you are agreeable. Dublin is probably the best place to try. They have all sorts of oddities in some of their homes.'

Johnnie was incensed. 'Don't call the child an oddity. Whatever her colour, she's still a baby, an innocent baby.'

'Aye, well, her mother's no innocent,' Seamus growled. 'Opening her legs for a bleeding nigger, begging your pardon, Sister.'

'She was attacked.'

'Aye, so she said.'

'Why don't you believe her?'

'Why don't you grow up, son? You can't let yourself see anything bad in her, because you always thought the sun shone out of her arse.'

'I've never known Lizzie lie. It was the blackout. She wouldn't know who attacked her, or what colour or creed he was.'

'There was no bloody attack.'

'Of course there was.'

'Does it matter?' Catherine said wearily. 'Whatever way our Lizzie got pregnant, she was, and has given birth to a child not wanted nor welcomed anywhere.'

'You're right there,' Seamus said. 'And don't call her 'Our Lizzie', she's no daughter of mine. I doubt I'll ever want to clap eyes on her again.'

'Don't say that, Daddy,' Johnnie protested. 'We are looking after her children.'

'Aye, and a fine example she is for them,' Seamus said. 'She'll not see them for some long while, if at all.'

'Daddy . . .'

'I agree totally,' Sister Jude said, cutting across Johnnie. 'She is in the infirmary now and will have no contact with the other girls. As for the child, she couldn't be taken into the nursery. That is where the parents come to collect their babies and we have two more girls due any day now. What if the prospective parents came in and saw a black baby? Anyway, the nuns can barely bring themselves to touch it.'

She didn't tell the family that the baby had been born dead. Sister Benedict had told her that. 'It was still, Sister,' she said. 'It just lay there, not crying or moving much. It was the doctor revived it and then it began to cry. God forgive me, Sister, but I did wonder why he bothered. I mean, what sort of life will it ever hope to have?'

'I expect Pansy to be taken from the place when the doctor deems her fit to leave,' she said now. 'Do I take it you want me to find an orphanage to take the child?'

'Aye. It's the only thing to do.'

'How does Lizzie feel about it?' Johnnie asked.

'Lizzie!' Seamus bawled. 'She has nothing to say in this. God Almighty, if this got out.'

Johnnie knew the time for any more talking was past and decisions were being made over Lizzie's head. Never mind, he thought, he'd see her for himself the following afternoon. Suddenly, the whole thing sickened him.

'Where are you off to?' Seamus demanded as Johnnie

snatched his jacket from the hook behind the door.

'Out!' Johnnie said. 'For the air in here stinks.'

When Lizzie came round, the first thing she asked about was the baby. The doctor, weary though he was, had waited for her to wake, because he'd seen the revulsion the nuns had for the wee child and wanted to explain to Lizzie when she came to.

'You have a wee daughter,' he told her.

'Is she all right?' Lizzie asked in alarm, for the doctor was sitting on the side of the bed, holding her hand and talking to her in the kind of voice people use when they have bad news to impart.

'She is absolutely fine,' the doctor said. 'But you have to prepare yourself for a shock, my dear, for the child is coloured.'

'Coloured?'

'Half-caste.'

'Half-caste! Oh Jesus Christ.' Lizzie sank back on the pillows as she assimilated what the doctor had said. So, it was a black man that had attacked her. If she had known that, the police would have soon hunted him down, she imagined, though little good that would do her now. She didn't know how she felt about the child at all. She'd geared herself to feel as little as possible so that she could give it up hoping it would have a good and happy life, but now . . .

'Can I see her? Is she in the nursery?'

'No,' the doctor said grimly, and then, because Lizzie needed to know the score, he went on, 'The nuns refused to have her in the nursery. In fact, they refuse to touch her at all. Your baby is in the crib.'

When the baby was laid in her arms, Lizzie was entranced. She pulled back the shawl and marvelled at the child's dusky skin, her tiny feet and toes and flexing fingers and the black downy hair on her head. The baby opened large eyes ringed with thick, dark eyelashes. There was a little frown on her brow as she tried to focus and Lizzie was engulfed suddenly by a fierce and protective love for the wee mite.

She knew in that moment she could never leave the child behind when she left this place, for it would be condemning it to purgatory. How could she plot and plan Celia's escape and leave an innocent and unprotected baby to these vile nuns.

Exhaustion and the sick feeling in her throat left her, and she wriggled to sit more upright on the bed, her arms tightening around her child. Then she unbuttoned the bodice of her nightdress and put the baby to the breast where she soon settled on the nipple and sucked contentedly.

Sister Jude, coming in at that moment, remembered seeing the beam of approval on the doctor's face. Stupid man! What did he know? But at least if Pansy took to the infant it would solve the problem for now anyway, until something could be sorted.

There was a veil of secrecy drawn over Lizzie, and Celia was worried to death about it. Too anxious to sleep the day Lizzie went into labour, she'd seen the doctor's car arrive just after midnight and the next morning she glimpsed the taxi pulling up at the front door and Sister Jude getting into it.

None of the other girls had seen that, for Celia had

only spotted it when she popped upstairs for the clean rag that did as a hanky after Mass. The nuns seemed more than usually edgy that morning and Celia saw a cluster of them on her way to the laundry, talking in agitated but low voices. She wondered if the doctor had been called for Sister Jude and not Lizzie at all.

'Huh, she's too full of badness to get sick,' one said under the cover of folding sheets when Celia mentioned what she had seen.

'Well, if she is, and very sick, I'd know then God answers prayers,' Celia hissed back.

'Is there someone talking?' Sister Carmel said. 'Let's start the rosary.'

But what's happened to Lizzie, Celia thought, as she recited the familiar litany. She must have had the baby by now, and yet no one has said a word. Even when Cora had died they were told, she thought, with a cold little shudder.

Sister Jude returned from her jaunt and looked far too healthy to be sick, and so it had to be Lizzie the doctor had come to see, but still the girls were told nothing. By Saturday, Celia was frantic and had been daring enough to ask Sister Carmel directly that morning, knowing it was of little use. The nun looked at her coldly and said it was not her concern and that she'd be better employing her energies at the wash tub.

However, later that day, Celia was hanging clothes in the garden. She thought it a pointless exercise to hang out anything on a day so dank and cold, but they were there to do as they were told, not question authority. How many times had that been said to her?

Then she heard the car crunch on the gravel drive and, leaving the basket on the grass, she stole down the side of the convent to the front, where she hid behind one of the privet hedges that bordered either side of the path and watched. It was Lizzie's brother Johnnie.

'Pst, pst, over here.'

He bent to see who spoke and Celia said, 'Don't bend towards me. Stand straight, or if anyone's looking they'll guess that someone is here.'

Johnnie obediently straightened up, but not before he'd glimpsed the most beautiful girl he'd ever encountered. She had enormous eyes, almost green in colour, encircled by the longest eyelashes he'd ever seen. Even in the awful clothes and with the cap rammed on her head, she was exquisite, and when she said, 'My name is Celia,' he knew this was the girl Lizzie wanted to help escape from this place. He knew too that he would do all he could to ensure she did.

But Celia wasn't thinking of her escape just then and had no idea of the effect her appearance had had on Johnnie, for her mind was filled with worry about Lizzie.

'She's all right, I believe,' Johnnie said when asked. 'I mean, I've not seen her, but Sister Jude said she's a bit weak but she's okay.'

'Sister Jude went to your house?'

'Aye.'

'Why?'

'I suppose they're trying to keep it from you,' Johnnie said, 'but I don't know why. It was hardly Lizzie's fault. She had a wee girl, but the child is black – well, half-caste.'

'Half-caste! Oh God.' Celia was shocked, certainly, but there was no disgust in her voice, only sympathy. 'The poor cow. Oh Christ. What's she going to do?'

'Well, she's to get to the boat as arranged, as soon as the doctor says she is fit enough, and you too if you're still up for it?'

'You bet.'

'The child will be taken to an orphanage.'

Celia made a face. 'Not much of a life, but then what else can she do?'

Later, Johnnie was to face his sister across the room and say, 'Lizzie, you can't take her back with you.'

'I can't not.'

'She'll ruin your life.'

'I know that. I will write to Steve, not that I expect him to accept another's bastard and half-caste into the bargain. I will get rooms or something as soon as I can, but he has to know about her. I am his wife and he has rights. But, Johnnie, you don't know what nuns are capable of, these nuns at any rate, and to be honest I couldn't live with myself if I committed her to a life like that.'

Johnnie wondered if Lizzie was thinking rationally. She looked so incredibly frail, it was as if her skin was almost translucent. It made her eyes seem bigger than ever and she had large blue smudges beneath each one. He picked up one of the hands that was as white as the coverlet it rested on and saw the blue veins prominent under the skin. He wished he could take her back to the farm and let her rest, and have good, wholesome food and breathe fresh air and stay until she was completely better.

'You're not ready for this, Lizzie,' he said. 'None of this is your fault. Why should you suffer?'

'Why should the baby? She's totally innocent too.'

'How will you live?'

'We'll manage,' Lizzie said. 'I have money in the Post Office. Enough to rent a few rooms for a month or two. When Georgia is a little older . . .'

'Georgia?'

'Aye. It seemed to suit her. When she is older, I will get her a place in a nursery and start war work again. At least jobs are two a penny there still, and according to Violet the raids are over.'

'You've thought this through.'

'I've had little else to do.'

'And what of Celia?'

'She can come too, but when she finds out about Georgia she might want to make her own way once we reach England. At least she'll be safe there.'

'She knows about Georgia. I told her.'

'How?'

'She sneaked across from the laundry.'

'God, she was taking a risk.'

'Aye, but she thought it worth it,' Johnnie said. 'Apparently, the nuns haven't said a word about you and all the girls are concerned. Anyway, she wasn't the slightest bit disgusted, just sorry for you. You didn't tell me she was so beautiful.'

Despite her own problems, Lizzie had to smile at the dreamy look in her brother's eyes. 'Oh, someone is smitten.'

'Not at all,' Johnnie said, embarrassed. 'She's a nice girl, that's all. But, to get back to your problems, you know if you keep this child our parents will never let you come home, never let you see the children.'

'I know, and when I think of that the pain is like a sword piercing my soul, but when I look at Georgia I know I cannot abandon her.'

'You've abandoned the others.'

'No,' Lizzie said. 'They're with people who want them and love them and wish them well. You'll be there too, Johnnie. Maybe when they're older you'll explain it to them. Don't let them think too badly of their mammy.'

'Oh, Lizzie, I'll do that and gladly,' Johnnie said, and he kissed his sister on the cheek.

The baby, Georgia Marie, was christened secretly when she was a week old while the other girls were in the laundry. Lizzie was too weak to walk and had to be taken into the chapel in a wheelchair, and two younger nuns were her sponsors. Lizzie burned at the contemptuous way they handled the child and she saw the same look on the priest's face.

He had a nerve, she thought. Since his attack on her, she'd refused to let him hear her confession. The thought of going into that confined space with the man made her feel sick. Anyway, she thought, how can he judge me and intercede for me before God and give me a penance? What right has he?

She'd been taken to Sister Jude, of course, who said she wouldn't stand such disobedience. Lizzie had faced her unafraid and told her the power that the nuns held over them all only stretched so far. 'You can beat me black and blue, Sister, but no one has the power to make me speak.'

'You won't be able to take Communion,' Sister Jude said.

Lizzie thought of that man placing the host on her tongue that he'd had in his fingers, the same fingers that he'd used to play with himself in the sacristy, and felt revulsion rise in her. 'I don't want Communion, Sister,' she said, and added, 'not from that man at least.'

Sister Jude's eyes widened, but Lizzie met the glare levelly. She knew at that moment that Sister Jude knew all about the priest. How did she justify it in her mind? Did she think of it as just 'a little weakness', and to be understood, even condoned, when surrounded as the man was by sinful girls parading their sexuality before him?

She watched the nun's face grow puce with rage, and in the end Sister Jude satisfied herself with two slaps either side of Lizzie's face. 'Get out,' she'd screamed. 'Out, out of my sight.' Lizzie went, and despite the two scarlet handprints across her cheeks she knew she had scored a victory.

She didn't want that pervert to put his dirty hands anywhere near her pure and innocent child either, but she fought her distaste, for she feared even now that the child might be taken from her, for they'd tried that once before.

Unknown to Lizzie, the nuns had arranged for a Dublin orphanage to take charge of the baby and the man had come when Georgia was just five days old. Lizzie had refused to hand her over. 'It's what your parents want,' Sister Jude pointed out. 'They told me so.'

'It doesn't matter what my parents want,' Lizzie cried. 'I am over twenty-one. You, none of you, have rights over my baby.'

She was fighting a desperate battle, for she knew they could take the child by force if they had a mind. It wouldn't be the first time a baby was wrenched from a frantic, weeping mother. Lizzie wasn't sure what might have happened if the doctor hadn't come in then and asked why Lizzie was so distressed. When he heard what the nuns intended to do, he was appalled. 'What do you want to do, Lizzie?' he asked.

Lizzie wiped her eyes with the back of her hand and said, 'I want to take her back to Birmingham with me.'

'Then you shall,' the doctor declared, and he turned to the assembled people and said, 'Lizzie is under no one's jurisdiction but her own and the child too is hers. No one has the right to take the baby away, and no one shall take her away, for it will constitute kidnap. That is against the law and I would make quite certain the authorities were informed.'

Even then, though the nuns backed off and the man returned to his orphanage in Dublin, Lizzie remained nervous.

The following Saturday, Johnnie came again. He'd retrieved Lizzie's case from the nuns, to pack his sister's clothes from home for the next time he came, when Lizzie would be ready to leave. Lizzie wrote the all–important letters for Johnnie to post: to Violet telling her about Georgia and saying she was coming home, and one to Steve confessing everything.

'The doctor won't let me go for nearly a fortnight,' Lizzie told Johnnie. 'I don't want to stay here, but he says when I haemorrhaged I lost so much blood that I won't be fit before then.

'I know if won't be a good idea to collapse on the boat, so I'll do as he says. I'll be leaving on Friday the twenty-ninth. Can you get things organised for the baby? Just enough for the journey, for it is bound to be cold and I want her well wrapped up. I've got all Niamh and Tom's baby things once I get home, but I'll not take in one stitch of clothes belonging to this vile place.'

'I'll see to it,' Johnnie promised, 'But in Sligo, for it wouldn't do to be buying things like that in Ballintra.'

'I have money in the Post Office.'

'Keep your money, you may have need of it yet,' Johnnie said. 'I have money of my own. What about Celia?'

'The doctor will get word to her, don't worry' Lizzie said. 'She's waylaid him on the way out more than once if she hasn't seen me for a few days. Between them, they'll work it out somehow. You just be here to pick me up. Make sure the laundry van is in, even if it means waiting on the road outside for a while. I'll be ready and waiting for you.'

'Where will Celia be?'

'Probably hiding behind the hedge,' Lizzie said. 'Just make sure you bring something to cover herself up with in the back of the car.'

'I have that sorted.'

'Right then, give me the paper and I'll write the most important letters of my life.'

Celia was like a cat on hot bricks, when the doctor passed on the news of the escape plan. The others put in down to the news about Lizzie having a black baby and the fact that she was leaving soon. Some of them were inclined to be disparaging over the black baby till Celia took them to task. 'Don't curl your lip like that,' she snapped at one girl. 'I suppose you were a willing partner when your brother started his hanky-panky?'

'You know I wasn't.'

'I know nothing,' Celia said shortly. 'I know only what I'm told and I believed you when you said you tried to fight your brother off, just as I believed Lizzie. It's just her bad luck that the bastard who raped her was black. The majority of us here are victims of one kind or another, and don't you forget it. We're in a position to judge no one.'

There was a murmur of agreement, for everyone knew Celia spoke the truth. No one there had the right to condemn the girl, and they sympathised with her and were further disgusted by the nuns when Celia told them of their attitude to the baby, which had made Lizzie decide to take her back with her to England. They could scarcely believe she'd do such a thing and would have asked many questions, but Celia seemed not to want to talk about it. They put her reticence down to the fact that she would miss Lizzie, for they had been close, but whatever it was, something was making her as jumpy as a cat on hot bricks, and she'd often bite a person's head off for little or nothing.

Lizzie knew that timing was of the essence if this escape had any chance of success, and the doctor had passed this on to Celia. 'Get into the car as soon as you can,' he'd whispered to her, 'for Lizzie has no intention of lingering and will be ready and waiting for Johnnie.'

'I'll be there,' Celia had promised. 'Tell her not to worry.'

However, as the days rolled by she'd become increasingly nervous about what she intended to do, and she was berated often and beaten once for the slapdash way she'd ironed the clothes. She'd lain in bed that night smarting from the pain.

She knew that the beating was nothing to what the nuns would do to her if they were even to hear about the plan, and if she was discovered and brought back – dear God! It didn't bear thinking about and she shook in the bed in fear. And then she thought of the alternative, a lifetime spent in the convent, beaten and degraded, half-starved and worked to death day in, day out until she was old and grey and had lost all will to live. No, by Christ, she rejected that. She would go for it, and she hoped that the God who'd done little for them so far would help them this time.

Both Lizzie and Georgia were ready and waiting for Johnnie. Lizzie was dressed and her suitcase packed. Georgia had on a long woollen dress over a warm fleecy vest, with a matinee jacket over that and little leggings and bootees for her feet. Over the top of this was a thick pram-set. It was far too large for her, as she was just over six pounds, but Lizzie put it on her anyway: the more layers the better. 'The lady in the shop in Sligo was very helpful,' Johnnie said, watching Lizzie wrap the baby in the shawl he'd bought. 'I pretended I was an inept father-to-be and she was grand. I bought everything she recommended.'

'Johnnie, you're very good,' Lizzie said. 'I'll never forget this.'

'You owe me nothing,' Johnnie said. 'Come on, let's get out of this place. It gives me the creeps.' He gave Lizzie a peck on the cheek and said, 'I'll always be there for you, Lizzie, you know that.'

'I know it, Johnnie,' Lizzie said, and there was a lump in her throat. 'You've saved my sanity and I'm not joking, and all my life I will be in debt to you.'

'No,' Johnnie said. 'There is no debt to repay. I have done these things because I love you and think you have been very badly treated, so let's away out of here and hope your young friend is by now crouched in the back of the car, for if she isn't there is not a jot we can do about it.'

Celia had been outside waiting for the laundry van, and she heard Johnnie's car on the gravel path just a few minutes after she'd heard the laundry van chugging along from the back gate.

All the girls knew Lizzie was going that day and they also knew Celia would miss her. A few thought it madness to make a friend of anyone in that place, but sometimes these things just happened. When Celia said to one of the girls nearest to her, 'Will you cover for me if I slip across and say goodbye to Lizzie?' the girl's eyes were sympathetic. 'Aye, surely,' she said. 'Sister Carmel is not likely to be out in this mizzly rain either.'

She wasn't. Sister Carmel hated rain and would stay inside, directing action from there.

Celia slipped away, and if any saw her go, none made a sound. She crept along by the side of the convent, hidden by the bushes till she came to the privet hedge. Johnnie, bless him, had parked his car as near the hedge as he could, and for a while she crouched there and felt the rain begin to seep into her clothes.

She knew if any of the nuns should take this moment to look out of the window they would see her when she attempted to get into the car. But, she told herself, who would be looking out on that drab, rain-laden landscape? Anyway, was she going to allow fear to stop her from trying to make a bid for freedom? God knows, she might never have another chance.

This thought gave her the impetus to leave her place of hiding, speed to the car, open the back door, creep inside, and cover herself with the blanket she found there.

She lay panting, feeling the dryness of her mouth, hearing her heart pounding against her ribs, tasting the terror that was almost consuming her. She waited for a shout from the convent and almost felt the hard, vicious hands that would haul her out. They would kill her, she knew that. She could expect no mercy from them, none at all.

But no shout came, no clawing hands reached in for her. When the car door opened, it was the front door.

There had been no committee waiting for Lizzie when she emerged from the room, just Sister Jude and Sister Benedict who looked down their noses at her and her child and her decision to take the baby home. They were glad to see the back of Lizzie. She'd never conformed, not really, never seemed to be fully ashamed of what she had done, and now to find she'd done this with a black man! 'She could be a very corrupting influence on the other girls here,' Sister Jude had said. 'We have told them nothing, but rumour does spread.'

'Oh indeed,' Sister Benedict agreed. 'The sooner she is away from here the better.'

None of this had been said to Lizzie. It didn't need to be. The nuns' feelings were apparent by their manner and the looks in their malicious eyes. Lizzie had a bag on her shoulder and held the baby protectively in her arms while Johnnie dealt with the suitcase. She lifted her head high when she saw the nuns and met their gaze levelly, and her contempt for them was plain, though she said not a word. She wished she felt stronger, more able to cope, for she still felt incredibly weak and the doctor had been worried about her. 'You've had a tough time,' he reminded her, 'and God knows, even in the normal scheme of things you shouldn't be leaving your bed for another few days, let alone traipsing the country and attempting a sea journey as well.'

'Doctor, I'll begin to recover as soon as I am away from this place,' Lizzie said. 'Believe me.'

He believed her, he was no fool, and Lizzie did feel light-headed with relief at leaving the convent. She sank into the car seat gratefully and gave a sigh as

Johnnie got in beside her and started the engine. She fought the desire to turn around to see if Celia had made it and just asked instead, 'You all right, Celia?' as they pulled away.

Celia's voice was muffled under the blanket, but cheerful enough as she answered, 'You bet.'

Johnnie sighed in relief, but he glanced back as they drove out of the convent gates. 'We're not safe yet by a long chalk,' he said. 'There's clothes for you in the parcel on the back seat: change into them and tie the scarf around your head. If the Guards are sent to look for you, they'll be looking for someone dressed as you are now. There's boots too. They were an old pair of Eileen's, and they're better than the ones you have, but I hope they are the right size.'

Celia dressed in the things, knowing if she lived to be a hundred she'd never be able to repay the debt she owed Lizzie and her brother. It was amazing how different clothes could make a person feel, she thought later as she laced up the boots. They were too big, but that didn't matter.

'Thanks for all this,' she said. 'Thanks seems such a short and inadequate word to describe how I feel about what you've done for me this day. I hardly ever cry, but God knows I could bawl my head off right this minute.'

'I know just how you feel,' Lizzie said, turning at last to smile at her friend. 'You look just terrific, Celia,' she said, seeing the girl's beauty that had so captivated her brother. She had high cheekbones and a full, quite sensual mouth, but mostly it was the eyes, so large they seemed fathomless. And now there was a light dancing behind them that Lizzie had never seen there before, and it lent a glow to her whole face. 'Can I hold the baby, Lizzie?'

'Course you can.'

Celia too was captivated by the tiny baby, who grasped her finger in her little hand, and when she looked back at Lizzie her eyes were moist. 'Oh, Lizzie, isn't she just bloody marvellous?'

'Oh aye, bloody marvellous she is right enough' Lizzie agreed, but her own eyes glistened with tears, for she knew at that moment Celia was realising what she had given away.

CHAPTER TWENTY

They had to travel about seventy or eighty miles across Ireland to reach the docks at Dun Laoghaire in time to catch the evening ferry, and as the car Johnnie borrowed was not a powerful one, and he'd kept to back roads just in case they were pursued, he was not anxious to stop for long anywhere.

But eventually he drew to a halt under the cover of trees, some miles from the convent, and got out the picnic his mother had made up. He'd told his parents very little. Nothing about the baby, for they were adamant that they didn't want to hear. He supposed they thought the child had been packed off to some orphanage somewhere, and they knew nothing of Lizzie's decision to keep the baby, nor anything about the existence of Celia, never mind the escape they had planned for her.

The girls tucked into the food gratefully, for they'd had nothing but thin, lumpy porridge, and Lizzie's mother was acknowledged as a fine cook. Johnnie had something else to give Lizzie that had arrived that morning redirected from Violet, and that was a telegram. Violet had opened it as she thought Flo should be told if anything had happened to her son, and so all the family knew that Steve Gillespie would be buried in some foreign field, but Johnnie decided to let Lizzie eat her fill before hitting her with the tragic news.

Even when they were well-satisfied and the food washed down with sweetened tea from a flask that was heavily laced with whisky against the cold of the day, there was plenty of food left. Johnnie insisted they pack up what was left to sustain them on the rest of their journey.

'But what of you?' Lizzie asked.

'What of me?' Johnnie said. 'Aren't I a big man, well able to stop for a sandwich and pint anywhere along the road? And anyway, isn't this the land of plenty and any food can be had if a man has money enough? I'm not going to a land of restrictions and food allotted out. It might not be so easy for you. Take it to please me and stop me worrying about the pair of you.'

Johnnie was anxious to get going as quickly as possible, for they had a long way to go yet, but the baby was protesting and Lizzie said she must be fed and so she'd sit in the back of the car with Celia. Until that point, Johnnie had not bothered himself with looking at the child. He'd thought Lizzie mad to saddle herself with it, but now, as Lizzie unwrapped the baby a little before putting her to the breast, Johnnie, catching sight of it in the mirror, saw it was a baby like any other. Her skin was slightly dusky and her eyes large and dark too, and she had a down of curly black hair on her head.

'You have a fine child there, Lizzie,' he said.

'You might say that but you still think Lizzie wrong to take her back with her, don't you?' Celia challenged. 'I've seen it in your eyes. You think she should have delivered her to some orphanage and forgotten all about her?'

Johnnie couldn't deny it. 'It's not that I don't feel sorry for the baby,' Johnnie said. 'I do. Anyone would. But I don't know the baby, and I do know my sister and I worry for the life she will have.'

'However bad it is, it can't be worse than the bloody convent.'

'I know it was a harsh regime,' Johnnie said. 'And I don't know why they made you wear those hideous clothes and cut your hair until it was like stubble.'

'You don't know the half of it,' Celia said bitterly. 'Did you not tell your brother, Lizzie?'

Lizzie shook her head. 'Why waste our precious time together talking about something Johnnie could do little about, but would only fret over.'

Celia could see the sense of that. 'Tell me now,' Johnnie said. 'I'd like to hear how it was.'

Afterwards, he almost wished he hadn't asked, for he listened to a tale of such brutality, such depravity, that it was scarcely believable. But he had only to look at Celia's eyes to see every word was true, that and hear the comments from his sister supporting her.

'Now,' Celia said at last. 'Those same order of nuns are in charge of most of the orphanages in Ireland. What chance would a wee, half-caste baby have, brought up by sadistic buggers like those, Johnnie?' She didn't wait for a reply and said, 'You know what's

400

laughable, or would be if it wasn't so tragic: we worked dawn till dusk six days a week doing all the laundry for the townfolk and we never saw a penny piece of the money paid out.'

'Aye,' Lizzie put in, 'it all went to the black baby heathens in Africa, but when a half-black child was born to me, they couldn't bring themselves to touch it. Now d'you see why I couldn't just walk away from my baby, for I know the sad, frightening and often painful childhood she would have had. She won't have an easy road to travel anyway, I know that, but at least this way she will have one person to love and cherish her.'

'Two,' Celia put in.

'Celia, I didn't go to the trouble of planning your escape from that prison to encase you in another. You are a free agent.'

'I'm a free agent because of you,' Celia said sincerely. 'I can't forget that. It will take a lifetime to repay that debt to both of you, and I will stay as long as you want me to and love Georgia as if she were mine.'

Lizzie was too choked to speak and Johnnie was glad his sister had a staunch friend by her side. He now understood more of the dilemma she'd been in with regards to the baby, and why she had taken the decision she had, and now he had to hit her with more bad news. He waited until the baby had been fed, changed and wrapped up again in her shawl before withdrawing the letter from Violet with the telegram folded inside it that he had in his pocket. 'This came this morning,' he said.

He saw Lizzie open the letter from her friend, thinking it odd it had been addressed to Johnnie, but when the telegram fluttered out from the pages she understood why. 'Violet explained it went to your house and she opened it so that she could tell his mother before she'd hear it from someone else,' Johnnie said.

'Aye,' Lizzie said, scanning it. 'So you know and she knows that Steve is dead.' And she felt a sudden, almost violent sense of loss; a yawning emptiness inside.

Dead! Steve was too vibrant, too alive to be dead. 'Killed in action', it said. She wondered what action and whether he'd received her letter before he died, or was it part of his effects that would be sent back to her. She hoped he hadn't received it, that he didn't know about the rape and the result of it. Her intention had never been to shame Steve, nor to flaunt her sin in front of him, but it was how he would see it, she knew that, so it would be better if he'd died with his image of her intact.

She wondered at the lack of tears, but she seemed numb inside; and yet she knew she would miss him dreadfully, for in his own way he had been a good husband, a good provider, a good lover most of the time, even if she had to share that part of him with others. 'The children will be devastated. Have they been told?'

'Not yet,' Johnnie said. 'Mammy is telling them today.'

'It will be hard to soften a blow like this,' Lizzie replied. The tears came then. She cried for the loss of Steve the husband and father, and she cried too for Flo, who'd lost a treasured and favourite son. Celia held her till the spasm of grief abated a little and the guilt began. 'What if he got my letter,' she said through the tears, and then, 'Oh God, what if what I had to tell him was the cause of his death?'

'How do you work that out?' Celia asked.

'He might have been upset over it, not watching himself, you know.'

'Stop beating yourself about the head for something you know nothing about,' Celia said quite sharply. 'The man was in a war, for Christ's sake. It's a tragedy and awful for you and your children, but that's what happens in war. Think of it this way too, at least he isn't to be shamed by the appearance of Georgia.'

But Lizzie couldn't rid herself from this feeling of guilt. And, in a way, she had been right.

Steve had been in North Africa when the letter came, and battle-weary like they all were. They were all overdue a spot of leave, but they had to hold the city of Tobruk until reinforcements got there.

He was sick of the place; sick of the unrelenting heat, which ensured that he was damp with sweat in minutes so that his uniform stuck to him. His head had a constant ache and his eyes stung and watered.

And the sand! God, the sand! He was fed-up to the back teeth with sand: miles of it – as far as the eye could see. It got everywhere: he'd eaten and drunk it now for months. It got into his hair, stung his eyes, gilded his eyelashes and seeped into his mouth and nose. It was ingrained in his hands and under his fingernails, inside his clothes, itching him or raising rough, raw patches. And his feet! Walking hour upon hour in heavy boots on that uncompromising sand that filtered through his army-issue socks so that the blisters were rubbed raw.

The heat and brightness seemed never-ending, and then, in an instant, it was black night. No gradual sunsets in this Godforsaken place. And the nights were cold, sometimes very cold. That had surprised him at first. Nothing did any more.

They'd suffered heavy casualties in the opposition they'd encountered as soon as they reached North Africa. Every time he came through the battles unscathed he was amazed. Each hour he was left alive was a bonus.

He was a seasoned fighter now and had been in this bleeding hole for going on fourteen sodding months. But soon, and it couldn't come too soon, they'd be taken to a port and shipped home to Blighty, back to their loved ones, he thought wryly.

He wasn't sure about his loved ones at all, his wife at least. She'd been sending weird letters for weeks now. Even when he'd asked how Tom liked school it took her over a fortnight to answer and then it was very vague and giving one excuse after the other why she couldn't come home. It was just pathetic.

Mike said both Tressa and Lizzie were better off where they were for the duration. Course, he had reason to say that. Seemingly he'd only have to catch sight of Tressa and she'd get pregnant again. Steve doubted that with the children's demands she'd have time to wish Mike the time of day, or even notice he was there. Lizzie was different. She always made a fuss of him when he was home, didn't complain overmuch when he went out each night and came home bottled, or even smelling of perfume when he'd had a bit of slap and tickle with some hot bit of stuff.

Took it in her stride did Lizzie, and she never refused his advances either. He wanted her back in their house when his leave came up, ministering to his every wish as a good wife should.

His mother kept on saying he should decide who was master in that house, who wore the trousers. Well, by Christ he'd show Lizzie who that was all right. If she wasn't back at home in Birmingham when he got leave, he'd go to Ireland and fetch her back if he had to drag her every inch of the way.

And now there was another letter from her. Once he'd longed for her letters. They'd been his lifeline. Many he knew had received 'Dear John' letters, as if their women couldn't do without sex with men away and they'd take it from whoever was available. It was understandable that fighting men would take any diversions offered them, but wives and mothers. God, it was disgusting!

At least he'd never expect behaviour like that from Lizzie. Her letters had been odd, but not worrying in that sense. She wasn't that kind of woman.

But this letter was like no letter she'd written before. Open-mouthed, he read of the attack on her the previous February. He'd known about it of course, his mother had told him, yet when he'd mentioned it to Lizzie she'd been quite dismissive and said there was nothing to worry about.

But it wasn't just an assault, it was a full-scale attack, a stabbing with a knife that could have been fatal. She painted a good picture too of the blackness of that night, and he remembered how horrendous the blackout had been at times from his days at home with his bad leg and arm. Course, other times the blackout had been a blessing, when he'd not wanted to be seen.

And this man hadn't wanted to be seen. He wondered why she'd told him it all now and why the man had picked on Lizzie; or was it some random choice, could it have been anyone? He read of Lizzie being rendered unconscious and of Violet finding her, and he stiffened when he heard of Violet also noticing Lizzie's knickers beside her still body.

He'd interfered with her, the dirty sod. His mother had never mentioned that. Course, Lizzie might not have told her.

But, as he read on, his mouth dropped open and he was unaware of it. Almighty Christ, the sod had done more than interfere with her, he'd made her pregnant!

He read of her shame and initial revulsion for the child. Now he understood her flight to Ireland, but knew his mother was unaware of the reason, though he could bet that that bitch Violet was in the know. He scanned the letter further, taking in how Lizzie's parents had sent her to a place run by nuns.

The nuns take the children away and give them to Catholic childless couples. And it was what I wanted, I welcomed the chance to get on with my life.
I gave birth to a girl a few days ago. And she is quite, quite beautiful, but also half-caste.

Steve jumped up and threw the letter away in disgust. A nigger. How in God's name had she let a nigger up inside her? He remembered for a brief moment the one black woman he'd had that he'd lusted after since he'd first caught sight of her. There was an element of curiosity there too. Everyone said a black man's dick was bigger than a white man's and he wanted to take a black woman and see if they were any way different as well.

She'd fought like a tiger, he remembered, but that had just excited him more; and the sex afterwards – on God, it had been wonderful. Course, she'd cried and carried on, but God, he could have started all over again and might have done if she'd have shut up. He knew the neighbours might easily come round to investigate and he'd told her to shut her gob, but when that had no effect he'd given her a smack in the mouth and taken off through the night, melting into the darkness.

That had been the first time he had taken a woman by force and he'd found it more exciting than those who were willing. He had the physique to subdue most women and that thought excited him further.

He had little control over his life now. He belonged to the army and had to go where he was sent and do as he was told, whether he liked it or not, but he could have some control over his sex life. When he saw women out alone in the blackout, shining their piddling little torches to light their way, he would feel his crotch harden, and the more they struggled the better it was.

But that was different. That was just a man getting his end away; this was his Lizzie and some bloody randy nigger. He didn't know if he'd ever want to touch her after this – dirty trollop. He began to wonder more about the attack. Was it the first time she'd been with the man? Maybe it had been going on for months and she'd tried to end it and he'd attacked and violated her. Funny that it had happened to no one else. She said extra police were drafted in, but no one was found, and as there were no further assaults they were stumped. Funny that. Jesus, he'd get the truth out of Lizzie when he got home.

And going on about some nigger bastard, as if he cared. He lit a cigarette and tried to control his shivering frame. He sat down on the bunk again and picked up the letter and read on:

> *I know you probably won't understand this, I barely understand it myself, but I've found myself loving the child. I have called her Georgia Marie and she was baptised not long after she was born. The nuns don't want a half-caste baby, and no one else would either. She would linger in an orphanage all her life, picked on because she is different. I'm not asking you to accept this baby, but I must bring her back to Birmingham, for I have nowhere else to go, for Mammy won't let me go back to her house. Once I am in Birmingham, I will look around for lodgings somewhere and take a job to support us both.*

Jesus Christ! Steve leapt to his feet once more. Was she stark staring mad? What loony bin did she think he came from? He knew if she was before him now he'd grind his cigarette out on her before beating her to a pulp. No way was she bringing that nigger brat to Birmingham, and if she attempted to he'd break every bone in her body and that of the child's too.

He shook as if from the ague as he began pacing the small room. God Almighty! Her mother wouldn't let her home, well, neither would he. She could go on the streets for all he cared. In his mind she was already halfway there. But no way would she get near Niamh and Tom. She'd given up all rights to them and he'd not have them cared for by her, or associate with a nigger bastard. He'd talk to his mother. She'd take them on if he asked her to, and she'd said Birmingham was safe as houses now.

He shoved the letter into its envelope and put it under his pillow before he went outside into the brightness and blistering heat, for he was too agitated to stay in. His mind was full of his wife's duplicity. How she'd played him for a fool. She'd gone one step further than the other cheating wives in the unit. At least they'd chosen white men. She'd chosen a nigger, and if the man was a stranger, as she maintained, and the attack as vicious as she described, would she want to keep the child? No way on God's earth would she.

He was going over the letter he would write to her in return and didn't seem to see his surroundings, or the comrades he passed, or those who called out to him. Some of them noticed his wild eyes, hair on end, his dishevelled appearance, and asked him if he felt all right. He didn't answer them and two were concerned enough to go for Mike. 'Not surprising really,' Mike said. 'He needs a break. God, we all need a break. I'll see if I can find him and have a word.'

Steve by then had reached the outskirts of the city, where the watch had been positioned. He had no idea where he was going. His head was filled with roaring sounds and he saw Lizzie's face before him and his fist pounding it over and over. 'Hey, mate, what's up with you?' one of the watch stationed on top of a building shouted to him. 'Don't go no further. There was sniper fire just a while ago.'

Steve didn't hear them. Didn't even turn his head. He just kept on walking and the two on watch looked at one another horrified. They couldn't leave their post, and anyway, it would take time to get off the roof. There was no one else in sight. 'Must have gone off his rocker,' one of the watch remarked to the other.

'Wants to watch his rocker don't get blown clean off his shoulders,' the other replied.

The words had just left his lips when the rifle shot cracked into the still air. Steve jerked and fell to his knees. Another shot laid him out on the sand. The two watchmen swivelled around the machine gun and were soon pounding the area where they'd seen movement, but for Steve Gillespie their response came too late.

Mike was devastated by the news of Steve's death. Although they walked with death daily, somehow this wasn't the same. From what he was told, he just walked out into the desert as if . . . as if he was inviting death. But why? Steve loved life.

It became clearer to Mike when he read the letter. As Steve's mate, he was asked to collect his effects to send home and he read the letter that Steve had left. As he read he found he had to sit down, for his legs trembled so much. He cried then for the mate he'd known all his life, who'd almost gone as far as taking his own life because he'd not been able to stand the shame of Lizzie coming home to Birmingham with a black bastard child she'd given birth to.

Steve had loved Lizzie with a passion in his own way, though he had never been faithful to her, but carnal desire was not something he imagined 'good' women, the sort men married, had in abundance.

He knew Lizzie had been attacked, for Tressa had written and told him, and it had been an horrendous assault by all accounts. But what if it had happened to Tressa instead and she'd carried and given birth to a child she wanted to bring home, as if it was the child born from a loving relationship? He'd not stand it, not even if the child was white. He'd never understand why Lizzie would want to keep such a child.

She wasn't stupid and she knew the manner of man she'd married. How had she imagined he'd react when he got that letter? God Almighty, he thought, Lizzie killed Steve just as if she'd pulled that damned trigger.

But then, he thought, at least Lizzie hadn't given herself freely to the man. Clearly he had been unhinged. Added to that, Mike liked Lizzie and knew Tressa thought the world of her.

Steve was dead and nothing would alter that fact, but Mike thought little would be gained by letting Lizzie take the blame for Steve's death on her own shoulders, as he knew she would if she knew he'd read the letter before he died. In many ways she had been suffering for months herself, and Mike replaced the letter and sealed the envelope carefully so that it didn't look like it had ever been opened. Then he got to his feet, wiped his eyes and began to collect his mate's stuff together for the last time, already composing in his head the letter he would write to Tressa about the whole business.

What consternation there was when it was discovered Celia had vanished. It was immediately suspected she'd climbed into the laundry van, for that had been done before. It certainly wasn't connected to Lizzie leaving that day, for the girls had covered for Celia well and it was some time before her disappearance was noted. Lizzie was well gone by then, and most girls thought if Celia had managed to sneak away too, then good luck to her.

The laundry van had almost finished distributing the laundered clothes to those in the town who took up the convent's services, and Sister Maria and Sister Benedict were despatched to find the girl and bring her back.

The day was cold and blustery and the rain continued to fall as the nuns walked quickly. They were none to happy in their errand and promised themselves Hetty would pay dearly for it when they did find her.

The laundry-van driver and his mate were none too happy either. Since the one girl had sneaked into the van they had been more vigilant. 'There was no girl in our van.'

'It's been done before.'

'Aye, but it hasn't been done this time.'

'Did you check?'

'We didn't need to check. We were at the van all the time.'

'The van's near empty now,' the driver said. 'Have a look if you like.'

'She'll hardly be there now,' Sister Benedict snapped. 'If she managed to get into the van, she'd leave it when you were delivering.'

'I tell you . . .'

'And I tell you, the priest will take a very dim view of anyone helping that girl escape, or anyone harbouring her in the town,' Sister Maria said. 'And she'll be found, don't doubt it. Such a girl, with a shorn head and in convent clothes, will stick out like a sore thumb, and some God-fearing soul will feel it their duty to tell us if they see her. I just hope it is not linked back to you.'

'It won't be,' the driver said, mentally casting his mind back to any time the van had been left un-attended, even for a brief second. But he displayed no doubts before the two nuns glaring at him accusingly, nor was he prepared to argue the toss any more. 'I've said all I intend to about the matter,' he told them. 'But now, if you'll excuse me, I have a job of work to attend to.'

They didn't believe him of course, but had no option but to return to the convent. They were angrier than ever, wet to the skin, and their thoughts about Hetty bordered on the murderous.

They waited all day and evening for someone to arrive at the convent and tell them they'd seen one of their girls, or even someone to use the phone, but nothing happened. The girls, who knew full well Hetty had climbed in no laundry van, were questioned but claimed they knew nothing and had seen nothing. If

413

the chance had been given to them to leave that accursed place, they would have grabbed it, and they'd give the nuns no information to help them track Hetty down.

By the time the Guards had been called, black night had fallen, and by then Lizzie, Celia and Georgia were aboard the mail boat to take them to England, where Lizzie would be safe from the nuns, but exposed to ridicule, scorn and prejudice. She knew Johnnie would be on the quayside till the ship pulled away, but in the darkness she could barely see him.

There were few passengers travelling at that time of year and Lizzie didn't wonder at it, for the cold ate into a person, and as soon as the engines began to throb causing black smoke to escape from the two funnels with a shriek, she took the baby inside. Celia followed with a sigh of relief at leaving her native land behind.

Later she was to tell Lizzie that even the seasickness was worth it. They kept to themselves as much as possible, not wishing to draw anyone's attention, glad of the small numbers travelling with them. They were thankful too of the darkness of the boat, as it was approaching the north Wales coast where blackout restrictions were in force, and Lizzie knew that without Celia it would have been a lonely and miserable crossing.

The shaded lamps in the station at Holyhead barely pierced the gloom of the place, and they were glad to get off the draughty platform and on to the train. Even there, the carriages were only dimly lit and the windows had thick blinds drawn across them, but Lizzie sank on to the seat, suddenly aware of how tired she was. She closed her eyes but dared not sleep, for she had Georgia in her arms. 'Give her to me,' Celia said, seeing the fatigue etched on Lizzie's face. 'You've barely recovered from the birth, no wonder you are worn out.'

Lizzie passed the baby over thankfully and was soon fast asleep. Celia sat taking comfort from the feel of the baby against her and knew with every clatter of the train's wheels the distance between her and that accursed convent increased. She felt the weight between her shoulder blades ease.

Lizzie woke as the baby made little complaining snuffles prior to waking properly. 'Where are we?' she asked as Georgia fastened on to one of her breasts.

'How would I know?' Celia replied. 'When I did peep past the blind a while ago, the station name was blotted out.'

'That was done to confuse the enemy,' Lizzie told her. 'Particularly after Dunkirk, when the whole country seemed to be perched on the edge of invasion. People were told to disable cars, and bikes too, and hide maps, and were discouraged from moving far at all, particularly on the trains, which were for the troops. Posters screamed at you: 'Is Your Journey Really Necessary?' I tell you, Celia, with the station names blacked out, some signposts removed totally, and the stop-start nature of the wartime train service, you'd go nowhere unless it was a matter of life or death.'

Celia laughed, though she sympathised. 'It must have been hard for you all.'

'You sort of get on with it,' Lizzie said. 'I mean, everyone was in the same boat.' She changed the baby to the other side and said, 'Anyway, it can't be long now.'

'But what if we go past the station?'

'We won't go past it,' Lizzie assured her. 'Remember, I am a seasoned traveller on this route and I'll not miss the station even in the dark.'

And she didn't, and later, outside in the velvety darkness, Celia stood and looked about her. There was nothing to see, just blackness and a sooty sour smell in the air, and it was so cold it was making her teeth ache. 'We'll have to take a taxi,' Lizzie said. 'No buses will be running.'

'Have you money enough?'

'Aye, Johnnie gave me some,' Lizzie said. 'I have my Post Office book too. I'll see about it tomorrow. I'll have to get new ration cards, mine have expired anyway and we both need to register with a grocer. We'll do it all tomorrow.'

There was no traffic on the roads and there wasn't a soul on the streets at that very early hour in the morning. The taxi drove effortlessly, its headlights catching the odd shuttered shop windows. It was eerie, like a ghost town, Celia thought, and she felt suddenly apprehensive of what lay ahead.

The ride was short, and when they were on the pavement again Lizzie bitterly regretted not asking Johnnie to bring a torch for them. Oh well, she thought, I didn't and that's that. 'Come on, Celia,' she said. 'Touch the walls and you'll know when you come to the end.'

The end of what, thought Celia, waving her arms forward.

'There's an entry here,' Lizzie told her, but quietly, knowing how sound carried in the stillness of the night. 'I'd hold your arm, but I can't with the bag and the baby.'

They each had a bag. Lizzie carried baby things and Celia carried Lizzie's clothes that Johnnie had brought. But at least Celia had a hand free and she held on tight to Lizzie's coat as they shuffled their way slowly forward.

When they stepped into the yard, Celia could quite understand why Lizzie had been unable to identify her attacker, why she'd had no idea he was black. Lizzie had cautioned her to be quiet and so she whispered, 'Have you let anyone know you'd be coming home today?'

'Only Violet next door. She'll leave the door unlocked for us, she said.'

Violet had done far more than that. The gas lamps were turned down low and when Lizzie turned them up she gasped in surprise and pleasure. The little room shone and there was no smell of neglect about the place, more a hint of polish. The grate had been black-leaded and embers glowed to take the chill from the room.

On the stove was a pan of stew, cold now but just to be heated, and on the oilskin covering the table was a jug full of milk covered with a circle of lace with beads hanging from it. There was a twist of tea, and another of sugar, and Lizzie marvelled at Violet's generosity, for she knew what rationing was like. There was also a bit of a loaf wrapped in greaseproof paper and another little packet with margarine in it.

A note was propped against the milk jug:

Welcome Home, Lizzie. Here's a few bits to give you a start. I'll pop in tomorrow.
Love, Violet

'She doesn't know about me, does she?' Celia said.
Lizzie shook her head. 'How could she know? I daren't write that while we were at the convent. God, if there had been a hint of what we intended the two of us might never have got out.'
'Oh Lord, just think of that.'
'Are you hungry?' Lizzie asked. 'I think I'm too tired to eat.'
'Me too, but I'd sell my granny for a cup of tea, I'm parched,' Celia said.
'I'll put the kettle on, and if you make us a cup I'll get the cradle down from the attic for Georgia.'
'Go on, I'll have a cup waiting when you come down.'
'All right,' Lizzie cautioned. 'But go easy on the tea and we might be able to get another couple of cups in tomorrow.'
Upstairs, Lizzie found that Violet had warmed the bed with a hot-water bottle and she put the baby in there and ran up for the cradle. When she came back down with it, Georgia looked so peaceful she decided to leave her where she was. The room was like an ice box anyway and she had no way of warming the cradle. 'We'll all have to sleep together for tonight at least,' she told herself. 'The nuns would be scandalised, but what do I care for their opinion.' And she kissed

her sleeping daughter and slipped downstairs for a cup
of welcome tea before she turned in for what was left
of the night.

CHAPTER TWENTY-ONE

Lizzie was roused by the wails of the baby, which sliced effectively through the shreds of sleep still clinging to her, and she struggled to sit up and then hauled the baby onto her knee.

Celia too had woken and, pulling a coat around her that was hanging behind the bedroom door, she went to the window and lifted down the blackout shutters to look out. What she saw appalled her so much she almost gasped out loud, but she swallowed the gulp.

Never had she seen so many houses crowded together around a yard. A tall gas lamp stood in the middle of it, little good now of course, with a squat building behind it. Dustbins were grouped against the wall on her left side, the contents spilling onto the cobbles, and beyond the squat building she could see the doors of the lavatories. God, what a way to live.

She'd been almost too tired to take in the room below when they'd come in just a few hours previously, noting only that it was small, very small and cramped, but this . . .

'Awful, isn't it?' Lizzie said from the bed. 'When I

first saw these houses, I could scarcely believe people lived like this, but,' she shrugged, 'you get used to it. I don't think of it now, but I knew you'd be surprised.'

'I am.'

'And there's nowhere to hide here,' Lizzie went on. 'I would have said my neighbours were, in the main, the salt of the earth, but now . . . Well, we'll see, and quickly too for I need the lavvy. Will you watch the child?'

'You don't need to ask.'

It was one of the hardest things Lizzie had ever done to step out into the yard, dressed in the clothes she'd worn to travel in, donned hastily with a coat over them, her bare feet thrust into boots and the fierce wind whipping at her legs.

Ada caught sight of her first, and then Gloria as Lizzie passed her window, and they stepped into the yard.

'We know about the babby,' Ada said. 'Violet told us.'

'Oh,' Lizzie said, not sure if she was pleased or not.

'Thought it would be less of a shock, like,' Gloria explained.

'And . . . and how do you feel about it?' Lizzie asked, knowing it was better to get that into the open straight away.

'I think it's a bloody shame and that's the truth,' Ada said. 'We all do here, because we knew you, like, and we knew about the attack. I mean, we saw how you were, and the police involved as well.'

'Aye, but not everyone will feel the same,' Gloria warned. 'Did you have to bring the babby back?'

'Aye,' Lizzie said. 'I had no choice. One time, when I have a spare few hours, I'll tell you tales about the place my mother sent me when I told her I was pregnant that will make your hair curl.' She sighed and went on, 'The nuns wanted to send my baby to an orphanage in Dublin, run by nuns of the same order. I couldn't risk letting my poor, innocent baby go there, where she'd probably have spent her life being mocked and bullied because she is different.'

Ada nodded sagely. 'I see that. Anyroad, it's a terrible thing altogether to give a kid away.'

'We was all sorry to hear that Steve was killed,' Gloria added.

'I know,' Lizzie said. 'I was bitterly upset, for he was a good man and a terrific father. The children will be heartbroken.'

'Didn't you tell them?'

Lizzie shook her head. 'I wasn't allowed to go home. My brother had to collect me from the convent and drive me straight to the boat.'

'So you didn't see your kids?'

'Not for long,' Lizzie said. 'As soon as I told Mammy I was pregnant they couldn't get rid of me quick enough.'

'D'ain't you tell them you was attacked?'

'Aye, I told them, and they refused to believe it. Daddy was the worst. The priest was there too and he didn't believe a word I said either, and that was that really. When my baby was born half-caste . . . Well, you can imagine the rest.'

'You poor cow.'

The sympathy in Ada's voice brought tears to Lizzie's

eyes, but then Gloria said, 'Have you thought that if Steve hadn't . . . I mean, what if . . . ?'

'I've thought of little else since I held the child in my arms and realised I could never let her go,' Lizzie said. 'I wrote to Steve to tell him everything, but I don't know if he'd received the letter before he was killed. I wasn't asking him to accept the child, but I thought he had to know. In a way, though I wished him no harm, at least this way he is saved the shame of it.'

'Aye,' Gloria said. 'But there's still Flo to contend with.'

Lizzie gave a shudder. 'Don't remind me,' she replied. 'But at least I can tell her what I think of her now. If I'd done that in the past, she used to write and tell Steve I'd done this or that, dreadful things I'd not done at all, worrying him unnecessarily. Oh,' she added, 'I have a young friend with me, name of Celia. She's minding Georgia for me while I go to the lavvy.'

'Georgia, is that what you call her?'

'Aye.'

'Can we go and have a wee look at her?'

'Of course,' Lizzie said, and added sharply, 'but look at her as you would any wee baby, not as if she is some sort of peep show. She hasn't two heads.'

'Lizzie,' said Ada gently, putting a hand on her arm. 'We're your friends, not enemies.'

And they were, and how much Lizzie needed friends. 'I'm sorry,' she said. 'I'm touchy at the moment. Go up to the house and Celia will be delighted for you to see the baby, I'm sure.'

While Lizzie took herself to the lavvy, the news

flew around the court, and when she returned it was to see the small house crowded with the women from the yard. They were passing the baby around and oohing and aahing over her, while Celia stood watching them, a smile on her face at their positive reaction.

Violet stayed on after the other women had gone and said quietly to Lizzie, 'I have Steve's effects, if it won't upset you to see them. They came next door like the telegram and I signed for them, knowing you were coming back, like.'

Lizzie wanted to see Steve's things, in particular to find the letter she'd sent him, for if he'd received it she'd always feel as if she had a hand in his death. But Mike had done a good job of resealing the envelope and when Lizzie pounced on it, she cried, 'It's not been opened yet. Oh, thank God! Thank God!'

'I told you Steve's death had nothing to do with you,' Celia remarked. 'The man was fighting a war, wasn't he, for God's sake.'

'Yeah,' Violet put in, 'I'd say you have quite enough on your plate already.'

'You think she was wrong to bring Georgia home with her, don't you?' Celia said, just as she'd asked Johnnie the previous day. 'She wasn't. You don't know what those nuns are capable of. I'll show you just one thing they did to us, as soon as we entered that place,' and with that she pulled off the scarf.

Violet looked at Celia's hair, cut roughly and only about half an inch from her scalp all over. She'd wondered why Celia had kept the scarf on in the house.

'But Lizzie's hair isn't like that?' she said. 'It's shorter than it was, I'll grant you, but . . .'

'Johnnie stopped them cutting mine,' Lizzie said. 'Before that, mine was like Celia's. He said I'd not be able to take up the strands of my life again if I had my hair shorn.'

'And what of you, Celia?'

'Oh, there was no brother or uncle to come for me. I'd have languished there for years, and for what? For eventually giving in to my fiancé's urging to let him have sex just the one time. When I found myself pregnant, I told him and he skedaddled off to England. I thought my father would kill me when he found out. He beat me black and blue and then went for the priest. I was in the convent before I had time to draw breath.

'But far, far worse than the pain of the beating was that of being thrown out, disowned by the family. I'd never felt sadness like that. I have three brothers and three sisters and we were all brought up together in a farmhouse in West Meath. Suddenly, it was as if I didn't exist any more, as if Mammy and Daddy had a list of their children and my name had been rubbed out.'

Celia's whole face was filled with sorrow, and even Lizzie, who'd heard the story, was moved afresh, and she saw tears glistening in Violet's eyes.

'I learnt to cope eventually,' Celia said, 'because you have to. Then I gave birth to the child, a little boy. Everything that had gone before, even being incarcerated in that bloody awful place, worse than any prison, was nothing to how I felt when my son was eventually removed from the room. It was as if they'd removed part of my heart. I thought I would die, the pain was so bad. I wanted to die. There's not a day goes by when I don't think about my little boy and miss him and wish with all my heart I hadn't had to give him up.'

The tears were running down Violet's face, and Celia's. Lizzie had never seen Celia cry before. She was like a hard nut, one the nuns could never crack, but now Lizzie realised the hard shell was how she had survived. Inside, she was aching with loss and rejection and Lizzie put her arms around her.

'Oh God, Celia, I never imagined you felt this bad,' Lizzie cried. 'You told me about your son, but . . .'

Celia grabbed Lizzie's arm, which was resting on her shoulder, and looked at her. 'You didn't dare show emotion in that place,' she said. 'If you did, they'd won. You know that as well as me.'

'I too had a son I lost,' Violet told Celia. 'His name was Colin and he was a fine boy. He was a sailor and died when his ship was blown out of the water and I miss him too. It's like an ache that never goes away.'

'The nuns would ridicule you for shedding tears, showing you cared,' Celia went on. 'I don't think any heartache will ever be greater than the loss of my baby, and I survived it. I told myself, if I could survive that, I could survive anything.'

'Was it really so bad?' Violet asked.

'Worse than you could ever imagine,' Lizzie said. 'I dared write nothing of it in the letters I wrote to you, just in case the nuns asked to see them. I dread to think what they would have done to me then.'

'Do you mean they actually hit you? Grown women hitting other grown women?'

Celia sighed. 'If that was all it was,' she said, and together the two young women began telling Violet about their life in the convent.

When, eventually, the tale drew to a halt, all the women's eyes were bright and their cheeks wet. 'You see now why I couldn't leave a wee baby in such a place?' Lizzie said.

'Yeah, I see it,' Violet answered. 'But few will, and you've paid a high price for her.'

'I know that,' Lizzie said grimly. 'My home is forbidden to me too.'

'Your home? You mean, you can't go home again?'

'No!' Lizzie said sadly. 'My children are lost to me, Violet, for now at least. If their father had lived he might have had other plans, but as it is, even if I were to go to court to try to claim them, to all intents and purposes I am a fallen woman, unfaithful to my husband and him a serving soldier, and unfaithful with a black man. That is what society sees and a court would never release the children to me, but might take them from my parents, who do love them, and put them with strangers who'd care not a jot, or place them in an orphanage, the very thing I rejected for their half-sister. I can't risk rocking the boat. I know it and my parents know it.

'However, despite the way that Georgia was conceived, I have grown to love her with the same passion I felt for the other two, and I will never desert her now. I just wish I could build a high wall around her. I know I can't, but I will protect her as much as I can.'

And I will help you, Celia thought. She knew she would never forget what Lizzie had done for her and she would stay with her as long as she was needed, for inside, Lizzie was still soft, capable of being hurt. She needed to harden herself to survive.

'I bet that there's one you didn't tell you were coming back and you're not really keen on meeting either,' Violet said.

'Aye, Flo Gillespie,' Lizzie said. 'I'm terrified of her, to tell you the truth.'

'Is this the harridan, Steve's mother?' Celia asked.

'The very same.'

'She knows about Steve, though, doesn't she?' Lizzie asked.

'Yeah,' Violet said. 'After I redirected the telegram to your mother's place, I set off for Pershore Road. I've never had much time for Flo, you know that, but God, when I told her I did feel sorry for her. The colour drained from her and she gave one small cry and fell like a stone. The doctor had to be called out, and people say she lies like one dead, according to her sister, anyroad.'

'But someone will feel it their duty to tell her I am back and living with a black bastard in Steve's house,' Lizzie said.

'Oh, bound to,' Violet agreed. 'Mind you, they might not get to see Flo herself, cos Gladys might not allow it; but no odds to that, if they tell Gladys it will be bad enough.'

Lizzie gave a sigh. The confrontation with Flo was

one thing she'd been dreading since she decided to return home.

'Well, the old sod can rant and rave all she likes,' Violet said, 'and call you all the names under the sun, but remember, when she does, you ain't responsible for any of it. Nothing you can do can change Steve's death either, and you must go forward. You have a child to rear and a life to live.'

Violet's words roused Lizzie, for there were things to do that couldn't wait. There were just coppers left from the money Johnnie had given them and she had to sort out ration cards, and a gas mask and an identity card for Celia. Maybe they could also get some clothes from the Mission Hall. Lizzie's clothes hung on Celia's slender frame, and anyway, there was scarcely enough for the two of them.

'I'll mind the babby if you like,' Violet said when Lizzie said what she must do. 'Don't want to be dragging a baby about, and certainly not in this weather. That wind would cut you in two.'

At the same time that Lizzie and Celia were setting out on their errands, Tressa had waylaid Johnnie, who was whitewashing the cow shed. He hadn't reached home until well after midnight the previous day, and this had been the first chance Tressa had had to see him. 'Is it true Lizzie's baby was black?' she said, her lip curled in repugnance and disbelief.

'Who told you?'

He hadn't denied it. Despite Mike's letter, she'd expected Johnnie to pooh-pooh the whole notion of it, for it was incredible.

'Is it true?'

Johnnie looked around to see if anyone was in earshot, and then realising it would be stupid to deny it, said, 'Aye.'

'So, it was a black man that assaulted her that time.'

'Obviously. According to what she told me, the man could have been pink with yellow spots, for she could see nothing.'

'Why didn't she leave the child with the nuns?' Tressa asked. 'They find homes for them. According to Mike she wants to take this child back to Birmingham with her.'

'She's taken her,' Johnnie said. 'I left her at Dun Laoghaire yesterday. The nuns didn't want the child. Apparently, there's few homes for half-caste bastards, and Lizzie wouldn't let them take her to an orphanage.'

'Oh Jesus, Johnnie, they'll crucify her.'

'I know that and she knows that,' Johnnie said. 'But she's been through the mill with those nuns and she said she couldn't leave a wee, innocent baby in their clutches.'

'Does she know Steve's dead?'

'She does now. How do you know?'

'Mike told me. He had to collect his effects and the letter from Lizzie, telling him all, was on the bed.'

'I don't have to ask you to keep this to yourself?'

'No,' Tressa said. 'I'll not spread it around, don't you worry, and neither will Mike. Steve just walked out of the city, you know, and was killed by a sniper. Many thought it was battle fatigue that sent him over the top, but when Mike read the letter he knew what had tipped the balance for Steve. He blamed Lizzie in

430

a way at first. I mean, Mike was his mate after all. But still, he thought she'd gone through enough and he resealed the letter, so Lizzie never needs to know Steve ever received it. I'm glad he did that, for she has enough on her plate and she is a great one for feeling guilty is our Lizzie.'

'Don't I know it,' Johnnie said. 'Write to her, Tressa. I think she'd value your support.'

'I will,' Tressa promised. 'I'll tell you what, though, she's one unlucky sod.'

'You can say that again,' Johnnie said. 'I'm worried sick about her, and the bloody thing is I'm helpless to do anything about any of it.'

Lizzie and Celia came home in good humour, pleased with their achievements for the day, for they'd registered with Moorcroft's on Bell Barn Road for their rations and Lizzie had also drawn some money out of the Post Office and picked up some lovely clothes from the clothes bank at the Mission Hall. They'd also been issued with new ration books and identity cards, and at the Town Hall Lizzie found she was entitled to a pension of fifteen shillings and sixpence. Although it wasn't a fortune, Lizzie was glad of it. She would also be getting eight shillings and sixpence for Niamh, and six shillings and thrupence for Tom. 'I'll get that made up into postal orders and send it to my mother,' she told Celia.

'Will she accept it?'

Lizzie shrugged. 'I don't know. If she doesn't I'll open an account for the children here and put the money in.'

'Do they know?'

'About Steve?' Lizzie asked. 'They will by now. My mother was going to tell them. That was hardly the sort of news I could break to two weans by letter.'

'No, I see that.'

'I will write to them, though, and tonight if possible,' Lizzie said. She gave a sigh. She knew she really should be there beside them to support them, but there was nothing she could do about that.

They'd dumped all their packages on the table and collected the grumbling, hungry baby from Violet's. Lizzie was just about to feed her when there was a knock at the door.

Celia opened the door to Father Connolly. He made no greeting to her, but strode across to Lizzie where she sat in a chair with the baby on her knee. She would not hide her daughter away, and so when the priest's long, bony fingers prised the shawl away from the baby's face, she made no move to stop him.

She saw his lip purse so tightly that creases appeared each side of his long, thin nose, and in his eyes she saw blazing anger and disgust as they raked over Lizzie and the young woman behind her. He didn't know who Celia was, and didn't much care. His business was with Lizzie. 'I was told,' he said, his voice cold and clipped, 'and I scarce believed it. There are women I wouldn't have been surprised to find carrying on like that, as soon as their husbands were out of sight, but you . . . and then to give yourself to a black man.'

Anger coursed through Lizzie's body. This was not to be borne. She stood up and handed the baby to Celia before facing the priest. 'Look here, you. Don't you dare go around preaching and judging me. That wee baby is the result of the attack that you know all about.'

The priest cast his mind back and said, 'I remember the attack, but you said nothing about any other type of assault.'

'I wasn't sure,' Lizzie said. 'That is, I was unconscious and I had no recollection of it. When I found I was pregnant, I went to my mother's. The idea was to give my child up for adoption, but when she was born she was half-caste, as you see, and they could barely bear to touch her, never mind care for her. The man who attacked me I hate with a passion, and my greatest wish would be to have him before me this minute and a knife in my hand. But that isn't the baby's fault and I love her with all my heart and soul. I will rear her to be decent and honest and respectable and proud of herself for who she is.'

Father Connolly was struck by Lizzie's words, for he guessed every syllable was true. If it was, the woman had suffered twice and would continue to suffer, he knew. However, it wasn't in his nature to feel sorry for anyone, and to give himself time to collect his thoughts he turned to look at Celia. He wondered what her relationship was to Lizzie, was she a sister maybe, or a cousin? 'And this is?' he said, and his very tone annoyed Celia.

'My name is Celia Hennessy and I'm a friend of Lizzie's.' The words were said as a challenge and Celia gave a toss of her head at the same time. She wasn't privy to the priest's thoughts, but she'd heard his rebuke and Lizzie's heart-rending response. After her own experience, she had little time for the clergy, and she owed this man nothing.

'I'm pleased to meet you.'

''Fraid I can't say the same,' Celia retorted. 'In fact, if you've said your piece you best go now.'

The priest had never been spoken to like that, and by a young girl too, and he bristled in annoyance. 'Really, I . . .'

'Celia's right, Father,' Lizzie said. 'Everything worth saying has been said.'

The priest looked from one young woman to the other and decided he would leave. Nothing would be achieved by his insisting on staying. As neither woman opened the door for him, he opened it himself, and once there he turned back. 'Will I see you both at Mass?'

'No,' Lizzie said. 'Not at St Catherine's anyway.'

'Lizzie, I'm sure . . .'

'Goodbye, Father,' Celia cried and she sped across the room with the baby in her arms and shut the door with a resounding crash, almost before the priest was through it. 'Sanctimonious prig,' she said with venom as the baby's hungry wails rent the air.

CHAPTER TWENTY-TWO

Flo awoke from her grief-ridden stupor on Sunday morning, feeling stronger than she'd done in a long time, and she decided to go to eleven o'clock Mass at St Catherine's. Maybe she'd have a Mass said for Steve while she was about it; not that he needed it of course, and yet prayers never went amiss and maybe a mass said in Advent would have special significance.

The news about Lizzie hadn't got as far as Pershore Road, and so Gladys encouraged her sister to go out into the air, seeing it as a positive measure. There were many, though, who'd heard the rumours about Lizzie and been disgusted by them. Seeing Flo at Mass, they made it their mission to tell her what that Lizzie Gillespie had been up to, in case she was ignorant of the fact. And Flo listened open-mouthed to the tale of her daughter-in-law, who'd seemingly opened her legs for a nigger when her own fine husband was doing his duty, fighting and dying for his country.

'She's up at the house, now, this minute, her and the child,' one said. She didn't mention Celia for she

didn't know about her, but anyway, Flo was only interested in the little sex-crazed wanton her son had had
the misfortune to marry. The brazenness of it, shaming
the memory of Steve's name in that way, caused Flo's
rage to increase with each step she took towards Bell
Barn Road.

Those who'd told her and those who'd heard it told
scurried home to spread the news. Even the women
who'd not been told knew something was afoot when
they saw the determined stride of Flo and caught sight
of the malevolent look on her face. Few felt sorry for
Lizzie, feeling she deserved all she got, and as Flo passed
they came to their doors, arms folded across their chests,
to discuss it with their neighbours, who'd done the
same thing.

Flo thrust Lizzie's door open with such force it
crashed against the wall, waking the sleeping baby
who began to cry. Lizzie was on her own in the room
for Celia had gone upstairs to put the clothes away
that they'd got the previous day. The crash alerted her,
though, and she began to descend the stairs rapidly.

Lizzie had turned from what she was stirring on the
cooker and she stared at Flo. This was the meeting
she'd been dreading, and yet she knew it had to come.
She almost welcomed it, and as she looked at the old
woman she suddenly lost all fear of her. She saw her
for what she was, wizened up with bitterness and badness and now bereft of the one person she held dear
in life. She'd coped with nuns ten times worse than
Flo and they'd not broken her, and neither would
Florence Gillespie.

'You dirty, stinking trollop!'

Lizzie allowed herself a sardonic smile. 'Good morning to you too.'

Celia opened the stairs door but didn't step into the room. Instead she just watched.

'How dare you! I'm surprised you can hold your head up.'

'It's easy,' Lizzie said, 'for I've done nothing wrong.'

'Nothing wrong!' Flo cried, so angry she could barely get words out. She sprang over to the pram, but Lizzie had anticipated that and got there before her, scooping out the crying baby, which she laid against her shoulder. 'You stand there, bold as brass, and tell me you ain't done nothing to be ashamed of, when not only have you been playing fast and loose with your favours, you were left with a belly full of a nigger's bastard.'

'I never played fast and loose, never,' Lizzie said. 'I never willingly went with any man but Steve, nor wanted to. But I agree, the man who raped me must have been black.'

'Rape! What's this talk of rape?'

'You must remember the attack on me?'

'You said nowt about rape.'

'No, I chose not to.'

Flo thought about this for a second or two and then spat out, 'Come on, Lizzie, think I was born yesterday. Christ Almighty, if you'd been raped, as you claim, why bring the child back here? I'd have thought you wouldn't want to even cast your eyes on it.'

'Well you're wrong, and what I choose to do or not to do is my business.'

'We'll see about that,' Flo said emphatically. 'I'll go

up and see the landlord in the morning. See what he has to say.'

Lizzie knew the threat was real. If the man thought she was living immorally she could easily be put out, but to portray fear in front of Flo was the very last thing to do. Lizzie knew this and so she said, 'You do that, Flo. There is a police file on me about that attack, and of course a doctor's report. I'm sure when he sees the documentation he will see I have no case to answer.'

Flo was silent. She didn't know Lizzie hadn't told the doctor about the rape. If the police and doctor confirmed the stabbing and bang on the head and went on to say Lizzie had been tampered with, she'd be the one to look the fool.

With a shriek of rage, Flo threw herself on Lizzie, and Lizzie tried only to protect the baby as the woman punched and kicked at her and raked her face with long, dirty nails. Suddenly, Flo's arms were pulled from Lizzie and held firm behind her back and Celia said in a tight, no-nonsense voice, 'Okay, you bloody old vixen. You've said your piece, so get going.'

'I'll go when I'm ready.'

'You'll go now and you'll either walk out the door under your own steam or go with the aid of my boot up your arse,' Celia said, forcing the woman towards the door that was still open, and Flo knew the girl meant every word.

'This ain't the end of this, Lizzie,' she shrieked.

'Oh yes it is,' Celia said. 'We don't want to see you here again.'

'Lizzie is my daughter-in-law.'

'Well isn't she the unluckiest bugger in the world

then,' Celia commented grimly, and she gave Flo a push as she released her arms so that Flo ended up in the yard.

Flo stood rubbing at her arms, glaring at Celia. 'You'll pay for this, Lizzie,' she screamed. 'You'll wish you'd never been born by the time I'm done.'

'Oh bugger off, you old bag of wind, before I completely lose my temper,' Celia snarled, and she shut the door with a bang and looked across at Lizzie, who was automatically rocking Georgia with tears rolling down her face.

But they were tears of laughter. 'Oh God, I shouldn't laugh,' she said. 'Really I shouldn't, but I've never seen Flo meet her match before. Haven't you a nerve in your body?'

'No,' Celia said with a grin. 'They were all shrivelled up in that bloody convent. But, later, as Celia bathed the scratches on her cheeks, Lizzie knew that the encounter could easily have repercussions, for it would only have fuelled Flo's anger and her need to get even.

The next morning, Lizzie went for the rations leaving Georgia in Celia's care. The two women had registered with Gerald Moorcroft on Saturday. His wife Dinah had been upstairs and hadn't been aware of this, nor had she heard anything about Lizzie. She knew now all right, though, for the news had flown around, and those in for their rations earlier had given Dinah Moorcroft a blow-by-blow account of their version of it, and so she stared at Lizzie as she came in the door as if she couldn't believe her eyes.

Lizzie had never taken to the dumpy, plump woman, her head barely reaching her husband's shoulder and her face hard and set with thin, pinched lips. But now, cold grey eyes flashed fire and two spots of colour appeared on her cheeks as she spat out, 'What are you doing here? This isn't the shop for whores and trollops. Get out!'

'Now, Dinah,' Gerald put in ineffectually.

Lizzie just stared at her for a moment or two, taken aback, and then demanded, 'Who d'you think you are to call names?'

'I think I'm the shopkeeper,' Dinah sneered. 'And I can choose who comes into the shop and who doesn't, and we don't want your sort in here, so hop it.'

'But I registered here on Saturday.'

'Well, un-register yourself.'

'Like hell I will,' Lizzie said angrily, and, appealing to the man who'd registered her and Celia without problem, she asked, 'What d'you say, Mr Moorcroft?'

Before the man was able to speak, Dinah cut in. 'I make the decisions here, and like I said, it's my shop and you are not welcome.'

'You make a mistake, my dear,' Gerald said, his voice unusually loud. 'This is my shop, as it was my father's and his father's before him, and I decide who comes in and who doesn't. I registered Lizzie, who's already been with us years anyway, and her friend on Saturday, because I wished to do so, and I will serve them.'

'Don't you get on your high horse with me, Gerald Moorcroft,' Dinah snapped. 'Fine shop you'd have left if I hadn't taken charge of it. And if you serve the likes of her, you'll drive respectable people away.'

'I doubt it, my dear,' Gerald said mildly. 'It's not a straightforward job, un-registering. Few will want to bother doing that and then go further for their shopping. And now, if the sight of Lizzie so offends you, may I make the suggestion you go up and put the kettle on while I attend to her.'

The glare Dinah shot Lizzie's way should have killed her stone-dead on the floor, but she didn't argue further and Gerald just remarked quietly when he was sure Dinah was out of earshot, 'It might be better for the next few days at least, till the gossips have someone else to discuss, if you only come into the shop when you can be sure I am here.'

'I'll take care to,' Lizzie said. 'And I'm sorry if I have brought trouble on your head.'

'Don't fret yourself,' Gerald answered. 'Trouble is never far away when you are married to a woman like Dinah, but her words roll off me like water off a duck's back. Now, my dear, let's see to your groceries.'

A couple of days later, Celia said to Lizzie, 'What's the matter with you? You've done nothing but sigh since you came in.'

'Have I? Sorry.'

'Well, what's it over?'

'Nothing specific,' Lizzie said. 'A bit of everything, I suppose. The way no one speaks to me when I pass in the street. Sometimes they stand on the doorsteps and stare, and other times they talk about me after I've passed. Today, I was coming along the top end of Bell Barn Road and a woman spat at me.'

'Spat at you?'

'Aye, a big blob of spittle landed on my coat.'

'People like that are ignorant,' Celia said. 'I've told you, people like that don't matter: their opinions don't, nor their attitudes. Anyway, surely to God you knew what you were coming back to? Are you going to fall at the first post?'

Lizzie had accepted, in her mind, that many people might be shocked and disgusted by her actions, not knowing the facts at all, but she found coping with the reality of this and the animosity directed at her day in, day out was upsetting. She wished she was more like Celia and could shrug her shoulders about it all, but she found that hard to do and it was beginning to wear her down.

Lizzie and Celia had been back in Birmingham just over a week when one Sunday evening on the wireless they heard about the American fleet being annihilated by the Japanese at a place known as Pearl Harbour. America would now be pulled into the war they'd ignored so far. 'About bloody time,' most people said. But Lizzie wondered bleakly if it would make any real difference. The war seemed no further forward, and though the threat of invasion had been lifted, cities were still getting bombed, killing civilians indiscriminately, and the sight of the telegraph boy still brought terror to people's hearts.

Many of the Royal Warwickshires came home on leave a week later. By then, Lizzie was used to getting her shopping in when it was at least dusky, and there was less likelihood of her being seen skulking around outside Moorcroft's till she could be sure there was no one in the shop but Gerald behind the counter, though she could never be totally sure through the shuttered window.

Mike, stopping off to see his mother before travelling to Ireland, went to see Lizzie as well. His mother had regaled him already with the loose morals of Lizzie that had caused her to stray from her wifely duties as soon as her man's back was turned: '. . . and to lie with a black man no less . . .'

Mike had also heard about the young, aggressive hussy whom Lizzie had living with her, but, for all that, they were two women living on their own and Mike was glad Celia was there, for she was a stronger character than Lizzie. Celia refused to go out in the dark, and though most people knew she was a friend of Lizzie's her step was firm and determined, her head held high and the look she cast on those glaring at her was defiant, even challenging.

Mike felt sorry for Lizzie, though he didn't tell her this, knowing it would serve no purpose, and he was almighty glad he'd been able to get to the letter before anyone else had got hold of it. He no longer blamed her. 'And the child is beautiful,' he was to tell Tressa later. 'Not black at all, just dusky brown and with the largest brown eyes you've ever seen. And she's just begun to smile, and when she does it makes your heart turn over. I feel for her too, for all Lizzie is a great mother.'

'She always was a good mother,' Tressa said. 'And if she could see Tom and Niamh now, she'd be heartbroken so she would. I thought of writing to tell her, but what could she do about it.'

'Nothing,' Mike agreed. 'Best say nothing.'

Someone else was worried about Lizzie's children, and that was her brother Johnnie. Apparently, when Catherine had told them of the death of their father, they'd both suddenly gone very still. Neither could quite believe it. Their daddy had been big and strong and afraid of nothing. They hadn't seriously thought any real harm could come to him. Niamh could only dimly remember the time after Dunkirk when he'd hurt his leg. He said he got it crushed between two army trucks and Niamh could see you wouldn't feel that great after such an experience. But bullets! Hadn't her daddy said bullets bounced back off him? That he'd catch them in his teeth and spit them back? But he couldn't have, because her granny said her daddy had been shot.

Tom didn't understand the finality of death, but he knew he wouldn't see his daddy for a long time. He'd heard grown-ups around him talk about the cities bombed to bits, ordinary people going about their business and doing no harm at all to anyone, people like his mother. And, suddenly, he needed his mammy, wanted her arms around him, her hands gently pushing the hair back from his face, holding him tight and telling him how much she loved him, to know she, at least, was safe. 'I want my mammy,' he cried.

His tears came like a torrent and Niamh knew she wanted her mother too, badly, and she wept with her young brother. When Catherine attempted to comfort the children, Tom pushed her arms away. 'Not you, I don't want you. I want Mammy.'

Niamh was more polite and she submitted to her grandmother's embrace, but held herself rigid so it was like hugging a lump of wood. Things hadn't really improved since then, for the children seemed burdened down with sadness and loss. Others noticed it, particularly Tressa and the children's aunts and uncles. Even the teacher at the County School in Ballintra had expressed concern, and their schoolwork began to suffer as they lost interest in it.

'They'll get over it,' Catherine snapped when Johnnie expressed concern.

'Aye, and at what cost?' Johnnie pointed out. 'Can't you see you are punishing the children because of something Lizzie has done, and which I firmly believe was not her fault.'

'What you believe is of no account,' Catherine said. 'As for the children, I am keeping them away from their mother for their own good. They can't be expected to understand this. They are only children.'

Lizzie was unaware how much her children suffered, but she sent them a letter every week, dredging up incidents to amuse them. She wrote to her parents too, enclosing the postal orders. She never mentioned Georgia. She couldn't bring herself to. She wanted to win her mother round and thought mentioning Georgia would not help her case, and so Catherine remained ignorant of the fact that she had a granddaughter residing in Birmingham, England.

All his life, Neil had sought his mother's approval. He'd had little time for the father he resembled and often thought his mother didn't like him because of it.

He'd resented his brother, yet he knew he would have been his willing little slave if Steve had ever given him a kind word. But Steve had followed his mother's lead in disregarding him and had pushed him away.

When his father died, Neil had shed no tears; and later, when Steve was killed, he'd thought, at last Ma has no one but me.

It was a blow for him to learn that her affections could not be transferred just like that. But she wanted someone to blame for Steve's death, and her hatred was redirected from the sniper who'd shot him to the wife who'd betrayed him and taunted his memory by flaunting her bastard for all to see, and without a bit of shame about it.

Neil was disturbed by all his mother told him about the half-caste child, and although he thought Steve probably had many offspring peppered around the place he said none of this. For the first time, his mother was relying on him, looking to him for some solution. 'Are you not shocked, son? Are you not incensed with that wanton defiling your brother's good name?'

'Yeah,' Neil said, and he was shocked that Lizzie could do such a thing in the first place, and then doubly shocked that she'd brought the child back with her and thought she could just carry on as if nothing had happened. 'What d'you want me to do, Ma?'

'See to her, son, what else?'

'Okay, Ma,' Neil said. 'I'm your man.'

Later, in the pub, Neil met Stuart, who had called to see Lizzie as a good mate's duty to her late husband. He'd been unaware of the set-up at all, as he'd been unaware of Lizzie's heart thumping in her chest, her clammy hands and her voice so dry she could barely speak. He told Neil she was, 'As cool as a cucumber about the whole bloody thing.'

Mind you, he hadn't studied Lizzie much at all. He couldn't seem to keep his eyes off the dark-skinned child and he'd thought fervently, *Thank God that Steve knows nothing of this*.

'If Steve had lived he'd never have allowed it,' Neil said. 'He'd have killed her if she'd tried that sort of caper.'

'Don't I know it,' Stuart said with feeling. 'She said she'd intended getting rooms, but that wouldn't have saved her. He couldn't and wouldn't have stood for it.'

'My mother thinks she shouldn't be allowed to get away with it.'

'Yeah, and she's bloody right as well.'

As the night wore on, the two men were joined by another mate of Neil's called Roy, and, in the course of many pints, towards closing time Neil told him about his sister-in-law. 'What she needs is a good seeing-to,' Roy said. 'If she'll open her legs for a nigger, she'll open them for anyone.'

'Yeah,' Stuart added. 'Bet she'd welcome good, honest white boys with open arms. Have her begging for it.'

'Begging for mercy more like, before I'm done,' Neil said. 'Come on then,' he announced, draining his pint. 'What are we bloody waiting for?'

Lizzie and Celia were both fast asleep, curled up together in the double bed, when the knock came at the door. Lizzie struggled to sit up. Beside her, Celia murmured sleepily, 'What is it?'

'Nothing,' Lizzie answered. 'Go back to sleep.'

She lit the lamp beside the bed. It was almost half past eleven. Who but someone bent on mischief would call at this time of night? Well, she'd not go down, she thought. Let them knock all they liked, and she thanked God she'd not got out of the habit of locking and bolting doors since the time she was attacked.

Outside in the yard, Neil was annoyed to find the door locked. Few bothered doing that, but he'd got this far and wasn't going to go home now. 'Hide in the entry,' he told Roy and Stuart in a whisper.

'Why?' Stuart said, wondering if the idea, formulated over many pints in a congenial pub, was so good now, here in the icy black yard. 'She's locked up and gone to bed, man.'

'Well, she can bloody well wake up,' Neil hissed. 'I reckon I can get her to open the door, but she won't if she sees you.'

'I don't know.'

Roy, however, was turned on by the whole experience. He hadn't had a woman in weeks and his groin ached with desire; he was in no mood to go home unsatisfied. 'Give him a chance, man.'

Stuart was still doubtful. He shook his head. 'I dunno.'

'Well, go home if you've lost your bottle,' Roy said.

Stuart couldn't go home. He lived miles away. He'd only intended staying at The Bell for the one that night to settle his nerves after his encounter with Lizzie earlier. It was Neil's offer of a bed for the night that had encouraged him to stay on. And so, now, he had little choice and he melted into the darkness alongside Roy.

Neil banged the door again, but this time he called, 'Lizzie, it's me, Neil.'

Neil! Lizzie eased herself out of bed to avoid rousing Celia, pushed her feet into slippers and grabbed a warm shawl from the wardrobe to cover herself, for the room was like an ice box. She lifted the blackout shutters from the window and peered out, but could see nothing.

With a sigh of annoyance, she got the lamp from the side of the bed and lit it. She slid up the window, letting blasts of damp, sooty air into the room. Risking the warden, she leant out, her arm extended, and in the light she saw Neil standing swaying in the yard. He was drunk, she realised, and she wanted no tête-à-tête with him in that condition. 'Neil, go home!' she pleaded. 'Whatever it is can wait until morning.'

'No, it won't,' Neil insisted. 'It was summat our Steve wanted me to tell you. This is the first chance I've had.'

If Lizzie was suspicious at all, she thought it only a little odd that Steve could have instructed his brother with any message of importance. But it probably wasn't that important – in his drunken state it just appeared so.

'Neil, it's late.'

'Come on, Lizzie. It will only take a minute.'

Lizzie gave a sigh. She had no wish to go down-stairs and speak to Neil, but she guessed he wouldn't be easy to persuade to go home, at least not without raising the court. And she couldn't stand at the window all night, letting the night air waft over those still sleeping, not to mention risking a two-hundred-pound fine if the warden was to catch sight of the light and could trace its source. 'All right,' she snapped. 'You are a nuisance, Neil, and a couple of minutes is all you'll have.'

She closed the window and snuffed out the light and Neil allowed himself a smile of triumph. Roy and Stuart had heard the conversation and moved into position behind him. Lizzie considered dressing, but decided against it. If she did that, Neil might take it as an indication to stay later, so she held the shawl wrapped about her while she ran down the stairs. She poked life into the fire and lit the gas lamps, but turned them low before she went to open the door.

Her first impression of Neil, whom she'd not seen for nearly six months, was that the army had made a man of him. He'd never be tall, but the way he stood so straight made him appear taller. His eyes seemed darker and even his skin more defined, but his mouth was slack and his words slurred. 'Hello, Lizzie.'

'Neil.' Lizzie inclined her head and opened the door wider. She wasn't afraid of Neil, but she was cautious. She knew Flo would have wasted no time telling her son about the half-caste child and might not have told him anything at all about the attack, either when it happened or since, but at least the message from Steve wouldn't have any connection with that.

But, suddenly, Neil's arm shot out and sent the door crashing open, yanking it from Lizzie's grasp. It twisted her hand so that she cried out with the pain of it, and she lost her grip on the shawl, which fell from her.

'Told you,' Neil said to his two mates, who'd crowded in after Neil and closed the door behind them. 'Gagging for it, she is. Even dressed for the part.'

Paralysing fear gripped Lizzie, but she forced herself to remain calm and she said angrily, 'How dare you burst in like that. And you, Stuart, is this any way to behave, abusing the hospitality you've received here many a time?'

Before Stuart could answer, Neil sneered, 'Like you abused your marriage vows, playing the field while my brother risked his life daily, until in the end you gave birth to a black man's baby.'

'That wasn't how it was, Neil, really it wasn't,' Lizzie said, desperately trying to pierce through his befuddled brain. 'I'll tell you what really happened sometime. When you're sober perhaps.'

It was a mistake telling Neil he was drunk. Neil grabbed Lizzie suddenly by the front of her nightdress and said in a voice full of venom, 'You'll tell me nothing. I don't want your version of anything because I wouldn't believe a word you say, anyroad. You're a lying whore.'

Even as Lizzie protested, Neil pushed her away a little and powered his right fist into the side of her cheek. The suddenness of the assault caused Lizzie to stagger slightly and she put a hand to her throbbing cheek as tears trickled from her eyes. Her mind was telling her to stay upright, not let herself fall, but she couldn't keep upright after the second blow to the other side of her face and she sank to her knees.

Maybe this was it, she thought. This was what Neil wanted, to beat her because of the false tale Flo had told him, or at least she must have omitted to tell him the whole truth so he'd assumed the rest and he'd come to avenge his brother. But still she would not allow herself to show fear. By God, she thought wryly, that convent was a good training-ground for most situations.

She'd seldom seen a man so angry as Neil that night. Even when she'd annoyed Steve in some way, she'd never seen him look as murderous as his brother did at that moment. And that was the word, *murderous*: from his dark, forbidding eyes in a face brick-red and swollen in temper, to the spittle forming around his mouth. It caused a shudder of fear to trail down Lizzie's spine like an icy finger and she swallowed the lump in her throat. Her own voice was slurred because one of her lips was split as she said, 'Well, Neil, I hope you're satisfied. I expect there was no message from Steve at all. I would say that all this has the markings of your mother on it.'

'You sodding bitch!'

The third blow caused Lizzie to fall to the ground with a groan. Blood was running from her lip and gushing from her nose and Stuart looked from her to Neil with distaste. 'There was no need for that.'

'There was every need.'

Roy, on the other hand, had been excited by the violence of it, and his erection was so strong it made him say, 'For God's sake, hurry. If you aren't man enough to take her, then I will.'

'Piss off!' Neil said. 'That pleasure is all mine. You take your bloody turn.'

Lizzie forced herself back to reality and she told

herself she couldn't lose consciousness. She was about to be violated a second time. Jesus Christ! She'd fight this time. And she fought, valiantly, lashing out with her hands and nails, which she raked down Neil's face, and then kicked at him as he came nearer.

But, eventually, Roy held her legs and Stuart had a hand over her bruised mouth, so that the scream she gave changed to a strangled yelp. Neil was astride her, her nightdress pulled up to her shoulders, and he was fingering her with one hand and unzipping himself with the other. Panic coursed through Lizzie for she knew she was helpless to do anything to stop this.

But the yelp Lizzie gave had roused Celia. In the darkness Celia felt the bed beside her and, finding it empty, she struggled to sit up. The child still slept peacefully, she could hear her shallow breathing, so the sound hadn't been from her. She lit the lamp beside her bed and in its light saw the blackout shutters had been removed from the windows, and she remembered the knock earlier at the door.

Surely now she could hear the mumble of voices in the room below. And she could, for Neil had his throbbing penis between his hands and he was saying to Lizzie, 'By Christ, I'm going to enjoy this and we'll take you one by one till you cry for mercy.'

Celia got up and, without stopping to cover herself and not owning slippers, she ran across the room and down the stairs, hardly feeling in her sudden anxiety the icy chill of the lino. She stopped for a brief second in the doorway and took in the scene. Some man she'd never seen before was astride Lizzie; no prizes for guessing what he was at and he'd already left his mark on her, or someone had. Her face was a mass of bruised pulp covered in blood, and her two eyes were like mere slits.

She only recognised one of the men and that was the one with his hand over Lizzie's mouth. He was Stuart, who'd been at the house earlier. Lizzie had said he was a friend of Steve's and she'd not taken to him then, nor she'd seen had he believed Lizzie's story of the rape, so this visit presumably was to teach Lizzie a lesson.

Over her dead body!

No one had noticed Celia, intent only with Lizzie, and none of them knew Celia would be in the house. Even though Stuart had seen the girl with the beautiful face and shapely figure and straight, cropped hair earlier, her presence had not been explained, nor had she been introduced, and he'd presumed she was a neighbour.

Flo had thought the same and hadn't bothered mentioning the girl to Neil at all, so when Celia cried, 'Get your fucking hands off her!' Stuart and Roy turned. Neil barely heard her words. He was rubbing his penis with one hand and so close to his goal, he was unaware of much around him and his breath was coming in short gasps. Then, catching sight of Celia, he burst out, 'Oh God. You want a bit, do you? You'll have to wait your turn.'

Only Stuart saw that Celia was enraged. Roy was too taken by her body to notice. He licked his lips. By Christ, he'd have this one first, whatever Neil said, and soon, before his aching dick exploded altogether.

'I said, get your fucking hands off her.' Celia sprang across the room as she spoke, picking up the poker as she ran, and as Neil continued to rub his penis between his hands she clouted him roundly on the head before he had recovered his wits about him to even try and protect himself.

Lizzie felt Neil's weight roll off her and she arched her back with such suddenness Roy let go of her feet. At the same time, she manoeuvred her mouth, for Stuart had relaxed his hold a little, and she bit hard between his thumb and first finger with all her might. He leapt up with a howl, his finger dripping blood, but Roy was more concerned with Neil comatose on the floor.

'You've killed him,' he said to Celia, who still held her menacing stance, poker at the ready, as Lizzie gingerly got to her feet and held on to the mantelshelf to steady herself as the room tilted and dipped before her.

Lizzie was shocked by Roy's words; not so Celia. 'If I have,' she said, 'it's no great loss.'

'Celia!'

'Have you seen your face, Lizzie, and that's not the only thing that bugger tried to do. And he brought his mates along to share the fun. Some loss to mankind, that man, whoever he was.'

'He's Steve's brother, Neil,' Lizzie said, and letting go of the mantelshelf she knelt on the mat where Neil lay and picked up one of his limp hands. 'He's not dead,' she said at last, 'but I would take him to hospital to be on the safe side.'

'What about me?' Stuart asked plaintively.

'What about you?' Lizzie repeated, as if in surprise, and then added, 'I'd get that seen to as well. Human bites are the most dangerous kind, I've heard.'

'We could have the law on you,' Roy said, and Celia

laughed. 'Oh aye, just try that,' she said. 'And we'll tell the courts how three big, strapping soldier boys inveigled their way in here.'

'We'd say you knew all about it. We arranged it and you were more than willing.'

And they'd be believed, Lizzie thought, and if there was any doubt the presence of Georgia would put the tin hat on it.

Celia thought the same, but wasn't going to admit it. 'We'll see about that,' she said. 'Tomorrow, Lizzie will visit the doctor, and whether she says she walked into a door or tells the doctor what really happened tonight is up to you.'

Stuart saw the steel in the young girl's eyes and heard it in the timbre of her voice, and he knew Lizzie had a strong ally in her camp. She didn't even seem to feel at a disadvantage because of the way she was dressed, and she flounced across the room and flung open the door. 'Now, fuck off before I brain the lot of you, and don't come back if you know what's good for you.'

'We can't go just like that,' Roy complained. 'What we gonna do with Neil?'

'That isn't my problem.'

'I can't carry him with my bad hand,' Stuart moaned.

'You'll have me in tears in a minute,' Celia commented sarcastically. She pushed her face right up to Stuart's and she hissed, 'I don't care how you do it, but if you don't all get out of my sight, and soon, you'll be lying beside your man, for I'll give you a clout an' all.'

'Come on,' Stuart said, 'we'll handle him between us. The night air might revive him a bit.'

Celia shut the door on them. She would have liked to have slammed it, but for the sake of their other neighbours she didn't. She heard the latch click and she turned the key in the lock and bolted the door top and bottom before turning to face Lizzie.

Lizzie had retrieved her shawl and was sitting before the fire. She'd put a few nuggets of coal on and she was shivering from head to foot. Celia knelt before her and held her and felt Lizzie's tears dampen her shoulder. 'Don't give in now,' she urged. 'This is what they want, you upset like this.'

Lizzie, knowing Celia was right, made an effort to control herself. 'Flo put Neil up to this,' she said. 'He'd never have thought about it himself. I thought she'd been too quiet for too long.'

'Aye, well I don't think you'll be troubled from that quarter again,' Celia said grimly. 'What d'you say to me making a cup of tea to settle our nerves, and I'll try and do something with your face.'

'You can't do much with bruises, Celia.'

'I can wipe off the dried blood that's smeared all over your face for a start, and warm water might soothe you. Are you sore?'

'Everywhere,' Lizzie admitted. 'And I could murder a cup of tea.'

CHAPTER TWENTY-THREE

The following evening, Violet called to tell her the tale of Neil and another man set upon by a gang as they left the pub, and Neil with a lump the size of a duck egg on his head and kept in hospital overnight for observation. But the words died in her throat as she looked at Lizzie's face. 'Who did this?' she demanded. 'What happened to your face? Is it at all connected with young Neil Gillespie and his injuries?'

Lizzie shrugged. 'You might as well know it, Violet. You know everything else.'

She told Violet, helped by Celia, of the events of the night before, and though it could have been far more serious, how Celia had reacted caused Violet to smile. 'Gawd blimey, girl, they should have had you in charge of the army,' she said. 'Missed an opportunity there all right. Germans would have turned tail and gone home by now, I reckon!'

'You're not far wrong,' Lizzie said with feeling, for she knew what might have happened if Celia hadn't arrived on the scene when she did. 'Celia's a grand person to have at your back.'

Lizzie refused to go to the doctor. 'What the hell can he do for bruises anyway?' She had no desire to go anywhere or be seen by anyone and she seemed struck with a kind of lethargy. Celia, who got on famously with Violet, spoke of her concerns when Lizzie had skulked inside for nearly a week. 'That last incident seems to have knocked the stuffing out of her,' she said. 'I mean, her face is near enough back to normal now.'

'Let's face it, she hasn't much to be cheerful about,' Violet replied. 'And I reckon she misses the kids more than she lets on, and with Christmas just around the corner it'll be worse, I should think.'

'I know what that feels like, to miss children,' Celia said, her voice wistful. 'But she never complains much about it.'

'Lizzie's not the complaining type.'

'She never talks of the money situation either,' Celia said. 'But our funds must be getting low and I have no intention of living off Lizzie. I'm going to go for a job in the new year. My hair might be shorter than is fashionable, but at least I don't look like an escaped convict any more.'

'No, you don't, girl,' Violet said. 'Your hair's not looking bad at all, and I think it will turn out to be wavy in the end.'

'It always was,' Celia said, 'in my other life, when I was somebody's daughter.'

Violet's heart constricted with pity for the girl; and that's all she was, just a slip of a girl. And yet she knew Celia would push away sympathy and so she said instead, 'You'll have a fine choice of jobs to choose from, anyroad. As long as this damned war goes on, at least.'

Two days after this conversation, very early one morning, Minnie tapped on the door. Lizzie had just come downstairs and she opened it cautiously as she seemed to do these days. 'Minnie!'

'I was on my way to the lavvy, Lizzie, but well . . . it's your wall.'

'My wall?'

'And your door, like,' Minnie said. 'I think it's bloody disgusting.'

Lizzie had opened the door as she spoke, and painted in black across it were the words: *Filthy Stinking Whore*.

Hoisting Georgia on one hip, she went into the yard. Across the front of the house was written: *Bugger Off – No Trollops Here*.

'Thought you'd like to know, like,' Minnie said.

Lizzie was shaken. The words were bad enough, but the menace and hatred, which a person or persons must have felt to write them, was harder to cope with. What was heartening, though, were those women from the court not at work, who turned out with mops, buckets and grim determination to help Lizzie and Celia remove every offending word in short order.

'God,' Celia said, after using the scrubbing brush on the brickwork. 'I bet this house thinks it's a birthday. I bet these bricks have never had such a clean since they were laid.'

But it wasn't funny, and no one was pretending it

was. Neither was the excrement pushed through the letter box on Christmas Eve, nor the woman who spat at Lizzie full in the face the same day as she was leaving Moorcroft's with the rations.

Christmas would have been an awful time if Lizzie and Celia had not spent it in Violet's house. Carol, who'd been told of Lizzie's problems, was full of sympathy for her and got on famously with Celia. She had with her a young pilot, Gavin Honeyford, and both young people seemed determined to make it somewhat of a special time for all concerned. Even Violet packed away her sadness that Colin was dead and gone, which still surfaced at special times like this, and everyone was enchanted with Georgia.

Carol knew all about the rape and felt really sorry for Lizzie. All the coloured people she'd met had, in the main, been American airmen, and as she'd said before, often more friendly and definitely more polite and respectful than their white counterparts. However, whoever had raped Lizzie and attacked her so brutally was a maniac, plain and simple, for no sane and sensible person would do such a thing.

'Do you ever think about it?' Carol asked as the three young women washed up in the scullery. 'You know, what he was like? Why he attacked you?'

'Carol, long before I knew the man was black, I tortured myself with thoughts like that,' Lizzie said. 'The only reason I care about the colour of the man's skin at all is because of Georgia and how it will affect her and make life harder for her.'

Carol acknowledged that that was probably the case,

for while Georgia was beautiful and delightful, she was different. 'Sometimes,' Lizzie confessed, 'I wish she could stay a baby, so that I can always be there to protect her.'

'She'll be all right,' Celia cut in. 'Whatever bastard fathered her, she has a bit of you in her and that means grit and determination as well as kindness.'

'I couldn't agree more,' Carol said with conviction.

'Give over,' Lizzie protested as her face flushed with embarrassment. 'But as we are singing people's praises, I do like your young man, Carol.'

'Is he your young man?' Celia asked. 'You just introduced him as a friend.'

Now it was Carol's turn to blush. 'He is a friend,' she said, 'though I'd like him to be more. I've tried to hold back from attachments while the war rages, because some of the boys I even half-liked never came back, but I can't seem to stop myself falling for Gavin.'

'That's the way of it when love lights,' Celia said with a wide smile. 'No telling where it will end up.'

Carol gave Celia a push and the three women laughed together.

'Is there any washing up being done in there at all?' Barry shouted through. 'There's too much hilarity for my liking, and here's us gagging for a cup of tea.'

'Hark at him,' Carol said with mock indignation. 'I'll take his tea in and tip it over his head if he's not careful, and then I'm going for a walk with Gavin.'

'Don't blame you, girl,' Lizzie said, and hoped for Carol's sake that Gavin would be one of the war's survivors.

*   *   *

Early in the New Year, Celia opened the door to a woman she'd never seen before.

Lizzie was at the stove and she turned as the woman walked in. 'Auntie Doreen,' she exclaimed, pleased to see her because they'd always got on so well. She introduced Celia as a friend and said she was staying with her for now. Doreen, noticing how short the girl's hair was, assumed she had been ill and asked no further questions.

Instead, she accepted the cup of tea Lizzie offered her and had it in front of her before she said, 'Tressa has told me how things are, my dear, and I just wondered if you'd like to come and stay with us for a bit – your friend too, of course.'

Lizzie longed to accept. It would be marvellous to be away from the streets, away from the antagonistic people who tried in all ways to make her life a misery. But, practically, it was not a solution. Celia had got a job in Fisher and Ludlow's factory in nearby Rea Street, which she was starting the following Monday, and she would be hesitant, Lizzie knew, to give it up.

But, more importantly, Lizzie knew that eventually Tressa would come back from Ireland. She'd have to when the war finally ended and Mike was demobbed and took up his old job in the car industry, and she now had six children. However big Arthur and Doreen's house was, it would not take all of them, and by then if Lizzie had given up this house she'd never get another.

And so she thanked Doreen for the offer but had to refuse. Doreen could see her reasoning, especially with regards to the house, for accommodation was hard to get, but she felt bad that she could do nothing to help. When she voiced this, Lizzie said, 'You have helped, just by coming to see me.'

'The way I heard it,' Doreen said, 'you were sinned against rather than being a sinner, and I know you as an honest and respectable girl. No woman can be held responsible, in any way, for a violent rape. And now, before I go, could I see the baby?'

Lizzie could have kissed Doreen for her understanding, and later, as Doreen sat and held the baby, she was as entranced by her as others had been.

Celia had been at work just three days when Minnie came to tell Lizzie that Flo was coming down the street. 'Someone's gone to get Gladys, because Flo looks set to murder someone. If I were you, I'd lock your blooming door and not open it, whatever she does.'

Lizzie thought it good advice. She had been almost waiting for Flo, for she'd known she wouldn't just let things drop, but now she was here Lizzie didn't feel up to dealing with her. She locked and bolted the door and crept upstairs with the baby and prayed the child wouldn't cry and betray them.

Flo firstly tried the door and then, annoyed to find it locked, she hammered on it shouting, 'Come out of there, you bleeding trollop.' Annoyed at no response to her knocking, she then let forth a string of obscenities at Lizzie and what she termed her 'carry on'. Lizzie risked a peep from the bedroom window. Flo was wearing a long and shapeless coat and just had slippers on her feet, while her hair was unkempt and her eyes wild. In her clenched hand was a rock and, with a cry, Flo suddenly threw the rock at the living-room window whereupon it shattered with a crash, sending splintered wood and glass spilling out onto the yard.

Gladys arrived then, taking in the scene immediately. By then, Flo was weeping great, gulping sobs, and the women of the yard, alerted by the crash, had come to their doors to see what was going on.

'Seen enough, have you?' Gladys demanded, glaring around at them. 'Piss off, the lot of you. We all know whose fault this is and that's the sodding whore in there.' She jerked a thumb at Lizzie's house and, raising her voice, shouted, 'I know you are in there, Lizzie Gillespie. That rock should have been used on your face, and by God I wish it had found its mark.'

Then Gladys turned to her sister and said crossly, 'Put a sock in it for Christ's sake our Flo. God Almighty, you're blarting every time I look at you. Give us your bleeding hand and let's go home.' Flo lifted her hand as if she were a child and Gladys took it and led her out of the yard, just as Georgia began to cry.

Lizzie's legs were trembling and she had the urge to sink onto the bed and, like Georgia, cry her eyes out, but she resisted it and instead she went downstairs to inspect the damage to the window. 'Soon clear this up,' Ada said, moving the debris around with her boot. 'Then you need a bit of cardboard for now, like, and have a word with the rent man in the morning. Repairs is their job.'

Lizzie nodded and gave a sigh.

'Don't you mind her, ducks,' Ada said. 'Nutty as a fruitcake, her is. That business with Neil being beaten up has sent her over the edge right and proper. Everyone knows. People say her's one body's work to watch. Might be Highcroft Loony Bin for her before she's much older.'

And then, seeing the guilty look on Lizzie's face, Ada said, 'Stop that. It ain't your fault, none of it. Small wonder the old cow's gone doolally tap, anyroad. All the badness she had inside is bound to send you mad in the end.'

Although Lizzie couldn't help feeling somewhat responsible for Flo's collapse, she was relieved when Violet heard on the grapevine that Flo had been taken to the mental home when she got too much for Gladys.

Father Connolly also visited one day, and Lizzie hid from him too. Gloria, seeing him at the door, told him Lizzie was now working. He was surprised, but had no reason to disbelieve Gloria and he thanked her for letting him know and never came back.

After their traumatic experiences at the hands of nuns and priest, neither girl was in any hurry to return to the bosom of the church. As Celia put it, 'I'll take my chance with the man upstairs when my time comes, and the first thing I'll ask him is why he allows such evil people to do such awful things in his name. We've all heard of the wrath of God. Why didn't he use a bit of that? Well, I'm finished with the clergy, nuns, priests, monks, the whole lot of them, and I imagine I'll get on just as well.'

'You will,' Lizzie said. 'You're a survivor.'

'You and me both,' Celia replied, and she gave Lizzie a punch on the arm and the two laughed together.

*   *   *

The third Friday evening in February, Celia came home from work to a little bundle of cards for her eighteenth birthday. Seeing how pleased she was, Lizzie was glad she'd told Johnnie about the impending birthday in her last letter. He'd sent a card to her himself and Tressa had too. She didn't know the girl, but wished her Many Happy Returns as a friend of Lizzie's. Lizzie gave Celia a card of her own, but although there was no money for presents, and nothing to buy anyway, there was something else and she told Celia to shut her eyes and not peep.

Lizzie had carefully saved a little of her margarine and sugar ration for the last fortnight, and that previous day Mr Moorcroft had given her two eggs. She knew if Mrs Moorcroft had been around she wouldn't have had sniff of them, but as it was she was able to make a satisfactory sponge cake. She even rummaged in the drawer of the cupboard set into the fireplace alcove for the candles she'd used on the children's cakes in the past.

Celia threw her arms around Lizzie in delight and tried not to remember that her previous birthday had been spent alongside a stern father who was driving her to a living death – the convent near Sligo. She remembered how she'd ached and throbbed all over from the beating her father had given her and that not even her face had escaped. Her mother, terrified she would miscarry, had bathed the weals where the belt had bitten into the skin and refused to let Celia go until they'd healed somewhat, but her eyes had still had yellowing around them from the punches and her bottom lip had been puffy, while the lower one had a scar from the vicious punch that had split it open.

Celia remembered she'd stood and faced Sister Jude, so scared she badly wanted to pee and her hands were clammy with sweat, and Sister Jude had looked her up and down. 'I see,' she said at last. 'Your father has already chastised you.'

Resolutely, Celia pushed such memories away. What good did it do recalling such things? This was another life, living with Lizzie, and the sumptuous baby, Georgia, as well as all the women in the yard, who always had a cheery word. And so she laughed and joked as though she hadn't a care in the world.

Lizzie knew it was no life for Georgia, staying inside day after day until dusk fell, and she talked to Violet about it one evening. 'She's young to leave in a nursery, ain't she?' Violet asked.

'Violet, she'd have a better life than she does here, when I am afraid to cross the threshold of the door,' Lizzie said. 'Anyway, I'm not thinking of now, this minute, I was thinking more of after Easter. I could have her weaned by then and she'll be five months in April.'

'I do see what you mean,' Violet said. 'Where was you thinking of going, like, cos I reckon you could have your old job back if you wanted. They know about Georgia, like, but they all remember the attack and the police coming round and they don't hold you responsible, not one bit – at least not those who were there at the time. They have sent you their regards, like. Wouldn't you consider going back there?'

'I did,' Lizzie said. 'But I rejected it. See, I've never left any baby at a nursery school and I feel I'm better

468

staying close to her. The factory where Celia works in Rea Street is just up the road from the day nursery. She is making wings for Lancasters and says they can't get enough people. All I need to do is go down to the nursery and see if they will have a place for Georgia.'

Violet didn't argue further. None of hers had been left in a nursery either, but these were strange times. 'Won't you miss her?'

'Every time I think of it, my stomach gives a lurch. But we need the money and this will be better for Georgia. Everything I do is for her sake.'

'I know that, bab,' Violet said softly. 'No one would ever doubt that.'

Lizzie visited the nursery in mid-March, for it was an early Easter that year, and the Matron in charge said places were available for mothers undertaking war work. She looked at Georgia sitting on Lizzie's knee opposite her on the other side of the desk and asked, 'Was your husband an American, Mrs Gillespie?'

Lizzie knew the reason the woman asked was because the few black men about were linked to the American forces, so she said, 'My husband was a serving soldier in the Royal Warwickshires and he was killed in North Africa.' She went on, for she knew she had to tell the truth about Georgia, before rumours were dripped into the woman's ear, 'Georgia is not my husband's child. She is the result of a brutal rape I suffered last year in the blackout.' And then, as the woman continued to stare at her, she asked, 'Will that matter?'

'Not to me, or any of the staff here,' the matron said. 'We treat the children equally, wherever they've come from. It might upset some of the mothers, but shall we cross that bridge when we come to it?' The matron smiled encouragingly and Lizzie felt her shoulders relax and knew she was believed. 'You get your job, Mrs Gillespie,' the matron went on, 'and we'll be pleased to see your little girl on Tuesday, 7th April when we reopen after the Easter break.'

Even knowing she was doing the best thing, it upset Lizzie to deliver her baby into a stranger's arms that first morning, however kind they appeared to be. She thought about her all day, and was glad of Celia's company.

But, in the end, she got used to it, and what helped was that no one at nursery seemed to be the slightest bit fazed by the colour of Georgia's skin. In fact, she was quite a favourite. None of the mothers seemed to mind either. She'd seen one or two of them look askance at her, some with plain disgust apparent on their faces, but they didn't transfer this to the baby and Lizzie could cope with that.

By the early summer of 1942, the sight of GIs in the streets of Birmingham was not uncommon. There were a fair few black servicemen amongst them and Lizzie was usually cautious in her dealings with them, which Celia and Violet felt quite understandable in the circumstances.

Not everyone felt like Lizzie, though. In a world virtually starved of young men for so long, many girl's were intrigued by the young GIs. They dressed smarter and seemed to have more money than the average Tommy; they brought a splash of colour into an England wearied by the restrictions of war, and caused many to remark wryly that, 'They're overpaid, over-sexed and over here.'

Many British people couldn't get over the disparaging way some white Americans treated their black companions. It upset the British attitude of fair play. 'I mean, ain't it enough to fight the Germans, Japs and Eyeties without rowing with one another,' Violet grumbled. 'I was stood in a queue in a ciggy shop on Bristol Street and these white blokes came in and told these black blokes, who had stood there ages, mind, to get to the back of the queue.'

In a country where queuing had become a way of life, jumping that queue unfairly was seen as a dreadful thing, and so Lizzie asked, 'What happened?'

'Oh, the man serving in the shop called the black fellers back and let the white chaps have the rough edge of his tongue,' Violet said. 'Said *he* decided who to serve and when in his shop.'

'Quite right,' Celia said. 'I understand why you don't like the coloured men and you have every reason, Lizzie, but any I've met have been really polite.'

'Our Carol says that,' Violet agreed, and went on with a nod of her head at Lizzie, 'Anyroad, little Georgia mightn't be the only half caste babby in the area soon, human nature being what it is.'

'What d'you mean?'

'Obvious, ain't it?' Violet said. 'I mean, the girls are all over the Yanks. Carol says it's the same at the dances. Often they dance more with the blacks than the whites and . . . well, you don't get chocolate, chewing gum, and especially nylons from shaking hands with a feller.'

'Violet!'

But Celia knew what Violet said was true in many cases. Nylon stockings were a dream for most people. Lizzie still didn't think a girl would do that for a pair of nylons, but when she said this both Celia and Violet laughed.

'When was you born?' Violet asked. 'Some of the young lasses now have not had a proper courtship at all. Any bloke they liked was often whipped off and some have never come back. Added to that, girls are working in greater numbers than before. They've more money in their pockets and more freedom as well, and then the place is flooded with Yanks, out to sample the local talent in their free time.'

'And some of them are good-looking,' Celia put in. 'And charming and, so I believe, generous. Some of the girls I work with have said so.'

'Why don't you go to the dances?' Lizzie asked. It was a matter that had been preying on her conscience for some time. It seemed wrong Celia should closet herself away, being content each night to sit in the house listening to the wireless or reading.

'I'm happy enough.'

'It's not right, Celia.'

'I tell you, I'm fine. Once bitten, twice shy.'

'Not for the rest of your life, surely to God,' Lizzie said. 'Our Johnnie more than likes you.'

Celia blushed and looked even prettier, especially when she protested, 'He barely knows me.'

'Isn't that what he's trying to do, get to know you in his letters?' Lizzie said, for since Johnnie had sent the card and Celia had passed her eighteenth birthday, he'd written a weekly letter to her. In the beginning, she'd shown them to Lizzie, but for the last few weeks she'd been more reticent, though she wasn't going to admit that or commit herself to anything. 'You're reading too much into that,' she protested. 'Johnnie is just being kind.'

Lizzie knew it was more than kindness, but she might make things worse instead of better to press Celia further and so she dropped the subject.

She watched Celia feeding Georgia the bottle she'd heated for her and knew Georgia was going some way towards helping the healing process for Celia, for Lizzie knew how much Celia missed her own baby. Since Georgia had been weaned, Celia often fed her and she would do anything else for her too.

Georgia had changed too. Abundant jet-black curls topped a face the colour of milk chocolate. She had huge dark eyes, a button nose and a rosebud mouth that turned upwards so it looked as if she was constantly amused by something.

She had little to grumble about of course, as yet anyway. She loved nursery, and when taken home Celia would spend hours playing with her. She had her astride her leg playing horsey, or teaching her pat-a-cake, or would trace her finger across Georgia's palm, reciting 'Round and round the garden . . .'

Georgia was fortunate in having the toys Niamh and Tom had left behind, and as she learnt to sit up, the truck with bricks that Niamh had had for her first birthday came into play. Celia would spend hours building towers for Georgia's podgy hands to destroy, and they'd hoot with laughter each time.

All the women in the yard, except for Sadie, who'd

kept her distance since Lizzie's return, had taken to little Georgia. But Lizzie knew that wouldn't be the case everywhere and, despite what Violet said, she'd hate people to think she'd just forgotten her principles for a pair of nylon stockings.

American soldiers, both black and white and miles from home, were often invited to share a meal with a family, and as one woman at work remarked, 'Never thought I'd see my old man sit down at the table with a couple of coloured blokes. But he did, and afterwards he said they was the same as us underneath and ended up standing them both a drink down the boozer.'

All this was well and good, Lizzie thought, but she couldn't think that way about them and no one who knew her would expect her to.

CHAPTER TWENTY-FOUR

To say Scott McFarland was more or less in shock since he'd come to England would have been putting it mildly. In America they'd had boys and men going off to war, but apart from that, for ordinary Americans, life had gone on as before. He'd heard of the blitzing of ordinary British cities, seen pictures in the papers and on the news reels back home, but he found it was one thing to see it in a detached way and another thing to be there: to see the gaping holes where shops, houses etc. once stood, and the craters in some roads making them impassable. Sometimes there would be a sea of rubble where whole streets had been destroyed.

And the people. He couldn't get over the people. Many were war-weary, their faces often grey with fatigue and their clothes shabby, but their humour and courage made him admire them greatly. But now he'd set off with a heavy heart to try and make amends for something dreadful and terrible that his brother had done.

Bell Barn Road was relatively easy to find, and when he'd gone up Bristol Passage, as the lady conductor on the tram advised, he stood at the top and stared. One side of the street was a mountain of debris; contents of many houses spilled out and smashed to fragments and mixed with bricks and charred beams, roof slate and brick dust. The shell of one house opposite a small shop still stood, its neighbour leaning against it drunkenly one side and the roof lifted from it.

This was Scott's first experience of back-to-back housing, for, as far as he was aware, they had nothing like this in the States and he'd been in England just a week. This pleasant, warm Saturday in June was the first time he'd been able to come here. Certainly there were no houses like this around St George's Barracks in Sutton Coldfield, where he was based.

He took a grip on himself. He wasn't here to judge and criticise but to try to right a wrong. He remembered what his brother had written in the letter he'd left.

I did it to avenge Shirley, but I know I did a grievous and shameful thing, and although I wasn't in my own mind there is no excuse. It's certainly not what Shirley would have approved of.

I intended to see to this myself, to see the family and confess, try and recompense them in some way, but if I don't come back could you do this, Scott? I can't trust anyone else to see this through.

I don't know if Steve is still alive, but as well as his wife who I violated, he spoke of children. Those children have haunted me and the great tragedy I inflicted on them, and they were innocent of everything. If I don't return, find them,

*Scott. You'll know what to do when you see how
they are.*

Scott looked about him. They mightn't be here at all,
he thought, if their father is overseas – or perhaps
dead. The children were maybe being cared for by
grandparents, or, failing that, in one of the city's orphanages. But Matt's involvement began in this street and
he glanced at the address he'd written down: *2, back
of 301.* He found 301, it opened onto the street, but
he had no idea how to find the back of it.

He made his way up the street to the shop he could
see, intending to seek information there before he
began knocking on strangers' doors.

Gerald Moorcroft was in the shop when he saw the
young black American soldier almost hesitate before
pushing the door open. Gerald saw that he'd removed
the cap from his head as he entered and he liked that:
it showed good breeding, respectable in Gerald's book.
And the man was smart. His beige jacket and trousers
were the sort of thing British officers wore and the
shirt beneath was pure white. Added to that, his
trousers were well-pressed and his shoes shone so
Gerald imagined you could see your face in them. The
whole attire and the man's manner pleased Gerald
Moorcroft and he smiled. 'Yes, sir, what can I do for
you?'

'I'm looking for information,' Scott said. 'Seeking a
family called Gillespie.'

Immediately, Gerald was wary. In his opinion,
enough had happened to that bonny Lizzie Gillespie
and he wanted no further trouble landing at her door.

What business could she have, or want to have, with a young black American soldier.

'What would you be wanting with Lizzie Gillespie?' he asked.

'Lizzie Gillespie!' Scott repeated incredulously. Could it be . . . ? But he had to be sure. 'Is that Steve Gillespie's wife – Lizzie?'

'Yes, though Steve's copped it, like,' Gerald said. 'North Africa.'

Now Scott was confused. He'd thought the woman dead. A faint hope began burning inside him, but he had to be certain. 'I really need to speak to this Lizzie Gillespie.'

'What makes you think she'll want to talk to you?' Gerald asked.

'I think she will,' Scott said earnestly. 'It's of utmost importance.'

'I don't know.'

'Please, I mean her no harm.'

'Look,' Gerald said. 'Let's put things on the line here. I like Lizzie Gillespie and she's had a rough deal at the hands of a black bloke like yourself. This isn't owt to do with the half-caste baby Lizzie had after she was attacked, like?'

'Half-caste baby?' Scott repeated in horror, while his mind went into overdrive. Ah, God, surely not. He noticed the shopkeeper looking at him, noting his agitation, and he asked, 'This baby, when . . . when did she have it?'

'Dunno, sometime before Christmas,' Gerald said, scratching his head. 'Cos she was home before that Pearl Harbour was bombed.'

'Then it's even more important I see her,' Scott said, and then as Gerald's eyes widened he said, 'No, I had nothing to do with anything that might have happened. I've been in Britain just one week, but I may know who it was that attacked her, and hasn't this lady a right to know that?'

Gerald nodded his head. He could see she had.

'And I need to know where the baby is.'

'What you on about? Where you'll find Lizzie, there you will find Georgia.'

'She kept it?' Scott said. 'She didn't leave it in some orphanage somewhere?'

'No,' Gerald told him. 'She kept it. Wouldn't do owt else, so I heard tell. Gone through it as well because of that decision.'

Scott could bet on that. Mixed marriages, and therefore mixed-race children, weren't common in the States, but it did happen. He'd not seen it in Britain, though, in fact black people were almost like a novelty to them; and though in the main they were friendly enough, he'd seen few of the black soldiers dating white girls, though he'd heard they were popular at the dances.

But for a woman to bring a half-caste child back here. Why had she done that? Why hadn't she hated the child and wished rid of it almost as soon as she'd given birth? He had to speak to her.

'You swear you mean her no harm,' Gerald said.

'I swear it,' Scott replied. 'I just wish to speak to her.'

'Right,' Gerald said. 'Now, if I'm wrong about you and anything happens to Lizzie because of it, you'll wish you had never been born. I've made a note of your number and I'll have your name before you go.'

'Scott, Scott McFarland,' Scott said, extending his hand.

Minutes later, Violet spotted Scott passing by the window to knock on Lizzie's door and she said, 'Barry, there's a big coloured bloke knocking on Lizzie's door. Get out there and see if everything is all right.'

Gloria and Ada had been having a conflab on their doors and giving an eye to Gloria's small son and Ada's daughter playing in the yard, but the words died in their throats as they saw the man.

Scott had been quite appalled by the cobbled area he'd stepped into and he took in the smell and saw the overflowing dustbins and the dirt and grime. The only clean thing he could see was the washing on the lines criss-crossing the yard, held on tall props. He nodded to the women watching him open-mouthed, but they made no response. They didn't know what he wanted with Lizzie Gillespie, and until they did know they were making no friend of him.

When Barry stepped from the house next door he wasn't smiling either, but Scott would not allow himself to be intimidated and the knock he gave was loud and imperious.

Lizzie sighed, certain it was the priest, and really she could do without the man. But when she saw the black GI standing there she was transfixed by terror. She didn't take in his smart appearance as Gerald Moorcroft had, she only saw his colour and she said sharply, 'What d'you want?'

Her voice, high in surprise and fear, alerted Celia who was upstairs putting Georgia down for a nap.

Anxious for Lizzie, she pulled the child back from the cot and pounded down the stairs with her.

Lizzie was so alarmed by the man's appearance she barely heard him say, 'I'm sorry to bother you, Mrs Gillespie – you are Mrs Gillespie?' She just stared at him and so he went on, 'My name is Scott McFarland.'

All Lizzie could think of was that this was the man who had attacked her come to finish her off. Common sense would have told her he'd hardly do that in broad daylight in full view of everyone, but a person in such intense fear doesn't listen to common sense and Lizzie could have wept in relief when Barry came into view. 'All right, Lizzie?'

He saw the state of Lizzie, so he addressed the man. 'What do you want?'

'Just a word with Mrs Gillespie.'

'I have nothing to say to you.' Barry's solid presence had given Lizzie the power of speech again. 'Go away. Get away from my door.'

And then Celia joined Lizzie at the door with the baby in her arms. She was beautiful, bonny and well-dressed, and obviously well-cared for, and Scott was, for a moment, awed by the sight of her.

'So, if that's all.'

'No,' Scott said, thrusting his foot in the door so it couldn't shut.

'How dare you!'

'Just say the word, Lizzie,' Barry said, 'and I'll throw him out.'

'Please listen,' Scott implored. 'I mean you no harm, I want you to know that, but I need to talk to you about the baby. Is it your child?' he said to Celia as

481

she was holding her. He had to be sure what the shop-keeper had told him was accurate.

'No, Georgia is mine,' Lizzie answered, lifting her from Celia's arms as she spoke.

'And how old is she?' Scott asked.

'I don't think that is any of your business,' Lizzie said angrily.

Celia, seeing Lizzie getting agitated, said, 'She's seven months, and why should you want to know that?'

Scott didn't answer. Instead he asked another question. 'Who is her father?'

'Okay'. Lizzie declared. 'This has gone far enough. You come to my door uninvited, force your way in here and then ask personal and intrusive questions. I don't know what your game is, but you go and play it someplace else. You are not welcome here and I want you to go.'

'You heard,' Celia said. 'Get out!'

Scott knew if he was to leave now he'd never come back. His own innards were complaining of what he had to do and he wanted to run away and forget all about it, but he knew if he did his conscience would never let him rest. He owed it to everyone involved, and this woman most of all, to tell her the whole truth. 'Please give me a few minutes?' Scott begged. 'I didn't come here to annoy or harass you and I'm sorry if it seems that way. I will ask you no more questions, but tell you a little bit about myself and then maybe you will understand. Please, I honestly think I might have information for you and it is about your child.'

Lizzie started. 'And is it information I'd want to have?'

'I can't answer that,' Scott said. 'But it is information you need to have.'

The man's words and the sincere way they were spoken caused Lizzie's limbs to shake. Could it be that after all this time she could find something out about the man who attacked her? 'This information you have, is it . . . does it concern the attack made on me?'

Scott nodded.

Barry was startled. Could it be that this man could clear up some of the mystery surrounding the attack on Lizzie? He'd certainly come on a special errand for something. 'Maybe you should hear what the chap has to say,' he said. 'I'll come in with you if you like.'

'No,' Lizzie said. 'I think Violet would be best.'

Ada and Gloria watched the interchange at the door and then Barry going into his own house and Violet coming out of it. 'What d'you make of that?' Ada said when Lizzie's door had closed.

'Dunno,' Gloria replied. 'But it'll be summat all right. Tell you what, the goings-on at Lizzie Gillespie's are more entertaining than a play.'

Inside the house, Scott was looking around the room, noting how small it was and yet how cosy. The three women were ranged opposite him and he could almost feel their animosity. He hadn't been asked to sit down and Lizzie stood watching him with eyes full of trepidation, rocking the child in her arms. Violet glanced at her and then said to the man, 'Come on then, say your piece and then you can sling your hook.'

Scott drew his hand through the springy curls on his head nervously, aware that his legs were shaking and his mouth was incredibly dry. 'What I am going to say first may seem irrelevant,' he began.

'Just get on with it.'

'Okay,' Scott said with a sigh. 'My family own a hardware store and timber merchants in Baltimore and in 1927 my father died. I was seventeen and the eldest and I quit school. My Mom had gone to pieces and I ran the business, and my sister Carla, who was two years younger than me, took on the house and looking after Ben, who was only two years old. No one had time to bother about Matt. He was thirteen and had adored our father. He was Dad's favourite too. Kindred spirits, Dad used to say they were.

'After Dad died, Matt hit the skids big-style. I tried to hide as much as possible from Mom, but when he disappeared altogether at fifteen I was relieved. I think everyone was, though Mom did make efforts to find him.'

He gazed across at Lizzie and she met his gaze dispassionately. 'You'll see the relevance of all this shortly,' Scott said, and went on, 'No one heard anything of Matt till 1936. He'd joined the American Air Force and wanted to marry a nurse called Shirley who'd nursed him through some illness he'd had.

'Not long after their marriage the Air Force asked for volunteers for a force that would be based in Britain, and Matt, with Shirley's encouragement, enlisted for this and was eventually based in a place called Castle Bromwich in the summer of 1938.'

Lizzie thought of Carol telling her of the Americans at the base. Generally she'd said many of them thought a lot of themselves, and in the main she preferred the black airmen. One of those could have been this man's brother, but she still couldn't see where this rambling account was leading. The man was speaking again and she forced herself to concentrate. 'Matt sent for Shirley as soon as he found an empty house to rent in a little village to the back of the aerodrome called Minworth in the autumn of the same year. War seemed inevitable then, and Shirley wanted to do her bit and enrolled as a nurse in one of the hospitals in the city centre.'

'Look,' Lizzie said impatiently, 'is this anything at all to do with me?'

'I'm just painting the picture for you,' Scott said. 'The next part of this concerns your husband.'

'Steve?'

Violet watched the blood suddenly drain from Lizzie's face and said. 'Why don't we all sit down? That baby must be a ton weight.'

She was. Lizzie's arms felt like lead, but she had no desire to make this interloper more comfortable, and when Celia asked, 'Shall I make tea?' Lizzie shook her head violently.

But before she could speak, Violet put in, 'Just the ticket, girl. My throat feels like the Sahara Desert.'

Defeated, Lizzie sat, the child still in her arms, and Scott sat beside her. 'I'm sorry,' he said. 'It must seem very long-winded, but I wanted you to get a little of the background. Can I go on?'

'Oh, please do,' Lizzie said sarcastically. 'Seems like everyone else makes the decisions here anyway.'

'That ain't fair, Lizzie,' Violet admonished. 'Just let him tell the tale and then judge whether it was

485

beneficial or not.' She nodded at the man and said, 'Go on, Mr . . . whatever your name is?'

'McFarland. Scott McFarland.'

'Go on then, Mr McFarland, tell us about Steve, and it had better be good.'

'Right,' Scott said. 'By early September 1940 the Battle of Britain was over and Matt was given a few days, leave. As he and Shirley were having a drink together in The White Horse, which was the bar nearby – you call them pubs, I know – they got talking to two men there. I'm afraid one of them said his name was Steve Gillespie and both he and his friend had girls with them.'

'Mr McFarland, you're telling me the road I know,' Lizzie said. 'Steve was never faithful to me all the years we were married.'

But for all Lizzie's valiant words, she felt suddenly cold inside and sick, like she used to feel when she smelt the perfume and make-up on Steve's shirts or skin, or, even worse, saw the strange marks on his neck. She was glad of the tea Celia gave her, though her teeth chattered against the rim of the cup.

'Matt said even then your husband seemed very attracted to Shirley, but he thought nothing of it as he had a girl of his own and they all enjoyed the evening.'

'This Shirley was probably a little flattered by the attention,' Lizzie said. 'Most women were. People have told me women sort of fell at his feet and sometimes he didn't have to try all that hard. There was a sort of sexual magnetism about Steve.'

Scott nodded. 'Matt too thought him a fine man and three days later they met again. This time they

486

had no women with them. Matt had taken Shirley to the pub for dinner – as his spot of leave was over he was returning to the camp the following morning for a period of duty. They saw the two men as they were leaving and asked them up to the house for a drink.

'It was as Matt was putting the coats away that a hospital appointment card fell out of your husband's coat pocket.'

'Aye,' Lizzie said. 'He was having treatment for the leg injury he got at Dunkirk.'

'One thing puzzled Matt about your husband, Mrs Gillespie,' Scott said. 'That night, he spoke more about where he lived. In the States we'd never see houses like these, for example. But what he spoke about most was you, how beautiful you were, how kind and gentle and how much he loved you, and yet you say that he had always been unfaithful.'

'I think Steve didn't see the sex he had with other women as important and certainly it was something quite separate from our marriage,' Lizzie said. 'I don't know how he would have reacted, or even if he would have understood, if I'd ever told him how worthless he made me feel when he went with other women.'

'So didn't you ever tell him?'

'Never,' Lizzie said. 'We never discussed it at all. Don't look at me that way, or feel sorry for me, for I didn't have an unhappy marriage. In his way, Steve loved me and he told me often. In the main, he was kind and generous and often good company, as your brother found out. I had also married for better or worse, and even if I'd wanted to I could never have separated him from the children he adored. But what

I want to know is how do you know all this. Was your brother a prolific letter-writer and he wrote and told you this trivia?'

'He did write often,' Scott said with a smile. 'But when he joined the Air Force, because it was something he'd so wanted to do from being a child, he started a journal to record it and wrote everything down there.'

'Then I'll tell you what he wrote in the journal next, shall I?' said Lizzie suddenly. 'I know the manner of man my husband was. He went with this Shirley, didn't he?'

'He raped her.'

'Are you sure?' Lizzie said. 'He seldom had to use force on a woman.'

'I'm sure,' Scott answered grimly. 'He drove her to despair.' He removed a letter from his inside pocket and held it out to Lizzie. 'Read it for yourself.'

Lizzie passed the drowsy baby to Celia, who took her upstairs while Lizzie took the letter from Scott with trembling fingers, not at all sure she wanted to read it. But she knew she should and so she began to read it aloud.

> My dear, darling Matt,
> This is the hardest letter I have ever had to write and I know that if you are reading it I have had the courage to take my own life. I want to explain to you why I felt driven to do such a dreadful thing.
> It is to do with Steve Gillespie, the Dunkirk veteran that we met in The White Horse public

house and invited home for a drink with his friend Stuart. You noticed that he was flirting with me and I said you had no need to worry, you were the only man for me. I spoke the truth and that is what I told that same man when he returned alone and drunk the following night.

I was in bed and asleep when I was roused and wouldn't normally have opened the door, but with you just recently returned to camp I thought something had happened to you.

I was incredibly surprised and annoyed to see Steve, but not alarmed at all. I told him you weren't there and he said he knew, that it was me he'd come to see, that I had known he would, and he was glad to see I was ready and waiting for him, for all I had on was a nightdress and a wrap. He was like a stranger and he pushed his way past me and held me so that I couldn't move. I told him to get out and I fought him as hard as I could, but I couldn't free myself. Nor could I shout out as he had one hand clamped across my mouth, and in the end he forced me to the floor.

All the time he talked, telling how he'd lusted after me since the first time he'd seen me and he knew that I was fully aware of how he'd felt. He asked me disgusting things like if his dick was as big as yours. There was more, vile and obscene things that I won't even write. I wanted to die as that man took what he wanted, pummelling his way into me till I cried out and sobbed with the pain of it and the shame engulfing me.

Afterwards, I sobbed further as he said that if

I complained at all he'd say I had been a willing partner, that it was something cooked up between us the night before, and how I had been ready and waiting for him in my nightgown. I knew that he, a white man and a hero from Dunkirk, would be believed before a black woman and I let out a scream.

Immediately, his hand was once more over my mouth and he told me to shut up, but I couldn't. Even as he clamped the sound, the screams were inside me still and coming out as little choking sounds, and that was probably why he punched me.

When I came to, the house was in darkness and Steve had gone, and I ran a bath. Even when I had scrubbed myself almost raw I could still smell that man on my skin and I thought I would never be really clean again. I knew too I could tell no one what he had done to me.

I remember you worrying about me when you came home a few days later, and when I refused you in bed you were hurt and confused and I am sorry about that. It was just that I couldn't bear it.

When I knew I was pregnant I was frantic. I can't even begin to explain the fear. I knew for certain it had to be that man's child.

Lizzie stopped reading then, for she knew, could feel this girl's terror and humiliation, which was written in almost every line. The tears were running down her cheeks. 'Oh God,' she said. 'I know what she was going through. I lived and breathed that same panic for months. But this poor girl had no network of friends to support her and her family were on another continent entirely. No wonder she was desperate.'

And this was Steve's doing, she thought. He'd done this vile thing to this young woman and driven her to take her own life.

'I quite understand why she killed herself,' Celia said with a shudder. 'I considered it myself and more than once.'

Lizzie saw Scott give a startled glance at Celia, but she didn't explain what she had meant. That was Celia's tale to tell and none of Scott's business. Instead, she picked up the letter again.

Eventually, I knew what I had to do and that was to end my life and prevent you being shamed further. I love you too much to allow that to happen, so though it breaks my heart I must say goodbye, my darling Matt, the one true love of my life.

Lizzie could barely read the last words. Her eyes were blurred and the lump in her throat threatened to choke her. Celia wiped her own eyes with the back of her hand and said, 'How did she die?'

'She hung herself,' Scott said. 'Matt found her lifeless body hanging from the stair-rail on the landing when he came home for a spot of leave. It was estimated she had been there for three days.

'The military told me that after the police had been informed, Matt disappeared for thirty-six hours.' He looked Lizzie full in the face and said quietly, 'That's when the attack on you must have taken place.'

Lizzie's eyes opened wide in horror. 'Your brother was the one who attacked me?'

Scott nodded. 'I'm afraid so.'

Lizzie's head was reeling. 'What was it?' she said. 'A sort of tit for tat?'

'It turned out that way,' Scott said. 'Although Matt hadn't gone looking for you, but Steve. He made that quite clear in the journal.'

'How did he know where to find him?'

'The appointment card,' Scott said. 'He'd taken little notice of the address at the time, but when he found Shirley's body and read the letter it was as if the card was in front of him it was so clear. And then the last time they'd met Steve had told him so much about the type of house and area he lived in.'

Steve! It all came back to Steve, who liked to put it about a bit, who saw no harm in it, thought it just a bit of fun. But then he'd met a woman who wasn't attracted to him sexually, who'd spurned his advances. That must have dented his ego. That's if he believed her and didn't think she was playing hard to get. In the end it didn't matter, for he took her anyway, and according to the letter punched her into silence. That was out of character, for since the night he had grabbed her when she'd tried to break off the relationship, before they were married, or the time when he had shaken her when she'd had a go at his mother he'd not laid a finger on her. He'd shouted and got cross, but he had never touched her and was always gentle with the children.

However, she knew it was an unfeeling and quite callous man who'd come back from Dunkirk. Had the war brutalised him? Could the war be blamed, or some facet or flaw in Steve's make-up? 'It's so hard to take in,' she said.

'I understand that,' Scott replied. 'Believe me, when I read the journal I could scarcely believe the words on the page.'

'Why didn't he come here himself?' Violet demanded. 'Why send you, and months after the event?'

'Matt was shot down on his first mission after he returned to duty,' Scott said. 'He was a rear gunner and the whole plane was blasted to bits. When his effects were sent over, Mom couldn't bring herself to look at them at first and I didn't even know they'd arrived. By the time she felt strong enough to go through his things, America was in the war. She sent the parcel Matt had left for me with the journal and the letters, but I was in the army and could do nothing until we were drafted over here to share an army barracks with some British units in a place called Sutton Coldfield. I came the first chance I had.

'Matt wasn't a bad man, really he wasn't. That's why I told you all that stuff at the beginning so you might understand.'

'Oh, don't worry yourself,' Lizzie said bitterly. 'I understand all right. Anyone would understand a vicious attack and violent rape.'

'How was he so sure it was Lizzie he went for anyway?' Celia said. 'In the blackout couldn't it have been just about anyone?'

Scott shrugged. 'I can only tell it as he wrote it,' he

said. 'Apparently, after finding Shirley like that he took off into the night, walking for miles until the grief subsided a little and was overtaken by furious anger and hatred for the man who had violated Shirley and caused such a tragedy.

'Sometime in the early hours he set out to find Steve. He hid in your yard that morning and watched you leave for work and tailed you. Then he returned to the house to search for Steve and was frustrated at finding the house empty.

'All day he hung about the streets, but was careful to keep out of sight. His intense grief and anguish probably needed some outlet, I would think, and it was towards afternoon, he said, when he thought of you. That, as you said, would be a form of tit for tat, because just as Shirley, who he loved dearly, was taken from him, he decided to take Steve's wife, whom he had claimed he loved.'

'This is crazy,' Lizzie cried. 'People, well, normal people at any rate, don't do that sort of thing. People can't and usually don't take the law into their own hands. This isn't the Wild West, but a civilised country. Didn't he think to tell the police what Steve had done and let the law deal with the one person who was at fault here?'

Scott sighed. 'He wasn't thinking in a rational way at all I shouldn't imagine. He wanted revenge. Anyway,' he said, 'you read the letter. Would the law believe that Shirley hadn't welcomed Steve's advances. He was white and a hero, and she was black and had opened the door and let him in and was dressed just in a nightdress and wrap.'

Lizzie remembered the night Neil had broken into her house and tried to have sex with her, and how he'd tried to frighten her by saying she was ready and waiting and more than willing if she complained. She knew he'd be believed, for not only did she have a child in the house that was not her husband's, but that child was a half-caste. Any court would have made mincemeat of her, and this Shirley wouldn't have been around to try and defend herself when her name and reputation were being dragged through the mud. No law would help, Lizzie realised, and she understood a little of the helplessness any husband would feel.

'I don't think he thought it through in a logical way at all,' Scott went on. 'He never wrote that down, anyway.' He looked into Lizzie's eyes and said earnestly. 'By the time I came over for Shirley's funeral, I believe he was on the edge of madness.'

'What I want to know,' Violet put in 'is, if this brother of yours was so doolally tap, like, how come he could write it all down in a blooming diary.'

'He didn't do it then,' Scott said. 'That came later with remorse and dreadful guilt and shame at what he had done.'

'Did he not admit it all when you arrived for his wife's funeral?' Lizzie asked.

Scott shook his head. 'Like I said, Matt was on the edge – he was saying nothing that made sense. I think he couldn't live with what he had done. The doctors were very concerned for his mental state, and the day after the funeral he was admitted to the psychiatric ward of the military hospital and he was there for over a month.

'When he sort of came to, he was most concerned about the children that Steve had told him about.'

'Why just the children?' Lizzie said. 'Didn't he think, this brother of yours, that there could have been consequences to the rape. I mean, his own wife became pregnant.'

'He didn't think you'd live to face any consequences,' Scott said softly. 'He thought he'd killed you.'

Lizzie gave a shudder. 'He nearly did,' she told him. 'Two things saved me: my thick winter coat, and Violet finding me before I turned into a stiff.'

'Well, Matt didn't know that. As far as he was concerned, he had killed you,' Scott said. 'When I read the journal and the letter he'd left for me, I felt sick with the shame of what he had done, and the stain on our family. 'Sorry' is an inadequate and overworked word, but I am truly sorry that you have suffered so much, Mrs Gillespie.'

'You don't know the half of it,' Celia said, for she saw the shock of it all had got to Lizzie and she was rocking herself backwards and forwards in agitation.

Violet had her arms around Lizzie, holding her close as Celia said to her, 'Tell him how it was, Lizzie?'

Lizzie shook her head. She had no intention of exposing the life she'd endured to this stranger. Instead, muffled against Violet's shoulder, she said, 'I don't want you here any more. You've had your say, now get out!'

'I can't just walk away.'

'Oh yes you can,' Lizzie cried. 'You can't help me. In coming to find me and telling me it was your brother who attacked me and why, you have probably destroyed

496

any shred of reputation I had still clinging to me.'

'The child is my niece. I feel some responsibility.'

At that, Lizzie's head shot up and she pulled herself from Violet's embrace angrily and leant forward, so her face was level with Scott's.

'Now, listen to me,' she hissed. 'Georgia is nothing to you. Do you hear that? Nothing! She is my child, the child I had no love for while I was carrying her, the child forced on me, the child I was going to give up for adoption until she was born half-caste, the kind of child no one wants. But I want her and love her and she has no need of you, nor any of your family.'

Behind the angry words, Scott was aware of the deep, deep hurt reflected in Lizzie's large and beautiful eyes. Maybe if he knew everything he could find a way of easing things a little. 'Please tell me how it was?' he said.

Lizzie shook her head vehemently. Violet looked from Scott to Lizzie and back to Scott. 'I'll tell you,' she said.

Lizzie opened her mouth to tell Violet not to say a word, but when she tried to speak the tears gushed from her eyes like a torrent and her body shuddered at the wretchedness of it all. Violet put her arm around Lizzie again, and though she cried too she patted Lizzie's back, saying, 'Come on, girl. You cry it out. It's about bloody time you let go.'

Scott got up and paced the room, embarrassed by the scene. Was he doing any good by staying? 'Maybe I should leave?'

'And maybe you shouldn't,' Violet snapped. 'You and your bloody family have brought this on. Sit down and I'll tell you.' And with her arms still around Lizzie's shaking shoulders, Violet told him how it was, going back to the raids in the war when the children had been taken to Ireland. She didn't know what happened after Lizzie's panic-stricken flight to Ireland when she found herself pregnant, but Celia did. Her own eyes were glistening as she told Scott of life in the Magdalene Laundry.

As Celia spoke she saw his horrified eyes widen and stretch, almost in disbelief. But he didn't disbelieve her; no one could disbelieve the passionate way she recounted their story. Every word she said was like a hammer-blow of guilt and shame in his heart. The woman left nothing out, from the rigid and unforgiving nature of Lizzie's parents to the reactions of neighbours when Lizzie brought the child she'd refused to condemn to a life of misery back to Birmingham.

Celia spoke of the insults levelled at them, the shouts and jeers, and of those who spat at them. She told of the daubing of filth on the wall and the shit pushed through the letter box, and lastly of the attempted rape by Steve's brother and two friends.

'I don't know what to say,' Scott said at last. 'How to convey . . .'

He knelt before Lizzie as Violet moved away and took her hands in his. Lizzie would have pulled her hands back, but she hadn't the energy. She looked up at him, her face awash with the tears still trickling from her eyes, and he said, 'I swear to you now, I will do all in my power to right some of the wrongs dealt you.'

'How?' Celia demanded, when it was obvious Lizzie still couldn't speak.

Scott had been thinking it over. 'Firstly, I will go to the police and give them Matt's letter, so that file at least will be closed. And then I will write to your parents, explaining everything.'

'Not her parents,' Celia said. 'Her parents might easily throw any letter you send in the fire. Her brother Johnnie would be the best one to contact. He's believed Lizzie from the beginning and I'm sure he'd be glad to get some concrete proof that the attack and rape really did take place to lay before the parents. I'll give you the address.'

Scott nodded. 'I'll be guided by you. I can't do anything about that damned laundry place, I don't think. I didn't know such places existed and the whole thing should be exposed, but that might rebound on both of you and you have already suffered enough. As for the neighbours, I'll tell them. I'll also go straight back to Moorcroft's when I leave here and tell him. That, I should imagine, is the quickest way to spread the truth of that awful night.'

'And the priest,' Celia said. 'A letter to him wouldn't come amiss.'

'I'll see to it, never fear,' Scott promised. 'As for the men who attacked you, I wish I had them before me this minute. However, if the situation ever presents itself for me to meet them then I will not forget, I promise you.'

Lizzie felt ill, truly ill, as if she might faint, and she willed herself not to. She had so many thoughts battering inside her head, she felt as if she might be going mad. She needed to be alone to think. She didn't want to talk, and least of all to Scott McFarland. She pushed him away and stood up, as if she were some kind of zombie, and said in a flat, expressionless voice, 'I need to go away.' And without another word to anyone, she crossed the room and mounted the stairs.

Violet looked across at Celia and said, 'Shock. Can't wonder at it really. Best place for her is bed. I'll take her up a cup of well-sugared tea and fill a hot-water bottle too. She was shivering as if she had the ague.'

Scott got to his feet and said, 'I must take my leave.' He smiled ruefully at Celia and added, 'This will be another black mark against the family, for my visit surely brought this on.'

Celia didn't deny it, but she did go on to say, 'Well, the point is, Lizzie had to be told, because no one likes blanks in their lives and she's wondered since it happened just why she was attacked.'

However, Scott wasn't sure he had done any good at all.

Lizzie, worn out by the emotion of it all, slept all the rest of that day and all night, and by the next morning she felt refreshed and better able to cope. 'For a time yesterday,' she confessed to Celia, 'I really thought I was losing my grip on sanity. But now I must accept what's done is done and I will get up and see to things and not lie in bed and feel sorry for myself.'

'What about Scott?'

'What about him?' Lizzie said. 'I owe him nothing, and for all I know we might never see him again.'

And Celia said nothing, for Lizzie could be right, and the man hadn't asked if he might come again.

CHAPTER TWENTY-FIVE

Lizzie had wondered if Scott's story would be believed, a coloured man and a stranger speaking out about a neighbour and a Dunkirk veteran, claiming he was a rapist. It had totally shaken her. To go with other women was one thing, but to force himself on someone else – especially a person he'd met but twice, and one who, according to her letter, had made it plain she was not interested – was an entirely different matter. It made her feel sick to think about it, though she knew if she had ever refused him he would probably have forced her. But that was different. A wife had to submit to her husband.

She lay back in bed and remembered Steve's tender moments, when he would tell her he loved her and kiss and caress her, raising her to heights of passion, and then go on to strive to please her as well as himself. She wondered where that kind and gentle man had gone.

Sometimes she would worry too that Shirley's attack was partly her fault. Maybe if she had complained to Steve about his dalliances, told him how it made her feel, involved the priest if necessary, he might have seen the error of his ways, and this incident with Shirley might never have happened.

But, in reality, she knew she couldn't really have changed Steve. He was as he was, and she had to accept him as that. He was a man's man, popular and well-liked, and she wondered if the revelation that Scott was about to make would make things worse for her rather than better.

It might have been that way with the women, who were, in the main, unaware of Steve's philandering, but as Gerald Moorcroft served the men their cigarettes and baccy and newspapers the next morning, he told them of the coloured man that had come into the shop with an amazing story. 'It's almost unbelievable,' one said. 'And yet Steve had always been that way inclined.'

'Aye, and marriage never changed him none either,' another put in. 'It were shameful the way he treated his missus.'

'Yeah,' another agreed. 'God, if I tried any of that malarkey, my old girl would have laid me out.'

'Lizzie just put up with it,' Gerald said.

'Maybe she d'ain't have no choice, like.'

'And you believe this coloured man?'

'Yeah, I do.'

'Course, Steve weren't never the same after Dunkirk. Bound to change a man, summat like that.'

'Lots weren't the same, but they d'ain't all go round shagging black women.'

'That's true an' all.'

And then Alice Cotterell came forward. She was no street woman, and with three children to see to she'd taken a job at the local chip shop. She'd been returning one night when she was set upon and raped by a drunken Steve Gillespie. There had been no repercussions to this and she had done nothing about it. Her man was overseas and she knew that any allegations she made would be relayed to him when he was not in a position to do anything. Anyway, she'd heard of women who claimed they'd been raped, but the men had said they'd asked for it, were willing partners, and they'd often been believed. She'd not put herself and her children through that, have that doubt lodged in people's minds. Best say nothing at all.

The second woman, Clara Guildford, was single and respectable and worked as a barmaid. She'd been raised in an orphanage, had no family, no support, and knew no one would take her word against Steve's. So although the assault was a violent one and the rape brutal, as soon as she realised there were to be no results from it she decided to keep her head down and say nothing.

But when these women heard of the rape of the young coloured girl that had led in the end to the attack on Lizzie Gillespie and the birth of a half-caste child, they came forward independently and told of their experiences. Gradually, the tide of opinion began to swing in Lizzie's favour. She was grateful that more spoke to her and were sympathetic towards her, though she was greatly affected by the new allegations about Steve and felt such shame that she had been married to a man who could do things so heinous.

'I feel a sort of responsibility to those women,' she said one day to Celia and Violet. 'As for Steve . . . well, it feels like I was married to a stranger, a man I don't recognise. I mean, you can blame the war, the things he saw, or any damned thing you like, but he had to have that bad seed inside him in the first place. Those poor women suffered in silence, just as I would have done if I hadn't found I was expecting.'

The women down the yard were incensed on Lizzie's behalf. 'We all said he was different after Dunkirk,' Minnie commented. 'And he was always yelling at Lizzie for summat.'

'She said she was glad when he went back to his unit,' Ada said. 'So I know she found him hard work.'

'Hard work is one thing,' Gloria said, 'but rape . . .'

'The old Steve would never have done such a thing,' Minnie put in. 'According to my Charlie he was always getting his end away. Not faithful to Lizzie, like, and never had any trouble getting a woman.'

'She must have known.'

'Probably. Never said owt, but then you wouldn't, would you? I wouldn't. I'd have been dead embarrassed.'

'I would an' all,' Minnie said. 'But Charlie said after Dunkirk you couldn't look at Steve wrong or he'd land you one. He was thrown out of The Bell a few times for fighting. As for drinking, well, he'd always liked a pint, but we all heard the state he was in many nights when he came home.'

'And Lizzie never said a cross word to him,' Ada remarked. 'Violet said he'd be shouting and bawling at her sometimes and she was always calm, trying to soothe him, like. Violet heard it all through the wall.'

'She never even moaned to us after, either,' Gloria said. 'And then there was the times he'd go off to his mate's and sometimes not come back for a couple of days or more. I think the woman is a bloody saint.'

'Yeah, at least thanks to that coloured bloke she's had her name cleared,' Ada added. 'That's summat, anyroad.'

Eight days after Scott had appeared at Lizzie's door the priest preached a gospel about not judging others, citing the woman taken in adultery and who was to be stoned to death until Jesus suggested that the man without sin should be the first to cast a stone. Lizzie wasn't there, but there were plenty to tell her about it. 'He might as well have said your name, like,' Minnie said. 'It'll make a difference, you mark my words.'

Lizzie was glad to see Scott the following Saturday because she wanted to thank him for keeping his word. She had more to thank him for too, as he'd brought with him tins of fruit, peaches and orange segments that made Lizzie's mouth water to think about. He also had three bars of chocolate, but what really made her cry out with delight were the nylons for each of the women. Nylons were like gold dust to get hold of and Lizzie's gratitude was sincere. She realised how much she owed Scott. He could have disregarded his brother's wishes. She'd never have known.

So, this time she asked Scott to take a seat and made tea and sandwiches for them both, as Celia had gone to the park with Georgia.

Scott told Lizzie something of his family and his

home, which he said he missed sorely at times. 'You never married?' Lizzie asked.

'Never found the right girl,' Scott said. 'Never really had the time to go looking either. The whole burden of the house and business was on my shoulders and I wanted to see the kids through school and college if they wanted it. Didn't work with Matt of course, but Carla went on. She's married now, though her husband's been drafted.

'Ben's a fine boy, only seventeen and due to go to college next year. I pray he'll make it and can then defer the draft till he graduates. I'd like to keep him out of this lot if I can.'

'I don't blame you,' Lizzie said with feeling. 'I'd rather fight the Germans and Italians any day before the Japanese. Somehow they don't seem quite human.'

They were silent, both thinking of Singapore, said to be impregnable, that had fallen to the Japanese in February. There had been terrific loss of life and seventy thousand allied troops had been forced to surrender. It had shaken the world and they realised Japan was a formidable adversary.

Eventually, Scott broke the silence to say, 'I think it's very good of you to agree to see me today. Many women in your position wouldn't want to have anything to do with anyone connected to Matt's family.'

'You can't be held responsible for what your brother did,' Lizzie said. 'I used to be like that once. Guilty about every damned thing, even about Steve's mother being committed to a mental home. In reality, though, she couldn't have borne this news and stayed sane, because she really did think Steve could never be at fault. And whichever way you look at it, when you take the catalogue of things that have happened to me right back to the beginning, it began with Steve not being able to keep his hands to himself.'

'In a way you're right.' Scott agreed. 'But there's no excuse for what Matt did to you.'

'No, but grief can do funny things to people,' Lizzie said. 'I thought once it would end my worries if I was killed in an air raid. But there were my other children to think of.'

'Which you're not allowed to see?'

'No.'

'Your parents can't stop you seeing your own children.'

'I've been through this,' Lizzie told him. 'And yet maybe now . . . The reason I didn't think I'd ever have access was because of Georgia. If the courts thought I was living an immoral life, for example, they might take them off me altogether. But if you were to write the letter you spoke about . . .'

'I wrote it the same evening I first told you,' Scott said. 'You should be getting a reply any day now.'

Ironically, while Lizzie and Scott were having this conversation, so Johnnie was facing his mother across the kitchen.

'Well?'

'Well what?'

'You know full well, Mammy,' Johnnie said. 'You've read the letter from this man Scott as well as me. If anyone is to blame for this it was Steve, and if anyone's blameless it's Lizzie. She tried to tell you that, but you wouldn't listen. She's been to hell and back.'

'I didn't know that.'

'You didn't try to find out,' Johnnie retorted. 'Out of sight, out of bloody mind.'

'What can I do?' Catherine cried. 'Especially now that you say she's kept the child.'

'Yes, she has, and I'm glad you accept that it is a child and not a Martian from another planet,' Johnnie said. 'And if you want more on your conscience, take two sick children, for that's what Niamh and Tom will be if you try and keep them away from their mother much longer. If you won't have her here, let me take them there. Don't look like that,' he yelled in anger as he saw the curl of Catherine's lip. 'Georgia is their half-sister, and Niamh and Tom have a perfect right to see their mother.'

Catherine looked at her grandchildren in the fields outside. She knew that they were unhappy. It oozed out of them, and neither ate enough to keep a bird alive. They were fading away before her eyes, and suddenly she knew she couldn't deny them what they craved any longer. She was punishing them and Lizzie for something that was not their fault.

'All right,' she said at last to Johnnie, 'do as you please.'

Johnnie immediately wrote to his sister suggesting he bring the children over to see her for a wee while as the summer holidays had begun. But before Lizzie received Johnnie's letter, the sirens blared out on the morning of 27th July. There had been no raids for a year and people looked at each other in trepidation – was it all beginning again?

Celia was unnerved enough by the explosions, even though they were some distance away and production at the factory continued.

But, that evening, just after they'd washed up from the meal, the planes returned and this time the first explosions were heard before the sirens shrilled out the warning. Lizzie saw that Celia was frightened, and why wouldn't she be. It would be her first experience of an air raid. Lizzie didn't want to share the public shelter with people who'd once abused and spat at her, so, 'We'll hide out under the stairs,' she told Celia. 'I've done it before. It's the safest place.'

Mindful of William Hearnshaw, who had been plucked from his mother's arms, Lizzie lifted up the drowsy Georgia and wrapped a shawl around the baby and herself and tied it tight. Celia wished she could go somewhere else, anywhere where they couldn't hear the raid, which was terrifying the life out of her. But she said none of this and continued to make tea in the flask with hands that shook.

Lizzie had just lifted her shelter bag when Violet popped her head round the door. 'Ain't you two going down the shelter?'

'No, we'll be all right here,' Lizzie said. 'Come and join us.'

'There'd hardly be room,' Violet said. 'Anyroad, Barry's not on fire watch tonight and he wants to go down the shelter.'

'See you later then.'

'Aye, more than likely.'

The raid wasn't as severe as many Lizzie had suffered, but she reminded herself that a person only needed one bomb to land on them, however heavy or light the bombardment was, and one did fall uncomfortably close, though the ack-ack guns alone were loud enough for Celia to quake in fear. She'd nearly jumped out of her skin a number of times when bombs landed nearby, and yet she noticed Lizzie barely flinched, and Georgia, tucked against her mother, slumbered through it all.

But although Lizzie was stoical about the raid, she hoped it wasn't a forerunner of another blitz. However, she didn't share her thoughts with Celia, who she saw was shaken enough.

Thursday 30th July found them once more spending the evening and into the night under the stairs, while clusters of incendiaries pounded the city centre and surrounding areas, starting many major fires.

Lizzie had, by then, received Johnnie's letter:

Dear Lizzie,

I've had a letter from a man called Scott McFarland, who told me what had happened the night you were raped and why. I believed you from the first of course, but this letter completely exonerates you. Mammy now knows you were completely innocent, and even Daddy's looking sheepish.

Anyway, they are agreeable to the children coming over to see you, for they miss you very much. But I know you are at work and need notice,

so if Friday, 6th August is too soon, please write
and say so and we will come a little later.

How Lizzie wanted to welcome her children and hold
them in her arms, listen to their lively chatter. And yet
. . . What if the raids were to continue? What if Johnnie
was to bring them back to the thing she'd taken them
to Ireland to escape from?

Celia agreed with her that to come home now wasn't
sensible, and so did Violet. 'It could start up again any
day,' she said.

Lizzie knew well that it could. It was the hardest
letter she'd ever had to write, telling Johnnie to stay
where he was with the children for the time being.

If there are no raids between now and, say,
Christmas, then it should be all right. So, much
as it breaks my heart to say it, for safety's sake,
bide a wee while longer in Ireland.

The summer sped by. Most women took all overtime
going, and there was plenty, and the days slid one into
another. Scott came most weekends and he and Lizzie
often took Georgia out, especially if the day was fine
and warm. Lizzie had coped with her embarrassment
of being seen with a black man and held her head high
as they walked.

Scott, she found, was good company, fun to be with,
and how she needed a bit of fun and laughter in her
life, which often seemed steeped in work, work and
more work. Then, one day in late September, Scott
came over to see Lizzie on a Friday night. 'We might

be moving out in the next few days and so I might not get over again,' he said in explanation.

'Oh.' Lizzie was surprised how disappointed she was, for Scott had become such a regular visitor and for some weeks now. 'Where are you bound for?'

'They don't tell us that, Lizzie,' Scott said with a smile. 'But most of us think it's somewhere in the Pacific. We know the Japs are meeting little resistance in the Philippines, and then the US troops have captured an airfield on the island of Guadalcanal in the Solomon Islands, so maybe we're being sent to reinforce that.' He shrugged. 'No one knows for sure.'

What Lizzie did know for sure was that whatever Scott was off to do, it would be dangerous, and she felt her stomach tighten with fear for him. 'Be careful, won't you. Don't try to be a hero?'

'I'll be as careful as anyone can be in a war situation,' Scott said. 'But I haven't come to talk about me, but you and Georgia.'

Celia made the inevitable tea and Scott took a gulp of it, before saying, 'The whole family feels somewhat responsible because of what happened to you.'

'There's no need,' Lizzie answered shortly. 'The incident happened and Georgia was the result. I wouldn't be without her for the world, and it isn't your fault or your family's. There is nothing to be gained by going on and on about it.'

'I agree,' Scott said. 'But the family worry about how you will manage financially. They want to make you a monthly allowance.'

'No.'

'It's to help you.'

'Thank you, but the answer is still no.'

'But why?'

'Look, Scott, I don't want you to be offended, but I don't want any of your family to have a stake in this child?'

'They want to help, that's all.'

'Aye,' Lizzie said. 'And what if, later, maybe when this damned war is over, they decide that they could give Georgia a better life and try and take her away from me. Your mother is Georgia's grandmother whether I like it or not. What clout would I have against her if she decided to fight for custody of Georgia through the American courts?'

Celia knew exactly where Lizzie was coming from, but Scott hastened to reassure her. 'That's far from my mother's mind, Lizzie. This was only suggested to help out, a salve for her conscience I suppose, but she has no intention of trying to take your child away from you.'

'That's what she says now, but if I accept money from her I am allowing her some level of influence.'

Scott saw that Lizzie was really seriously worried about this and so he dropped it, because it wasn't as if he could guarantee he'd be around to see fair play. He knew he was going to no Sunday School picnic, and in a way Lizzie was right about the money too. What if his mother had a yen to see the child – Matt's child? God, if they saw the house she was being raised in, they could make a good case for providing a better home for their granddaughter, and he knew it.

But he had to admit that the house wasn't half so important as the love Lizzie and Celia had for Georgia.

Lizzie hadn't the slightest resentment for the child and she was a wonderful mother. It was criminal that she should be separated from her own children and so he changed the subject. 'Have you thought of having your own children back home now?'

'Aye,' Lizzie said with a sigh. 'It's what I long for and dream about at night, and Johnnie was to bring them for a wee holiday in August, but in July we had those two raids and I wasn't sure if the blitz was starting again.' She looked at Scott and went on, 'You've no idea of the severity of the raids here in October, November and December of 1940 and other raids into the spring of 1941. I took the children home to Mammy to keep them safe. I couldn't risk them coming back and something happening to them.'

'Well, nothing has happened for a few months, so what now?'

'If we're raid-free by December, Johnnie is bringing them home here for Christmas.' She bit on her lip in agitation and went on, 'I don't know how to explain Georgia to them.'

'What d'you mean?'

'They are no longer babies, Scott. Niamh is eight and Tom going on for six. They'll know the child isn't Steve's. There is no way on earth I am going to tell them about that God-awful rape, but I'd not want them to think that I . . . well, you know.'

Scott knew full well and saw at once the dilemma Lizzie was in. The solution, when it came, was an obvious one. 'Tell them the child is mine.'

'Yours?'

'Aye, say you were friendly with my wife, who was

killed in an air raid, and you agreed to look after the child for me.'

'I couldn't.'

'Course you could. I wouldn't mind,' Scott said. 'Anyway, what's the alternative?'

Lizzie couldn't think of one. The problem of what to tell the children had driven sleep from her mind on a number of occasions. But still she hesitated.

'It can't hurt for now,' Celia put in.

'But what about after the war, when you go back home, Scott?'

'At the moment, that's like saying when the sun stops shining. God knows how long this war will go on for, and circumstances could change by then anyway. Let's not cross bridges till we come to them, and telling your children I am Georgia's father and serving overseas will fit the bill nicely.'

Lizzie turned to Celia. 'What d'you think?'

'I think it's just perfect,' she said.

Lizzie nodded. She could see it working. They would accept such a story, and Scott was right, it would do for now. 'Okay,' she said to Scott, 'and thank you.'

'Don't thank me,' Scott said. 'It's the very least I can do. And take my advice, Lizzie, go back to Ireland yourself and bring back the children. Make peace with your parents and your family soon, while they still remember the letter I sent them.'

'I couldn't do that. I couldn't take Georgia, it would shame them too much and not help my case any.'

'I would look after Georgia,' Celia said. 'You don't have to ask, and Scott is right again. You are in a much better position than I am. Haven't you a champion like

515

Johnnie in your camp, and your cousin that you told me about? You've not done a damn thing to blame yourself for. Go home yourself and bring the children home for Christmas.'

Lizzie looked from one to the other. 'I will,' she said. 'Aye, by God I will. I'll write to Johnnie this evening and suggest it.'

Lizzie worried about Scott more than she thought she would and wrote to him every week, something she'd promised him she would do, but his replies were erratic. In his first letter he included ten American-dollar notes, and when she remonstrated with him he said that if Georgia really was his daughter he would send money home. Wouldn't the children, Niamh especially, wonder if she received no payment at all? Surely it would make the whole thing more believable?

'I hate admitting he's right all the time,' Lizzie said.

'Then don't,' Celia suggested. 'Just accept the money with good grace.'

'There's nothing else for it, I suppose,' Lizzie said. But the reference to her children had turned her mind back to the goal she had, to have them with her for Christmas. Johnnie had been put fully in the picture, but in her letters home she told him to say nothing to the children.

Although she desperately wanted to see Niamh and Tom she hated the thought of leaving Georgia behind. She was adorable, and having passed the crawling stage by her first birthday she was now not so much walking as taking life at a run. Hastily, gates were erected at the top of the cellar steps and the door to the stairs was kept firmly closed, for Georgia could be whippet-quick when she chose to be. But it was hard to be cross with the child. Her smile would melt a heart of stone and her chuckles were infectious, and Lizzie knew she'd charm the children to bits. But the children knew nothing about Georgia either – she too was to be a surprise.

By the time November was drawing to a close, Lizzie knew she had to make a decision about her journey to Ireland. 'I want to be there a few days before the Christmas holidays,' she told Celia. 'There's things I have to say to the priest that's not for children's ears.'

Lizzie had never been as shocked as the day she stood at the farmhouse door and stared across the kitchen at the two children huddled before the fire. Because the day was raw and bleak, Johnnie had decided not to take the children with him to meet Lizzie, but to let the meeting take place indoors.

Lizzie had wanted to surprise them, but she was the one surprised – or, rather, shocked. They turned as Johnnie came in and Lizzie wondered where her robust, healthy children had gone, for these two were pasty-faced. Their eyes, which had been almost lifeless, held a spark of excitement as they viewed their mother across the room.

'Mammy!' The word was almost breathed, but neither ran across the room as they once would have done, but approached her slowly, almost as if they couldn't believe it.

Catherine turned from laying the table and felt tears

prick her eyes as she saw the children fall against their mother with a sigh. Lizzie felt the bones of them as she held them close and their thin arms and legs reminded her of the poor children of the destitute and unemployed in Birmingham.

Over the children's heads, her eyes sought first her mother's and then Johnnie's as he stood in the doorway, the cases in his hand, and her eyes were questioning. What had happened to her two children? Had they been ill and she hadn't been told? By God, she thought, there would be some questions for her family to answer tonight when the children were in bed.

'Ah, Mammy,' Niamh said. 'Why are you here?'

'Well, that's nice,' Lizzie answered. 'Didn't you want me to come over to see you and take you back with me for Christmas?'

'Back?' Tom asked. 'Back home, you mean?'

'Aye,' Lizzie said.

'Oh, Mammy, that would be grand,' Niamh cried. 'Wouldn't it, Tom?'

Tom nodded but didn't speak, and Lizzie saw the tears seeping from his eyes. The one thing he'd hoped and prayed for since his grandmother had told him his Daddy was dead had happened at last. His mother was here, holding him close, and he knew he didn't want her to go away again without him.

'What in God's name happened to them?' Lizzie asked that night as she sat before the fire with her parents and Johnnie after putting the children to bed. 'Have they been ill?'

'Yes,' Johnnie said, before Catherine could dismiss

Lizzie's concern. 'Not any sort of illness you could put your finger on, not like a dose of flu you would recover from. More a sort of pining away.'

'Pining away?'

'They missed you,' Johnnie said shortly. 'And it got worse when they were told of Steve's death.'

'They're so thin.'

'Aye,' Johnnie agreed. 'That dinner they tucked into with relish . . . well, I've not seen them eat like that for months. Have you, Mammy?'

'No,' Catherine replied with a sigh. 'They're usually good eaters, and you know there's no shortage of food here, but for months now they've just picked at their food.'

'You should have told me.'

'What could you have done? You wouldn't have them come home in the summer.'

'How could I risk it?' Lizzie asked. 'We were all fearful of the blitz beginning again. I couldn't bear it if anything had happened to them.'

'I know,' Catherine said soothingly, 'I'm not blaming you – and I haven't had a chance to say this before, but I'm sorry, Lizzie, that I disbelieved you, and sorry I sent you to that place. Johnnie described it to us both.'

'Aye,' Seamus said. 'We were so burdened down with shame we didn't listen to the whys or wherefores.'

'Maybe if Father Brady hadn't been so . . .'

'You can't blame him totally,' Seamus said. 'What he said might have had some bearing on the way we thought, and with the speed he moved you from the house we weren't able to discuss options – if there were any. Still, we must shoulder the blame, for we agreed to it.'

'And then you went on to keep the child,' Catherine said.

'Aye, Mammy.'

'Johnnie explained why you did that,' Catherine continued.

'Ah, Mammy, you wouldn't blame me if you could see her, for she's beautiful, Lizzie said. 'Thirteen months old now, and cute as a button and full of fun and mischief.'

Catherine saw in Lizzie's eyes and heard in her voice how she loved the child begot in such violence. 'What will you tell Niamh and Tom?'

'That she is Scott's baby,' Lizzie said. 'Scott is agreeable to it. We'll say his wife has been killed in one of the air raids and I'm minding her for him. I could hardly tell them about the rape, could I? And I wouldn't like them to think of me as a bad person.'

'What of the neighbours?'

'Well, the women down the yard have always believed my version of events. They saw me after I was attacked. Some of the others who once abused and spat at me have stopped now the truth has come out.'

'You know,' Catherine said, 'you'll never know of the nights I tossed and turned after sending you to that place. And to think it all began with Steve. It's hard to credit. When you were in hospital that time, the man was golden, all the nurses spoke of it. I would have said he worshipped the ground you walked on.'

'He did,' Lizzie said. 'In his own way, he did. In the main, he was considerate and very generous and would do anything for me, or buy anything I needed, and he would help with the children, often without being asked. But he had this need for other women. He was unfaithful just months after the marriage. I thought then it was just because I'd had a little scare when I was expecting Niamh and the doctor suggested we weren't to do anything – you know what I mean, Mammy?'

'I know,' Catherine said. 'But it didn't stop there.'

'No.'

'And you put up with it?'

'What else could I do, Mammy?' Lizzie cried. 'Especially when in all other ways he was a model husband.'

'How did he justify himself?'

'He didn't have to justify anything, for I never spoke of it.'

'Why not? God, if ever your father had strayed, I'd have wanted to know why.'

'You think that, but honest to God, Mammy, when it happens you don't know how you feel. Your mind is like a yo-yo. You feel dirty, cast aside, and yet you ask yourself if it could be your fault, something you've done or not done. In many ways, I lost respect for myself, felt unworthy to be loved. When Steve made love to me after he'd been with another, part of me wanted to push him away and part of me was grateful he still wanted me, that he hadn't shunned me totally by leaving me. How could I put any of this into words?'

'I find all this incredible, that he should make you a laughing stock.'

'He didn't really. I mean, he never flaunted his

women in front of me. I knew they weren't people I'd meet shopping or anything. But before this business with Shirley, he'd never, to my knowledge, been violent or forced a woman, but after his experiences at Dunkirk he was a changed man and some of the things I've been hearing about him have shaken me to the core. I think the man was damaged in some way. He had a much shorter fuse, for example, and drank like a fish. I always forgave him, for though he never spoke about his experiences he had dreadful nightmares. He'd wake with a scream or shout and would often be drenched with sweat, shuddering with fear, and the words he spoke in his sleep told of the horrors of just some of the things he had witnessed.'

'Are you trying to excuse him?'

'No, of course not,' Lizzie said. 'There is no excuse for what he has done, but I'm trying to come to terms with that myself and trying to explain to you why I believe he acted the way he did. For example, I think one of the reasons he attacked and raped Shirley was because she was black.'

'Why?' Catherine asked.

'I think Steve was curious,' Lizzie said. 'Got to wondering what a black woman was like. He'd have no idea of the chain of events he'd set in motion.'

'I still hold him responsible.'

'In the end I suppose I do too,' Lizzie admitted.

It was as Lizzie walked with the children to the school at Ballintra the next morning that Niamh said, 'When we go back with you, is it for good or just a wee holiday?'

'Just a holiday,' Lizzie said. 'For aren't you grand here with your grandparents?'

'We'd be better with you,' Tom put in quickly.

'Aren't you happy here? Don't you like it?'

'We like it fine,' Niamh said. 'But we want to come home with you.'

And why couldn't they? Lizzie thought. But of course there was her job. 'I work now, making new wings for aeroplanes, as I told you in my letters. I would have to give notice if you were to come home for good.'

'Would you mind that?' Tom asked.

Lizzie crouched on the road and looked into the children's eyes. 'I'd mind nothing if I get the chance to have you living at home again; if I can hold you in my arms and tuck you into bed at night.'

She held the children tight for a moment, and afterwards Tom scrubbed furiously at his damp eyes with one of his gloves. It would never do for one of the lads in the schoolyard to see him crying. They'd think him a sissy, but he was so excited he found it hard to stay still, for their mammy had promised that they were going home, back to Birmingham, and he could hardly wait.

CHAPTER TWENTY-SIX

As soon as Lizzie left the children at the school gates she went to seek the priest, and moments later she was facing him across the church.

Father Brady knew about the black baby born to Lizzie Gillespie. Sister Jude had seen fit to inform him of that. She'd also said it was being taken to an orphanage in Dublin and so he'd never mentioned the matter to any of the Clooneys and was totally unaware of the latest turn of events.

And now here was the brazen hussy, the cause of shame and embarrassment to her entire family, facing him as bold as brass. 'Hallo, Father.'

Even the tone of her voice had a challenging note to it, the priest observed. 'Good morning, Elizabeth.'

'Have you a few moments to spare for a chat?'

Father Brady owed no favours to Elizabeth Gillespie. 'I am a busy man, Elizabeth.'

'A few moments of your most precious time is all I ask.'

'Don't mock, Elizabeth, it doesn't become you.'

'I'll be the judge of that,' Lizzie snapped. 'And when

you listen to the tale I have to tell you, you might whistle a different tune too.'

'I really think . . .'

'I really think that for once in your life you should shut up and listen to the grave injustice you did me.'

Father Brady wanted even less to listen to anything Lizzie had to say after that comment. He would have liked to order Lizzie from the church and tell her never to enter it again.

However, he couldn't help but listen, though he wished sometimes as Lizzie told of her time in the convent that he could stop up his ears and not hear the vilifying words dripping off her tongue. He didn't doubt a word she said, for the truth was in her haunted eyes and impassioned voice, and that made it worse.

Lizzie didn't spare Father Brady, and when she began to talk of the convent priest's abuse, he held up his hand. 'Enough, please, Elizabeth.'

'Upsets you, does it, Father?' Lizzie said. 'What do you think it does to the girls, preyed on by this perverted and pathetic excuse for a priest? And before you ask, Father, they are not harlots and whores in that place, who lead the priest on.'

'You know,' she went on, 'I had months in there to think, and though we were told often how sinful we were, I don't think getting pregnant is the greatest crime in the universe. To hurt another human being is worse in my book, but the most despicable thing of all is surely to assault and pour scorn and degradation on fellow human beings and to enjoy doing it and know the same thing will happen again and again. That, Father, is evil. Those nuns are evil and the priest who condones it, as they condone his debauchery, is evil.

'Some of the girls incarcerated with me will never go beyond the convent walls. They will grow old and die in that corrupt and depraved place. They are the forgotten women of Ireland.'

The priest was shocked at last. 'Surely not.'

'Who will take them out, Father? My own family would have thrown me to the wolves if it hadn't been for Johnnie. One girl died in childbirth and her family would not allow her to go home to be buried – they never even came to the funeral. My friend Celia wasn't surprised. She was one of seven children and because of one mistake she was thrown aside by the whole family. Disowned. No longer to be considered a child of theirs. She had no family, no home, no future, and her baby son is being brought up by someone else.'

'But surely that is to the good?'

'Not all the girls in that place would agree with you, Father. Like the girl who threw herself off the laundry roof, for the pain of separating her from her baby was too great to take.'

'Ah, God,' Father Brady said. 'I didn't know. Please believe that. I'd heard rumours, but . . .'

'I'd say they were based on fact,' Lizzie retorted. 'Think of your worst nightmare and it won't come close to what we had to endure. And think too of the men involved – and there had to be a man involved – and they get away scot-free. Where in God's name is the justice in that?'

'But Sister Jude said your baby was black?'

'She is not black. My baby has dusky skin and enormous brown eyes and a smile that lights up her whole face and gladdens your day,' Lizzie said. 'And she is that colour because the man who attacked me was black. His name was Matthew McFarland and he was part of the American Volunteer Air Force based in Castle Bromwich.'

'I understood the man had never been found.'

'Nor will he be,' Lizzie replied. 'He is dead, but he had the foresight to write everything down in a journal, which his brother had charge of after his death.'

'And in it he admitted to having attacked you?' the priest asked incredulously.

'Aye, he did,' Lizzie said. 'You've got your disbelieving face on again, Father, but I assure you this is no figment of my imagination. The man's brother came to see me.'

'It does sound unbelievable, Elizabeth.'

'I agree, Father,' Lizzie said. 'But it all hinges on the fact that my husband went to the house one day and raped the man's wife. When she found she was pregnant she hanged herself and left a letter, saying why and naming her abuser. Her grief-stricken husband came for Steve and got me instead. He thought he'd killed me and very nearly did, and he wrote it down when he came to his senses and realised and was mortified by what he had done. Every word I told when I came home that time, each word that you ridiculed, was the truth.'

The priest was obviously shaken, Lizzie could see. 'How do you think it felt, Father, incarcerated in that bloody place for something I had no control over and was not my fault at all?'

'Lizzie, I just . . . I don't know what to say.'

'Sorry would be a good place to start,' Lizzie said sarcastically.

'I am sorry,' the priest said. 'Sorry for doubting you . . . but for such a thing to happen. It's incredible, and a tragedy for that young woman driven to take her own life. I met your husband only the once at the wedding, but your mother always gave a good account of him. For him to do such a thing,' the priest shook his head in consternation. 'And this terrible attack on you . . . But one thing puzzles me, Elizabeth. Why did you go on to keep the child? I understood she was going to be sent to an orphanage.'

'Do you think I would leave my wee, vulnerable baby in the care of nuns, in danger of being hurt and bullied and raised in fear? Anyway,' Lizzie said with her head held high, 'I love her, Father. Her name is Georgia Marie and I love the very bones of her.'

'Your courage and determination leaves me astounded,' Father Brady said. And he was astounded. This self-assured young woman before him was nothing like the panic-riddled one he'd delivered to the convent over a year before. There was no resemblance either to the young girl who used to be at the beck and call of her family, and especially her cousin. He had the distinct impression that this Elizabeth Gillespie would be at the beck and call of no one.

'All I can say – and from the bottom of my heart – is that I'm sorry for any part I played in this,' the priest said sincerely. 'And I will certainly make some enquiries about how the convents are managed.'

Lizzie wondered if it was enough to just make

528

enquiries, if he would be fobbed off. But for him to even listen, believe her and agree to take action, however limited, was more than she could have hoped for.

'Thank you, Father.'

'I couldn't do nothing,' Lizzie said later to Tressa as she recounted her talk with the priest. 'Outside of it now, I can't credit I allowed myself to be treated like that. If we'd have banded together we'd have been a match for any nun, but you are stripped of everything and ruled by fear and intimidation. I was a different person then. I hope I've done enough for the others left behind.'

'I think you've done all you could,' Tressa said. 'These people are powerful, remember.'

'Aye, and the arm of the Catholic church stretches miles. Really, I can't wait to get back now, and I'm missing Georgia like mad.'

'Mike says she is gorgeous.'

'She is, Tressa. I wish you could see her,' Lizzie told her.

'I just might,' Tressa said. 'I'm thinking of coming back in the New Year. I need to be on the spot now. Mike and I are going to look for a place of our own after the war. Anyway, sometimes Mike only has a forty-eight-hour pass, and really he's not here five minutes before it's time to turn round again. I worry about him going back to army life, and maybe active service, worn out by all the travelling.'

'You'll have to get on with producing the football team as well, won't you,' Lizzie said with a smile. 'For isn't Nuala three in February?'

'She is, thank God,' Tressa replied. 'That's one thing. With all the travelling, Mike is too tired to want to do much. I mean, he still gets the urge sometimes, but he's just too exhausted.'

'I'd stay on a good few years yet then,' Lizzie teased.

'Aye,' Tressa laughed, and added, 'you know I wouldn't be without any of them for the world, but it's marvellous to have them all out of nappies and sleeping through the night. God Almighty, some nights it wasn't worth going to bed at all. And Mike was never any help. Spoilt by his parents and sisters, see – he could barely make a cup of tea, and he's absolutely no idea with the children.'

Lizzie too thought Mike pretty useless and that was way before the war when he marched away to kill Germans, and was always glad Tressa had had Doreen to give her a hand, and now had her mother. And, she thought, six children were enough for anyone to rear – more than enough, in her opinion, no matter what the Church said.

It would be lovely to see Tressa back in Longbridge, Lizzie thought, and she told Tressa this before heading for home.

Catherine never asked her daughter how it had gone with the priest and so Lizzie never mentioned it either. She spent the day sorting out the children's clothes, for the next day, 19th December, was the last day at school and she intended to leave on the 20th. Both Susan and Eileen called in to see her, and she'd arranged to call up to see Peter and Owen the following day. She couldn't help but regard the welcoming home of the prodigal daughter wryly. She wondered what their attitude would have been like if Matt hadn't written down what he'd done or Scott hadn't acted on the information. She imagined the reception from them all would have been quite different.

But she had no reason now to fall out with any of them, and, all in all, the visit, though short, was pleasant enough.

'You'll come back in the summer, sure you will?' Catherine said, drawing Lizzie into her arms as she prepared to leave.

'I don't know, Mammy,' Lizzie said. 'There's Georgia.'

'Can't your friend look after her?'

'I don't know,' Lizzie repeated. 'I'd hesitate to leave her for longer than a few days. Anyway, one day I'll have to bring her with me. I'm not going to hide her away all the days of her life.'

To Catherine, who, despite Scott's letter, had not come to terms with her daughter giving birth to and raising a mixed-race child, the thought of hiding her away seemed a very good idea.

She knew better than to give voice to this and instead said, 'Well, maybe it's best left this summer. Get the children properly settled and all. Anyway,' Catherine whispered, 'Eileen thinks she's expecting. Early days yet, but if she's right it will be due in July. I'd like to be on hand really. She's a bit long in the tooth to be having her first.'

'Mammy, she's not old,' Lizzie protested. 'And I hope she's right, it would be good news, so it would.'

And it would be grand news, for poor Eileen and

Murray, married since 1932, had no children. Maybe it would take the sour look from Eileen's face if she held a child of her own, and stop her glaring at Niamh and Tom with such resentment and longing.

Her mother was right about Eileen's age, for she was four years older than Lizzie. She was already thirty-four and would be thirty-five when she gave birth, her birthday being in March, and though Lizzie knew her mother was using Eileen's possible confinement as an excuse against seeing and welcoming Georgia, Lizzie couldn't really expect less. It would take time.

They left very early in the morning because Lizzie wanted to sail in the daylight. Catherine got up to see them off and Lizzie kissed her and hugged her tight before making her way to the cart where the horse pranced on the cobbles and tossed his head in impatience to be off, his breath rising like smoke in the wintry air.

Johnnie was coming with them. Lizzie couldn't have managed without him, because as the children were leaving for good they were bringing everything home with them. Most of it was packed in a trunk, except for Niamh's doll Maisie, which she insisted on holding in her arms, and Tom had three of his favourite cars in his pocket. Then there was the small case Lizzie had brought and the larger one for Johnnie, for he was staying until the New Year – plus another full of food her mother had insisted she take.

It was all stowed away in the cart and Seamus was driving it to the station. As Johnnie helped his sister up into the cart beside the two excited children wrapped up in blankets, she caught sight of his face and knew he was looking forward to seeing Celia again.

Remembering Celia's shock, all the way home Lizzie tried to explain what Birmingham was like to Johnnie and the house she lived in and the destruction the war had brought everywhere. In a way, she was also reminding the children, for she knew a lot of the bomb damage would be new to them too.

Johnnie was the only one sick on the boat and so he stayed on deck most of the crossing. Though the day turned to night eventually, as the boat ploughed its way through the turbulent waters, the sky had been so grey and overcast it made little difference.

Lizzie knew even such little light would be gone by the time they reached Birmingham, the winter days being so short, and she was glad Johnnie had not only brought a flashlight but lots of batteries too. He wasn't sure the muslin Lizzie had tied around the flashlight was necessary, until she told him of the two-hundred-pound fine for breaking the blackout, whereupon he conceded she probably knew best.

As the train rattled its way to Birmingham they all tucked into the picnic that Lizzie had helped her mother prepare. She was glad to be going home and longing to see Georgia. 'I have a secret waiting for you at home,' she told the children.

'What? What?'

'If I told you it wouldn't be a secret, would it?'

'Ah, Mammy.'

'Don't ah Mammy, me,' Lizzie said with a smile.

'Will we like it?' Niamh asked. 'Is it a nice surprise?'

'I think so.'

'Will Tom like it, or will I like it more?'

'I imagine you'll both like it.'

'Is it something real or not?'

'It's something I'm not going to say another thing about, my girl, until we get there,' Lizzie said firmly. Johnnie crossed to the window and looked out. He knew they were passing the backs of houses. He could see the outline of them in the gloom and yet he could see no lights. As far as he could tell there was darkness. It was quite an odd feeling and one he'd never experienced before, and he pulled down the blind and fastened it at the bottom, shutting out the night.

Johnnie had never seen a railway station like New Street either, but then he had to admit he'd seen little past his own hometown. Apart from his sojourns to Sligo, and later leaving the girls at Dun Laoghaire, he'd never ventured far. He was glad Lizzie seemed to know her way around. She didn't seem bothered at all by the throngs of people, nor the noise of panting engines clattering into the station, coming to a halt with squealing brakes and the hiss of water that sometimes dribbled onto the tracks. Niamh didn't appear unnerved at all either, and nor did Tom, who seemed to care for nothing but holding tight to his mammy's hand.

Lizzie pushed her way through the raucous, noisy crowds and found the porter she was searching for. He piled their luggage on his trolley and took them outside to the taxi rank. There were still shoppers on the streets; Johnnie could see them scurrying from one shop to another, but the shops were in total darkness and it seemed odd to see no lights at all, no street lamps, and the lights on the taxi barely made an impression on the intense blackness.

When they alighted in the pitch-dark street, minutes later, Johnnie was more than glad he'd brought the flashlight. 'Where d'you live, ducks?' the driver asked.

'Down the yard,' Lizzie answered, jerking her head towards an entry.

'Right, guv'nor,' the driver said to Johnnie, 'I'll take the trunk if you have the cases. And you,' he said to Tom, 'leave go of your ma's hand so she can bring the bags and you cop hold of this instead.' He handed Tom the flashlight. 'Shine it in front so as you don't go arse over elbow,' he directed, and Tom walked importantly in front of them all.

Celia opened the door to them. 'This is a friend of mine, Celia,' Lizzie said. 'Say hello, children.'

But Tom's eyes were disappointed. 'Is that the surprise?' he asked, but then a little dusky face peered around Celia as she opened the door wider for the taxi driver to pass through.

'A baby,' Niamh breathed, and Tom cried, 'Oh boy, a baby. Is that the surprise, Mammy? Did Jesus send us a baby?'

The innocence of childhood, Lizzie thought. The taxi driver looked from Lizzie to Celia and then to the child and gave a shrug. It was none of his business. Lizzie left Johnnie to pay him while she was taking off the children's coats so they could play with Georgia. However, Georgia wanted no one but the mammy she missed and was unnerved by the strangers. Her big eyes brimmed with tears and she lifted her arms. 'Mammy, Mammy.'

'Sit down with her,' Celia advised. 'It's you she wants. I have some stew ready just to heat, but will you have a cup of tea to be going on with?'

'Aye, that will be grand,' Lizzie said, struggling out of her own coat to lift the child while the children plied her with questions. 'Give me a minute and I'll tell you all,' she said. She'd rehearsed this many a time and she told them, 'I'm minding the baby. Her name is Georgia.'

'She called you Mammy,' Niamh said.

Lizzie had forgotten the child could talk. 'She probably thinks I am, for she has no mother,' she told Niamh. 'Poor Shirley was killed in one of the air raids.'

'Ah, that's sad.'

'Isn't it?' Lizzie said. 'And her daddy is American and in the army and overseas at the moment.'

Georgia was regarding the two children solemnly and Niamh said, 'Isn't she brown, Mammy?'

'Aye,' Lizzie said. 'That's because her daddy is black.'

'Black?'

Neither child had ever seen a black man, Lizzie realised; nor Johnnie either, of course.

Johnnie was quiet for he was looking about the room in amazement. He never imagined his sister living in such an awful place, yet the children accepted it as a matter of course, had chosen to come back to it. And he had to admit it was clean and tidy, apart from the toys on the floor, and quite cosy with the fire roaring up the chimney and the spluttering gas lamps lit. He resolved to hide his shock and make this Christmas one to remember.

* * *

A parcel with American stamps on it had come for Lizzie while she'd been away, and she opened it immediately for the children were dying to see what was in it. From the box she lifted the most exquisite doll she'd ever seen. Its hands were china and the eyes opened and shut, and her tummy was soft but when pressed the doll said 'Mama'. It was wearing a red jumper and blue skirt beneath a navy coat and matching hat, and on its feet were leather boots and knitted socks. Lizzie could quite understand the exclamation of delight from Niamh and Celia. She had seen nothing like it.

'Who's it from?' Niamh said.

'There's a letter,' Celia commented, handing it to Lizzie. As she opened it, dollar bills fluttered to the floor, and Johnnie collected them up as Lizzie scanned the letter.

'It's from Georgia's grandmother in America,' she told the children truthfully, 'and as Scott – that's the name of Georgia's daddy – has told her I have two other children she has sent the money for the rest of us.'

'It's fifty dollars,' Johnnie said. 'But I bet that doll cost a pretty penny.'

'Aye,' Lizzie replied, 'and though I will, of course, write and thank her, how can I give it to a child of thirteen months – she'd have it destroyed before the day is out. I'll have to put it away till she is a good bit older.'

'She can have Maisie if she likes,' Niamh said.

'Ah, Niamh, that's kind of you, but . . .'

'And my teddy,' Tom said. 'She can have my teddy.'

Lizzie was overwhelmed by the children's generosity and their acceptance of Georgia, and she was so very glad she'd brought them home. It was where they belonged.

CHAPTER TWENTY-SEVEN

The children settled back to life in the inner ring of Birmingham as if they'd never been away, but Lizzie didn't know how far Johnnie had progressed along the line with Celia. She'd given them as much time alone as she could, without it seeming obvious, and once suggested a wee walk in the evening.

'What's the fun of walking in the blackout?' Celia said.

'Okay, what about the pictures then?'

'What about them?'

'Come on, Celia. You never go over the doorstep except to go to work.'

'Neither do you.'

'I'm a married woman with responsibilities.'

'You're a widow.'

'I still have the responsibilities.'

'You're not reneging on them if you take a few hours off to see a film.'

'Celia, stop being aggravating. Johnnie has never seen a film in his life and neither have you. *How Green Was My Valley* is on at the Broadway and

The Maltese Falcon at the ABC on Bristol Road.'

In the end Celia went to both, and raved on so much about *How Green Was My Valley* that Lizzie and Violet went to see it, leaving Johnnie and Celia listening out for the children.

'How's the romance going?' Violet said as they set off down the road.

'Search me,' Lizzie answered with a shrug.

Celia could have told her that she liked Johnnie a lot, although she didn't know whether she was attracted to him sexually, for she kept those feelings firmly under lock and key. Johnnie had confessed he loved her, had always loved her, but she wasn't ready for such a declaration.

'I'm not ready to settle down, Johnnie,' she told him. 'Not with you or anyone else, and I'll never leave Lizzie as long as she still needs me.'

'She'd not want you to feel this way.'

'How the hell do you know how she wants me to feel?' Celia snapped. 'Oh aye, she's selfless enough to tell me to go out and get a life for myself, but I'll not do that. As long as she needs me, I will stay with her.'

'That could be years and years, your whole lifetime.'

Celia shrugged. 'If it is, it is.'

'You're wasting your life.'

'I don't see it that way.'

'Is there any point in hoping?'

'No, not really,' Celia told him.

'I can still write to you, can't I?' Johnnie asked dolefully.

'If you want to,' Celia said. 'As long it's just as a friend.'

It wasn't what Johnnie wanted to hear and yet Celia spoke with such determination he knew there was no point in pleading further.

The day before New Year, Niamh said, 'Haven't we got to go and visit Granny?' She gave a shudder as she spoke, for the woman scared her to death. Tom, zooming his toy cars over the lino, stopped his play at Niamh's words.

Lizzie chose hers with care. 'Your granny's not too well at the moment.'

'Again?' Niamh said. 'Like she was before when you had to see to her?'

'No,' Lizzie said. 'It's not that sort of ill. This time her mind became sick when she heard of daddy being killed. She's in a special hospital and it's not a place children visit.'

Tom's sigh was audible and heartfelt. 'Oh, that's all right then,' he said, and returned to his cars.

Lizzie's amused eyes met Johnnie's over the children's heads, and she tried to hide her smile.

'You shouldn't say that, Tom,' Niamh said primly.

'Why not?'

'Well, it's like . . . it sounds as if you don't care.'

'Well I don't,' Tom said. 'I don't like her much. I don't see how anyone can like her. She's a bitch. I've heard people say so.'

'Tom! That's a bad word.' Niamh was scandalised.

Lizzie thought it time to step in. 'That's enough from the two of you,' she said. 'Now it's bedtime. Put your cars away now, Tom, there's a good boy.'

Tom did as his mother bade him obediently enough,

but as he passed his sister on his way to the stairs, he said, 'I don't want to visit her ever, ever, ever again, so there!'

'Tom!'

Lizzie shooed the children up the stairs and came down to see Johnnie and Celia trying to muffle their chuckles. Lizzie too was smiling as Johnnie said, 'I see Flo is a much-loved and valued member of your family.'

'Oh aye, she is,' Lizzie replied sarcastically. 'And you can't blame the child totally either. He's just expressing how we all feel.'

'I'd use more colourful language if I was asked to describe her,' Celia said.

'No doubt,' Lizzie replied. 'But I just thank God she's in a place where she can hurt no one any more.'

'Amen to that,' Celia agreed with feeling.

Johnnie returned home, and before the schools opened Lizzie went up to see Father Connolly about enrolling her children at St Catherine's. 'I haven't seen you at Mass recently,' he said, regarding Lizzie across the desk.

'No, Father,' Lizzie replied. She offered no reason, no excuse.

'Why is that?'

'You know why, Father. Why ask the road you know?'

'And yet you want your children to have a Catholic education?'

'Of course I do, Father,' Lizzie cried. 'None of this is their fault.'

'It isn't God's, Lizzie, and yet you choose to punish him.'

'Not God, no,' Lizzie said. 'I still pray. But d'you know, Father, I no longer fear the cloth and I'm afraid I also have little respect left in me, particularly for the clergy.'

'And yet you want the children . . .'

'It is their immortal souls at stake now, Father. And for their sake I will go to church, go through the motions at Mass and endeavour to bring them up good Catholics.'

Father Connolly knew that really he could expect no more and so when Lizzie said, 'So will you take my children into the school, Father?' he nodded his head.

Now that Lizzie was at home every day she was grateful for the money Scott sent. There had been little in the shops to buy Niamh and Tom for Christmas, so in February she took up Violet's offer to mind Georgia and used some of the money to buy tickets for a pantomime – a first for the children and Celia too. Lizzie remembered her first experience of this type of entertainment and wondered what the others would make of it.

It was *Cinderella*, and from the first moment Niamh and Celia sat transfixed with delight. They loved everything: the setting and costumes seemed almost magical and Niamh thought Cinderella so beautiful in her shimmering ball gown it almost hurt to look at her. All the risqué jokes went over the children's heads, but they laughed uproariously at the funny parts and booed and hissed as loud as any when the baddies entered the stage.

When eventually the show drew to a close, Lizzie didn't have to ask the children if they'd enjoyed it, for their eyes shone with excitement. 'Oh, Mammy, that was terrific,' Niamh said, and Tom nodded his head enthusiastically. 'Can we come again?'

'Maybe,' Lizzie answered. 'But not a pantomime necessarily. There are other things to see. Maybe now Niamh is old enough to look after you, you could go to the pictures at the Broadway on a Saturday morning.'

'I can look after myself.'

Lizzie didn't argue, but Niamh knew that unless she went with her brother he wouldn't be allowed to go on his own. She didn't mind; it was the lot of elder sisters and she'd always wanted to go to the thrupenny crush herself, for lots of her friends in the streets and school had spoken of it. So when Lizzie said, 'What d'you say, Niamh?' she nodded her head enthusiastically.

'I'd love it, Mammy,' and she added quietly, seeing Tom was discussing the merits of *Cinderella* with Celia, 'I'll keep an eye on Tom, never fear.'

'How did you like it, Celia?' Lizzie asked as they boarded the tram for the short ride home.

'It was grand, wonderful,' Celia said, and added, 'almost as good as dancing lessons.'

Lizzie smiled. Worried about Celia and remembering her own loneliness in the city after Tressa had got married, she'd booked a set of dance lessons at a place in Digbeth and had given it to Celia for Christmas.

Celia had been almost speechless with pleasure and she had enjoyed the lessons immensely. Lizzie had come to a decision. If they were to live in Birmingham,

544

they'd embrace city life, not hide away from it. True, there was still the blackout and rationing, men were still getting killed and cities bombed, but there were the cinemas and variety halls and dance halls that the German planes hadn't attacked and maybe they should make use of them.

Just after the visit to the pantomime, Lizzie read in the paper that the Japanese had finally been repulsed in Guadalcanal by the Americans, who still held Henderson Airport. Lizzie wondered if that was where Scott had been sent. She couldn't ask him directly for the censor would never pass such a letter, nor could he reply with any definite information. In the end, she wrote a letter asking if things were all right, and in the reply he said things were more peaceful.

Scott's mother Sarah wrote too. Since the gift of the doll and the letter they'd been in regular contact, though Lizzie's senses were alerted when Sarah asked if she had any photographs of Georgia that she could spare.

'Why would she want photographs?' she asked Celia. 'Next she'll want to see the child herself and then they'll want to adopt her.'

'Aren't you jumping the gun a bit?'

'Even so,' Lizzie said. 'I'm giving her no snapshot, or anything else either.'

'That's your decision, and she'll probably write again,' Celia warned.

'She can write all she wants,' Lizzie said. 'But no snapshots of Georgia are crossing the Atlantic.'

By the time spring was really in the air, Celia was out twice a week at dancing class, and with friends she made there she'd often go to a dance on Saturday.

'She's living a more normal life now,' Lizzie said with satisfaction to Violet one evening.

'And what about you?'

'What about me?'

'Life isn't over for you, you know,' Violet said. 'I mean, I wouldn't mind going to the pictures a time or two, and Barry wouldn't mind. I mean, if he was down the boozer he'd never notice.'

And so once a week, with Celia quite willing to babysit, the two began going out, either to the Broadway or the ABC or into the city centre, a safer place now the raids were over. There had been an attack on 23rd April, but it had been just from one plane, the bomb landing in Little Bromwich, and neither Lizzie nor the others in the house had been roused and only read about it afterwards.

Lizzie was no longer self-conscious to be seen out with Georgia and this was mainly due to Niamh. Tom was always busy outside, building with the dust piles in the gutter or playing marleys up the street, or risking life or limb on the bombsites building dens and up to all kinds of devilment. Niamh, on the other hand, when she wasn't playing hopscotch or practising her skipping, liked nothing better than pushing Georgia up and down the road, or leading her by the hand to Moorcroft's.

There had been curiosity about this from the first, because the children outside of the court hadn't had a really good look at Georgia until then. She was at nursery every day and seldom taken out at weekends since Scott had been sent overseas, and one day Lizzie had overheard how Niamh dealt with the other children's questions.

It had been a fine Sunday afternoon in mid-January just a few weeks before and Niamh asked if she could take the baby out.

'Out where? It's cold, Niamh.'

'Just along the road,' Niamh pleaded. 'Please, Mammy, you can wrap her up well and I'll not keep her out long?'

And Lizzie realised Niamh was proud of her little half-sister, which was far better than her being semi-embarrassed by her. Georgia had plenty of clothes that had been Niamh's or Tom's, but Lizzie usually chose pastels, or better still white, to dress Georgia in. It looked so gorgeous against her dark skin, so over the top of her warm dress and leggings, Lizzie zipped her into a white all-in-one. It had a hood trimmed with white fur and Georgia's black curls peeped from under it. She looked absolutely gorgeous and Lizzie kissed her as she placed her in the pram and covered her up. 'Only about ten minutes, mind.'

Lizzie, watching through the window, saw that Niamh had not gone very far when she was stopped by two girls nearly the same age as herself. One of them was at St Catherine's and she'd heard the whispers of the black baby at the Gillespie house as soon as Niamh and Tom began at the school. But she saw this was no black baby and both girls looked at her in awe. 'That your sister?' one asked in the end.

'How could she be?' the other said.

'No,' Niamh told them. 'She's a babby my mammy

is minding. She has no mammy of her own. She was killed.'

'Ah.'

'Aye, and that's not all, Niamh said, seeing she'd got the girls' sympathy. 'Her daddy is overseas. He's a soldier.' There was a significant pause and then Niamh went on, 'An American soldier.'

That got the girls' attention soon enough. 'An American?'

'Aye. He sends ever so many dollars every week for Mammy to look after the baby. Her name is Georgia.'

'Georgia,' they repeated. It was an unusual name for a baby, but seemed to suit the child, who was gazing from one to the other as they regarded her solemnly.

'It's a shame, ain't it?' one said at last. 'Having no mom and that.'

'Yeah. Good job your mom took her in, like. Must be kind, your mom.'

'She is,' Niamh said shortly, and added, 'she's the best.'

That made the listening Lizzie flush with embarrassment and she wondered what would happen when the children told their tale about Georgia in their homes, where most adults would know it wasn't true.

But she needn't have worried. The general consensus was that if their children believed that, it was far better than them being told about the rape. More believed in Lizzie's innocence now, but some, seeing Scott at the door, had thought him to be Georgia's father. 'Come back to see the result of his handiwork and then off again,' one remarked, and added spitefully,

'Let's see now if he's filled her belly again.' But even these people didn't refute the tale their children brought home.

So Georgia became a regular sight on the streets, at first with Niamh, where girls would stop their games and nearly stand on their heads to get the baby to smile or chuckle at them. When she was out of the pram and toddling along the road, they vied with each other to hold her hand and pick her up and Georgia grew in stature and confidence.

Lizzie, who knew that not everyone would be kind to Georgia, hoped that confidence would stand her in good stead for the future. But she began to take the children out more, and fine weekend afternoons would find them away from the streets, she and Celia taking turns to push the pram and the children cavorting beside them.

Everyone began feeling more hopeful in 1943, especially after the fall of Mussolini on the 25th July. Everyone knew then, the surrender of the Italians was a foregone conclusion. 'No fight in the Eyeties,' Barry remarked.

'Bloody good job,' Violet retorted, 'for there's plenty of fight left in the Germans and bloody Nips.'

Violet was right, but everywhere there were successes, the Allies making inroads in Africa and the United States, taking over the Philippine Islands one by one. Italy officially surrendered on 3rd September, and just a few days later the paper reported the United States and Australian Forces in the Pacific had invaded New Guinea. In October, letters from Scott ceased.

At first, Lizzie wasn't too concerned, for his letters were spasmodic. Sometimes she'd have none for a couple of weeks or more and then a batch together. A month had passed before Lizzie received the letter from Scott's mother, and although she'd had many her hands felt clammy as she picked the envelope up from the mat.

Dear Lizzie,

I am writing to you with tragic news, for I received a telegram today to say that Scott is missing, presumed dead. I cannot begin to express the extent of grief I feel. Scott was my son, my friend, the rock I leant on, the one all the family looked up to, and he was loved so very, very much.

He talked of you often, my dear, in his letters, and I know he loved you too. Maybe he never told you. He never told me in so many words, but I know him so well and I could read between the lines, and I thought you had a right to know.

I know too, he was sending an allotment of his wages to you each week and I will continue to do that. I know he would want that done . . .

There was more, but Lizzie couldn't read it. Her eyes were blurred with tears and she crushed the letter in her hand and sank onto the chair. She felt so low and depressed with the news and yet there was something else disturbing in the letter. Had Scott really felt something other than friendship? And had she? She didn't really know the answer to either, and it wasn't as if it made any difference now anyway.

In this frame of mind she was almost unaffected by the news announced from the pulpit the following Sunday that Flo had died.

'Gladys was glaring at me,' she told Celia on her return from Mass, 'and a couple of her cronies too, but for God's sake the woman was evil and no great loss to society.'

'I'd go further,' Celia said, 'and say the world will be a better place without her.'

'And,' Lizzie continued, 'I don't care what anyone thinks, I'm not going to her funeral; though I might trot along later and dance a jig on her grave.'

'I'll come with you,' Celia said with a laugh. 'Let's do the whole hog and make it a highland fling.'

'You're on,' said Lizzie.

'The pair of you are clean barmy,' Violet put in, but she was pleased to see a smile on Lizzie's face, for she'd been more upset about Scott's death than she let on. 'I wonder,' she said, 'if Neil will be at the funeral.'

'Oh God,' Lizzie cried. 'That's a good reason not to go, for if I see his mean, sneaky face near me again, I won't be responsible for my actions.'

'We'd have to go armed with a poker and give him another crack of it.'

'Aye, and do the job properly and kill him outright this time,' Lizzie said. 'And then we could roll him in on top of his mother.'

Lizzie's laughter had a hint of hysteria to it, but Violet didn't wonder at it and hoped her life would be smoother from now on.

*   *   *

Tressa came back in November, when everyone was aware that something big was happening on the south coast. No one knew anything; the south coast was out of bounds to civilians and a veil of secrecy drawn over it, and yet by the New Year rumours were abounding.

'They say the roads are impassable, blocked with army trucks and such like,' Celia told them.

'That's what I heard an' all,' Violet said. 'And the fields covered with tents and the place full of soldiers.'

'They're building up for invasion,' Lizzie predicted. 'They have to be. Oh God, another Dunkirk.'

'Come on, girl, it needn't be like that,' Violet said. 'They'll be better prepared this time.'

'And so will the Germans,' Lizzie retorted. 'I mean, they'll hardly stand on the beaches and shake hands with the invading armies. No, Violet, whichever way you look at it there will be great loss of life.'

Violet was silent, knowing Lizzie spoke the truth.

And yet nothing happened, though everything seemed to be heading south. Tressa came to see her with four-year-old Nuala, the only one not at school. As the youngest at home, she was delighted to find Georgia was younger than she was and the two little girls got along famously.

Lizzie was glad to see her cousin. She also saw that Tressa, freed from the rigours of a pregnancy every year or so, had begun to get a grip on her life. She'd had her hair cut and a Marcel wave put into it and had begun using a little make-up.

'Only what I bought in Ireland,' she said when Lizzie commented on it. 'God knows what I'll do when this lot is finished. It's hard to get a bit of lipstick here.'

'They probably think lipstick isn't necessary for the nation's survival.'

'Probably not,' Tressa said with a chuckle and a nudge in Lizzie's ribs that reminded Lizzie of the time they'd been young girls together. 'But it gives a girl a lift.' She patted her ample waist and said, 'This has got to go too. It's all right Mike saying there's more for me to get hold of, but God – I'm beginning to look like Two Ton Tessie. Anyway, Mike will find me half the woman I was when . . . I suppose I should say "if" he comes back from this.'

'Course he'll come back.'

'There's no "of course" in this war, Lizzie,' Tressa said.

And Lizzie was silent. There was no certainty Mike would return. She remembered how she had felt when Scott had been killed, and yet the man was nothing to her really. How would Tressa feel if Mike, her first and only love and the father of her six children, was to fall in battle? And yet she wouldn't be in a unique position.

Lizzie decided to change the subject to prevent Tressa getting thoroughly depressed and they started to discuss Georgia.

'Do you still hear from the people in America?' Tressa asked.

'Aye. Well, Scott's mother writes a fair bit, and in nearly every letter she asks for photographs of Georgia. She even sent me a present of a camera. I suppose she thought I hadn't got one because I won't send her any photos.'

'Why not?'

'Look, Tressa,' Lizzie explained. 'They're moneyed people. God, you should see the lavish gifts she sent for Georgia's birthday and Christmas. The last was a dolls' house. It was in a kit and Celia and I spent ages putting it together, and it turned out to be an enormous place with furniture too, all beautifully made, and wee dolls. I tell you, I thought Niamh's eyes would pop out of her head and she's played with it far more than Georgia.'

'What's wrong with a gift like that?'

'I'm afraid that Scott's mother will try and take Georgia away from me.'

'Would she?'

Lizzie shrugged. 'Scott says not,' she said, 'but people are funny. I mean, whatever way the child was conceived, she is part of Matt, the only child he will ever have. Oh, Tressa, I went through so much for this child, I think I'd die if she was taken from me.'

'Ah Lizzie.'

'No, I mean it Tressa,' Lizzie said fiercely. 'I know people are losing their lives daily on the battlefield, and I know too your Mike is in the firing line, but I also know as long as the war goes on Georgia is safe.' She turned worried eyes to Tressa. 'I know it's selfish,' she said, 'but, in a way, the longer the war goes on the better. Sarah is kind, though, and every month forty dollars come for me with a wee note. I didn't want to accept it at first, only she said Scott would expect it of her and it was him that started it. He said Niamh would think it odd if he was to send nothing when Georgia was supposed to be his child.'

'Aye, she would, very knowing is that child.'

'Too knowing,' Lizzie said with feeling. 'I said to her yesterday, she's so sharp she'll have to watch she doesn't cut herself.'

When Lizzie heard the waves and waves of a planes flying overhead on the evening of 5th June, she knew with dreaded certainty that the invasion was imminent. She was out in the yard with everyone else, watching, for as Minnie remarked, 'It's like they're emptying every aerodrome in the bloody country.'

The news broke the following evening with a broadcast from Reuters News Agency:

'The official communiqué states – under the command of General Eisenhower – Allied Naval Forces began landing Allied Armies this morning on the northern coast of France.'

So that was it, the invasion had happened and everyone knew this was make or break, victory or defeat. There was no middle way.

The scale of the massive operation unfolded gradually as everyone scoured papers and listened to every news bulletin in the quest for news. It seemed Minnie was right about emptying the aerodromes, for 487 squadrons of the International Air Force had marshalled eleven thousand, five hundred planes.

The British people weren't told of the bloodbath, the carnage, the beaches littered with bodies, though they weren't stupid and the sight of the telegraph boy delivering tragic news compounded people's fears. And yet the sheer scale of the invasion awed most listening to or reading reports.

But the allied troops were pushing forward too. Pictures in the papers showed liberated towns and grateful people lining the streets to cheer them on, and hope began to flourish in many a heart that the end of this dreaded war was in sight.

And then on the 13th June a pilotless rocket landed in Kent. It did little damage and few knew then of the new danger that the Londoners would have to face. Called V1s, but termed 'doodlebugs' because of the high-pitched buzzing sound that would cut out seconds before impact, they were twenty-five foot long and carried a ton of explosives in their noses.

When these doodlebugs were joined by V2s that were completely silent, the effect on Londoners' nerves was catastrophic, especially as they'd barely got over the Blitz. There was a second evacuation of men and women as well as children, all going northwards in an attempt to find somewhere safer to live.

But, this apart, everyone was feeling more hopeful and many sentences began with, 'After the war . . .' However, Lizzie wasn't the only one who remembered the slump. Surely to God that couldn't happen again. All those lives would be thrown away needlessly if the future wasn't brighter for those that were left.

CHAPTER TWENTY-EIGHT

It was the Red Army that found Hitler dead in his bunker alongside the body of his mistress Eva Braun, who he had married just the previous day.

On 2nd May 1945, Berlin surrendered to the Red Army, and by 7th May the war in Europe was officially over. The people went wild with joy: the church bells chimed out the joyful news, bonfires were lit on every hilltop and many a bombed site in the cities. Shopkeepers produced fireworks they'd kept for years for such an event and people pooled resources to have street parties for everyone. Those that began in court-yards quickly spilled onto the streets, where people joined together in jubilation and happiness that the dark days were behind them.

Lizzie took joy in her children she had grouped around her and was sorry for Violet, who'd miss Colin afresh, and Minnie, whose husband Charlie was one of the D-day casualties. The death toll had been colossal and the bodies of Stuart and Roy were just two of the thousands left on the beaches of Normandy. Neil hadn't been killed, but had lost his left arm above the elbow and his left leg above the knee. The whole left side of his body had nearly been blasted away, and while the news brought Lizzie no satisfaction, she felt no pity either.

All in all, after V-E Day there was a bit of an anticlimax feeling. Lizzie felt it, for although the blackout had been lifted and the threat of bombs was no more, everything went on as before. She was also aware that the war with Japan was not over, and wondered bleakly one day, hearing fresh reports of battles in the paper, how long that carnage would linger.

Then, on 6th August, the Americans dropped a bomb on the Japanese city of Hiroshima. The British people were used to bombs – God knew, they had had their fill of them and thought they'd seen them all: high-explosive bombs, cluster bombs, parachute bombs. But no one in the world had ever seen a bomb of this magnitude.

One observer, placed in the rear of the plane, wrote of what he saw after the bomb was dropped, and this was reported in the paper:

> *There was a giant ball of fire, as if the bowels of the earth were belching forth enormous smoke rings. Next, there was a pillar of purple fire ten-thousand foot-high, shooting skywards with enormous speed. By the time our ship [aircraft] had done another turn towards the atomic explosion, the purple flame had reached the level of our altitude. Only forty-five seconds had passed. Awestruck, we watched it shoot upwards like a*

meteor from earth instead of outer space, becoming
more alive as it climbed skywards through the white
clouds. It was no longer smoke, or dust, or even
a cloud of fire. It was a living thing, a new species
being born right before our incredulous eyes.

'Oh my God,' Violet said, looking at the pictures in the paper. 'Them poor, poor sods.'

'Seventy-eight thousand of them, by all accounts,' Barry added. 'But don't forget, American soldiers are dying every day, and if this shortens the war it's got to be a good thing.'

'But still,' Lizzie said. 'Seventy-eight thousand.'

'It's hard to visualise that number of people,' Celia commented.

'Not half,' Barry said. 'But surely to God they'll surrender now?'

But Japan didn't, not even when a second smaller bomb was dropped in Nagasaki on 9th August and killed thirty-five thousand people. And so, on the 13th August, a massed armada of one thousand, six hundred allied aircraft attacked Tokyo and at last Japan gave in. The war that had dragged on for six years was finally at an end.

'Welcome Home' banners fluttered from many windows that autumn, and the men began filtering back in their light grey, chalk-striped demob suits with the booklet on 'Resettlement Advice' to help them live on civvy street.

Violet's daughter Carol came home too, but not for long as she was engaged to Gavin Honeyford, the young pilot she'd brought home the Christmas Lizzie had brought Georgia back. 'Didn't you get civilian clothes?' Celia asked her. 'Like the men.'

'Can you see women all settling for wearing the same dress?' Carol said with a laugh. 'We get clothing coupons and a bit of cash to buy our own stuff. Not that there's much to choose.'

Carol was only too right. 'And don't you just hate the word utility?' Celia said.

'Oh, too right I do.'

It wasn't just clothes in short supply, but foodstuffs too, and there was little in the way of festive fare. Lizzie looked forward to the first Christmas of peacetime with little enthusiasm. Sarah McFarland sent a dress to Georgia, based on the one Shirley Temple wore in *The Good Ship Lollipop*. Georgia looked exquisite in it for it was basically white. The bodice was a sailor-suit design and the skirt had three petticoats of lace to make it stand out. Inside the box was a card and money for them all and a request to see a photograph of Georgia wearing the dress.

'I don't think it's much to ask,' Celia said. 'Pity it won't be in colour now.'

Lizzie thought so too and Scott's mother had been very generous, and so she spent some of the dollars on taking Georgia to a proper photographer because he was able to take a coloured photograph of her. She used her Box Brownie to take photographs of family and friends, including Tressa and her children, for she wanted to show Sarah that the child was happy and settled into this life and surrounded by love.

*   *   *

Sarah knew as soon as she looked at the photographs what Lizzie was saying. She had secretly harboured a dream that Georgia would grow up with them one day, but now she saw and accepted that could never be. She couldn't pluck a child from a family where she was so happy, and she could only hope that Lizzie might bring her over to see them when the world was a more settled place.

It wasn't such a settled place in Birmingham, where too many people had lost everything belonging to them and taken shelter with friends or family. There was terrific overcrowding, while other families were camping out in deserted houses or church halls, and many servicemen came home horrified to find their families living in such conditions.

Prefabricated houses began being erected as a stopgap measure. 'What are prefabricated houses?' Celia asked, scanning the paper.

'They're built in sections and assembled on the site,' Lizzie told her. 'Not unlike that dolls' house Sarah McFarland sent from America that we had to put together. They don't need foundations. People say they're lovely inside, and with a bit of garden for the kids. I tell you, I wouldn't mind one myself.'

'People say they're for servicemen's families first.'

'I know,' Lizzie said. 'Fair enough, I suppose.'

Just then Violet popped her head around the door. 'Here,' she said, 'don't say I never give you owt,' and from behind her back she produced something that hadn't been on sale in the shops for six years.

'Bananas! Oh, Violet.'

'It weren't me,' Violet explained, 'it was our Carol. Couldn't resist them when she saw them hanging up. Wonder what the nippers will think of them?'

'The older two might remember,' Lizzie said. 'Niamh, anyway.'

But Niamh didn't and all three children regarded the bananas with suspicion. In her quest to eke out the rations and still feed her children nutritiously, Lizzie had produced many an odd concoction, and in their opinion this banana might be just one more.

'What are they?'

'I thought you might remember. They're bananas.'

Niamh shook her head, and Tom asked, 'What do they taste like?'

'It's difficult to explain,' Lizzie said. 'Anyway, you have to take the skin off first.'

'How?'

'I'll show you,' Lizzie said. The children's faces were a study as she unzipped Georgia's banana and cut it into pieces on the plate. They watched more intently as Georgia picked up a piece and popped it in her mouth. 'Mmm,' she said. 'S'nice.'

The two older ones lost no time in removing the skin from their own bananas and devouring them, and afterwards declared bananas were the best fruit they'd ever tasted and when could they have them again.

'They're easy to please,' Lizzie told Violet later. 'They don't see the headache I have each day to put food on the table – and now to talk about rationing bread! It's madness.'

The idea of bread-rationing had caused a national

562

outcry, for as many mothers said, you can fill the family up with bread, especially as butter, margarine and cooking fat were cut to wartime levels, and all meat, including poultry and even eggs, were to be considered luxury items. 'Make-do meals', were reissued in papers and magazines and read out on the wireless.

The only bright light on the horizon was the introduction of family allowances for every child after the firstborn, five shillings for each one, and paid to mothers in an order book that was due to come in to force in August. There was also talk of a National Health Service where visits and treatments from doctors, dentists and opticians were going to be free.

'Be bloody marvellous if it does come off,' Violet said.

'Aye,' Lizzie agreed. 'And rationing can't last forever. Tell you the truth, I'm thinking of getting a job in September when Georgia starts school.'

'I'll come with you,' Violet said. 'When our Carol gets married next month and moves down to bloody London, I'll not know what to do with myself.

'No sign of a man on the horizon for Celia yet?' she added.

Lizzie shook her head. 'She still goes dancing and to the pictures, but she says most men she knows or she's heard about have been untrustworthy.'

'God, girl, she couldn't have had that much experience,' Violet remarked. 'She was only a bit of a kid when she was put in that bloody convent.'

'I know, and that's the problem,' Lizzie said. 'Some of the tales the girls told us, well, you wouldn't credit it and it's put her off all men.'

'Yeah. Seems to have affected you as well. Never go anyroad but out with me a time or two.'

'I've got the children, Violet.'

'Oh that's it, is it? I've got kids and my life's over?' Lizzie grinned at her. 'Shut up, you. Stop nagging me. I'm not interested in any man and I can't see the situation changing, so don't hold your breath for me to go floating up the aisle.'

In early September 1946, Georgia started school as she would be five in November. It would be her first real foray out of the streets and courts where she was known and accepted. Now she had to stand alone against people who might pick on her because she was different.

There was no way Lizzie could prepare her for this, but she needn't have worried. Both Tom from the junior playground and Niamh from the seniors kept a weather eye on their little half-sister. Niamh ripped verbally into any she saw tormenting Georgia, while Tom was more physical. When he saw three bigger boys picking on her one day when she'd been at school less than a week, calling her names, pushing her over and laughing at her tears, his blood boiled and he let fly at them. Before the chant of 'Fight, fight, fight,' had alerted the teachers, one boy had a black eye and another a bloodied nose. It was worth three strokes of the cane on each hand, Tom thought, but he was no sneak and wouldn't say why he'd attacked the boys. However, there were plenty who would, and Mr Steele thought he should nip racist attacks in the bud and the three tormentors were given the same punishment as Tom.

'I'll get you for this, Gillespie,' one of the boys said, leaving the headmaster's office holding his burning hands under his armpits.

'Oh yeah? You and whose army?'

'I'll get my big brother on you.'

'Well get him,' said Tom. 'He'll think you're terrific, won't he, when I say you was picking on a little girl half your size. You just leave our Georgia alone or you'll get more of the same.'

After that Georgia had no further trouble, and Lizzie guessed much by the grazes on Tom's face and cane marks on his hands. 'Do you want to tell me about it?' she asked.

'No,' Tom said. 'Not really. Something had to be sorted out. Now, it is.'

Lizzie asked no further questions and was just glad Georgia had such great protectors in her two older children, who loved her so much.

By early October, Lizzie was alone in the house, and so far her and Violet had done nothing about looking for a job. This might be a good day to start, she thought, for it was fine and quite warm, with shafts of autumn sunlight lighting up the yard. 'I'm sure if I'm busier, with less time on my hands, I'll feel better,' she told herself.

There was a knock on the door at just that moment.

Lizzie sighed, wondering if it was the priest, virtually the only one who knocked on doors, and she held herself straighter and told herself she wouldn't be intimidated or browbeaten by the man.

When she opened the door she was so surprised she

had to hold on to the door frame for support. 'So . . . Scott?' It was said hesitantly and questioningly. The man was said to be dead, and this wasn't the Scott she remembered. Scott had been a fine build of a man, strong and broad without being fat, his face open and honest and his curls jet-black. This man appeared to have shrunk, his face was heavily lined and his hair peppered with grey.

Pity flowed all through Lizzie as Scott said, 'Aye, no wonder you are surprised. I'm not half the man I was.'

'But it's not only that,' she protested, drawing him inside the house as she spoke. 'Your mother said . . . I had a letter . . .'

'I know,' Scott replied. 'But I wasn't dead, though I might well have been when I was captured by the Japs. They didn't bother informing anyone, probably because they didn't think many of us would survive, and a fair few didn't.'

'Oh, Scott, I can hardly believe it,' Lizzie said. She'd thought this man dead and gone, lost to her, lost to them all, and for him to be here, alive! God, it was wonderful, marvellous! She wanted to touch him all over to convince herself he was real, hold him close, even kiss those lips. She flushed with embarrassment at the thought, for whatever his mother had written about his feelings for her, he'd never shown her he thought of her that way.

He looked at Lizzie and the pain in his eyes was so evident she forgot all her reservations and put her arms around him and felt him sag against her with a sigh of contentment. 'When did you get out?'

'The camp was liberated last year after the atomic bombs landed,' Scott said. 'The guards just took off one day. Some of the guys did too, but I was too sick and was airlifted to hospital.

'I wasn't with it for a long time and even when they fixed my body my brain was still addled, that's why Mom never contacted you. She didn't know if I'd ever recover. Some days I didn't even recognise her'

Scott was quiet, remembering those awful, scary days when he'd hovered in a sort of foggy half-life, and Lizzie disentangled herself and, taking Scott's hand, led him to the armchair by the fire. Then, thinking to give him a few minutes to compose himself, she gave his hand a squeeze, saying, 'Shall I make us a nice cup of tea?'

'No,' Scott cried, and he clasped Lizzie's hand tight again. 'This is more important then tea. When I was deemed to be on the mend and I was assigned to a psychiatrist, I confessed to him as I've never confided in anyone before, that what made me determined to survive during the hard times was the thought of here, this room, and Georgia and you.'

'I'm glad,' Lizzie said, not really understanding what Scott was saying. 'Everyone needs something to hold on to, to give you hope for the future. Johnnie coming to see me in the convent and bringing the letters did that for me.'

It wasn't really what Scott meant, but he knew the situation was different for Lizzie. He'd held her up as the vision to come home to, but any budding feelings she might have had for him would have been snuffed out at the news of his death, for Lizzie was nothing if not practical.

So he said no more of this in case it would disturb her further, but instead went on, 'The psychiatrist said I should come and lay the ghost. I wanted to anyway. It wasn't hard advice to follow.'

'Ah yes, and it's important for Georgia to know she has other relations,' Lizzie said. 'Even if she never gets to see them, it's nice for her to know. Everyone likes to know their roots.'

It wasn't just for Georgia I wanted to come back, Scott wanted to cry, but he didn't and went on, 'My mom was knocked out with the photos you sent. Me too. God, I mean, in my head I knew Georgia would now be going on for five, but in my mind I carried the image of the child when I left. She was just a toddler. And your own children look fine, Lizzie. I'm glad you brought them back.'

'Your letter made that possible.'

'They should have believed you anyway.'

'If they had,' Lizzie said, 'is there an alternative to the Magdalene Laundries? I've thought a lot about it since. Is there some place in Ireland girls can go when they find themselves in the position I was in, or are the laundries the only place?' She looked at Scott and went on, 'I told the priest all about it, you know, the priest in Ireland when I went for the children.'

'I'm glad. Was he shocked, surprised?'

'I'm not sure,' Lizzie said. 'Oh yes, he said he was, but you know, the priests, nuns and all, they close up, protect their own. The Catholic Church is a law unto itself and can get away with atrocities. Somehow, it seems to have little to do with the Jesus I pray to.'

'You still pray?' Scott said. 'You still believe in God

after the war the world is reverberating from, not counting what happened to you?'

'What could God do about the war, Scott?' Lizzie asked. 'Come down with a heavy hand like some avenging parent and give the Germans and Japs a good talking-to, or maybe throw in a few curses to bring them into line?'

'No, maybe not, but . . .'

'Some of those nuns had evilness like a canker in their hearts,' Lizzie said. 'The same as the Japs who treated you so badly and the Germans who herded the Jews into concentration camps and then on to gas chambers so that six million of them are not alive today. D'you know, I think when Jesus looks down on the mess of it all – that human beings, given free will, can act like this, and to one another – he just might weep himself.'

Scott lifted the hand he still held and kissed Lizzie's fingers lightly. He was so moved by her words, his voice was husky as he said, 'You are a very special lady, Lizzie Gillespie.'

Lizzie felt a stirring of her heart, which seemed to have lain dormant for so long, and she realised and acknowledged she cared deeply for this man sitting beside her, holding her hand and looking at her in such a way. God above, he was looking at her as if he loved her.

Their faces were very close and Scott bent towards her. What might have happened was interrupted by Violet coming in, saying as she came through the door, 'How d'you fancy taking a dander up the shops, Lizzie?'

Scott had dropped Lizzie's hand and yet the

atmosphere was still charged. Violet stared at Scott. 'Where the bleeding hell have you sprung from?' she said before she took in the situation properly. *Me and my big foot and bigger mouth*, she thought, and aloud she said, 'Sorry, Lizzie, did I interrupt something?'

Aye, Lizzie might have said, *a tender moment, a moment of awakening to feelings I didn't know I had, a moment when I might have kissed this man for the first time*. But how could she say this; her feelings were too new, too raw. Maybe she confused pity and sympathy for love. God knows, she'd had little experience of love between a man and woman, for she'd never felt this way about Steve, about anyone, so she said, 'No, it's all right, Violet.' She got to her feet. 'I'll make us all some tea and then we can sit down and let Scott, who's risen from the dead, I should say, tell us of all he's suffered since he left us.'

What Scott went on to tell the women left them stunned. His voice was the only sound in the room except for the ticking of the clock and the settling of the coal in the grate.

They listened to Scott telling them how their company had been surrounded in Java and forced to surrender. 'We were herded into the holds of ships,' Scott told them. 'Packed in like sardines, till there wasn't room to move or breathe; too low to sit up, we had to lie like that for days.

'Those of us who survived that were then put into tin boxes, they laughingly called railway carriages and again travelled like that for days.'

'Where were they taking you?'

'Thailand,' Scott said. 'And we were set to work on

570

the railway that people say runs from there to Burma. The work was back-breaking and on a starvation diet. People dropped like flies; buddies you'd just shared a word with sank to the ground. If they couldn't get up they were dragged away and shot. There were plenty to take their place.'

He closed his eyes for a minute and then said, 'It never leaves me, that time. Beatings were commonplace and could be for anything or nothing. Sometimes you felt so sick, so sore you could scarcely move, yet to stay in bed or even to linger would sign your death warrant and you would be in the yard, trying to stand straight, glad to be one of those marched off to the railway for another day of torture, because it was better than ending your life impaled on a Japanese bayonet, or shot through the head because you were too sick to be of any use.'

'It's diabolical to treat people like that,' Violet cried. 'Almighty God, I hope those people are brought to book for this eventually.'

'I doubt they will be,' Scott said glumly. 'I'll not hold my breath over it. The one thing they were frightened of was cholera, and that swept through the camp, quickly wiping out many who were too ill-nourished to fight any sort of disease. Every morning there were people who died in their bunks, or those who keeled over standing in the parade ground, or beside you working. Each day I marvelled that I was still alive.'

He looked at Lizzie and added, 'You said once you'd already visited Hell, and now I know what you mean.'

All the children were intrigued by Scott, who was supposed to have died in the war, and Tom's standing rose in the street because he had a real-life American visiting his house.

'It's cos he's our Georgia's daddy,' Tom told them proudly one day. 'She hasn't got a mammy so our mammy has been looking after her when her daddy was fighting and that.'

'Has he come to take her home then, back to America?' one boy asked.

Tom was suddenly very still. He'd never thought of that. He faced the fact that that was probably why the man had come, to take Georgia away with him, and he was filled with misery and sadness at the thought of Georgia leaving them.

Lizzie wondered why she hadn't anticipated this. She'd been so thrilled to see Scott alive she hadn't thought of anything else, but the children had accepted the lie that she had told them. She should have known this would come up sooner or later.

'Is he going to take our Georgia back to America or not then?' Tom asked, after recounting what the boy had said to him.

Lizzie didn't know what to say to the child, who was so obviously upset at the thought of losing Georgia, and he was still far too young to be told the truth. She parried, playing for time. 'It's not as cut and dried as that, Tom.'

'Why ain't it?' Tom said, scrubbing the tears from his eyes with his sleeve impatiently. 'I can't see any other reason for him coming here.'

'Georgia doesn't know Scott yet. He wants to get to know her again.'

'And then take her?'

Over my dead body, Lizzie thought, but didn't say this as she put her arms around her son. Normally he'd have pushed his mother away, thinking he was too old for such things, but he was grateful now for the arms around him as Lizzie said, 'Nothing is decided yet, really it isn't.'

She knew Tom wasn't satisfied, and when Niamh also attacked her that evening with similar questions, she knew they had been talking, understandably, discussing it. Celia had been home from work and she said when the children had gone to bed, 'What are you going to do?'

'I'll talk to Scott tomorrow. Maybe he'll think of something.'

However, Scott had no magical solution. 'Let me talk to them,' he suggested to Lizzie, 'after Georgia is in bed this evening.'

'Aye,' Lizzie said, and added, 'At least that is one who is very glad you are here.'

Scott smiled, for the little girl was totally enchanted to find she had a real live daddy after all this time. She remembered being told he had died, but they'd made a mistake, her daddy told her. He'd been in a camp, not dead at all, and she was very glad about that.

'The most important person here is Georgia,' Scott told the children. 'This is her home and you are her family. Oh, I know she is all over me at the moment, but that is because I am new, someone different.'

'But she's your little girl,' Niamh said.

'Yeah, I know, and one I haven't seen for four years,'

Scott said. 'That's what I meant by saying that Georgia and how she feels is the only important issue here, even more important than the fact I am her father. How could I take her away from all of you, especially your mother? You would be unhappy, but she would be distraught, I imagine.'

'So you won't be taking her away?'

'For a holiday maybe, when she knows me better,' Scott said. 'That's all.'

'So she can stay with us for always?' Niamh asked.

'It's where she is happiest,' Scott said simply.

It was Lizzie's greatest desire to feed Scott good, wholesome food to build him up. Within a couple of days the lines had begun to disappear from his face and he had become much more relaxed. He was still far too thin, but with rations how they were she was at a loss to know what to do about food. Not that Scott ate much at the house, taking most of his meals at the hotel.

Scott himself could remember well the shortages of wartime, and from what he'd seen, things were no better yet. He had a surprise coming any day that would, he knew, put a smile on Lizzie's face. He'd flown over to England, but the surprise had had to come by sea and there had been a little delay, for the only ships so far returned to civilian duties that trawled across the Atlantic were those detailed to bring the girls who'd married American servicemen back home to the States. But he was expecting news of it soon.

In the meantime he seldom came empty-handed. Hearing of the children's delight at their first sight of a banana, he started to bring fruit – not just bananas, but apples, oranges, pears, and even grapes. He bought them their first pomegranate and taught them how to eat the purple seeds inside.

But although Scott enjoyed spending time with the children, what he liked most was time alone with Lizzie. As one day slid into another they became easier with one another and Celia would often slip around to Violet's to give them time alone.

They could talk for hours and never run out of things to say, and Lizzie felt her feelings for Scott deepen, but she didn't know how she could tell him this for she didn't know how he felt. Sometimes he would reach for her hand as they sat together, or drape an arm around her, and she would snuggle against him and give a little sigh of contentment. Scott would hold her closer and feel himself relax and begin to hope that Lizzie was warming to him.

'And how is your lovely mother-in-law?' he asked her one day.

'Dead, thank God,' Lizzie said. 'Oh, and you remember the night I told you Steve's brother Neil and two of his mates tried to rape me and might have succeeded if it hadn't been for Celia?'

'I remember,' Scott said grimly. 'I said I would like to meet them some day and give them all a dust-up for what they did to you.'

Lizzie shook her head. 'They've had their just deserts,' she said. 'Roy and Stuart never came back after D-day and Neil was damaged all down his left side and has lost his left arm and left leg.'

'And did you feel sorry for him?'

'No, I didn't,' Lizzie said. 'I don't know what sort of person that makes me.'

'A normal one,' Scott replied, and kissed her lightly on the cheek, and Lizzie put her arms around Scott's neck and held him tight.

The next day Scott turned up at the door with a large tea chest, which he helped the taxi driver carry into the living room.

'What is it?' Lizzie asked, intrigued.

'You'll see,' Scott said, the smile nearly splitting his face in half as he anticipated Lizzie's delight.

He wasn't disappointed, for when the lid was prised off Lizzie was rendered speechless, for the chest contained food she hadn't seen for years, all in tins and packages, and so much of it. There was ham and pork and spiced sausages, even tins of sliced chicken and beef and lots of dried egg powder. There were cans of fruit, pineapple, oranges and peaches, and jars of jam of every flavour and others of honey and something else, which Scott said was peanut butter, and two large jars of coffee as well as many, many packets of tea. There were bars of chocolate, a tin of toffees, and a much larger tin housing a huge fruit cake, and tucked down the side a bag containing six pairs of nylon stockings.

'Oh Scott!'

'You're not crying?'

Lizzie gave a sniff and dashed the tears from her eyes with her fingers. 'Only a little,' she said. 'I can't find the words to tell you what all this means.'

'It had to come by ship, so that is why you've had to wait a while,' Scott said, and Lizzie was overcome by Scott's thoughtfulness, his kindness, and when he swept her into his arms she went without a moment's hesitation. For the first time their lips met and Lizzie felt an explosion inside her and knew that the things both were hesitant to talk about had been decided by that kiss.

Scott led Lizzie to the sofa and, sitting beside her, picked up one of her hands. 'We need to do some straight talking, Lizzie,' he said, 'because I know that you're the woman I have waited all my life to meet. I love you with every part of me. There isn't a way I could ever hope to show you how much I love you. I've known this since the first time I met you, I think, though those first few visits were tinged with guilt. I know for years you thought I was dead, lost to you, and I don't expect you to feel as deeply as I do, but have you any feelings for me at all?'

'Oh Scott,' Lizzie said. 'You don't know how I've longed for you to say something like this. I thought I'd misinterpreted the way you looked at me sometimes.'

'You mean there is hope for me?'

'More than just hope,' Lizzie told him. 'I too have never loved anyone before.'

'Not your husband?'

'No,' Lizzie admitted. 'He knew, I think, that I didn't. I married him because it was easier than trying to find a future on my own. Britain was a strange place then, and millions were out of work. I'd lost my job through illness, and my place to live too, because I worked in a hotel. Steve offered me marriage, begged me to marry him, and it was easier to agree than try and figure things out myself. But never before have I felt this fluttering in my heart that I get when I look at you. I want you to put your arms around me and hold me tight, and I want you to kiss me properly.'

'Oh God, Lizzie,' Scott said. 'You shall have all that, my darling. You'll have everything you want, but there are serious implications too. Tell me truthfully how you feel about the colour of my skin?'

Lizzie looked at this honourable and considerate man, his love for her reflected in those deep, dark eyes, and she said, 'You deserve honesty. When you appeared in my life and told me about your brother, I was devastated and, yes, embarrassed to be seen with you, embarrassed to walk the streets. But I see that as stupidity on my part and ignorance on the part of anyone else who views it differently. Now, I'd be proud to be seen with you.'

'Would you consider marrying me?' Scott asked. 'Please think carefully before you answer. All in all, we've known each other such a small amount of time, and marriage will mean us all living in America. And there's something else: I am not a Catholic.'

'I know that.'

'And I'll not turn,' Scott said. 'However, I'll not stop you practising your religion, nor any children we might have.'

'Scott, I want to marry you,' Lizzie said. 'I always understood that when a woman married a man she went with that man to the ends of the earth if necessary. The religion bit is difficult because, if I'm to be married in the eyes of God, it must be done in a Catholic Church, and they do not like mixed marriages. But we'll cross that bridge when we come to it. As for not knowing each other long, well, we're not a couple of teenagers who don't know our minds, are we? I have never felt this way before and I don't expect to ever feel this way again.'

'You don't know how happy you have made me,' Scott told her. 'I feel ten feet tall; I feel like telling everyone, shouting it from the rooftops, but I'll content myself by asking you if you will accept this and do me the honour of wearing it? I see you have no engagement ring.'

Lizzie had been given an engagement ring by Steve. As he'd boasted the night Tressa got engaged, the night she'd told him it was over, his ring for Lizzie was larger, more lavish, and, she guessed, far more expensive than the one Mike had bought, and Lizzie had never liked it. To her it was like Steve was showing off, showing the world how much he loved his wife. She would have appreciated Steve's company more, cuddling her before the fire, listening to the wireless, or just talking, or risking Flo's wrath, or going to the pictures, or taking in a show now and again, and not to have to share her husband with prostitutes.

She'd taken the engagement ring off and put it in her case the day the priest took her to the convent, and had never worn it again. She intended giving it to Niamh when she was older, but the one Scott presented her with was exquisite. The centre was a sparkling blue sapphire, surrounded by diamonds that twinkled in the lights, and she slipped it on her finger and kissed Scott on the lips. 'I'll be proud to wear it,' she said.

She felt incredibly lucky to have another chance like this. And yet she knew there were problems and possible heartache ahead. She didn't know how the children would take to Scott as a father figure, and more particularly whether they would view moving to America as an opportunity or something to dread.

But when Scott kissed her, all her apprehensions fled, and when he gently teased her lips open she groaned with longing, and how she wanted to take this further. But she knew that any minute the children would be in from school and she pulled away with difficulty. 'The children will be here soon,' she said in explanation. 'Can you help me put all this food away, and then . . . then I will cook a meal fit for a king. A meal to celebrate the fact that you have made me the happiest woman on God's earth.'

CHAPTER TWENTY-NINE

Niamh noticed the ring straight away, as Lizzie knew she would. Scott had gone out for a walk so that Lizzie could talk to the children alone. 'If I'm here they might feel constrained and not be totally honest about how they really feel, and after all it is a lot for them to contend with.' It was just another sign of his thoughtfulness that Lizzie so loved him for, so she sat with the children and told them all of their plans to marry. 'Scott will be your new daddy,' Lizzie told them. 'Will you mind that?'

Niamh considered this and eventually said, 'No, I don't think so, Mammy, Scott's all right. I suppose we'll have to live in America too?'

'Will you mind that?'

'No,' Niamh said. 'I'd quite like that.'

'Tom?'

'Scott's better than all right,' Tom grinned. 'He's great, but if we have to live in America then he'd better start teaching me baseball. I don't want to go over to America and be called dumb cos I don't know the rules.'

'You're dumb anyway,' Niamh said. 'Will you shut

up about sport. We're talking about Scott.'

'Well so am I, stupid.'

'Children!' Lizzie admonished. 'Stop arguing. Goodness, I'm not sure Scott will want to adopt you if you go on like this.'

'Adopt us?'

'To be your daddy, yes.'

'Right,' Niamh said.

'What is it, Niamh?'

'You'll wear his ring then,' Niamh said slowly, 'like, Scott's engagement ring now?'

'Aye.'

'What about the rings Daddy gave you?'

'They're still precious to me, Niamh,' Lizzie said gently. 'But, you see, I can't wear them when I'm married to Scott. I thought to give them to you when you're sixteen. Would you like that?'

'Ooh, Mammy, yes. Yes I would.'

'That's settled then.'

'Can I have our Dad's watch then?' Tom asked.

Lizzie remembered when Tom was sitting on Steve's knee he would always put the watch to his ear to hear the loud tick. Because Steve had been killed cleanly by a sniper's bullet, the watch on his wrist had been intact and returned with his effects. So she was able to say, 'Of course you can.'

'What can I have?' Georgia asked.

'Nothing,' Niamh said. 'He wasn't your daddy.'

'That's not fair.'

'Yes it is. You've still got your daddy.'

'Well then,' Georgia said mutinously, 'I'm not going to any America.'

'You've got no choice,' Tom taunted her. 'You're just a baby.'

'I'm not.'

'Oh yes you are'.

Lizzie scooped Georgia up just before her booted foot struck Tom on the shin. 'Stop it,' she said. 'And you stop teasing, Tom. God, you wear me out. Maybe I'll go to America and leave the lot of you behind.'

Lizzie was sorry she'd said that when she saw the look on Tom and Niamh's faces. They remembered a time when their mother hadn't been there. But it did ensure that for the rest of the evening they behaved like angels.

When Celia came home and was told, she too admired the ring and extended the warmest congratulations to them both, for Scott had returned from his walk. The sumptuous meal was followed by peaches with condensed milk dribbled over them, while Niamh and Tom plied Scott with questions about life in America.

'Why don't you two go out tonight?' Celia suggested to Lizzie as they washed the dishes while Scott tucked Georgia into bed. 'Sort of celebrate. You know I wouldn't mind seeing to the children.'

'You don't have to look after me,' Niamh protested. 'I can see to myself.'

'And me,' said Tom, and Celia was grateful Georgia was in bed as she would undoubtedly have chimed in too. 'Aye, well,' she said, 'I'm here anyway, so why don't you take advantage of it?'

Scott, coming into the room at that moment, said, 'We could go to the pictures if you'd like to. *Brief*

Encounter is showing at the Gaumont in the city centre.'

'How d'you know?'

'It's not far from the hotel where I'm staying,' Scott said, 'and I saw it when I took a walk out the other evening. I went to see the bomb damage. The city centre sure took a pounding.'

'Aye, it did,' Lizzie agreed. 'There were times I thought it might all be razed to the ground.'

'Well, would you like to see *Brief Encounter*?'

'I wouldn't mind.'

'Well get a move on then,' Celia said, and Lizzie made a face at her before opening the door to the stairs, but her insides were jumping with excitement. She was determined to make herself look good for this man of hers, and to wear a pair of the nylon stockings she'd received that day.

'D'you think it's all right, Celia, Mammy getting married and all?' Niamh asked when Scott and Lizzie had gone.

'Why not?' Celia said. 'Your daddy has been dead for years, and whatever your mammy does now she can't change that. But she's still young.'

'She isn't,' Niamh protested. 'She's over thirty.'

Celia laughed. 'Believe me, Niamh, thirty isn't old. When you're thirty yourself, you'll know this.'

But thirty seemed an impossible age to a twelve-year-old and Niamh still looked doubtful as Celia went on, 'Your mammy needs to begin to live a little, have a bit of fun in her life, and you do like Scott, don't you?'

'Yeah, he's all right.'

'He's a mean footballer,' Tom said. 'And he's going to teach me to play baseball.'

Niamh gave him a withering look. 'We're talking about important things.'

'So am I,' Tom said. 'Tell you what, though, I can't wait to go to America. It sounds terrific.'

Niamh had to agree with her brother about that, for Scott had gone out of his way to paint an exciting picture of the future awaiting them on the other side of the ocean. 'Yeah,' she said, hugging her knees with delight, 'I can't wait either.'

Later, after the children had gone to bed, Celia sat down in the room and tried to lift the depression she'd felt settle all around her and be happy for Lizzie. Hadn't she suffered enough, and shouldn't she have another stab at happiness? What sort of friend was she? All right, she knew Lizzie leaving and taking Georgia with her would leave a large, gaping hole in her own life, but she also knew she'd never tell her that, or admit how lonely she would feel.

Scott and Lizzie held hands all the way home, and when they got to the entry Scott turned Lizzie round. The look in his eyes turned Lizzie's insides to water and she leant against him with a moan of desire. The kiss was as tender as it was mind-blowing and Lizzie wanted more. Scott unbuttoned her coat and slid his hands over her body, but outside her clothes, and though Lizzie wanted him to go further she didn't press him. There was time enough. They would know each other's bodies intimately in the end, but they could wait and then their fulfilment would be all the more wondrous.

Violet was thrilled for Lizzie, though she knew she'd miss her sorely. 'It's not that I begrudge her, like,' she said to Celia, 'and it's not that I don't think she don't deserve some good luck, the poor sod, but Christ I'm going to miss her.'

Celia nodded. 'I feel exactly the same,' she said.

'What you going to do?'

Celia shrugged. 'I haven't really thought.'

'You can always bide here, you know,' Violet said. 'I got an attic room that will be going spare in a few months when our Carol marries, and she won't mind sharing with you for a bit.'

'Thanks, Violet,' Celia said. 'Lizzie asked me if I wanted to go to America with them, but you know I've never had a yen to see the place.'

'Nor me neither,' Violet said. 'Nasty horrible place, full of gangsters if the films are to be believed. Give me good old England any time, and that offer to stay here stands till I hear otherwise.'

Scott thought Lizzie deserved a proper courtship, and after that first time they went once to a variety show and a couple of times to the cinema and a fair few times out for dinner. Sometimes, just being near Scott made Lizzie's whole body tingle for his touch. She ached for the feel of his hands on her and longed for him to kiss her properly, and she knew no man had ever truly touched her heart before.

And yet sometimes she was beset with doubts for

all she was leaving behind: not the place, but the people. How could she just abandon Celia after all they had gone through? And what about Violet and all the others down the yard who'd always been on her side, and Tressa and her family in Ireland that she might never see again.

And then she'd see Scott, and he'd smile at her or catch her around the waist, or kiss her, and her doubts would vanish, for she knew if she didn't have this man her life would have no meaning.

Scott insisted they do the job properly. Father Connolly disapproved strongly of mixed marriages and so Lizzie asked the kindly Father Peters, the curate, to see them. He too disapproved, for the church dictated he had to, but he conceded that there were more mixed marriages now than before the war. 'You weren't thinking of taking instruction to be a Catholic,' he asked Scott.

'No, Father. I couldn't do that,' Scott said.

'You'll need to take instruction anyway if you want to marry Elizabeth. You need to understand what being married to a Catholic means.'

'I understand that, Father,' Scott said. 'And I'll put no obstacle in Lizzie's path. We have a Catholic Church and school not far from the store back home. I would never hamper either Lizzie or the children following their religion.'

Despite himself, Father Peters was impressed with the man, and so were Tressa and Doreen when they went up for tea one Sunday. As the cousins played in the garden, the women listened to Scott and Lizzie and their plans for the future. Later, with the men off to

587

the pub, Doreen and Tressa both said what a thoroughly nice and kind man Scott was. 'You don't mind about the colour and all?' Tressa asked.

'Not now,' Lizzie said. 'But I have to admit I did at first. No, I don't even see the colour, I see the man behind it.'

'Wonder what your mammy will say?'

'What can she say? I am over twenty-one.'

'Hmm. As if that ever made any difference in Ireland.'

Lizzie grinned at her, knowing her cousin was right. 'Anyway,' she said, eyeing her up. 'What's happened to you?'

'What d'you mean?'

'Well, Mike's been home how long now and you're not pregnant yet?'

'Nor won't be,' Tressa said with feeling.

'What d'you mean?' Lizzie said. 'Doesn't Mike fancy it any more?'

'As if it's any of your business,' Tressa replied, giving Lizzie a push. 'If you must know, he's using something.'

'Tressa!'

'I know,' Tressa said. 'But he said I haven't got to know anything about it, and then the sin is his, not mine.'

'Why, all of a sudden?'

'Why d'you think?' Tressa cried. 'We have got six already. Surely that's enough souls for the Catholic Church.'

'And he was all set to have a football team,' Lizzie said. 'Now you barely have enough to play five-a-side.'

'Aye, and that's the way it will stay,' Tressa commented grimly.

Scott insisted they go over to Ireland and meet Lizzie's parents. 'We don't need to ask permission, but it would be nice to get their blessing.'

Lizzie thought that that was like asking for the moon. 'Look at it from their point of view, Violet,' she said. 'The man I'm marrying is black and the brother to the man who attacked me and brought shame on the family, and, added to that, Scott's a Protestant.'

'That's a negative viewpoint to have, Lizzie,' Violet said. 'Think of Scott's good points.'

'I know his good points,' Lizzie said. 'I don't have to be convinced.'

'Neither do they. They're not marrying him.'

'I know that, but it's bound to be awkward.'

'Look, Lizzie, what odds?' Violet had said. 'You'll be there for a few days, and after you marry you probably won't see them again for one hell of a long time. You've coped with worse. Haven't the pair of you fine broad shoulders?'

Violet, as usual, spoke good sense. Lizzie didn't expect her parents to fall on her neck and say Scott was the very man they'd have chosen for their daughter, and welcome him as warmly as some favoured son. It would be unreasonable to expect anything like that.

Niamh and Tom were happy enough to be going back to Ireland when they knew they'd be returning from it, and Georgia was dreadfully excited at the prospect of going on trains and boats. It was Celia who was proving difficult.

'What are you afraid of?'

'Do you have to ask?'

'Come on, Celia, don't let those perverted nuns ruin your life.'

'I don't consider it ruined, just because I don't want to go to Ireland. Anyway,' she added, 'you'll hardly want me there.'

'Course we do. I've told my parents all about you. They'll be expecting you.'

Lizzie said nothing about the impassioned plea from her brother to bring Celia with her, and in the end, with the children and Scott adding their voices to Lizzie's, Celia agreed grudgingly to accompany them.

Lizzie's estimation of how her parents would feel were accurate, for Catherine thought it strange that her daughter was marrying a man with skin as dark as coal. 'I expect he's marrying our Lizzie out of a kind of duty, with his brother doing the dirty and all,' she said.

'Aye. That'll be it all right,' Seamus agreed gloomily. 'And all she can expect in the circumstances.'

'And of course he's no Catholic.'

'Well he wouldn't be, would he?' Seamus said. 'I suppose we're lucky he's not into some voodoo mumbo-jumbo.'

Johnnie was irritated by his parents' small-town mentality, but he said nothing. It wouldn't do to be at one another's throats and the atmosphere uneasy when the man came. God, it would be bad enough anyway.

*   *   *

Seamus and Catherine tried to welcome Scott, but their greeting was artificial and forced and Lizzie was glad Johnnie was there; and glad too of the children, who saw nothing amiss and fell upon their Uncle Johnnie eagerly and covered up the awkwardness.

Lizzie could see that while Seamus and Catherine welcomed Niamh and Tom they were more than reticent with Georgia. They didn't know the child, of course, but this was their opportunity to get to know her. 'This is Niamh's and Tom's granny and granddad,' she told Georgia. 'You can call them the same.'

Georgia, more sensitive to atmosphere than her half-brother and sister, regarded the couple solemnly, her finger in her mouth, a sure sign of nervousness. Catherine gazed at the pretty child, with the mass of black curls and big brown eyes in the dusky face, dressed in a red woollen skirt and a cream jumper, and she smiled. This was no monster. This was just a child, like any other. 'Come away,' she said, putting out her arms, 'and give your granny a wee hug.'

Georgia, still unsure, didn't move. She looked up at Lizzie, who gave the child a little push forward and Catherine took her in her arms.

Niamh and Tom were bouncing with impatience to take Georgia and show her around the farm. As Catherine released the child, the children struggled into their coats, helped by Johnnie, for the day was a cold one, and Lizzie introduced Celia to her parents.

All Seamus and Catherine knew was that Celia was a staunch friend of Lizzie's and Catherine acknowledged that after their treatment of their daughter it was a good job she had someone at her back, some measure of support. So they had no trouble making Celia feel welcome and Celia thought the situation might be different entirely if Lizzie's parents knew where the two had met up.

At the table, most of the talk was again carried by the children and Johnnie, although Scott gave a good account of himself and spoke of his mother, sister and brother and the business they owned.

Lizzie loved Scott's voice, the way he used his hands as he spoke, and Catherine, catching sight of Lizzie's eyes as she looked at Scott, knew that she was looking at a woman in love. In fact, seeing them together, it was obviously not a marriage of duty at all, and she was glad of it, though she thought it hard that her daughter would shortly be living so far away.

Celia thought it hard too, but knew her future was now in her own hands and she had to decide which way to jump. Her sexual feelings, which she thought she had securely under lock and key, had begun to surface when she met Johnnie again. She'd definitely not felt this way about him before, and had only seen him as a friend, but now . . .

It had begun in the station when their hands touched as Johnnie was stowing the cases into the cart, and it was a little like an electric shock passing up her arm and through her body. Johnnie had been aware of it too. Since then, as the days passed there had been other odd things: the way he smiled, laughed, even the way he held a glass or cup could send tremors through her.

She avoided being alone with him because she didn't want to talk about her feelings till she got them sorted out. She didn't want him to declare his either, because before they could take their relationship further, could have any future together, Catherine and Seamus had to know where she came from, what her background was.

She discussed it with no one, for she couldn't risk being talked out of it, and she chose a day when Johnnie had taken Scott, Lizzie and the children to Donegal town. She'd been asked too, but pleading a headache had said she would stay at home.

She thought the lie a necessary one and waited until she heard Seamus come in mid-morning for a drink before coming into the room.

'How's your head?' Catherine asked her.

'Never better,' Celia said. 'I never had a headache, and though I don't like lies and deceit I needed to see the two of you alone and without any listening.'

There was a puzzled look on Catherine's face. 'Is there something ails you?'

'No,' Celia said. 'Not in that way, but I think you should know that, though not a word has been said about it, I know your son Johnnie likes me. Maybe more than likes me.'

'We know of it,' Catherine said. 'How do you feel about him?'

'That's just it,' Celia replied. 'I could return those feelings and more, for I love your son with all my heart and soul, but before I say this to him there is something I must tell you, something about my background. When I have finished, if you feel you don't want such a person in your family, I will return to Birmingham and no harm done.'

Seamus and Catherine were thoroughly intrigued,

but as Celia's tale unfolded, beginning from being exiled from the family to West Meath, they understood. Johnnie had told them some things about the convent, but it was hard to picture the horror of it without experiencing it, and Seamus and Catherine listened to a tale they could scarcely believe. Celia pulled no punches, and yet didn't exaggerate or embellish, and they both knew she spoke the truth.

Seamus at first felt the same shock as he had when Lizzie had told him she was pregnant. It had been ingrained in him that it was by far and away the worst thing a girl could do to her family . . . but to treat the girls so brutally, surely that couldn't be right. Yet, he had to be honest with himself. If he'd been aware of it all would he have fetched Lizzie from the place and stood against the shame of it? Johnnie was right, out of sight was out of mind.

Catherine wept as she realised that everything Celia spoke about, her own daughter had suffered too, and she reproached herself and more, especially as Lizzie was an innocent victim. But Celia, even now, was little more than a girl. Should she suffer all the days of her life for a mistake made when she'd not left childhood far behind? 'I can't speak for Seamus,' she said, 'but I would welcome you to this family.'

'And so would I,' Seamus said. 'All in all, I think you have suffered enough.'

When Lizzie came back, Celia sought her out and told her what she'd done and how her parents had taken the revelation.

'Why did you do it?' Lizzie asked.

'I think, given the slightest encouragement, Johnnie will ask me to marry him, and I couldn't come here under false pretences. I'll have no secrets, no skeletons in the cupboard.'

'Do you love Johnnie?'

'Aye, I do,' Celia said. 'I didn't, I know I didn't one time, and I don't know why. Maybe it was too soon, maybe I was too young, but I know now. It's come upon me suddenly, but it's no less deep for that. I love him so much I long to be with him. I want to bear his children, children we can take joy in and watch grow up. I love him, Lizzie, more than I thought it was possible to love anyone.'

'Oh, Celia, I'm so happy for you,' Lizzie said in delight, and gave her a kiss.

Scott, Lizzie and the children left Celia in Ballintra when they returned to Birmingham, as she'd written to Fisher and Ludlow's giving notice. Lizzie felt it a strange house without her, particularly when Scott went back to America to tell his family and arrange their passage over for the wedding.

Sometimes, Lizzie was gripped by anxieties and concerns, and it was always Violet who calmed these fears and said it was natural to feel apprehensive.

Lizzie woke on the morning of her wedding in a fever of nervous excitement. She knew that soon Celia would arrive to sort out the girls and Tom for her, because she and Johnnie, with Lizzie's parents, had arrived two days before. Scott had arranged accommodation for them in the same hotel where he and his family were booked in, and the two families had got on famously. 'Fell on your feet at last,' Celia said. 'They're lovely people.'

'I know,' Lizzie said, catching up Celia's left hand. 'I've met them, and I'm not the only one to fall on my feet, you dark horse. It's a beautiful ring. When did you get engaged?'

Lizzie had never seen Celia blush before and it made her look more beautiful than ever. 'About a week after you came back,' she said. 'No point in waiting.'

'And the wedding?'

'No date set yet,' Celia said. 'I'd like it if you could come over.'

'I won't promise,' Lizzie said, 'but I'll do my level best. I would like to see someone make an honest woman of you.'

'That'll be the day,' Celia said. The two laughed together, and when that laughter turned to tears as they hugged one another, neither was totally surprised.

The house was quiet. Celia and the children had left and everyone else was waiting at the church. Only Lizzie and Violet remained.

'So,' Violet said, coming into the bedroom as Lizzie stood before the mirror, 'the future is going to be hunky-dory for you, I'd say, and about time too.'

'I know,' Lizzie agreed dolefully.

'So why the bloody long face?'

'Oh, Violet, I'm going to miss you so much,' Lizzie cried. 'We've been through so much together and you really are a very special person.'

'And so are you, Lizzie,' Violet said, and her voice

was husky with unshed tears. 'And much as I will miss you I'm glad you're going. You'll have a better life in America, the land of opportunity, they say, and the children can't wait.'

'I know. It would have been worse if they hadn't wanted to go.'

'Well, they do, and if we don't get going your man will have a heart attack in the church thinking you've stood him up,' Violet said.

'He'll know I'd not do that,' Lizzie replied.

'No, you're not a fool altogether,' Violet agreed.

Suddenly, it was too much for Lizzie. She was leaving all that she held dear for strangers, however kind they were, and Violet heard the gulping sob.

'You ain't crying?'

'No.'

'Liar,' Violet said, and then, as the tears dribbled down Lizzie's cheeks, she said, 'Oh, come here, you silly sod,' and she enfolded Lizzie in her arms. Lizzie cried out her fears and knew in that moment that no one would ever be able to take Violet's place in her life.

They were all there that beautiful Saturday in late January when Lizzie stood at the door of St Catherine's Church in a gown of blue satin, followed first by Georgia and then Niamh in bridesmaids' dresses of peach. The church was full, neighbours and friends on one side and relations on the other. Lizzie tucked her arm in her father's as the wedding march began and they walked slowly down the aisle.

And then Scott, standing beside Ben, who was his

best man, turned around, and his face had such love for Lizzie she felt it wash over her in a wave. Seamus delivered his daughter into Scott's keeping and she stood beside him just as a shaft of winter sun, shining through the stained-glass windows, bathed them both in myriad shades of light.

A Sister's Promise
Anne Bennett

Molly's life changes forever when her parents are killed in a horrific accident. Although her beloved grandfather wants to keep her and her little brother Kevin with him in Birmingham, the authorities decide it's best for the girl to live with her maternal grandmother on a farm in Donegal. So Molly is packed off to Biddy Sullivan, a hard, cruel woman who loves to bear a grudge.

Years of hardship follow and just as Molly begins to grow independent, war breaks out. She fears the worst for her grandfather – and what will become of Kevin? He's only ten. So the naïve country girl sets off for her home city, little guessing what perils are to befall her before she can discover her brother's fate…

'Anne Bennett draws on her own background to give emotional depth to an affecting story populated with rich, beautifully drawn characters'   *Choice*

ISBN: 978 0 00 722602 3